Küchlya

Decembrist Poet

A Novel

Cherry
Orchard
Books

Küchlya

Decembrist Poet

A Novel

Yuri Tynianov

Translated by Anna Kurkina Rush, Peter France, & Christopher Rush
Introduction by Anna Kurkina Rush

BOSTON
2021

Library of Congress Cataloging-in-Publication Data

Names: Tyni͡anov, I͡U. N. (I͡Uriĭ Nikolaevich), 1894-1943, author. | Rush, Anna Kurkina, translator. | France, Peter, 1935- translator. | Rush, Christopher, 1944- translator.
Title: Küchlya : Decembrist poet : a novel / Yury Tynyanov ; translated by Anna Kurkina Rush, Peter France, and Christopher Rush.
Other titles: Ki͡ukhli͡a. English
Description: Boston : Cherry Orchard Books, 2021.
Identifiers: LCCN 2021019230 (print) | LCCN 2021019231 (ebook) | ISBN 9781644696842 (hardback) | ISBN 9781644696859 (paperback) | ISBN 9781644696866 (adobe pdf) | ISBN 9781644696873 (epub)
Subjects: LCSH: Ki͡ukhel'beker, V. K. (Vil'gel'm Karlovich), 1797-1846--Fiction. | Poets, Russian--19th century--Fiction. | Decembrists--Fiction.
Classification: LCC PG3476.T9 K513 2021 (print) | LCC PG3476.T9 (ebook) | DDC 891.73/42--dc23
LC record available at https://lccn.loc.gov/2021019230
LC ebook record available at https://lccn.loc.gov/2021019231

ISBN 9781644696842 (hardback)
ISBN 9781644696859 (paperback)
ISBN 9781644696866 (adobe pdf)
ISBN 9781644696873 (epub)

On the cover: Oleg Korovin, "Meeting. Pushkin and Küchelbecker"
(Встреча. Пушкин и Кюхельбекер).
Reproduced by permission.
Cover design by Ivan Grave
Book design by PHi Business Solutions

Published by Cherry Orchard Books, imprint of Academic Studies Press
1577 Beacon Street
Brookline, MA 02446, USA
press@academicstudiespress.com
www.academicstudiespress.com

Contents

Introduction

Yuri Tynianov (1894–1943) has left an indelible mark on Russian literature of the twentieth century and beyond. In the early 1920s he carved his name as a gifted and influential Russian literary theoretician and Formalist critic. What is now known as the Formal School in Russia and Russian Formalism in the West started in St. Petersburg as the Society for the Study of Poetic Language (OPOYAZ) on the eve of the Great War. Its founder, Viktor Shklovsky, the leader of a circle of young intellectuals and literary theorists, boldly asserted that "the literary work is pure form, it is neither thing nor material, but a relationship of materials"[1]. Tynianov joined in autumn 1918 and together with Shklovsky and Eikhenbaum formed an intellectual nucleus of the group, its so-called "triumvirate." After OPOYAZ disbanded in 1923 Tynianov became a leading light of its successor, the Russian Formal School, in which he worked prolifically until the late 1920s.

The February and October Revolutions of 1917 swept away not just the tsarist regime but an entire Russian civilization. The harrowing experiences of the First World War and the political upheavals that followed brought along drastic and irreversible changes to the very core of society and its culture. Many avant-garde artists and literary critics close to them philosophically, and in some instances personally (like the Formalists who were close to Russian Futurism), were enthralled by the idea of revolution as a means of acquiring a "new vision." They believed that it is through new art that "modern, bourgeois, conventional man with his tired assumptions might be jolted out of his epistemological

1 Viktor Shklovsky, "The Resurrection of the Word," in *Russian Formalism: A Collection of Articles and Texts in Translation,* ed. Stephen Bann and John E. Bowlt (Edinburgh: Scottish Academic Press, 1973), 41–47.

rut and helped to 'see' and therefore '*be* anew.'"[2] The energies unleashed by the Revolutions were now directed at the radical transformation and momentous rebuilding of life and culture. The Formalists threw themselves into the struggle against the old academe and for the emphatically new "science" of literature studies. A post-Revolutionary "Renaissance man," driven by the firm conviction that social revolution should necessitate a profound transformation of culture and the arts, Tynianov was vigorously engaged in a variety of genres: he was an active critic, essayist, polemicist, public speaker, editor, translator of Heine, an innovative screenwriter, and theorist of the then still silent cinema. His main passion, literary theory, was never his exclusive concern. Formalists were empiricists, and in their view, theory could never be divorced from the *practice* of writing. Shklovsky famously argued that "to be an ichthyologist one doesn't have to be a fish." And then qualified his polemically categorical pronouncement by stating that he himself was "a fish turned ichthyologist, a writer analysing the art of literature."[3] His Formalist colleagues, Eikhenbaum and, in particular, Tynianov could easily describe themselves in the same terms.

Tynianov turned to historical fiction in 1925, after the authorities appointed a new director and restructured the State Institute of the History of Arts where he had been lecturing during the previous five years. The Formalists' approach to the study of literature had been officially denounced as isolationist and reactionary, and a full-scale campaign was launched against them by the Marxist-leaning Institute of Comparative History of Occidental and Oriental Literatures and Languages. Tynianov stayed on at the Institute until spring 1930 when the Institute was "reorganized" yet again (in practical terms, disbanded). On December 1, 1925 he published his first novel with an enigmatic title, *Küchlya,* about Pushkin's little-known fellow-student from their Lycée years, Wilhelm Küchelbecker. The choice of a protagonist from Pushkin's intimate milieu was emblematic of the Formalists' spiritual affinity with Pushkin's circle (significantly, Tynianov's own research into Küchelbecker began in Prof. Semyon Vengerov's Pushkin seminar). Like the Silver Age artists

2 Katerina Clark, *Petersburg, Crucible of Cultural Revolution* (Cambridge, MA: Harvard University Press, 1995), 30.

3 Viktor Shklovsky, *Bowstring: On the Dissimilarity of the Similar*, trans. Sh. Avagyan (Champaign, IL: Dalkey Archive, 2011), 295.

before them, the Formalists were keen to re-mythologize the experience of twentieth-century Russia in terms of an apparent cyclical return of the early nineteenth century with its European war and social upheavals and the flourishing of Romanticism and utopian idealism. The December uprising of 1825 had a particular fascination for the young scholar as the pivotal event of the literary period at the heart of his research.

Küchlya gained an instant success with readership and critics alike. Tynianov continued to write historical fiction, and when the atmosphere around him became more sinister and the political ambience increasingly more dogmatic, his novels provided him with a creative outlet and a means of clothing his theoretical constructs with the flesh and blood of historical characters. They also gave their author a safe vantage point from which he could analyse and obliquely comment on his own ever grimmer times. From 1928 on, feeling the academic ground slip from beneath his feet, Tynianov was forced to abandon theory; what replaced this, his novels, reflected his personal intellectual odyssey as well as the concerns and the disillusionments of the wider intelligentsia at the very moment when the trap of historical circumstance was being sprung. The novels that followed, *The Death of Vazir-Mukhtar* (1928) and *Pushkin* (1936–1943), and the three novellas, *Lieutenant Kijé* (1928), *Young Vitushishnikov* (1931), and *The Wax Effigy* (1933) cemented his fame as a historical novelist of extraordinary power and influence and, to a certain extent, eclipsed his renown as a scholar. These days for the general reading public in Russia Tynianov is known first and foremost as the author of outstanding historical fiction with its primary focus on Russian history and literature of the nineteenth century. And it all started with his first novel: *Küchlya* propelled Tynianov to fame and established his reputation as the founding father of the Soviet historical novel. It has been a fondly loved minor classic of twentieth-century Russian literature ever since, published in runs of millions.

Tynianov died young, at the age of forty-nine, leaving his last novel about Pushkin uncompleted and his readership wondering how many more historical characters he could have brought back to life and what artistic heights he could have reached had his life not been so cruelly cut short. For a couple of decades following his death from multiple sclerosis in 1943, Tynianov's scholarly works were out of print. Nor were they sufficiently studied. Official Soviet literary criticism rejected the Formalist concepts of the specificity and autonomy of poetic language and literature, and for many years Tynianov's artistic works, highly regarded by his contemporaries familiar with the theoretical principles of the Formal method, were read in isolation from the context of their creation.

The novel *Küchlya* was commissioned by an obscure publishing house, Kubuch,[4] on the instigation of the children's poet and literary critic Korney Chukovsky, as an educational novella for a teenage readership, although the book almost inevitably went its own way. Like many ventures in those times, it was dictated by dire financial necessity, decided by chance and due to be delivered at short notice (the publication was timed for the 100th anniversary of the Decembrist uprising that had taken place on December 14, 1825.) By all accounts, it was written in a remarkably short period of time, in fact, in a matter of weeks, rapidly evolving into a "proper" novel, considerably longer than anticipated. Shklovsky maintained that the novel "appeared to have already lived in Tynianov's imagination and he only flung open the door to where it had been waiting for him. . . He raised Küchlya from the dead."[5]

Indeed, Tynianov the literary scholar rediscovered Küchelbecker for his age and restored his name to the canon of Russian literature. He was the first to look into Küchelbecker's writings, which had remained mostly unpublished until the twentieth century.[6] He transcribed and annotated Küchelbecker's archive, which he had bought from an antique book dealer in 1928–1929. He wrote about Küchelbecker in his scholarly

4 Publishing house founded in 1925 in Leningrad by the Commission for the Improvement of Students' Living Conditions; published educational literature in various fields of knowledge, primarily in science and technology. Profits from the sales of publications went to student organisations; ceased to exist in 1935.

5 Viktor Shklovsky, *Yuri Tynianov: Pisatel' i uchenyi* (Moscow: Molodaia gvardiia, 1966), 67.

6 The fate of Küchelbecker's literary heritage is also peculiar. He first published while still at the Lycée but in his lifetime a relatively small number of his works saw the light of day (mainly in literary journals such as *Son of the Fatherland*, *The Neva Spectator*, *The Champion of Enlightenment and Charity*, and *Mnemosyne*). Before 1825 only one of his works, "The Shakespearean Spirits," was published as a book-length edition. After the defeat of the Decembrist revolt, political state criminals such as Küchelbecker were banned from publishing. A few of his works found their way into the press anonymously or under an assumed name of V. Garpenko in 1835, 1836, and 1839.

articles "The Sham Pushkin" (1922), "*The Argives*, Küchelbecker's unpublished tragedy" (1929), "The Archaists and Pushkin" (in *Archaists and Innovators*, 1929), "Pushkin and Küchelbecker" (1934), "Küchelbecker's French Contacts" (1939), and "The Plot of *Woe from Wit*" (published posthumously in 1946). In 1929 he edited Küchelbecker's diaries and in 1939 a two-volume edition of Küchelbecker's *Selected Works*, many of them hitherto unpublished, and supplied them with an introductory biographical essay. With some inevitable additions, amendments, and rectifications, every subsequent edition of Küchelbecker's works has been based on Tynianov's ground-breaking research. And yet, paradoxical as this may sound, and notwithstanding Tynianov's painstaking effort invested in his investigation of Küchelbecker's legacy, it is a work of *fiction*, the novel *Küchlya*, that remains the fullest, most vivid, and enduring testament to Küchelbecker.

Wilhelm Karlovich Küchelbecker (1796–1846) is possibly one of the most striking, contradictory, and tragic figures in all of Russian literature. Leo Tolstoy in a letter to the philosopher and publicist Nikolay Strakhov in 1878 described Küchelbecker as an "affecting" man of a specific type, men who are "not really poets but convinced that they are poets and passionately devoted to their make-believe vocation." Nabokov defined him as "a curious archaic poet, an impotent playwright, one of Schiller's victims, a brave idealist, a heroic Decembrist, a pathetic figure," who "only at the very end of a singularly sad and futile literary career, and in the twilight of his life produced a few admirable poems, one of which is a brilliant masterpiece, a production of first-rate genius—the twenty-line long 'Destiny of Russian Poets.'"[7]

The novel *Küchlya* is often and somewhat misleadingly viewed as a preparatory and even auxiliary text to Tynianov's life-long ambition to write a novelistic biography of Pushkin. Pushkin already features as a supporting character in the first two novels of Tynianov's loosely termed *trilogy* about Russian poets (Küchelbecker and Griboyedov). Exploring the life of Pushkin's classmate and life-long friend was a godsend to Tynianov for the potential insights this could provide into Pushkin's formative years.

---

7 Vladimir Nabokov (ed. and tr.), *Verses and Versions: Three Centuries of Russian Poetry* (Orlando, FL: Harcourt 2008), 64.

The strangely sounding title of the novel immediately points to their shared *alma mater*, the Tsarskoe Selo Imperial Lycée, as "Küchlya" was Wilhelm's nickname provided for him by his fellow-students—among them some future poets and revolutionaries, such as Delvig and Pushchin. Some of the boys were fond of him, even though he was mercilessly tormented for his strange physical quirks (he was lean, deaf, and had a stammer), for his poor Russian (he spent his pre-Lycee years at a German-language school), for his fiery temperament, unbridled ambition, phenomenal diligence, and obsessive versifying. The comic and intriguing titles of the novel (*Küchlya*) and of its first chapter ("Willie") immediately undermine any expectation of a "canonical" biography like those of cherished national heroes or of men of greatness.

To the end of his life Pushkin remained deeply attached to what he considered his *real* home and his *real* family—the band of fellow-lycéens. The Tsarskoe Selo Lycée was founded by Alexander I in 1811 and at the time was the most innovative and academically advanced institution of education in the entire country: all teaching was conducted in Russian. Its egalitarian ambience, absence of corporal punishment, lenient and respectful treatment of the boys, highly knowledgeable professorial staff, some of whom became father figures for the pupils, whose own fathers were either neglectful (like Pushkin's) or dead (like Küchelbecker's)—all this made an appreciable difference to the boys' worldview and sense of identity, shaping their passion for intellectual distinction and hatred of mediocrity. The Lycée was established with a view to educating the Tsar's younger brothers, Grand Dukes Nicholas and Michael. But, significantly, the Lycée also offered free entry to any nobleman, even to a destitute small-fry. It placed on an equal footing representatives of the aristocracy, old and new, and the offspring of the families on the fringes of the nobility, such as Küchelbecker's, whose father was a university-educated minor Saxonian nobleman.[8] The ethos of the school, its challeng-

8 Karl Ivanovich Küchelbecker, a Baltic German, studied Law at Leipzig University at the same time as Goethe and Alexander Radishchev, the Russian writer later exiled by Catherine the Great for his harsh social critique of contemporary Russia. Unlike the also impoverished Pushkin, who on his father's side traced his roots back to the ancient boyars who served with the Grand Prince of Kiev and Vladimir, Alexander Nevsky (1221–1263), Karl Küchelbecker's nobility was very recent, received before his move to Russia in the 1770s. He died of consumption in 1809.

ing curricula, goals, and procedures were based on the State Secretary Mikhail Speransky's rationalist ideas on education: his faith in the power of education seemed unshakeable, not only in respect of the acquisition of knowledge, but also as a tool for society's moral improvement. At his suggestion the sciences were eliminated at the Lycée in favor of the humanities and of physical education; these aimed at producing civically minded members of society. Speransky envisaged that, after graduation, the students would be appointed to government posts according to their achievements, and promoted to high office in the military and civil services. Events would unfold differently from how Speransky had imagined them. The plans for the Grand Dukes' education changed. Tsar Alexander abandoned the course of reforms and turned instead to reactionary politics and religious mysticism. Speransky himself was replaced in his role of the Tsar's advisor by the strict Artillery General, Count Arakcheyev, then fell from grace, and was exiled to a minor administrative post in Siberia. The window of historical opportunity for change, progress, political and social freedoms, so much anticipated in post-1812 Russian society, was thus quickly shut. These frustrated expectations led to the formation of a network of conspiratorial groups, or secret societies, and the December uprising. The only way to change Russia's shameful backwardness, to abolish thriving serfdom and corrupt and inefficient bureaucracy, and turn towards large-scale social, judicial, industrial, agricultural, and administrative reforms seemed to be a constitutional monarchy in which the new tsar would turn his attention to internal affairs in order to address the serious issues of the empire.

The harsh suppression of the uprising and the unnecessarily humiliating execution of the main conspirators by hanging (tsar Nicholas was unwilling to spill blood) permanently alienated the progressive part of the Russian elite from the tsar and his government. In total, over five hundred men were investigated. Almost three hundred were found guilty; five were sentenced to death and executed (Ryleyev, Pestel, Kakhovsky, Bestuzhev-Ryumin, Muravyov-Apostol); a hundred and twenty rebels were exiled to hard labour or to a permanent settlement in Siberia. The Decembrists were amnestied thirty years later, on August 26, 1856, when Alexander II ascended the throne and restored their rights, privileges, and titles. But the amnesty arrived too late for Küchelbecker: after 1825 he spent ten years imprisoned in solitary confinement in various fortresses and the rest of his days in Siberian exile (as Tynianov puts it, "sentenced to death and condemned to life"), disenfranchised, expunged from the history of Russian literature, and largely forgotten.

By the beginning of the twentieth century, traditional historical fiction with its rigid conventions had fallen from favour while biography, on the contrary, experienced a marked increase in popularity. In search of a "new vision" in literature, Tynianov set out to write a "new novel." He revamped and blurred the boundaries of the rigidly structured traditional historical narrative, creating an experimental genre imbued with the aesthetics of high modernism. "I begin where the document ends," Tynianov famously stated, in an apparent contradiction; artistic truth for this particular scholar often seemed to have greater value than factual accuracy. In a letter to Shklovsky from March 31, 1929, Tynianov wrote: "I see my novels as experiments in scholarly fantasy. I think that *belles-lettres* on historical material will soon completely pass, and there will be *belles-lettres* on theory." His play with form may be broadly seen as a scholarly experiment that derives from his literary theories on literary genres and literary evolution. In this novel in particular, the genres of literary-historical research, biography and fiction most happily merge. Tynianov is least of all interested in eulogizing, defending, or excusing his protagonist, instead offering his reader artistic prose informed by a level of research unique in both depth and extent in a novel which provides penetrating and comprehensive insights into his subject, excluding any simplifications and generalisations.

A decade later in the preface to his novel *Pushkin* Tynianov would reassert his novelistic credo: "In this book I would like to approach the artistic truth about the past, which is always the goal of the historical novelist."[9] As this claim suggests, Tynianov's novel, though based on documents, is not their slave and is only true to the author's concept of the protagonist. A mere accumulation of facts without aesthetic distillation and qualitative transformation is worthless. The chronicle method in the studies of artistic lives had failed to show how the facts of lives and history relate to creativity. Tynianov sets out to prove that the biographical

9 Quoted in Yuri Tynianov, *Lieutenant Kijé* and *Young Vitushishnikov*, trans. M. Ginsburg (Baltimore, MD: Eridanos Press, 1990), 14.

novel could be true to history in its own way, even without always being true to facts, for the facts of life can be overwhelming, and may even hinder the achievement of a successful story. He has to fill in the blanks and to provide not a literal interpretation of a life, but rather a symbolic one. This argument can be traced back at least as far as the Romantics, with Keats maintaining that only "very shallow people take everything as literal. A Man's life of any worth is a continual allegory—and very few eyes can see the Mystery of his life. A life, like the scriptures, is figurative."[10] To see life as such an allegory, to grasp its essence through telling detail, was Tynianov's particular gift. He imbues his narrative with literary texts created in the period he describes, in order to suggest deeper, timeless meanings; they assist his artistic imagination in filling in the gaps between the confirmed facts to suit his concept of Küchelbecker's persona. And when long-established facts do not conform to the concept, these are sometimes reshaped, chronology changed, motives reinterpreted.

With admirable flair and confidence, Tynianov presents a picture of Russian society, political intrigue, and large-scale historical events of the time. His novel is populated with the historical characters of the period: royalty and aristocracy, military leaders and secret service informers, statesmen and politicians, political rebels and their denouncers, peasants and serfs, all coming together in rich and lively tableaux. But the main character of the novel is Russian literature; its true heroes are writers, poets, philosophers, hack journalists, and the frivolous hostesses of literary salons. In this sense *Küchlya* is unashamedly "literature-centric." Tynianov makes the history of the literary process the propulsive force of the plot and explores complex concepts and ideas, as opposed to merely illustrating certain ready-made doctrines imposed on the writer by the political establishment. Furthermore, he enters into a polemic with the existing accounts of Küchelbecker's life—the reminiscences of his contemporaries and other factual sources. In his lifetime, and for a long time afterwards, Küchelbecker had been perceived as a laughable and inept third-rater. The imagination of the novelist arrives at a different version of the poet's personality and firmly establishes Küchelbecker's contribution to the formation of the Russian poetic tradition, to the Decembrist

10 Robert Gittings, *The Nature of Biography* (London: Heinemann, 1978), 13.

literary output, and to the literary process of the 1820s, including his influence on Pushkin's development as a poet.

Tynianov leaves his reader in no doubt that great writers emerge from the creative environments with which they engage, and Küchelbecker was the marginal figure who had a profound influence on Pushkin at the stage that mattered most—at the point of the burgeoning of Pushkin's own poetic genius. Tynianov's Küchlya is a tragi-comic and elusive character, an ideal protagonist for the Formalist technique of estrangement, which saw the major quality and function of art as provoking and prolonging a sense of wonder at the world, otherwise old forms of literature turn into a "convention, like a necktie," and become desensitized "like gums numbed by cocaine." True literature is engaged in *retardation* or *defacilitation*, "overcoming" old forms by devices, whether semantic, syntactic, or phonological, that force the reader to follow the text with intense conscious effort and thus sharpen perception. Küchelbecker provided ample material for the technique, as he was already a strange individual, a perceived abnormality, a freak. His strangeness was testified to by various people who knew him throughout his life. A lycéen, Baron Korf, for one, described him as having "an eccentric mind, fiery passions, an unbridled hot temper; he was almost half-crazed and was always up to the funniest of escapades." In "The Literary Fact" (1924) Tynianov discussed "freakery" [*urodstvo*] as the moving force of art and the source of new forms: "Every 'ugliness', every 'mistake', every 'irregularity' in normative poetics is potentially a new constructive principle."[11] And as it happened, Tynianov's strange protagonist who wrote freakish verses also strenuously asserted the necessity for poetic innovation. Tynianov plays on the two meanings of the word "weird" [*strannyi*]: anomalous (or atypical) and distinctively unique. In the same way as Pushkin was aware of his "African ugliness" and creatively reimagined it as a positive feature, so Wilhelm knew the effect his freakish appearance had on other people ("He was well aware of his ugliness and was used to curious looks") and, though feeling hurt, reconciled himself with this mark of distinction.

Linguistically the word *urod* ("freak") with its prefix signifying rejection by *rod* (the Slavic root meaning "kinsfolk") defines someone who is excluded from the kin, who has broken away, become isolated, having

11 Yuri Tynianov, *Literaturnyi fakt* (Moscow: Vysshaia shkola, 1993), 129.

chosen for himself a life without love, without relatives, and hence lost vital reference points. In Tynianov's novel, Pushkin tells Wilhelm: "I love you like my own brother, Küchlya, but when I am no longer here, mark my words: you'll never have either a sweetheart or a friend. You're a difficult one." And Küchelbecker's freakery steadily increases as the novel unfolds. By the time we see him on the eve of the Decembrist uprising, he looks not just weird [*urodlivyi*] but, as Tynianov suggests, like a *yurodivyi* or Holy Fool. Such Fools for Christ in Orthodox Christianity renounced worldly possessions upon joining a monastic order, or deliberately flouted society's conventions to serve a religious purpose. In Küchelbecker's case, service to literature is a cult similar to a religious one. It demands self-abnegation and sacrifice. At the Lycée the boys refer to their dormitory rooms as "monastic cells" and to themselves as "monks," "sages," or "wise men," who lead lives of austerity and venerate the Muses. They are brothers (or brethren) of a fellowship of a particular kind. As Tynianov points out both in his biographical essay on Küchelbecker and even more so in his novel, Küchelbecker extolled the joys of friendship, as other poets extolled the joys of love. Küchelbecker's choices in later life are distinctly reminiscent of a *yurodivyi*—he is rootless and homeless, and he consistently challenges social norms by eccentric, shockingly unconventional behaviour.

Indeed, "eccentric," for Tynianov, is redolent with multiple significant connotations. Apart from the usual meanings of being off-centre, deviating from an established pattern or norm, or strangely fascinating, eccentricity interested Tynianov fundamentally as a characteristic of true revolutionary art, which broke away from the established habits of perception. This went back to his collaboration with the young Petrograd film directors, Trauberg, Kozintsev, Yutkevich, who, in their obsessive search for a new form, set up a group called FEKS (Factory of Eccentric Actors). Their manifesto "Eccentricity" (1922) outlined five basic principles based on negations—of the past, of the old, of the ossified, of high bourgeois culture, and of any authority, proclaiming instead clownery, spontaneity, and carnivalization as the main aesthetic principles of art.

The "de-automatizing" effect in *Küchlya* is further achieved by a rethinking not only of the protagonist but of the traditional artistic means such as plot and composition. This is mostly accomplished by extensive use of the literary equivalent of cinematographic techniques:

interchanging close-ups of the characters and lingering panoramic views of large-scale events, Eisensteinian rapid "shock-cutting" to create symbolic montage, metonymic use of detail and a system of highly visual recurrent leitmotifs, which create a particular narrative rhythm, such as road, sea, window, coffin, jail. Tynianov plays with the cognates of the Russian word "strange" [*strannyi*], and suggests yet another one, that of a "wanderer" [*strannik*] rejected by his country [*strana*]. The motif of wandering emerges as an important element of the novel's composition. Küchelbecker's travels to Europe are interpreted as a pilgrimage to the Europe of his Romantic dreams, the Europe of strong traditions of revolution and freedom-fighting, where Küchelbecker delivers lectures on Russian literature and history and is enthusiastically received as an equal by French and German cultural elites. At the same time, his trip represents his farewell to once cherished Romantic ideas, as he turns away from "gothic nonsense" and "that fearful Europe, the Europe of romantic visions, like the dreams of a drunk asleep in a dungeon." He's had enough of this: "Out into the fresh air!"—to the rougher and more authentic "language of the streets." Whatever Küchelbecker's personal literary evolution was, he was always the bearer of creative daring and ambition, and even when calling for a return to national roots, was paradoxically guided by a modernizing impulse. This idea was later developed by Tynianov in his collection of essays *Archaists and Innovators* (1929) and in particular in its central essay, "The Archaists and Pushkin." There, Tynianov introduced the concepts of a literary "archaist" and of an "innovator" in Pushkin's time and defined the main characteristics of literary "archaism."[12] The homogenous literary camp of the archaists is further divided, with all due caution, into "senior" and "junior" ones. The senior "archaists" (Shishkov, Khvostov, Shalikov), and the other members of the literary group "The Colloquy of the Lovers of the Russian Word," were opponents of Pushkin, while the junior ones (Griboyedov and Küchelbecker among them) were Romantics with nationalist leanings.

---

12 The "archaists" traced the origins of the Russian language either to Church Slavonic or directly to Greek, showed interest in lexical archaism, folklore, and the common language; rejected "smooth," "literary" style, which was associated with "eloquence" and "beauty"; emphasized the spoken rather than the written word, valued archaic syllabic poetry; and indulged in translation of foreign words into "genuine" Russian with often hilarious results.

Shklovsky half-jokingly suggested that Tynianov should have entitled his book *Archaists-Innovators.* In his opinion, this would have more clearly reflected Tynianov's thesis: in spite of bitter rivalries and harsh polemics there were certain similarities between some branches of the seemingly irreconcilably opposed literary camps; the "junior archaists" were linguistically and often politically radical, perhaps even revolutionary, and unmistakably innovative in their approach to the renewal of poetic language. The heart of the matter, as Tynianov sees it, is that both the senior *and* the junior archaists were utopians, unhappy with the existing state of affairs—in literature, the state and society. Such paradoxes of literary evolution fascinated Tynianov, for whom the history of Russian literature was a chain of negations, a road offering no smooth transitions, for literary evolution in Tynianov's understanding has a non-linear character, where succession is never peaceful and occurs "not from father to son but from uncle to nephew."

The motif of travel, first introduced in the beginning of the novel with the fourteen-year old Wilhelm's failed escape to meet his sweetheart, Minchen, continues in a succession of travels that increasingly turn into the enforced flights of an outcast or a pariah, fleeing from persecution. Some of these travels fail to materialize or get aborted, like the elopement with Minchen, but throughout the novel Küchelbecker's inability to settle and his impulse for restless and almost irrational movement are always there. Wilhelm perceives this perpetual travel as a punishment and even a curse, like that of the wandering Jew. The strong sense of identification with that biblical character is highly appropriate: later, in his Siberian exile in 1840–1842, Küchelbecker would write a narrative poem, *Ahasuerus, the Wandering Jew*, remarkable even "despite its odd archaism, awkward locutions, crankish ideas, and a number of structural flaws, a major piece of work, with a harshness of intonation and gaunt originality of phrasing."[13] This imprecation appears to afflict not only Küchelbecker but also Pushkin and Griboyedov, who in the novel experience something like a curse, "as if with the prophecy: Thou shalt move from every place under the skies." They are dispatched to the margins of the empire (Küchelbecker and Griboyedov have to travel to the

13 Nabokov, *Verses and Versions*, 65.

war-ravaged regions of the Caucasus, where they could easily perish) or into the vast empire's impassable depths (Pushkin's exile into his Pskov region estate). These are the regions that Griboyedov in the novel calls the "ultimate extremity," "the land of oblivion." As a result of these enforced wanderings, all three poets arrive at a stark conclusion that in spite of their best efforts their lives "do not come out well" ("How sad," muses Pushkin in the novel, "God's my witness, how sad!").

Relentless movement with an unclear goal perfectly resonates with Küchelbecker's biography, full of frenetic, almost compulsive movement. By further combining the motifs of "noble" insanity (in Grech's characterisation of Küchelbecker in a conversation with Griboyedov) with that of wandering, Tynianov arrives at his portrayal of Küchelbecker as a quixotic tragi-comic personage who prefers glorious fantasy to quotidian reality. Cervantes's famous novel is about an idealist and his futile desire to change reality, and like Alonso Quixano, Küchelbecker is spurred into action by prodigious reading (in Küchelbecker's case not of chivalric romances but of Romantic poetry) and decides to set out to revive chivalry, undo wrongs, and bring justice to the world. Pushkin with his earthy wit and Griboyedov with his jaundiced scepticism act as Küchelbecker's Sancho Panzas, attempting to bring him down to earth and to pour cold water on their overheated friend, even though they cherish his ardour as "an elevating deception," which, in Pushkin's famous line, "is dearer to us than a host of low truths." As for Küchelbecker, he sees himself as more than a hapless knight. He is a poet aware of his calling, one with a mission, a herald of higher divine truths. In his "Prophecy" (1822), Küchelbecker set up a theme picked up by Pushkin in his own renowned "Prophet" (1826). Tynianov inflects his portrayal of Küchelbecker from the harmless idealistic Don Quixote to the homeless, peripatetic prophet who fights the Pharisees and who is scorned as an imposter. The prophet poet combines writing with political struggle and mystical service to an unknown God. He sees himself as a conduit for God-inspired creativity and transmitter of messages between the living and the dead.

The tragic motifs of unrecognized talent, suffering, and redemption develop throughout and grow stronger towards the devastating finale of the novel. Thus, the novel becomes Küchelbecker's spiritual odyssey: he begins his journey as a ridiculed character who endures mockery, rude jokes, and cruel pranks, but as the novel unfolds and he suffers spectacular failures and catastrophic defeats, he eventually turns into a flawed but quasi-saintly figure. His life is an endless chain of misfortunes, and he can only endure it because he has an unshakeable belief in literature and his service to it. Death comes when doubt in his creative powers creeps in. Not physical deprivation but emotional torment hammers the last nail into his coffin. His death is portrayed as a return to the garden of Eden, which is reminiscent of the Tsarskoe Selo gardens where he and his friends roamed, full of youthful ardour and idealistic dreams. It is a paradisiacal space for a reunion with the dear departed in the bosom of nature, the gentle sound of water trickling to the lamenting song of the nightingale, the emblem of Russia, and the Russian nightingale—Pushkin, his curly head, laughter, merriment, and the final moment of affection: the dear dead calling, "brothers" reunited. A symbol of love, the nightingale in Christian symbolism stands for pain and longing for Heaven. And Tynianov seems to be saying that there *is* no death, there is transcendence (or flowing) from one state to another, and what survives are "the intangibles": love and art. It is a tender ending to the relentlessly unlucky and unhappy life of a pure-hearted, passionate, and gifted man.

Originally, the novel had a subtitle: "The Tale of a Decembrist," which implied that it focused on the portrayal of the protagonist's path to Decembrism. Tynianov the historian pieces together and provides a striking account of the historical events triggered by the 1825 interregnum and of the uprising itself. The historical backdrop of his narrative is saturated with additional meanings. The motif of wandering continues to feature prominently in the Decembrist chapters of the novel to convey the disarray and irresolution in the ranks of the conspirators on the eve of and in the course of the uprising. To convey the idea that the rebels' activities were well-intentioned but inconsistent, and to an extent suicidal, Tynianov describes them in Shakespearean terms as "travellers who had only five minutes left before they departed for an unknown country, from which there was unlikely to be any return." The uprising was not sufficiently prepared and was to take place at a later date, in March 1826, but due to the sudden death of Alexander I it was moved to December 14, the day for which the official ceremony of swearing allegiance to the new Tsar was scheduled.

The uprising chapters are a painstakingly researched artistic reconstruction of one of the critical events in Russian history, which has preserved its powerful and lasting hold on the Russian imagination. The outcome was violent and inglorious, but had a profound inspirational effect on generations of future revolutionaries. At the time when the novel was written, the new-born socialist state found it crucial to identify itself with the progenitors of the revolutionary movement and their indisputably altruistic service to noble ideals. Soviet writers were expected to highlight the threads stretching from the heroic past of a century ago to the no less heroic present. Tynianov was praised for his felicitous choice of protagonist, sincere and impractically quixotic, and thus well suited to reflect the idealistic illusions of the Decembrist ideology. But the author appeared ambivalent: in the final analysis, his protagonist was a poet, and the novel was primarily about his attempts to revolutionize *literature*. The entire essence of Küchelbecker's character is his striving for innovation, for what the Lycée's second headmaster Engelhardt called his "gargantuan projects," referring to his encyclopaedic knowledge of literature and history: "he has read all the books on earth about all things on this earth; has much talent, much diligence, much good will, much heart and much feeling"; "unfortunately all this lacks taste, tact, gracefulness, and measure." Pushkin, who in his Lycée years was the most prolific lampoonist targeting Küchlya, later in life extolled Küchelbecker as an intellectual and the most significant personality in the literary criticism of the 1820s. "Be it right or wrong, he always gives the reasons for his point of view and evidence to substantiate his judgments, which is rather rare in our literature. Nobody has ventured to contradict him, either because everyone agrees with him, or because nobody feels he can contend with an athlete who is, apparently, both strong and experienced."[14]

By removing the subtitle from the subsequent editions of *Küchlya* Tynianov seemed to admit that he has failed to produce a *celebratory* piece. The tenor of the novel is too sombre and too dark. The reader is left with the lasting image of the rebels' confusion, betrayals within their ranks, the deaths of innocent civilian onlookers, and the sinister aftermath of the uprising when the bodies of the dead are submerged beneath the ice on the Neva, the blood is scraped from the ground, and sprinkled over with fresh snow in a literal cover-up. The novel is written

14 Alexander Pushkin, "Notes on Küchelbecker's Articles Published in *Mnemozina*," in *Pushkin on Literature*, trans. T. Wolff (Evanston, IL: Northwestern University Press, 1998), 169.

by a witness and a survivor of the huge historical traumas of the early twentieth century, and this striking piece of Decembrist iconography is, in effect, a startling meditation on the unrealized potential of the revolution and its human cost. Tynianov argues that Küchelbecker's disastrous poetic fate and literary oblivion were "possibly, the most striking example of the destruction of a poet by autocracy." This poignant reference to events a century before reflects the anxieties of the Soviet collective unconscious. It also expresses the fear of Tynianov's immediate circle and of his generation that they were being denied biography and ousted from history, if not ruthlessly destroyed by it.

A year before the publication of *Küchlya*, in a survey of contemporary Russian prose Tynianov observed that "literature is not a train that arrives on time at a particular destination and the critic is not the station master. Russian literature has been given many assignments. It is an ungrateful task: tell the Russian writer to sail for India and he will discover America."[15] Setting off to write the tale of a Decembrist, Tynianov arrived at the portrait of one of the most touching and memorable characters in Russian literature who cannot but win over the sympathy of the reader. This strange and erratic, awkward, ardent, and utterly unheroic hero fails to match the ideal of the Decembrists cultivated in Soviet Russia, which had given the Decembrists a hyperbolically legendary status. Instead, Küchlya is a failure. Artistic failures seem to fascinate Tynianov for the same reason as abortive uprisings: for their generative power and forcefully audacious modernising impulse ("the spirit of transformation," as one of the rebel leaders, Pestel, put it). Tynianov asserted that Küchelbecker's failures were an enduring phenomenon and the literature of the 1820s was not unresponsive to them. Küchelbecker thus emerges as much more than the minor figure he was once believed to be. Tynianov portrays him as brimming with far-reaching ideas, and although he lacked the superior artistry of Pushkin to translate these ideas into consistently good writing, he nonetheless enabled a much greater poet to draw on these ideas and to suck inspiration from them, sufficient to turn them into magic. That a bright spark like Küchlya created such

---

15 Yuri Tynianov, "Literaturnoe segodnia," in his *Istoriia literatury. Kritika* (St. Petersburg: Azbuka-klassika, 2001), 458.

sparkle among his fellow poets but died in such sad obscurity certainly raises his stature and takes his story close to the level of the tragic.

Ultimately, *Küchlya* is a novel about the inspirational power of delusions, about the interplay of sense and obsessions, about a Russian Don Quixote, a poet-prophet, and a man who looms larger than his talent and rises up as an equal to his destiny. No one can know exactly what Küchelbecker's life was really like, but when reading *Küchlya* one is convinced that this is precisely "how it was." Insightful, compelling, complex, detailed, and erudite, this work is a joy and a gem—one of the most rewarding Russian novels of the mid-1920s.

Anna Kurkina Rush
Edinburgh

The Characters

FAMILY AND HOUSEHOLD

Wilhelm Karlovich Küchelbecker (Küchlya, Willie, Tapeworm, Gesell, Küchel, Sea Biscuit) (1797–1846).

Karl Ivanovich Küchelbecker (1848–1809), Wilhelm's father, minor Saxonian nobleman.

Ustinya Yakovlevna Küchelbecker (née Justine Lohmen) (1757–1841), Wilhelm's mother.

Ustinya (Ustinka) Karlovna Glinka (née Küchelbecker) (1786–1871), Wilhelm's sister, wife of Grigory Andreyevich Glinka.

Anna Ivanovna von Breitkopf (1747–1823), Wilhelm's aunt, former headmistress of the St. Catherine's Institute for Noble Maids.

Ioanniky Fyodorovich Nicolai, baron, friend of the family.

Pavel Petrovich Albrecht, Ustinya Yakovlevna's cousin, Wilhelm's uncle.

Senka (Semyon Balashov), domestic servant of the Küchelbeckers, later Wilhelm's valet.

Minchen, daughter of Wilhelm's tutor at his boarding school in Werro.

Mikhail Karlovich Küchelbecker (Misha, Mishka) (1798–1859), Wilhelm's younger brother.

Grigory Andreyevich Glinka (1776–1818), Wilhelm's brother-in-law, his sister Ustinya's husband.

Mitya Glinka (Mitenka, Dmitry), Wilhelm's nephew.

Drosida Ivanovna Küchelbecker (née Artyonova) (1817–1886), daughter of the Barguzin post-master, Wilhelm's wife, mother of his four children, only two of whom, Mikhail and Ustinya, survived into adulthood.

LYCÉE STAFF AND PUPILS

Broglio, Silvery Frantsevich (Sylvester, Silver) (1799–early 1820s), count, lycéen, after graduation will be killed in the Greek War of Independence.

Danzas, Konstantin Karlovich (1800–1870), lycéen, after graduation will become an army officer; Pushkin's second in the fatal duel with D'Anthès.

De Boudry, David Ivanovich (David Ivanych) (1756–1821), professor of French and brother of the notorious French Revolutionary figure Jean-Paul Marat.

Delvig, Anton Antonovich, baron (1798–1831), life-long friend of Pushkin; poet and journal editor (*The Literary Gazette*, *The Northern Flowers*, *The Snowdrop*).

Engelhardt, Egor Antonovich (1775–1862), headmaster of the Lycée from 1816.

Galich, Aleksandr Ivanovich (1783–1848), professor of Russian and Latin, 1814-15.

Gorchakov, Aleksandr Mikhaylovich (Sasha), prince (1798–1883), lycéen, will become a diplomat; Foreign Minister (1856-82).

Illichevsky, Aleksey Damianovich (Olosinka) (1798–1837), lycéen, will become a civil servant and a writer.

Kartsov, Yakov Ivanovich (1784–1836), professor of physics and mathematics.

Komovsky, Sergey Dmitriyevich (Little Fox) (1798–1880), lycéen, will become a civil servant, eventually Deputy Secretary to the State Council.

Korff, Modest Andreyevich, baron (1800–1876), lycéen, will serve in the Ministry for Justice; author of hostile reminiscences of Pushkin and the Lycée.

Koshansky, Nikolay Fyodorovich (1781–1831), professor of Russian and Latin.

Kunitsyn, Aleksandr Petrovich (1783–1841), professor of moral philosophy, sacked from the Lycée in 1821 for free-thinking.

Malinovsky, Vasily Fyodorovich (1765–1814), first headmaster of the Lycée.

Myasoyedov, Pavel Nikolayevich (1799–1869), lycéen, will become a scholar and maritime adventurer, and in 1867 an admiral.

Pushchin, Ivan Ivanovich (Vanya, *Jeannot*) (1798–1859), lycéen, Pushkin's dormitory neighbor and close friend.

Pushkin, Aleksandr Sergeyevich (Sasha, Frenchie, Monkey with Tiger) (1799–1837), lycéen, poet, novelist, and playwright, considered to be the founder of modern Russian literature.

Yakovlev, Mikhail Lukyanovich (Misha, Jester, "Jester of two hundred tricks") (1798–1868), lycéen, amateur composer and talented impersonator; will become a civil servant, member of the Privy Council and Senator.

Yesakov, Semyon Semyonovich (1798–1831), lycéen, will become an army officer.

Zernov, Aleksandr Pavlovich (b.1781), assistant tutor at the Lycée from 1811 to 1813.

WRITERS AND POETS, ARTISTIC MILIEU

Batyushkov, Konstantin Nikolayevich (1787–1855), major Russian poet of the early nineteenth century, much admired by the young lycéens for his hedonistic and satirical poems.

Bludov, Dmitry Nikolayevich (1785–1864), Russian imperial official and diplomat who filled a variety of posts under Nicholas I; also famous for his friendship with Zhukovsky and Karamzin.

Bulgarin, Faddey Venediktovich (1789–1859), writer, journalist, publisher of the journals *Northern Bee* and *Son of the Fatherland* (together with Nikolay Grech). From 1826, an agent of the secret police.

Chaadayev, Pyotr Yakovlevich (1794–1856), hussar and philosopher, author of the *Philosophical Letters* written in French in 1826–1831.

Derzhavin, Gavriil (Gavrila) Romanovich (1743–1816), major Russian poet of the eighteenth century.

Glinka, Mikhail Ivanovich (Misha) (1804–1857), a pupil of Küchelbecker, composer, founder of Russian classical music.

Gnedich, Nikolay Ivanovich (1784–1833), poet and publisher, translator of the *Iliad*.

Grech, Nikolay Ivanovich (1787–1867), leading Russian grammarian of the nineteenth century, primarily remembered as a journal publisher (*Son of the Fatherland* and *Northern Bee*).

Grech, Varvara Danilovna (née Müssar, 1787–1861), Nikolay Grech's first wife.

Gribov, Aleksandr Dmitriyevich, Aleksandr Griboyedov's footman, possibly his half-brother.

Griboyedov, Aleksandr Sergeyevich (1795–1829), diplomat, poet, composer, and playwright, famous for his verse comedy *Woe from Wit*; Russia's ambassador to Persia, where he and the embassy staff were massacred by angry Tehrani mob.

Izmaylov, Aleksandr Efimovich (1779–1831), the last major literary figure of Russian Enlightenment; government official, publisher of literary journals *The Flower Garden* and *The Man of Good Will*, novelist and poet, lauded for his satirical fables.

Karamzin, Nikolay Mikhaylovich (1766–1826), prominent writer and linguistic reformer, Imperial Historiographer, author of the monumental twelve-volume *History of the Russian State*.

Karatygin brothers: Vasily Andreyevich (Vasya) (1802–1858), tragic actor, and Pyotr Andreyevich (Petya) (1806–1879), dramatist and actor.

Katenin, Pavel Aleksandrovich (1792–1853), army officer, poet, playwright, translator of classical French tragedies, and literary critic, a close literary associate of Pushkin.

Kaverin, Pyotr Pavlovich (Pierre) (1794–1855), hussar who fought in the Napoleonic Wars and in 1816 was stationed at Tsarskoe Selo, an intellectual, a prankster, and a rake.

Khvostov, Dmitry Ivanovich, count (1757–1835), senator, prolific and ambitious poet of little talent, member of the traditionalist literary circle; often mocked by Pushkin and his literary associates.

Knyazhnin, Yakov Borisovich (1742–1791), Russia's foremost tragic author during the reign of Catherine the Great. His tragedies are imbued with the pathos of patriotism and hostility to tyranny.

Krylov, Ivan Andreevich (1769–1844), Russian playwright, poet and fabulist in the style of La Fontaine.

Panayev, Vladimir Ivanovich (1792–1859), an official, Privy Councillor, as well as an author of poetic idylls and sentimental prose.

Pletnyov, Pyotr Aleksandrovich (1792–1865), minor poet and literary critic who rose to become a professor and the dean of the St. Petersburg University (1840–1861) and academician of the Petersburg Academy of Sciences; a friend of Pushkin.

Ponomaryova, Sofya Dmitriyevna (Sofia, Sophie) (née Poznyak, 1794–1824), hostess of a literary salon SDP ("Society of the Friends of Enlightenment") frequented by minor literary figures of the time; an amateur woman of letters.

Pushkin, Lev Sergeyevich (Lyova, Lyovushka, Spew) (1805–1852), Aleksandr Pushkin's younger brother.

Pushkin, Sergey Lvovich (1767–1848), Aleksandr Pushkin's father.

Pushkin, Vasily Lvovich (1760–1830), Aleksandr Pushkin's uncle, a poet who introduced his nephew to the leading Russian poets of the time.

Shakhovskoy, Aleksandr Aleksandrovich, prince (1777–1846), poet and playwright (mostly of comedies), the first professional Russian stage director.

Trediakovsky, Vasily Kirillovich (1703–1769), Russian poet, playwright, literary theoretician, and advocate of poetic reform. The view of Trediakovsky as a mediocre writer was reappraised long after his death.

Turgenev, Aleksandr Ivanovich (1784–1845), senior civil servant in charge of the Department of Religious Affairs under Prince A. N. Golitsyn, 1810–1824; an enlightened man, a wit, a friend of Zhukovsky, Karamzin, Vyazemsky, and Pushkin.

Vyazemsky, Pyotr Andreyevich, prince (1792–1878), poet, critic, and humorist known for his sharp wit.

Vyazemskaya, Vera Fyodorovna, princess (1790–1886), the wife of Prince Pyotr Vyazemsky; her name is closely linked to the literary circles of the time—she was related to the Karamzins, a friend of Zhukovsky and Pushkin's confidant.

Zhukovsky, Vasily Andreyevich (1783–1852), respected Romantic poet, translator, and man of letters.

DECEMBRISTS

Arbuzov, Anton Petrovich (d.1848), Mikhail Küchelbecker's fellow naval officer, member of the Decembrist Northern Society.

Bestuzhev(-Marlinsky), Aleksandr Aleksandrovich (1797–1837), a Decembrist exiled to the war zone in the Caucasus; a Romantic poet, short story writer, and novelist; killed in a skirmish with the Circassians.

Bestuzhev, Mikhail Aleksandrovich (1800–1871), Staff Captain of the Life Guards (Moscow Regiment) and an active participant in the Decembrist uprising; sentenced to hard labor in Siberia; a writer.

Bestuzhev, Nikolay Aleksandrovich (1791–1855), a Russian naval officer, writer, inventor, and portrait artist; associated with the Decembrist uprising.

Glinka, Fyodor Nikolayevich (1786–1880), poet, essayist, novelist, officer.

Kakhovsky, Pyotr Grigoryevich (1797–1826), army officer and active participant in the Decembrist uprising; known for the murder of General Miloradovich and Colonel Ludwig Niklaus von Stürler.

Kornilovich, Aleksandr Osipovich (1800–1834), captain of the Guards General Staff, writer, historian.

Obolensky Evgeny Petrovich, prince (1796–1865), an officer, an active participant in the Decembrist uprising; elected chief of staff on the eve of the uprising and on the day commanded the insurgent forces.

Odoevsky, Aleksandr Ivanovich (Sasha) (1802–1839), Russian poet and playwright, one of the leading figures of the Decembrist uprising; sentenced to hard labor in Siberia.

Pestel, Pavel Ivanovich (1793–1826), the founder of the Decembrist Southern Society and the mastermind of the revolutionary project for reforming Russia, *The Russian Truth*.

Rosen, Andrey Yevgenyevich, baron (1800–1884), an officer of the Life Guards Finnish Regiment; sentenced to hard labor in Siberia.

Ryleyev, Kondraty Fyodorovich (1795–1826), poet, one of the five Decembrist leaders who were hanged.

Shchepin-Rostovsky, Dmitry Aleksandrovich (1798–1859), Staff Captain of the Moscow Life Guards Regiment; on December 14, 1825, together with the Bestuzhev brothers led his regiments to the Senate Square.

Shteingel (Steinheil), Vladimir Ivanovich, baron (1783–1862), a member of the Northern Society, assisted in organizing the Decembrist uprising; was sentenced to twenty years of hard labor in Siberia; essayist, memoirist, author of historical and ethnographical works.

Sutgof, Aleksandr Nikolayevich (1801–1872), army officer who led the Second battalion of the Life Guards Grenadier Regiment to join the rebels in Senate Square.

Trubetskoy, Sergey Petrovich (1790–1860), one of the organizers of the Decembrist uprising, on the eve of the uprising declared the rebels' leader (Dictator).

Tsebrikov, Nikolay Romanovich (d.1866), lieutenant; participant in the Decembrist uprising; was demoted to the rank of private.

Turgenev, Nikolay Ivanovich (1789–1871), economist and political theoretician, cofounder of the Northern Society of the Decembrists; was abroad during the uprising; chose never to return to his homeland, where he was tried in absentia and sentenced for life to hard labor in Siberia.

Voyeikov, Nikolay Pavlovich (d.1871), army officer, adjutant to Yermolov; from 1816 served in the Caucasus; was involved with the Decembrists.

Yakubovich, Aleksandr Ivanovich (1792–1845), army officer who took an active part in the Decembrist uprising; sentenced to hard labor then transferred to the Caucasus.

OTHER CHARACTERS

Adlerberg, Vladimir Fyodorovich (1790–1884), from 1817 adjutant to Grand Duke Nicholas, later Minister of the Imperial Court.

Albedyll, Pyotr Romanovich, baron (1764–1830), adjutant to Alexander I.

Alexander I (Aleksandr Pavlovich) (1777–1825) Grand Duke, the oldest son of Paul I, reigned as Emperor of Russia (1801–1825).

Anna Ioannovna (1693–1740) Empress of Russia (1730–1740), niece of Peter the Great.

Arakcheyev, Aleksey Andreyevich, count (1769-1834), brutal martinet, virtual ruler of Russia for ten years after being appointed deputy chairman of the Committee of Ministers.

Barclay de Tolly, Mikhail Andreyevich (Michael Andreas) (1761–1818), Russian Field Marshal and Minister of War during Napoleon's invasion of Russia in 1812 and War of the Sixth Coalition (1813–1814). Later Governor-General of Finland.

Benckendorff, Aleksandr Khristoforovich, von (1783–1844), one of the most reactionary statesmen of Nicholas's reign; from 1826 Chief of the Gendarmes and Head of the Secret Police.

Bistram, Karl Ivanovich, von (1770–1838), a German Baltic nobleman; commander in the imperial Russian Army during the Napoleonic Wars.

Catherine II, "The Great," (1729–1796) Empress of Russia (1762–1796), her reign is popularly remembered as the period of stability, territorial expansion and cultural, intellectual, and administrative advances.

Cloots, Anacharsis (Jean-Baptiste du Val-de-Gráce), baron (1755–1794), a Prussian nobleman and a significant figure in the French Revolution. Executed on the insistence of Robespierre for implication in a foreign plot.

Constantine (Konstantin Pavlovich) (1779–1831), Grand Duke, second son of Paul I, heir presumptive of his elder brother Alexander I.

Diebitsch, Ivan Ivanovich, count (1785–1831), German-born Russian Field Marshal; from 1824 Chief of the General Staff; assisted in suppressing the Decembrist uprising.

Dzhankhotov, Kuchuk (Old Kuchuk) (1758–1830), the last Supreme Prince of Kabarda (1809–1822).

Dzhankhotov, Dzhambulat (Jambot), (d.1825) youngest son of Kuchuk Dzhankhotov, Supreme Prince of Kabarda.

Elizabeth (Elizaveta Alekseyevna) (1779–1826) born princess Louise of Baden (1779–1826), Empress of Russia during her marriage to Emperor Alexander I.

Filaret (1782–1867), Metropolitan of Moscow (in 1823–1825 Archbishop) and head of the Russian Orthodox church; keeper of the secret Manifesto of 1823 in which Alexander I changed the order of succession to the throne.

Fleury, Papa, the name given to a few early nineteenth-century religious and political thinkers in France; here an invented character.

Fock, Maksim Yakovlevich, von (1777–1831), State Councillor in charge of the secret police in Russia, the specially created Third Department.

Golitsyn, Aleksandr Nikolayevich, prince (1771–1844), Minister for Religious Affairs and National Education (1816–1824), president of the Bible Society, a conservative reactionary.

Grudzinska, Jeanette (Joanna), princess (1791–1831), second wife of Grand Duke Constantine of Russia, the *de facto* viceroy of the Kingdom of Poland.

Karazin, Vasily Nazarovich (1773–1842), founder of the Ministry of National Education; petitioned Alexander I with his views on government development and wrote denunciations of Pushkin and Küchelbecker.

Kotzebue, August Friedrich Ferdinand, von (1761–1819), German dramatist and writer, consul in Russia and Germany, assassinated by Karl Sand, a militant member of the student fraternities.

Krüdener, Barbara-Julia, baroness (1764–1824), Baltic German religious mystic and Lutheran theologian who exerted great influence on Tsar Alexander I of Russia.

Kuruta, Dmitry Dmitriyevich, count (1769–1833), childhood friend and confidante of Grand Duke Constantine; general of infantry.

Lobanov-Rostovsky, Dmitry Ivanovich, prince (1758–1838), Russian general, Minister for Justice (August 1817–October1827).

Louvel, Louis Pierre (1783–1820), an anti-royal Bonapartist, who, at the Paris Opera, stabbed and mortally wounded Charles Ferdinand d'Artois, Duke of Berry, the youngest son of the future King, Charles X of France.

Maria Fyodorovna (1759–1828), Empress Dowager, the second wife of Paul I.

Metternich, Klemens, von (1773–1859), diplomat, one of the most important statemen of his era; Austrian Foreign Minister 1809–1821, then Chancellor.

Michael (Mikhail Pavlovich) (1798–1849), Grand Duke, the fourth son of Paul I.

Miloradovich, Mikhail Andreyevich (1771–1825), from 1818 Governor-General of St. Petersburg; mortally wounded during the Decembrist uprising.

Minkina (Shumskaya), Nastasya (Anastasiya) Fyodorovna (1782–1825), cruel and corrupt peasant lover of Count Arakcheyev

Nader Shah (1688–1747), one of the most powerful Iranian rulers in the history of the nation (reigned 1736–1747).

Naryshkin, Aleksandr Lvovich, prince (1760–1826), great chamberlain, chief operating officer of the imperial theaters (1799–1819); Marshal of Nobility of St. Petersburg (1818–1826).

Naryshkina, Marya Alekseyevna, princess (1762–1823), wife of Aleksandr Naryshkin; one of the favorite ladies-in-waiting of Catherine the Great.

Nesselrode, Karl-Robert (1780–1862), from 1816 Russian Foreign Minister, implemented the reactionary policies of the Holy Alliance.

Nicholas I (Nikolay Pavlovich) (1796–1855), Grand Duke, the third son of Paul I, younger brother of Alexander I; Tsar of Russia (1825–1855).

Novosiltsev, Nikolay Nikolayevich (1761–1838), Russian statesman and close aide to Alexander I.

Orlov, Aleksey Fyodorovich, prince (1787–1862), brother of the Decembrist Mikhail Orlov; was in charge of suppressing the Decembrist uprising.

Paskevich, Ivan Fyodorovich (1782–1856), general, appointed Governor-General of Georgia after Yermolov's forced retirement; after the Persian campaign of 1827–1828 received the title of the Count of Erivan.

Paul I (Pavel Petrovich) (1754–1801) Emperor of Russia (reigned from 1796 till his assassination in 1801).

Peter III (Pyotr Fyodorovich) (1728–1762), Tsar of Russia for six months in 1762 before he was deposed and possibly assassinated as a result of a conspiracy led by his wife who succeeded him under the name of Catherine II.

Photius (Pyotr Nikitich Spassky) (1792–1838), archimandrite, an influential reactionary Russian priest and mystic; in 1823–1825 he and Arakcheyev plotted the downfall of Arakcheyev's political rival, Prince Golitsyn, Minister for Education and Spiritual Affairs.

Pokhvistnev, Nikolay Nikolayevich (d.1828), minor official in the Ministry of Justice, adjutant to General Yermolov.

Pushchin, Pyotr Ivanovich (1723–1812), admiral, senator, uncle to a friend of Pushkin and Küchelbecker, Ivan Pushchin.

Pushkina, Avdotya (Eudoxie, Dunya) a distant relative of Aleksandr Pushkin, Küchelbecker's fiancée (from 1822).

Razumovsky, Aleksey Krillovich, count (1748–1822), Minister for Education (1810–1816).

Rostovtsev, Yakov Ivanovich (1803–1860), as a young officer was invited to join the secret society; reported the Decembrist plot to Grand Duke

Nicholas; went on to hold posts in military education reaching the rank of Full General.

Rückert, Friedrich (1788–1866), master of thirty languages, translator, poet, professor of eastern literatures.

Sand, Karl Ludwig (1795–1820), radical and nationalist German theological student who assassinated the German writer and playwright Kotzebue in Mannheim in March 1819, in outrage at his reactionary views; was arrested and in 1820 executed by beheading.

Schwarz, Fyodor Efimovich (1783–1869), Russian general infamous for his cruelty, commander of the Life Guards Semyonovsky Regiment.

Shishkov, Aleksandr Semyonovich (1754–1841), admiral and statesman; President of the Russian Academy and Minister for People's Education; a writer notorious for his proto-Slavophile sentiments; the founder of The Colloquy of Lovers of the Russian Word.

Shkarov, Yakov, Zhukovsky's servant of many years.

Skobelev, Ivan Nikitich (1778–1849), adjutant to Kutuzov during the Patriotic War against Napoleon in 1812.

Smirdin, Aleksandr Filippovich (1795–1857), prominent Russian publisher of all the best-known works by Karamzin, Zhukovsky, Pushkin, and Krylov; played a key role in the development of Russian literature in the early nineteenth century.

Sukhozanet, Ivan Onufrievich (1788–1861), Russian military engineer and artillery general active in dispersing the troops loyal to the Decembrists with artillery fire; rewarded with the rank of adjutant general.

Suvorov, Aleksandr Vasilyevich (1729–1800), Field Marshal; Russian national hero and military leader who in his fifty-eight years in the military fought sixty battles and won all of them with his brilliant tactics.

Teleshova, Ekaterina Aleksandrovna (1804–1857), famous ballerina.

Trubetskaya, Ekaterina Ivanovna (née de Laval (1800–1854), princess, the wife of Prince Sergey Trubetskoy; followed her husband to Siberia.

Toll, Karl Wilhelm, von (1777–1842), Baltic German aristocrat and Russian subject; general-adjutant to Alexander I in 1823; infantry general (from 1825).

Vasilchikov, Illarion Vasilyevich (1776–1847), general of cavalry, favorite of Nicholas I; during the Decembrist uprising persuaded the tsar to use harsh measures for its suppression.

Velho, Sophia (1793–1840), daughter of the banker Joseph Velho; Alexander I's mistress.

Vogel, Gustav Lvovich (1805–1859), police spy.

Volkonsky, Pyotr Mikhaylovich (1775–1852), military commander, General-Field Marshal, Adjutant General to Alexander I, member of the State Council (1821).

Yermolov, Aleksey Petrovich (1777–1861), general, who distinguished himself in the Napoleonic Wars and led the Russian conquest of the Caucasus.

Zakharzhevsky, Yakov Vasilyevich (1780–1865), general, commandant of Tsarskoe Selo.

Küchlya
Decembrist Poet
A Novel

Georg Wilhelm Timm, *Life Guards Horse Regiment During the Uprising of December 14, 1825 on Saint Isaac's Square*. Courtesy of the Hermitage Museum, St. Petersburg

Willie

I

Wilhelm graduated from boarding school with distinction.

He returned home from Werro considerably taller, strolled about the park, recited Schiller, and maintained an enigmatic silence. Ustinya Yakovlevna would watch him declaiming verse and then, suddenly, turning around and when there was no one nearby dabbing his eyes with his handkerchief.

Without thinking about it, Ustiniya Yakovlevna would later place a juicier morsel on his plate at dinnertime.

Wilhelm was already grown up, in his fourteenth year, and Ustinya Yakovlevna sensed that something had to be done about him.

A council was organized.

Wearing the tight breeches of the Guards, her young cousin Albrecht came to visit her in Pavlovsk, Aunt Breitkopf arrived, and a little gray-haired old man, a family friend, Baron Nicolai, had been invited. The old man was completely decrepit and kept sniffing a little vial of salts. Besides, he had a sweet tooth and every now and then would pop into his mouth a boiled sweet from an old *bonbonniere*. This kept him so busy he could hardly concentrate. Generally he behaved with great dignity and only occasionally confused names and events.

'Which school is Wilhelm to be sent to?'

Ustinya Yakovlevna looked at the council with some apprehension.

'Wilhelm?' the old man asked very graciously. 'Is he to be enrolled at a new school?' And he sniffed the little vial.

'Yes, he is,' said Ustinya Yakovlevna wistfully.

Everyone was silent.

'Military service, the academy,' the baron said suddenly and with great firmness. 'Wilhelm should enter military service.'

Albrecht narrowed his eyes slightly and said:

'But Wilhelm would not appear to have any particular disposition toward military service.'

Ustinya Yakovlevna seemed to detect that the cousin was speaking with a degree of condescension.

'Military service is the be-all and the end-all for young people,' the baron said weightily, 'although I personally have never been a military man. . . . He must be enlisted in the academy.'

He pulled out his *bonbonniere* and sucked on a sweet.

At this moment Ustinya junior came running into Wilhelm's room. (Both mother and daughter bore the same name. Aunt Breitkopf called the mother Justine and the daughter Little Ustinka.)

'Willie,' she said turning pale, 'come and listen, they're talking about you in there.'

Willie glanced at her absent-mindedly. For the last two days he had been whispering in dark corners with Senka, the domestic servant boy. During the day he wrote a lot in his notebook; he was silent and mysterious.

'About me?'

'Yes,' whispered the wide-eyed Ustinka, 'they want to send you to the war or to the academy.'

Willie jumped up from his chair.

'Do you know this for sure?' he asked in a whisper.

'I've just heard the baron say that you need to be sent to do your military service at the academy.'

'Swear to God,' said Wilhelm.

'As God is my witness,' said Ustinka hesitantly.

'Very well,' said Wilhelm, pale and resolute, 'you may go.'

He went back to his notebook, no longer paying any attention to Ustinka.

The council continued.

'He is a boy of rare abilities,' said Ustinya Yakovlevna, growing more and more anxious. 'He has an inclination to writing verse, and I don't think military service would suit him.'

'Ah, verses,' said the baron. 'Well, verses are quite a different kettle of fish, you know.'

He paused and added, looking at Aunt Breitkopf:

'Verses are literature.'

Aunt Breitkopf spoke slowly, hammering out every word:

'He must enter the Lycée.'

'But isn't it in France—the Lycée?' said the baron distractedly.

'No, Baron, it's in Russia,' Aunt Breitkopf snapped indignantly. 'It's in Russia, in Saarskoe Selo,[1] half an hour's walk from here. It is going to be a noble institution. Justine must have heard about it: I believe the grand dukes themselves are expected to be educated there,' and the aunt made a triumphant gesture toward the baron.

'Splendid,' said the baron resolutely, 'so he will enter the Lycée.'

Ustinya Yakovlevna thought:

"Oh, what a wonderful idea! It's so close to home."

Then she remembered:

'Actually, the grand dukes will not be educated there after all; there has been a change of heart.'

'And all the better,' the baron replied unexpectedly, 'all the better. Who cares if they won't? Wilhelm will enter the Lycée.'

'I'll have a word with the Barclays.' Ustinya Yakovlevna glanced at Aunt Breitkopf. (Barclay de Tolly's wife was her cousin). 'We shouldn't bother Her Majesty too often. The Barclays won't turn me down.'

'There is no way,' said the baron, thinking of something else, 'that they can possibly turn you down.'

'And once you've spoken to Barclay,' added the aunt, 'we'll ask the baron to take Wilhelm there and enrol him.'

The baron grew confused.

'Take him where?' he asked in bewilderment. 'The Lycée is not in France, it's in Saarskoe Selo. Why on earth does he need to be *taken*?'

'Good Heavens,' the aunt said impatiently, 'they are taken to the minister, to Count Aleksey Kirillovich. You are an old friend, baron, and we rely on you; it will be more appropriate if you go to the minister's.'

'I'll do everything I can, absolutely everything,' the baron said. 'I'll personally take him to the Lycée.'

'Thank you, dear Ioanniky Fyodorovich.'

Ustinya Yakovlevna raised her handkerchief to her eyes.

The baron also shed a tear and became very agitated.

'He must be taken to the Lycée. Pack his things and I'll take him to the Lycée.'

The word "Lycée" fascinated him.

'Dear Baron,' said the aunt, 'first of all he needs to be introduced to the minister. I shall bring Wilhelm to your place and you'll accompany him.'

She was treating the baron like one of her charges—Aunt Breitkopf was the headmistress of the St. Catherine's Institute for Noble Maids.

The baron stood up, looked wistfully at Aunt Breitkopf, and bowed:

'Trust me, I shall be greatly looking forward to seeing you.'

'Dear Baron, you are staying the night with us!' said Ustinya Yakovlevna and her voice trembled.

The aunt half-opened the door and called out:

'Wilhelm!'

Wilhelm came in, staring at everyone with a strange expression.

'Now pay attention, Wilhelm,' Aunt Breitkopf said solemnly. 'We have just decided that you will enter the Lycée. It is being opened not far from here at all, at Saarskoe Selo. You'll be taught various subjects there—including poetry. You will also make friends.'

Wilhelm stood as if struck dead.

'Baron Ioanniky Fyodorovich has been kind enough to agree to take you to the minister in person.'

The baron stopped sucking his sweet and looked at the aunt with interest.

Then, without saying a word, Wilhelm walked out of the room.

'What's wrong with him?' asked the aunt in amazement.

Ustinya Yakovlevna sighed:

'He must be upset, poor boy.'

Wilhelm was not upset. The thing was that tonight was the night when he and Senka had planned to escape to the town of Werro where Minchen, the daughter of his respectable tutor, was waiting for him. She was only twelve years old. Before leaving, Wilhelm had promised that he would abduct her from her father's house and marry her secretly. Senka would accompany him, and then, when they got married, all three would live in a hut a bit like a Swiss chalet, pick flowers and strawberries all day long, and be in a state of perfect bliss.

At night Senka quietly knocks at Willie's window.

Everything is ready.

Wilhelm takes his notebook, puts two pieces of stale bread into his pocket, gets dressed. The window hasn't been locked since the previous evening—deliberately. He carefully walks around the bed of little Mishka, his brother, and climbs out of the window.

It feels eerie in the garden, even though the night is light.

Quietly they turn the corner of the house, where they will climb over the fence. Before leaving his family home Wilhelm kneels down and kisses the ground. He read about this somewhere in Karamzin. He feels sad and holds back a tear. Senka waits for him patiently.

They take another two steps and come across an open window.

Dressed in a gown and a nightcap, the baron is sitting by the window gazing indifferently at Wilhelm.

Wilhelm freezes on the spot. Senka disappears behind a tree.

'Good evening. *Bon soir, Guillaume*,' says the baron indulgently and rather vaguely.

'Good evening,' says Wilhelm, suddenly breathless.

'Fine weather, almost like in Venice,' says the baron and sighs. He sniffs the vial. 'They say that such weather in May happens only in a leap year.'

He looks thoughtfully at Wilhelm.

'Although this isn't a leap year. How are you getting on at school?' he asks Wilhelm, showing some interest.

'Thank you for asking,' replies Wilhelm. 'My German is good and so is my French.'

'Are they indeed?' the baron asks in amazement.

'And Latin too,' says Wilhelm, feeling the ground going from under his feet.

'Ah, that's another matter.' The baron lapses again into indifference.

A startled Ustinya Yakovlevna in a nightcap shows up at a window that opens nearby.

'Good evening, Ustinya Yakovlevna,' the baron greets her courteously, 'wonderful weather, isn't it? You have *Firenze la Bella* over here. One can breathe so deeply.'

'It is.' Ustinya Yakovlevna sounds dumbfounded. 'But what is Wilhelm doing here in the garden at night?'

'Wilhelm?' the baron asks absent-mindedly. 'Ah, Wilhelm!' he remembers. 'Wilhelm is also enjoying the air. He is out for a stroll.'

Ustinya Yakovlevna's eyes are wide open with astonishment:

'Come here, Wilhelm.'

Wilhelm approaches, his heart in his boots.

'My dear boy, what are you doing here?'

She looks at her son apprehensively, stretches out a dry hand and strokes his coarse hair.

'Come to me,' says Ustinya Yakovlevna, looking at him with alarm. 'Come through the window.'

Hanging his head, Wilhelm climbs into his mother's window. Her eyes well up. Seeing these tears, Wilhelm gives a sudden sob and tells her everything, everything. Ustinya Yakovlevna laughs through her tears and strokes her son's head.

The baron sits by the window for a long time yet, sniffing the little vial of salts. He remembers an Italian actress who died forty years ago and almost imagines that he is in *Firenze la Bella*.

II

The baron puts on an old-fashioned uniform with decorations, pulls on his gloves, leans on his stick, takes Wilhelm's arm, and they head off to see the minister, Count Aleksey Kirillovich Razumovsky.

They enter a vast hall with columns, with huge portraits all over its walls. There are about a dozen adults in the hall, each accompanying a boy. Wilhelm passes by a diminutive lad standing beside a dull man in the uniform of a government official. The baron sinks into an armchair. Wilhelm looks around. Next to him stands a boy, black-haired and fidgety, like a monkey. Holding him by the hand is a man in a black tailcoat, wearing a decoration on his lapel.

'Keep still, *Michel*,' he says with a Parisian accent when the boy begins to make faces at Wilhelm.

This is the French tutor of the Moscow University Boarding School, who has come to enrol Misha Yakovlev.

Not far from them is a little old man in the dress uniform of an admiral. His brows are knitted in a frown and like the baron, he leans on his walking stick. He seems cross and avoids looking at anyone. Next to him is a boy: ruddy, plump, blue-eyed, and fair-haired.

On spotting the baron, the admiral brightens up.

'Ioanniky Fyodorovich?' he says in a deep hoarse voice.

The baron stops sucking his bonbon and stares at the admiral. Then he approaches him and shakes his hand.

'Ivan Petrovich, *cher amiral*.'

'Pyotr Ivanovich, if you don't mind,' grumbles the admiral. 'Mixing up names, aren't we, my dear fellow? It's Pyotr Ivanovich.'

Not in the least embarrassed, the baron plunges into a conversation. This is an old friend of his—the baron has plenty of old friends—Admiral Pushchin. The admiral is not at all happy. He has been waiting for the minister for half an hour. Another five minutes go by. Wilhelm stares at the rosy-cheeked boy, who looks back at Wilhelm with some surprise.

'Vanya,' says the admiral, 'go and stretch your legs in the hall.'

The boys walk awkwardly round the hall, peering at one another. When they pass by Misha Yakovlev, Misha swiftly sticks out his tongue at them. Vanya says to Wilhelm:

'What a monkey!'

Wilhelm responds:

'A complete clown.'

The admiral is beginning to lose patience. He knocks on the floor with his stick. The baron knocks with his at the same time. The admiral calls the duty officer and inquires:

'Is His Excellency intending to see us today?'

The official responds:

'Apologies, Your Excellency, His Excellency is finishing his *toilette*.'

The admiral loses his temper:

'What I need is Aleksey Kirillovich, not his *toilette*.'

'I shall report at once.'

Half-bowing, the official slips out into the next room.

A minute later everyone is invited into the inner rooms. The meeting begins.

A fop in a black frock coat and with an extraordinary jabot, strongly perfumed and tightly corseted, approaches the admiral. His little eyes are lively and slightly crossed, he has a bird's nose, and despite being corseted like a wine glass, the dapper man has a bit of a belly.

'Pyotr Ivanovich,' he says in a remarkably pleasant voice, and begins to shower the admiral with French phrases.

The admiral cannot stand fops and all their French nonsense, and looking at the dandy he thinks: "You scoundrel," (he calls all fops "scoundrel"); nevertheless, the admiral enjoys honors and respect.

'Who is this with you, Vasily Lvovich?' he asks agreeably.

'My nephew, Sergey Lvovich's son.' He calls out: 'Sasha!'

Sasha Pushkin approaches. He is a curly, quick-eyed boy, he scowls and lounges around. Seeing Wilhelm, he laughs with his eyes, observing him quietly.

At that moment a high-ranking official comes out of the minister's office; he is holding a sheet of paper in his hands and calls out the names:

'Baron Delvig, Anton Antonovich!'

A pale plump boy with a sleepy face approaches reluctantly and uncertainly.

'Komovsky!'

A tiny boy minces up with small neat steps.

'Yakovlev!'

The little monkey almost runs to the call.

The official calls Pushchin, Pushkin, Wilhelm.

They feel rather overawed in the minister's office. There are important people sitting at a desk covered with a gold-fringed blue tablecloth. The minister is a man with a sash over his shoulder, stout, wavy-haired, curled and pomaded, with a pale face and a sour smile. He jokes indolently with a tall man in a uniform, who looks like either a seminarist or an Englishman. The tall one is the examiner. This is Malinovsky, the newly appointed headmaster of the Lycée. He asks them questions, as if tapping them with a little hammer, and waits for an answer with his head cocked to one side. The exam ends late. Everyone leaves. On parting, Yakovlev pulls such a face that Pushkin bares his white teeth and quietly nudges Pushchin in the side.

III

On October 19, Wilhelm took his time donning his full dress uniform. He pulled on a pair of white breeches and a dark blue jacket with a red collar that was too high, tied his white tie, smoothed down his white waistcoat, put on a pair of Hessian boots, and examined himself in the mirror not without some pleasure. In the mirror stood a tall thin boy with bulging eyes, looking pretty much like a parrot.

When everybody lined up in the Lycée corridor, Pushkin glanced at Wilhelm with laughing eyes. Wilhelm blushed and kept shifting his head, as if the collar was making him uncomfortable. They were ushered into the hall. The inspector and the tutors bustled about arranging the boys in three rows and stood before them, like majors during the changing of the guard.

Between the columns in the Lycée hall there was an enormous table covered with red cloth, its golden fringe reaching the floor. Wilhelm blinked—there was so much gold on the uniforms.

The pale, podgy, quiffed minister sat in an armchair talking with an old man he didn't know. He looked blankly at everybody, then said something in the pale headmaster's ear, at which the latter grew even paler, and left.

Silence.

The door opened and the tsar came in. His blue eyes were smiling to all and sundry, a foppish frock coat clung tightly to his plump flanks. He made a gesture with his white hand to the minister, pointing to the seat next to himself. Ungainly and tall, Grand Duke Constantine was walking beside him. His drooping lower lip made him look sleepy and he was hunched over, his uniform hanging like a sack. White lace foam glided alongside the tsar on the other side—the Empress Elizabeth—and the crisp silk of the Dowager Maria Fyodorovna rustled all over the hall.

They sat down. With a sheaf of papers in his hand, trembling with excitement and barely moving his long legs, the headmaster stepped out in front and, stammering, in a hollow voice, began to speak about the feelings of allegiance to the throne, which had to be implanted, developed, and affirmed in certain persons. The sheets of paper danced in his hands. He stared as if bewitched into the blue eyes of the tsar who, raising his eyebrows and biting his lips, did not listen to a word of what he was saying. Admiral Pushchin gave a series of loud coughs; Vasily Lvovich sneezed dramatically and blushed with embarrassment. Only Baron Nicolai looked at the headmaster with approval and sniffed his vial.

"His Majesty" was heard among the murmuring and then again: "His Majesty," and more murmuring. The headmaster sat down; the admiral breathed freely.

The headmaster's speech was followed by one from a young man, upright and pale. Unlike the headmaster before him he did not look at the tsar, he looked instead at the boys. This was Kunitsyn, professor of moral philosophy.

At the first sounds of his voice the tsar pricked up his ears.

Kunitsyn sounded disapproving:

'The education of social beings does not imply the ability to shine with external qualities, which are often the specious mask of gross ignorance, but genuine formation of minds and hearts.'

Stretching out his hand toward the boys, he spoke almost gloomily:

'The time will come when your fatherland will entrust you with the sacred duty of preserving the public good.'

And not a word about the tsar. He seems oblivious to his presence. But no, here he is, half-turning toward him:

'The social man never rejects the cry of the people, for the voice of the people is the voice of God.'

And again he looks only at the boys, his voice reproachful again, and his hand movements rapid.

'What is the point of taking pride in titles not acquired by merit, when one sees in everybody's eyes scorn or reproach, animadversion or censure, hatred or curses? Should one seek distinction so that having attained it one would fear disgrace?'

Wilhelm cannot take his eyes off Kunitsyn, whose immobile face is pale.

The tsar listens attentively. He has even raised his white hand to his ear: he is slightly hard of hearing. His cheeks have flushed, his eyes follow the speaker. The minister looks at Kunitsyn with a sour, weighty expression—and sideways at the tsar. He wants to know what impression the strange speech is producing on His Majesty. But the tsar's eyes are devoid of expression, his forehead is frowning while his lips are smiling.

All of a sudden, Kunitsyn as if involuntarily glances at the minister. The minister is listening closely to the professor's tense voice:

'Imagine a statesman without knowledge, who has only a nominal understanding of the duties of state, and you will see how sad is his situation. Not knowing the inherent causes of the rise and fall of states, he is unable to give a permanent course to public affairs; at every step he is mistaken, while at every action he changes direction. While correcting one error he makes another; eradicating one evil he lays the foundation for another; instead of essential improvements he strives for peripheral ones.'

The pale sagging cheeks of the minister flare up. He bites his lip and no longer looks at the speaker. Baron Nicolai in the audience takes a good strong sniff at his vial. Vasily Lvovich listens agape, which makes his face look remarkably stupid.

Kunitsyn's voice rings out; he no longer looks at the boys, he addresses empty space—so as to avoid looking at the minister and the tsar:

'Exhausted by futile labors, tormented by conscience, driven by general indignation, such a statesman gives himself over to chance or becomes a slave to other people's prejudices. Like a reckless swimmer, he is swept onto the rocks, surrounded by the sad remnants of multiple shipwrecks. At the very time when he should harness the whirlwinds of threatening clouds, he surrenders himself instead to their onslaught and, seeing the yawning abyss, seeks shelter where the sea has no limits.'

Calm, taut as a string, the young professor sits down. His cheeks are burning. The minister directs a sideways look at the tsar.

The reddish head gives a sudden bow of approval: the tsar has remembered that he is the foremost liberal in his country.

He casually leans his head toward the minister and speaks in a loud whisper:

'Recommend for distinction.'

The minister bows his head, his face expressing joy.

The list returns to the headmaster's hands and begins to dance in them again. The boys' names are being called out.

'Küchelbecker, Wilhelm.'

Willie, leaning forward with his upper body and getting entangled in his legs, approaches the intimidating table. He forgets the ceremonial protocol and bows so absurdly that the tsar brings the lorgnette to his lusterless eyes and looks at him for a second. Only for a second. The reddish head nods patiently to the boy.

The baron says to the admiral:

'This is Wilhelm. I've enrolled him at the Lycée.'

Then the boys are led to the dining room. The dowager empress tastes the soup.

She approaches Wilhelm from behind, leans lightly on his shoulders and asks graciously:

'*Karosh zup*?'[2]

Taken by surprise, Wilhelm chokes on a pie, attempts to get up on his feet, and, to his horror, answers in a thin voice:

'*Oui, monsieur*.'

Sitting next to him, Pushchin swallows the hot soup and makes a desperate face. Pushkin pulls his head into his shoulders, and his spoon freezes mid-air.

Grand Duke Constantine, who stands by the window busying himself pinching and tickling his sister, hears everything from afar and roars with laughter. His laugh is barking and wooden, as if someone was clicking on an abacus.

The empress suddenly takes offense and majestically glides past the schoolboys. Then Constantine comes up to the table and stares at Wilhelm with curiosity, his lip drooping low; the grand duke positively likes him.

As for Wilhelm, he feels that he is about to burst into tears. He is trying not to. His face with its bulging eyes is turning crimson, and his lower lip trembles.

Nevertheless, all ends well. His Imperial Highness goes back to the window—to tickle Her Imperial Highness.

October 19, 1811 comes to an end.

Wilhelm is now a lycéen.

The Bechelkückeriad

I

"Do you know what the Bechelkückeriad is?

"It is a long strip of land, a country engaged in large-scale trade in the ghastliest verses; it includes the Tin Ear province, which the other day fought a big battle with the neighboring Donkey-Doyasomev[3] state; the latter kingdom, wishing to demean the former one, with a great shout attacked the Bechelkückeriadian Tin Ear province, for which the latter avenged herself in the most terrible way . . ."

Wilhelm didn't read any further. He knew that he would pay dearly for his fight with Myasoedov, that the *Lycée Sage* would make a big deal of it, that they would read about the Bechelkückeriad all day long, roaring with laughter and fighting each other for the sheets of the school magazine.

Komovsky, nicknamed Little Fox, a clever little sneak who told on his fellow-students to Küchlya and on Küchlya to his fellow-students, and reported everything confidentially to the tutor in the evenings, looked at him eagerly and whispered:

'Illichevsky assures me that it's only the beginning, that they're really going to write such things about you that . . .'

Wilhelm stopped listening. He ran upstairs to his room and locked himself in.

He sat down at the desk and buried his face in his hands.

He had been bullied at the Lycée. His deafness, quick temper, strange manners, stammering, his entire figure, tall and stooped, provoked uncontrollable laughter. But this week he seemed to have been harassed especially ruthlessly. Epigram after epigram, caricature after caricature, "Tapeworm," "Küchlya," "Gesell"[4]!

He jumped to his feet, a tall, thin boy, made a ridiculous gesture, and, all of a sudden, calmed down.

He still had his poems, his writing. He didn't need people. He thought a bit, then suddenly realized that he really did need a friend. He sighed, picked up his ballad about Almansor and Zulma, which he had been composing for a fortnight, crossing out, redrafting and starting again. He pondered. Should he show it to Pushkin?—no, Frenchie would certainly write an epigram about it, he had already written enough of those!

Strangely enough, Küchlya could not bring himself to be angry with Pushkin, not really, not entirely. No matter what Frenchie did, Küchlya forgave him everything. He would fly into a temper and rage at him, but he was fond of him. When Frenchie suddenly stopped in a corner of the hall, his eyes shining, thick lips puffed out, gaze fixed grimly on one point, Wilhelm would timidly and tenderly let him be: he knew that Frenchie was composing poetry.

He was drawn to him.

But Frenchie would quickly raise his darting brown eyes to him and suddenly start laughing, while racing about and carrying on. Most crucial for his pride was not that he was good at writing poetry, but that he could run faster than anyone and was better at jumping over chairs. Pushkin's poetry was appreciated at the Lycée for the very same reason as Illichevsky's—for its smoothness. But Küchlya enjoyed it for a completely different reason and would say about Illichevsky's verses: 'They may be good, but they're not poetry.'

'And what is poetry?' Delvig asked him wistfully.

'I bet yours are better, old boy,' Pushkin said with a wink.

Küchlya knew that his poems were worse, but he didn't want to write like Illichevsky. So what if they were worse?—no matter; and he went on composing his ballads and folk songs. His poems were called "Klopstockian" at the Lycée. "Klopstock" was something thick, something oakish, some sort of a clumsy lump. In essence, the only person in the whole Lycée who understood Küchlya was Delvig. This lazy, dozy boy could listen to Küchlya for hours when he recited Schiller in a wild voice. Then the little grin that scared Küchlya to death would disappear from behind Delvig's glasses.

Wilhelm went back to the ballad. Somebody knocked on the door. Once again it was Komovsky. He was holding the all-important issue of the *Lycée Sage*. Sighing, but looking intently at Küchlya—he was secretly pleased to see Küchlya losing his temper—Little Fox said in the most pitiful voice:

'Wilhelm, you haven't finished reading, there's more.'

Wilhelm opened the magazine: the very ballad over which he had been toiling in total secrecy for the last two weeks had been copied almost entirely, and alongside it in a tiny hand was written the most devastating critique of every word!

Küchlya furiously jumped to his feet and asked, gasping:

'Who stole the ballad from my desk? Who dared steal the ballad from my desk?'

The only people who knew about the ballad were Komovsky and Delvig. Little Fox cringed, but glanced at Küchlya with enjoyment.

'Must have been Delvig,' he said with a sigh.

'Delvig?' Küchlya rolled his eyes.

This was the most heinous betrayal in the world—if it had been Yakovlev or anyone else—but Delvig!

Not looking at Komovsky or listening to him, Küchlya ran along the corridor.

He burst into Delvig's room. Delvig was lying on his bed staring at the ceiling. As he did for days on end—his laziness was legendary at the Lycée.

'Willie?'

Küchlya said breathlessly:

'I want a word with you.'

'What's wrong?' Delvig asked calmly. 'Have you lost your mind or just written a new song?'

'And you dare talk to me like that?' said Küchlya and stepped toward him.

'Why not?' Delvig yawned. 'Listen,' he said, stretching, 'you know what, don't go to the headmaster's tonight—Pushkin is suggesting a walk instead.'

He looked at Wilhelm, suddenly surprised:

'What's the matter with you, Willie, are you ill, is your tummy sore?'

Wilhelm was trembling.

'You are a dishonorable person, you are mean,' he said. 'I'm no longer your friend. If your name wasn't Delvig, I would give you a good thrashing. And I might still do so.'

'No idea what you are talking about,' Delvig said, dumbfounded.

Wilhelm wailed:

'You pretended to be my friend in order to steal my ballad and to mock me! This is the work of a mean-minded schemer!'

'You are out of your mind,' Delvig said calmly and finally got out of bed. 'I can see one thing clearly—that you are out of your mind. Funny, isn't it!'

When he was greatly hurt or felt sad, he always said "Funny, isn't it?"

Pushkin burst through the door without knocking, dragging Komovsky behind him. He was grimly cheerful. Komovsky struggled with his hands and feet to get out of his grip.

'The sneak has been eavesdropping again,' he announced, slapped the back of Komovsky's head and turned toward him. 'If you report this to the tutor, Little Fox, he might give you a second helping of dinner.'

Having spotted Wilhelm standing with his fists clenched. Pushkin went up to him and gave him a sideways shove. Wilhelm growled . . .

'Oh my!' said Pushkin and burst into laughter.

Delvig quickly blocked the door:

'Come here now, Little Fox. Who told Wilhelm I'd pinched his ballad?'

Komovsky's little eyes darted all over the room.

Pushkin pricked up his ears.

'You see,' Delvig explained to him and his voice trembled, 'this madman says I took advantage of our friendship and stole his ballad for the *Sage*. Funny, isn't it?'

Pushkin assumed a serious look:

'We'll hold a court. I'll bring the publisher over here. Arrest Little Fox.'

The publisher was Danzas, who had copied the magazine. Pushkin ran out and a moment later dragged in the mighty Danzas.

Wilhelm stood utterly uncomprehending.

Komovsky addressed Pushkin ingratiatingly:

'Listen, Monkey with Tiger. I need to go, I'll be right back.'

At the Lycée Pushkin was called either "Frenchie" or "Monkey with Tiger." The second nickname was more honorable. Little Fox was trying to wriggle out of it.

'No, you can't. We'll resolve the matter here and now. What have you to say, Danzas?'

Looking straight at everyone, Danzas said that Little Fox had handed Küchlya's ballad over to him three days earlier.

Komovsky shrank into a ball.

Küchlya remained standing there, utterly confused.

He forgot to get angry with Komovsky. The latter hunched his shoulders and slipped out of the room.

Then Pushkin put his arms round Küchlya's and Delvig's waists, pushed them toward each other and said peremptorily:

'Make peace.'

II

Alas, the peace did not last long. That day was a miserable one for Küchlya.

Before dinner, Yakovlev was clowning. Yakovlev was the Lycée's favorite buffoon. There were a few of these lively, fidgety boys who joked, pulled faces, and eventually became the Lycée jesters. But Misha Yakovlev made foolishness a subtle and high art. He was "the jester of the two hundred tricks"; he mimicked and impersonated two hundred people. This was his pride, this was his niche at the Lycée.

Dark-haired and quick-witted, with a droll little snout, he transformed himself before everyone's eyes. When he gave a "performance," he grew taller or shorter or stouter or thinner and the open-mouthed lycéens saw before them Delvig, Kunitsyn, or the Lycée sexton. He imitated horn music so well that once a tutor carried out a special investigation into how the students had acquired horns. He also imitated the sound of the flute and played on his lips well over half of Field's *Nocturne*—he had an ear for music. However, he could just as easily grunt like a piglet or impersonate a lecherous cockerel.

Today was his gala day. The jester had prepared a new number.

The boys crowded together and Yakovlev started. To warm up, however, he chose to execute a few old numbers. He paused and looked at the boys around him. He was waiting for suggestions.

'Yesakov.'

Yesakov was a quiet boy with blushing cheeks, shy, with a peculiar gait: he shuffled and nodded as he walked. He was very fond of Küchlya and, after Delvig, was his best friend. Yakovlev shrank, gave a little grunt, grew shorter, began to nod in a special humble way and suddenly walked with that peculiar shy gait that Yesakov had. Yesakov smiled.

'Broglio.'

This was a quick number. Yakovlev squinted and screwed up his right eye, threw back his head, and began to twirl his fingers at the sides of his uniform as if searching for a decoration. (Some decoration or other had recently been brought to Broglio from Italy; he was an Italian count.)

'De Boudry.'

Yakovlev stuck out his belly, his cheeks puffed and sagged, he frowned, half-closed his eyes, and began to howl softly, shaking his head. In front of the Lycée students stood David Ivanych de Boudry, their teacher of French and a lover of recitation.

'The priest, the priest!'

'The sexton, with tremolos!'

Yakovlev stretched his neck, his eyes became dull and at the same time began to dart about swiftly and stealthily, his cheeks were drawn in, and a sexton very much like the Lycée sexton began to drone in a tremulous voice:

'Lord, have mercy, Lord, have mercy, Lord, have mercy.'

'A monkey.'

This number was the easiest for Yakovlev. He already looked like a monkey. He sat down on the floor, spread his legs, and began quickly, not like a human being, to scratch his armpits. Yakovlev's little eyes darted here and there with that meaningless and tranquil expression that he had seen on the monkey of a wandering Italian who had once looked into the Lycée.

'Now the new number.'

Yakovlev announced:

'The new one is Minchen and Küchlya.'

Wilhelm was bewildered. His betrothal with Minchen was a secret, which he had entrusted only to Delvig.

He watched Yakovlev.

Yakovlev grew taller. His neck stretched out, his mouth opened, his eyes bulged. Wobbling and twisting his head, he took two steps, kicked his foot in the air, and stopped. A faithful and wicked replica of Küchlya.

The lycéens rolled about laughing. Pushkin laughed with a staccato barking laugh. Oblivious to everything in the world, Delvig moaned in a thin voice.

Now Yakovlev squatted as if he were sitting on a bench. He puckered his lips into a Cupid's bow, raised his eyes to the sky, dropped his head to one side, and began to fumble with an imaginary plait that lay on his chest. Then "Küchlya" stretched his neck like a giraffe, pouted hard, and fiercely rolling his eyes, smacked his lips, after which, with a sudden kick of one leg, he jumped away to the side, as if burnt. "Minchen" pushed out her lips in the most pitiful way, also kissed the air, jerked her head, and hid her face in her hands.

The dormitory roared with laughter.

Wilhelm turned crimson and advanced toward Yakovlev, but this move had been anticipated: he was immediately picked up by the arms, pushed into his cell, and the door shut behind him and barricaded.

He squealed and threw his whole body at it, pounding it with his fists and shouting: 'Swine!'—and finally sank to the floor.

Outside the door, a duo of voices was singing:

Ah, I feel sick, alas,
On a bench a lonely lass.
Nothing pleases me, everything disgusts me,
There is no Küchelbecker next to me!
Küchelbecker is not there.
At the big wide world I stare—
Every seat and every bench
Reminds me of my charming wench.

And immediately the chorus responded in concert:

No, it is no wrench
For me, this alien bench.
Everything delights me, nothing disgusts me,
Küchelbecker is not with me!
Küchelbecker is not with me
The big wide world I see
And all the benches, every one
Tells me I'm the happy one.

Wilhelm did not cry. He knew now what he had to do.

III

The dinner call.

Everyone runs up to the dining room on the second floor.

Wilhelm waits.

He peeps out of the door and listens. A vague rumble comes from below—they are all sitting themselves down.

No one has noticed his absence yet. He has a minute or two.

He runs down the stairs, past the dining room, and, a second later, he is rushing through the garden.

One of the tutors has spotted him through the dining-room window. His astonished face flashes for a moment before Wilhelm. There's no time to waste.

He runs as fast as he can. He catches a glimpse of the mushroom-shaped arbor, in which only yesterday he wrote his poems.

Here it is at last—and with all his might Wilhelm hurls himself into the pond.

His face is smeared all over with slime and mud, and the cold stagnant water reaches up to his neck. The pond is not deep and has grown even shallower during the summer. The garden is filled with screams, the sounds of stamping feet and general commotion. Wilhelm sinks into the water.

Sunlight and green slime close over his head. He sees some iridescent circles—then hears the abrupt stroke of oars, very close to his head, and voices, howls.

The last thing he sees is the closing circles of a rainbow, the last thing he hears is someone's desperate shriek, probably a tutor's:

'Over here, over here! Bring a boathook!'

When Wilhelm opens his eyes, he is lying on the grass by the pond. He suddenly feels chilled.

An old face with glasses leans over him; Wilhelm recognizes him, it is Dr. Peschl. The doctor puts some strong-smelling spirits under his nose; Wilhelm trembles and makes an effort to say something.

'Be quiet,' says the doctor sternly.

But Wilhelm has already sat up. He sees the frightened faces of his fellow-students standing next to Kunitsyn and the Frenchman, de Boudry. Kunitsyn says something in a low voice to de Boudry, who nods disapprovingly. Engelhardt, the new headmaster, has folded his hands on his belly in bewilderment and stares blankly at Küchlya.

Küchlya is taken back to the Lycée and put to bed in the sick-bay.

At night Pushkin, Pushchin and Yesakov creep into the ward.

Yesakov, shy and red-faced, smiles, as always. Pushkin is gloomy and anxious.

'What's got into you, Wilhelm?' asks Yesakov in a whisper. 'You can't act like that, old boy.'

Wilhelm says nothing.

'You've got to understand,' Pushchin says reasonably, 'if each of us starts drowning himself because of Yakovlev's every joke, there won't be enough room in the pond. After all, you're not Poor Liza.'[5]

Wilhelm still says nothing.

Pushkin unexpectedly takes Wilhelm's hand and squeezes it uncertainly. Wilhelm tears himself off the bed, hugs him, and mutters:

'I couldn't take it any more, Pushkin, I just couldn't.'

'Very well then,' Yesakov says calmly and confidently, 'enough of this nonsense. They are actually fond of you, old boy. And if they laugh at you—it doesn't matter.'

IV

In spite of all this, life at the Lycée went on in its usual way.

Grievances were forgotten. The lycéens grew older. After the pond incident, only Illichevsky carried on with his mockery of Küchlya. Küchlya even acquired admirers. Modest Korf, a neat good-looking German, claimed that although Küchlya's verses were peculiar, they were not without merit, and perhaps no worse than Delvig's.

Küchlya was a good pupil and developed a new trait—ambition. When falling asleep, he imagined himself a great man. He would be making speeches in front of a crowd that was roaring ecstatically, or he would become a great poet and Derzhavin would kiss his head and declare either to the same crowd or to the lycéens that he was handing over his lyre to him, Wilhelm Küchelbecker.

Küchlya was stubborn; if he was sure of something, no one could compel him to change his opinion. The mathematics teacher, Kartsov, wrote in his progress report, that he was "thorough, but liable to error due to overconfidence." Three people understood him well: the teacher of French, David Ivanovich de Boudry, the professor of moral sciences, Kunitsyn, and the headmaster, Engelhardt.

Kunitsyn noticed Küchlya grow pale in his lessons when he spoke about the Gracchi brothers[6] and about Thrasybulus's[7] struggle for freedom. Despite his wild nature the boy had a clear head and Kunitsyn even enjoyed his doggedness.

The headmaster, Yegor Antonovich Engelhardt, was an orderly man. When he referred to "our dear Lycée," his eyes would assume an almost devout expression. He could understand and explain everything under the sun and when faced with a puzzling individual, would take pains to pigeon-hole him; it was only after he had finally done so and the person was correctly labeled that Engelhardt would calm down.

Everything was in order and what a wonderful order it was: the entire world was well arranged. Universal goodness lay at the heart of creation.

Pushkin hated Engelhardt without knowing why. He would lower his eyes when talking to him. He would laugh rudely when Engelhardt ran into trouble. And Engelhardt was lost before this disorganized creature. Deep in his soul he hated him too and, worst of all, he was afraid of Pushkin. The heart of this young man was empty, not a single spark of true good nature was there, only undisciplined levity together with certain sounds in his head, and at the same time negligence, frivolity, and, alas, immorality! Yegor Antonovich bore absolutely no responsibility for this pupil; he really could not find a label for him.

And yet Yegor Antonovich understood the chaotic Küchel (Yegor Antonovich called Wilhelm Küchel, not Küchlya: to refer to him as such was in the Lycée spirit and yet slightly different from the boys, the lycéens), Küchel who was also given to frivolity and extremes. Oh yes, Yegor Antonovich understood this crazy young man from a good German family. This was a Don Quixote, extremely wild but at heart a good-natured soul. Yegor Antonovich knew for sure that Küchel was a muddle-head with a lot of trouble in store for him in later life—but all the same, a good-natured soul. And this was enough for him: Küchel did not threaten the goodness that lay at the heart of the entire creation.

Engelhardt was apprehensive of Pushkin because he could make no sense of him; he was fond of Küchelbecker because he understood him even though both were chaotic creatures.

David Ivanovich de Boudry was a stubby, chubby old man with a greasy, lightly powdered wig; he had sharp black eyes, he was strict and even nit-picking. He dropped remarks genially and nimbly, joked sarcastically—and the whole class split their sides. But his chief joy was recitation. When with his eyes half-closed, he recited *Le Cid*, in a long drawn-out shout, the lycéens froze in their seats, which did not prevent them afterward from roaring with laughter when Yakovlev mimicked him.

Küchlya had a special feeling for him; he was not fond of him, but observed de Boudry with a strange sort of wonder, almost with awe: Kunitsyn had told him in great confidence that David Ivanovich was the brother of Marat, the man himself, and that he had been forced to change his last name. Nothing about the little old man was reminiscent of Marat—terrible to Küchlya but somehow seductive, from the portrait of him he'd seen in a book.

Once he summoned up his courage, went quietly up to David Ivanovich, and asked him softly:

'David Ivanovich, could you tell me please about your brother?'

De Boudry turned around quickly and gave Küchlya a piercing look.

Then he replied calmly: 'My brother was a great man, and in addition to that, a wonderful doctor.' De Boudry then pondered a little and smiled. 'Once, wishing to warn me against the pleasures of youth—if you know what I mean—he took me to a hospital and showed me the sores of mankind.' He moved his lips and frowned. 'They write a great deal of nonsense about him,' he added quickly, avoiding looking at Wilhelm. And suddenly, taking him in in one glance, he ended quite incongruously: 'And you are vain, my friend. You are ambitious. This does not bode well for you.'

Wilhelm gave him a surprised stare.

De Boudry was right. It was no accident that when falling asleep Wilhelm imagined a crowd roaring ecstatically.

V

Soon an opportunity presented itself for the gratification of Wilhelm's vanity. It was December 1814. The end-of-year examination was approaching. The annual exams at the Lycée were always a big event. Important people arrived from the city, and before the exams the school authorities experienced a fever of ambition, endeavoring to impress as much as they could.

This time the news that Derzhavin would attend spread throughout the Lycée. The news was soon confirmed.

Galich, the teacher of literature, and the most kind-hearted of drunkards, assumed a most solemn appearance and one day announced during a lesson:

'Gentlemen, I would like to warn you that this year the examinations will be attended by our famous lyrical poet, Gavrila Romanovich Derzhavin.'

He grunted and gave a particularly meaningful look to Pushkin:

'I advise you, Pushkin, to take this into special consideration and greet Derzhavin with a bardic gift.'

At that moment Pushkin was chatting with Yakovlev. Hearing Galich's words, he suddenly turned pale and bit his lip.

Küchlya, on the contrary, looked extremely flushed.

After the classes, Pushkin became gloomy and withdrawn. When asked about something, he would answer reluctantly and almost rudely. Küchlya took him discreetly by the arm:

'What do you think, Pushkin? I want to offer some poems to Derzhavin too.'

Pushkin reddened and withdrew his arm. His eyes suddenly went blood-shot. He made no reply, and Wilhelm stood open-mouthed and uncomprehending, while Pushkin left for his room.

The next day everyone knew that Pushkin was writing verses for Derzhavin.

The Lycée was in a state of ferment.

They forgot all about Wilhelm.

There came the day of the exams.

Since morning Pushkin had been silent and abrupt in his behavior. He moved about listlessly and dozily, oblivious to everything around him, even bumping into things. He went to the hall with everyone else, still in a lethargic state.

The uniforms and black tailcoats sat in the armchairs; Vasily Lvovich Pushkin's jabot was very conspicuous by its dazzling magnificence—the "rascal" attended examinations without fail and was more interested in his nephew than was his brother, Sergey Lvovich.

Delvig stood on the stairs waiting for Derzhavin. It was high time to go upstairs but he continued to stand and wait. To see the author of "The Death of Meshchersky," to kiss his hand!

The door flew open; a small, hunched old man came into the vestibule, all wrapped up from the cold in an ample fur overcoat.

He cast his eyes around. The eyes were whitish and opaque, as if totally unseeing. He was cold, his face was bluish with frost. His features were rugged, his lips trembled. He was old.

The doorman rushed toward him. The star-struck Delvig waited for him to ascend the stairs. For some reason, he was no longer looking forward to the meeting, indeed, it seemed rather frightening.

And yet he was determined to kiss the hand that had written "The Death of Meshchersky."

Derzhavin dropped his overcoat into the doorman's hands. He had a uniform on and warm fleecy high boots. Then he turned to the doorman and, staring at him with the same empty eyes, asked in a rattling voice:

'And where is the jakes here, old chap?'

Delvig was dumbfounded. He heard the sound of footsteps on the stairs—the headmaster was rushing to greet Derzhavin. Delvig quietly climbed the stairs and entered the auditorium.

Derzhavin was seated at the table. The examination began. Kunitsyn was the examiner in Moral Philosophy. Derzhavin paid no attention. His head trembled, he fixed his dull eyes on the rows of chairs. Vasily Lvovich's jabot caught his eye. Vasily Lvovich started to fidget in his chair and gave him a deep bow. Derzhavin never saw a thing.

So he sat there, napping and rocking, propping up his head with his hand, detached from everything, staring absent-mindedly at the white jabot. His lips drooped.

Küchlya looked at Derzhavin with an inexplicable shudder. For some reason this frightening senile face with the bluish nose reminded him of the pond overgrown with weeds in which he had wanted to drown himself.

The literature examination began.

Galich said with a stammer:

'Yakovlev, could you recite the ode on the death of Prince Meshchersky, composed by Gavriil Romanovich Derzhavin?'

Derzhavin took his arm off the table. His lips closed. His whitish eyes gazed at the lycéen. Yakovlev was a good reader. De Boudry's lessons had not been lost on him. He recited, wailing slightly, not stressing the meaning, but emphasizing the sonorous rhymes.

Metallic clangor! Tongue of time!
Your fatal voice oppresses me.

Derzhavin closed his eyes and listened.

Tomorrow or today we die,
Perfilyev, this is our destiny.[8]

Derzhavin raised his head and nodded slightly, either with approval or as if finding the answer to a question.

'Küchelbecker.'

Wilhelm went up to the table neither dead nor alive.

'Explain the essence of the ode.'

Wilhelm began to answer following Koshansky's textbook; Derzhavin made a gesture for him to stop.

'Could you tell me,' he said in a cracked voice, 'what is more essential for an ode—poetic inspiration or regularity of style?'

'Enthusiasm,' said Wilhelm ardently, 'poetic inspiration, which excuses the weaknesses and imperfections of the style and fills the soul with high aspirations.'

Derzhavin looked at him with approval.

'Excuse me,' said Wilhelm, not in his usual voice, 'allow me to read a poem dedicated to Gavrila Romanovich.'

Galich was embarrassed. Küchelbecker had not mentioned his verse. No, it might be risky. He had probably concocted something outlandish.

'The first stanza, if Gavrila Romanovich permits.'

Derzhavin made a gesture with his hand. The gesture was wide and unexpectedly elegant.

Wilhelm read in a trembling voice:

A flash of forked flame from up on high,
A thunderous rumbling under the vault of sky,
A prow is split, upon the rocks to die.
The wild waves of ocean raged and surged,

On the savage shore a swimmer is disgorged,
His fearful eyes searching the night that raged
About him. He calls for his companions from his heart's core,
But deep dead silence is the only door,
Opening on fierce far winds and the lion's roar.

He finished and in confusion looked straight into space.

Derzhavin commented: 'Quite strong. And lively. Needs more fire. Obvious though that you have read Derzhavin,' he added, with an insipid smile.

Galich smiled too, seeing that everything had gone off well.

Küchlya returned to his seat with his head bowed.

'Pushkin.'

Pushkin came forward, pale and resolute.

Galich knew about Pushkin's "Derzhavin poem." The whole Lycée knew it by heart.

Pushkin began to recite.

From the very first line Derzhavin became agitated. He fixed his eyes on the boy. Dark lights began to flicker in the white eyes under the frowning eyebrows. His large nostrils flared. His lips moved noticeably, repeating the rhymes after Pushkin.

There was silence in the hall.

Pushkin could hear his own tense, resounding voice and submitted to it. He did not understand the words he was reciting, the sound of his voice drew him along.

Derzhavin and Petrov a heroes' song would sound
On strings of lyres, sonorous and proud.

The voice rang—on the point of breaking.

Derzhavin leaned back in his armchair, closed his eyes, and listened like that to the end.

There was silence.

Pushkin turned and fled.

Derzhavin jumped to his feet and ran from behind the table. There were tears in his eyes. He was looking for Pushkin.

Pushkin ran up the stairs. He reached his room and hurled himself onto the pillows, crying and laughing. A few minutes later Wilhelm burst inside. He was white as a sheet. He rushed to Pushkin, embraced him, pressed him to his chest, and muttered:

'Aleksandr! Aleksandr! I'm so proud of you. Be happy. Derzhavin is passing on his lyre to you!'

VI

But over Illichevsky Küchlya managed to win.

Aleksey Illichevsky—or as he was called at the Lycée, Olosinka—was an intelligent and scholarly boy, he was friends with everyone and no one in particular and was pretty sharp.

He was considered a great poet at the Lycée.

And he did have "a good command of versifying"—so, at least, the teacher of rhetoric, Koshansky, said about him. His poems read smoothly, without a hitch, his handwriting was small, slanting, with elegant flourishes. He wrote fables: he liked the genre, considering it the most reasonable one; Illichevsky's were moral fables. He invented a pseudonym for himself, a meaningful one, "the Bestest." He ridiculed Küchlya, patronized Delvig, and was prepared to consider Pushkin his equal, but secretly was bitterly envious of him. He was cautious, prudent, and never entered into the conspiracies of his comrades. Olosinka was top of the class. After Küchlya's attempt to drown himself in the pond, Olosinka drew a fine caricature in the *Lycée Sage*; it portrayed a pale-faced Küchlya with a thrown back-head (the nose in the picture was huge) being dragged with a boathook out of the water. Küchlya saw the caricature, but, strangely enough, he did not get angry; he disliked him too much to be mad at him.

Illichevsky knew this and, in turn, could not stand Küchlya. He wrote a rather malicious epigram about him and called it, not without grace, "The Refutation":

Enough of you, sages, who often deceive,
Declaring perfection is hard to achieve
In any mortal creature on this earth.
So come, dear Willie, and prove by your worth

That with body so weird and soul so weak,
You're exactly that—the perfect little freak!

But for Pushkin and Delvig the perfect freak with his freakish poems was more attractive than the perfect Olosinka. And one day the freak gained a victory over him. Foaming at the mouth, he attacked Illichevsky.

'I can hire a master of calligraphy,' he shouted, advancing on Illichevsky, 'and in three lessons he will teach me to compose as you do!'

Olosinka smiled sarcastically:

'I doubt it.'

'You're never mistaken, you're perfect, you write flawlessly—God knows that's no big deal. After Batyushkov, is it that hard to write smoothly?'

Olosinka snapped: 'You are a living proof that it *is*,' and looked around defiantly, inviting a laugh.

No one laughed.

'I'd far rather write with mistakes than dish up your tasteless gruel!' shouted Küchlya. 'I'm not ashamed of my mistakes. To hell with the correctness of a corpse! Pushkin,' he said with an unexpected challenge, 'I'll disown you, if you follow Illichevsky!'

Everyone turned to Pushkin, who was biting his lips. He was frowning and serious.

'Calm down, dear Willie,' he said, 'why all this bluster? Each of us has his own way.'

He grabbed Küchlya by the sleeve and dragged him away.

'Is he offended, do you think?' Küchlya asked Pushkin and sighed heavily. 'No matter. He can be offended as much as he likes.'

VII

Meanwhile, the Lycée spirit was changing. Whether it was because they were maturing or because of changes that were taking place around them, but there now appeared at the Lycée something called "liberty."

In the evenings they would discuss who was ruling Russia—the tsar, Arakcheyev, or Arakcheyev's mistress, his serf concubine, Nastasya Minkina. And the subjects of the lycéens' epigrams were no longer Küchlya or the Lycée cook.

Of the 1812 war the lycéens retained the memory of the bearded Russian soldiers passing through Tsarskoe Selo, who scowled at them gloomily and responded wearily to their greetings. The times had changed. The tsar either prayed or had his fortune told at Mme. Krüdener's, a name whispered by one lady to another, or he drilled the soldiers with Arakcheyev, of whom the men spoke with fear. The name of the obscurantist monk Photius spread from one living room to another. There were dark rumors of who would prevail—Photius over Minister Golitsyn or Golitsyn over Photius, or whether Arakcheyev would gobble them both up. And nobody knew what would be better or worse. A secret scrapping and scuffling was starting for posts, money, and influence; everybody quoted what Arakcheyev had said publicly in broad daylight to General Yermolov, whom he feared and loathed:

'You and I, Aleksey Petrovich, won't start scrapping like a couple of dogs.'

And this rippled in waves and circles all over the country—and these waves reached the Lycée.

The Lycée was an indulgent institution—it had been set up without flogging or drill.

Grand Duke Michael kept repeating someone else's quip: "*Les Lycenciés sont licencieux*."[9]

But soon the Lycée too experienced first-hand what everyone was feeling.

One day the tsar summoned Engelhardt and asked him—amicably enough:

'Do you have any students who are intending to pursue a military career?'

Engelhardt thought for a moment. There were so few of them, that, strictly speaking, there were none at all. But it was not so easy to give a straightforward reply to the tsar, who spent his days drilling regiments and immersed in unfathomable reflections about changes in military uniform.

Engelhardt frowned and said:

'Just over ten people, Your Majesty.'

The tsar nodded purposefully.

'Very well. In this case they must begin military training.'

Engelhardt was stupefied. "Drill, barracks, and Arakcheyev will spell the end of the Lycée,"—flashed through his mind.—"This will be the end of our beloved Lycée." He bowed in silence and left.

There was a long discussion at the Lycée council meeting, known to all the lycéens, who were treading carefully these days.

De Boudry gave a quizzical look.

'So, this means going over to martial law, does it?'

Kunitsyn was pale and determined:

'If drill and standing to attention is implemented, your humble servant will have to tender his resignation.'

Engelhardt finally decided to laugh it off. This could sometimes work. Joking was encouraged at court even under Emperor Paul, who rewarded witticisms with posts. Grand Duke Michael did his utmost to be known as a wit.

Engelhardt went to the tsar:

'Your Majesty, permission to leave the Lycée if there is to be military drill.'

The tsar frowned:

'And why is that?'

'Because, Your Majesty, I have never carried and never will carry any weapon except the one that I have in my pocket.'

'And what kind of weapon would that be?' asked the tsar.

Engelhardt pulled a gardening knife out of his pocket and showed it to the tsar.

The joke was lame and fell flat. The tsar had already accustomed himself to the idea that he would watch the Lycée drill out of his windows. For him it would be a relaxation, a summer entertainment. He was drawn to this kind of toy drill, just as his grandfather Peter III had once been drawn to toy soldiers. They bargained for a long time, and the tsar finally agreed with an acid smile that for those who wished, there would be a class devoted to the military sciences. They agreed on that.

On another occasion in summer the tsar summoned Engelhardt and informed him loftily that the Lycée students should be on duty when the tsarina, Elizaveta Alekseyevna, was staying at Tsarskoe Selo.

Engelhardt was silent. Without looking at him, Alexander said:

'This kind of duty will teach young people to be more relaxed in their conduct.'

Sensing that he had said something inappropriate, he added hurriedly and crossly:

'And it will be good for them.'

The news of this duty caused a stir at the Lycée. The students divided into two camps. All for the duty was Sasha Gorchakov, a short-sighted, fresh-faced boy with a jerky walk and that particular carelessness of manners and absent-mindedness, which he considered essential for every aristocrat.

They had to start a career somewhere, and it would be a mistake not to take advantage of the proximity of the palace.

'Good idea,' he said indulgently, expressing his approval either of the tsar or of Engelhardt.

The pretty-looking German, Korf, who followed Gorchakov, and Little Fox, Komovsky, stated firmly that they approved of the new arrangements.

'I never performed a lackey's duties and I am not about to start,' said Pushchin calmly, but his cheeks flamed.

'We're not talking about lackeys, but about pages,' objected Korf:

Pushchin countered:

'But pages *are* royal lackeys.'

'Only a scoundrel can be a lackey to the Tsar,' Küchlya blurted out and turned purple.

Korf shouted:

'Those who don't want to don't have to go on duty, but it's mean to call somebody a scoundrel.'

Yesakov smiled:

'Go ahead, Korf, they'll give you an extra helping for it.' (Korf was a glutton.)

'If they want us to acquire relaxed manners,' said Pushkin, 'they can teach us horse-riding. Much better than being a page.'

Gorchakov considered it absolutely unnecessary to argue. Let Korf do the debating. As far as Gorchakov was concerned, the argument was utterly *comique*. He raised his short-sighted eyes at the disputants and smiled calmly.

Both parties went to Engelhardt.

Seeing that the Lycée was divided, Engelhardt went to see the tsar again. On this occasion the tsar looked distracted and barely listened to him.

'Your Majesty,' said Engelhardt, 'in our most loyal opinion, court service will distract the Lycée students from their studies.'

Paying no attention, the tsar glanced at Engelhardt and gave him a nod. Engelhardt waited a little, made a bow, and left.

The lycéens were forgotten and left in peace.

But the jester Yakovlev no longer impersonated just the sexton with his tremulous voice. On one occasion he performed a "mystery scene."

Having combed his forelocks over his temples, he placed his legs apart, spread his uniform on his shoulders, glanced enigmatically at the lycéens—and they froze: he was the spitting image of the emperor!

On another occasion, with a chamberpot as his prop he acted out an indecent scene: how Modest Korf serves the empress.

At the Lycée there was an usher called Aleksandr Pavlovich Zernov, actually not an usher, but an "assistant tutor" according to the Lycée table of ranks, a man of rare ugliness: lame, red-skinned, with a ginger stubble on his chin, and, to complete the picture, a broken nose. And an epigram went into circulation among the lycéens:

TO TWO ALEKSANDR PAVLOVICHES

A. P. Romanov and Zernov (you beggar!),
You're both the same, it's said:
Zernov, you have a weakness in your leg; er . . .
Romanov, it's your head.
But how to end with wit, do you suppose,
This parallel? No bother!
The kitchen floor gave one a bloody nose,
And Austerlitz the other.[10]

Soon two political incidents took place at the Lycée: one with Wilhelm, another one with a bear cub.

VIII

The bear-cub was quite big, with a black muzzle and intelligent eyes; he lived in a cabin in the Lycée courtyard. He belonged to General

Zakharzhevsky, supervisor of Tsarskoe Selo palace and the palace gardens. Every morning the Lycée students saw the general patting the bear cub on the lead, before making a round of the premises, with the bear cub trying to break the chain and follow him. Pushkin was especially fond of him and always stopped to say hello. The bear cub would give him his thick paw and peer into Pushkin's face, begging for sugar.

And one day the lycéens witnessed an event, which ushered the bear cub into the political history of the school.

The bear cub escaped.

Walking past the sentry-box, General Zakharzhevsky was horrified to find it empty. The bear cub had broken from his chain. A search was carried out—without success. He was not to be seen either in the courtyard or in the grounds. The general completely lost his head: the palace gardens were just a few steps away—what if . . . He was out of his mind with worry.

And with good reason.

The tsar was out for a stroll in the gardens. He unbuttoned his uniform, stuck his hand under the lapel of the waistcoat, and walked slowly through the gardens. The lycéens knew where he was heading: to visit "pretty Velho," a young baroness, with whom Alexander had regular assignations at the Babolovo Palace in Aleksandrovsky Park.

It was late afternoon.

Regimental music was playing at the guardhouse. The lycéens could hear it from the palace corridors.

Suddenly the tsar stopped. The curly spaniel, who always went on walks with him, gave a desperate, shrill bark. The tsar jumped sideways and cried out in surprise. A young bear was advancing toward him. The bear stood up on his hind legs begging for sugar. The yapping dog kept jumping up at him and bouncing back to his master.

Then the tsar silently turned around and made for the palace at a gentle trot. The little bear hobbled after him unhurriedly.

The lycéens observed all this with their mouths agape. Yakovlev even crouched with delight. The figure of the emperor quietly puffing along the garden paths absorbed his attention. Watching the retreating tsar, he opened his mouth and involuntarily reeled from side to side.

The tsar disappeared from their view.

Kicking up a racket, the sentinels and some petty officers ran swiftly from all directions, the shaken general racing ahead of everyone with a pistol in his hand.

One shot—and, with a deep roar, the bear cub stretched out on the ground.

Pushkin turned to his fellow-students:

'Finally, one good man was found, even if he happened to be a bear.'

In the evening Yakovlev gave an impersonation of "the villainous attempt on His Majesty's life," showing a bear on his hind legs, the tsar jogging along the path, and the general as savior.

Such was the political incident concerning the bear cub.

The incident that featured Wilhelm was somewhat reminiscent of the bear cub affair.

One day Wilhelm was walking in the grounds; he remembered Pavlovsk, Ustinka, his mother's eyes, and her dry hands—and felt terribly homesick. At that point he came across a young officer in a dapper frock coat.

'Pavel Petrovich! *Oncle* Paul!' exclaimed Wilhelm, recognizing his mother's cousin Albrecht, who had taken part in the family council, at which it was decided that Willie should be enrolled at the Lycée. 'What brings you here? Fancy meeting you here!'

He gave the officer a hug.

The officer pushed him away coldly. In the heat of the moment Wilhelm did not notice this.

'Been here long?'

'Erm,' mumbled the officer.

'Have you been to Pavlovsk lately?'

'Erm,' the officer said through his clenched teeth.

'Have you seen Mama recently?'

'Erm,' said the officer, glaring angrily at Wilhelm.

Uncle Pavel Petrovich did not deign to answer him. Wilhelm was offended. He made a stiff but dignified bow. The officer did not reciprocate, watched the retreating Küchlya, shrugged his shoulders, and continued on his way.

Küchlya stumbled upon some lycéens, who looked at him in dismay. Pushkin asked:

'What has got into you, Wilhelm? You stop grand dukes and appear to give them hugs.'

'What grand dukes?'

'You've just been chatting to Michael Pavlovich and holding him by the sleeve.'

'But it was my uncle, Pavel Petrovich Albrecht,' muttered Wilhelm, 'what do you mean, Mikhail Pavlovich?'

Pushkin burst out laughing:

'No, it wasn't. Pavel Petrovich was the *papa*, and this is his dear son, Mikhail Pavlovich.'

Such was the political anecdote with Wilhelm—the bear cub attacked the tsar, Wilhelm embraced a grand duke.

IX

On one occasion Pushkin said to Wilhelm:

'Küchlya, why do you never go out? Let's go to the hussars tonight; they've heard about you and would like to meet you.'

Küchlya agreed, not without some trepidation.

In the evening, they tipped the usher pointedly, went out of the Lycée gates, and headed for Kaverin's.

Kaverin's windows were wide open; you could hear laughter and the sounds of a guitar. A high tenor was singing "The Gloomy Tones of a Pianoforte."

Pushkin and Küchlya were welcomed heartily.

Kaverin, in an unbuttoned pelisse and a snow-white shirt, was sitting in an armchair with a guitar on his lap. Kaverin's eyes were pale blue, his flaxen hair curled on his temples. A tall black-haired hussar was standing before him, regarding him gloomily at point-blank range, and singing in a high-pitched voice. He had had a few already. The table was noisy, cheerful, and drunk.

A short broad-chested hussar rose from behind the table and, jangling his spurs, rushed to Pushkin, and lifted him into the air. Pushkin climbed onto his shoulders like a monkey and, without supporting him with his hands, the hussar ran around the table, stamping on his strong short legs.

'You'll drop him!' they shouted from behind the table.

Pushkin leaped down onto the table between the bottles. The hussars clapped.

'Pushkin, give us your song.'

And, standing on the table, Pushkin began to recite:

Let it be known in Russia
(What's elsewhere long been known):
For Austria and Prussia
New uniforms I've sewn.
Russians, rejoice! I'm well, replete, with larger waistline;
I've won loud plaudits in the press;
I've eaten, drunk, made promises—
On those, though, I shan't waste time.[11]

The black-haired hussar, the one who had just sung the romance, abruptly burst out laughing. Pushkin leapt lightly off the table. They poured him some wine.

The glasses were clinked. Küchlya, as a newcomer, was poured a huge cup of punch. Kaverin shouted to him:

'To liberty, Küchelbecker! Bottoms up!'

Wilhelm drained the cup, and his head began to spin. Everything seemed wonderful to him. Surprising himself, he reached out to Kaverin and embraced him. Kaverin kissed him hard. Everyone around them burst out laughing.

'He's in love,' said the short hussar and winked. 'I know them when I see them: when a man in love has a drink, he starts kissing.'

The black-haired hussar asked Pushkin:

'Is that your *bon mot* about the palace bear cub—that one good man was found in Russia even if it was a bear?'

Pushkin nodded smugly:

'Mine.'

'Maybe there *will* be a man,' said the black-haired hussar solemnly.

Pushkin raised his glass high:

'To you and to the bear cub.'

The black-haired hussar frowned.

But Pushkin was already laughing, whirling around him, tickling him, and pulling him about. He was always like this when he was a bit embarrassed.

'*Pierre*,' he shouted to Kaverin, '*Pierre*, be my second. We are going to fight a duel.'

Kaverin laughed and his eyes twinkled, then he instantly performed his thunder and lightning trick, twisting his face sideways and opening his mouth. This was his favorite one.

He left the table. Quite drunk now, he kept his feet firmly on the ground, perhaps too straight. His white teeth parted in a half-smile. He walked like this round the room with light dancing steps. He stopped and sang, wryly and sadly and joyfully all at once:

Ah, why the fence around your vegetable-patch?
And why have you planted that goddamn cabbage batch?

He squatted and began to kick his legs in the air. The black-haired hussar forgot about Pushkin and leaned toward Kaverin:

'Ah, *Pierre*, you Göttingen soul, *Pierre*!'

Kaverin came up and slapped him on the shoulder:

'Bring more *Getränke*![12] Try the Chambertin—it's damn good!'

Küchlya was intoxicated. He was unusually despondent. He felt like bursting into tears.

Looking at him, a short, broad-shouldered hussar remarked:

'He's definitely in love. He's just about to cry.'

And surreptitiously poured him more wine.

Küchlya wept, saying that he utterly despised the base materialism of life and complaining that no one loved him. The short man winked to his friends. Küchlya saw this, he was a little ashamed. The candle-light was turning yellow—day was breaking. The hussars at the table were pensive.

Pushkin was no longer laughing. He sat in a corner chatting quietly with a pale hussar. The hussar's forehead was high, his eyes were cold and gray. Smiling caustically with his thin lips, he was trying to dissuade Pushkin from something. Pushkin looked gloomy, glanced quickly at him, biting his lips, and shrugged. Only now did Küchlya notice the hussar. It was Chaadayev, the philosopher hussar. He wanted to approach

Chaadayev, to talk to him, but his feet were not holding him up and his head was buzzing.

It was time to leave; Kaverin poured everyone a last glass.

'To Küchelbecker. We accept you into our band. Let's drink to the common cause, *res publica* . . .'

He drank, then suddenly pulled his saber out of its scabbard and hurled it into the wall.

The blade sank into the wood, quivering, Kaverin laughed happily.

Outside was cool and damp. The trees in the alleys were fresh and wet. The intoxication was soon gone. It was morning, their heads were pretty empty and weary. Pushkin asked Küchlya:

'Good, isn't it?'

'Too drunken,' Küchlya answered gloomily. 'They're all jokers.'

He remembered how the short hussar had winked in his direction and felt uneasy about it. Pushkin stopped, exasperated, looked at his friend's pale oblong face, and said angrily, pressing his hand to his chest:

'You're a difficult one, Küchlya, old chap.'

Küchlya looked at him reproachfully. Pushkin spoke to him harshly, like a senior:

'I love you like my own brother, Küchlya, but when I am no longer here, mark my words: you'll never have either a sweetheart or a friend. You're a difficult one.'

Wilhelm suddenly turned and ran away. Pushkin felt confused, watched him leave and shrugged.

After that Küchlya went no more to the hussars.

X

That last month before graduation from the Lycée everyone felt differently, they lived a month ahead; there was indeed some awkwardness between them. Prince Gorchakov was impeccably courteous with his comrades; his light springy gait grew even easier, he was already imagining himself in high-society salons, and, narrowing his eyes, he scattered witticisms, rehearsing his appearance in the *beau monde*. Pushkin seemed anxious, Korf was business-like, and only the little monkey Yakovlev stayed the same, clowning around and singing romances.

In the evenings in the gardens they talked about their future careers.

'What are you going to do after graduation, Little Fox?' asked Korf patronizingly. Recently he had been close to Gorchakov and had adopted his condescending tone from him.

Komovsky squeaked:

'I've been promised the post of head clerk at the Department of Public Education.'

'I'm going into jurisprudence,' said Korf. 'The fastest way up the ladder is in justice.'

'Especially if you do the necessary backscratching,' said Yakovlev.

Gorchakov kept silent. Everyone at the Lycée knew that he was starting out in foreign affairs. Gorchakov had high connections.

'Unlike you head clerks,' said Pushkin quickly, 'I am joining the hussars. Don't care too much for a desk job. But Illichevsky will certainly carve out a career in finance.'

Everyone laughed. Illichevsky was stingy. He answered in a cross voice:

'We can't all be hussars, can we? Some of us have to work for a living.'

Only Pushchin and Küchlya were silent. Still patronising, Korf asked:

'And what about you, Pushchin?'

Pushchin responded calmly:

'I am going to be a police constable.'

The lycéens burst out laughing.

Korf wouldn't let go:

'No, seriously, what are you going to go in for?'

Pushchin replied:

'I *am* serious. I'm going to be a police constable.'

Everyone laughed. Wilhelm looked at Pushchin, perplexed.

'Any post in the state should be treated with respect,' Pushchin said slowly and looked around at everyone. 'There is not a post unworthy of approbation. One must show by example that it is not about ranks and money.'

Korf gaped at Pushchin in bewilderment, completely uncomprehending, but Gorchakov, looking quizzically at him, said in French:

'Doesn't this mean that a lackey's post is also worthy of recognition, and yet you wouldn't want to be a lackey?'

Pushchin explained drily:

'There are different kinds of lackey. For some reason, to be the tsar's lackey is not considered a humiliation.'

Gorchakov grinned but did not say anything. He turned to Wilhelm with a tongue-in-cheek expression:

'And you? What are *you* going to do?'

Puzzled, Wilhelm looked at Gorchakov, Pushkin, and Komovsky and shrugged.

'I have no idea.'

XI

June 8, 1817. Night. No one can sleep. Tomorrow they will say farewell to the Lycée, to their fellow-students and then, and then . . . Nobody knows what is out there.

The air is dark outside the Lycée walls, a thin pink dawn is glowing, there are some sounds, something sweet and terrifying, and a glimpse of a woman's face.

Like all the rest, Küchlya is awake, alone in his room. His heart is beating fast. His eyes are dry. Some vague fear haunts his imagination.

A knock on the door. Pushkin enters. He is not laughing as he usually does. For some reason his eyes are half-closed.

'I've composed a poem for you to remember me by, Wilhelm,' he says quietly. 'It's called "Parting."' His voice too sounds different, muffled and trembling.

Küchlya turns toward him and looks at him with an unaccountable melancholy:

'Could you recite it to me, Aleksandr?'

Pushkin recites quietly and slowly:

These final words, as I face loneliness,
I write to you, companion of my heart.
You gods that guard our schooldays, bless
Our happy fellowship—now torn apart!
The years of comradeship have passed;
Our league of friends will meet no more.
Farewell! We two—heav'n keep us

United, friend, for evermore,
With liberty and Phoebus!
May love be yours, the love I've never seen—
Warm love, with hopes, and raptures and delights
To speed your life—like some enchanted dream—
And bless your days and soothe your peaceful nights.
Farewell! I vow—be it in battle, fire, or fear,
Or wandering safe at home beside a murmuring stream—
In brotherhood I'll still stand fast.
This is my prayer (but will capricious Fortune hear?):
May all my friends and yours find happiness at last![13]

He finished; Küchlya closed his eyes. He burst into tears, then impulsively rose to his feet, embraced Pushkin (who barely reached his shoulder), and so they stood for a minute, without saying a word, perplexed and abashed.

The Lycée was at an end.

Petersburg

I

The "kind-hearted headmaster," Yegor Antonovich Engelhardt, wrote about Küchlya in a letter to Yesakov:

> Küchelbecker is in clover: he teaches Russian literature to junior pupils of the newly established boarding school for the nobility at the Pedagogical Institute and recites his hexameters to the eight-year olds; in addition, he fulfils the duties of a tutor; in addition, tutors Misha Glinka (a lazy but very capable boy) and two others; in addition, he reads the French newspaper *Le Conservateur Impartial* and diligently attends the Society of Lovers of Literature; and alongside all this, produces a whole heap of hexameters for almost every issue of the *Son of the Fatherland*. When he was drowning in our pond who could have thought that he would turn out to be capable of all these things!

Aunt Breitkopf was equally delighted. When in the evenings tall Willie visited her at the St. Catherine's Institute on his way home after a literary meeting, she would look at him with pleasure and pour so much cream into his coffee that the absent-minded Willie choked on it.

Indeed, who would have thought that Willie would have such abilities, that the boy would be one of the leaders, that despite his *Dummheiten* he would be published in the best magazines and be friends with Zhukovsky and various other literati who occasionally carry some weight in society!

Ustinya Yakovlevna could calm down at last, even Aunt Breitkopf had faith in Willie. The young man would go far, and in general, with God's mercy, the children had been sorted out: the youngest, Misha, was serving in the Navy, in the Guards Company, and had also moved up the career ladder; Ustinka had married Grigory Andreyevich Glinka. Grigory Andreyevich was an eccentric, but he loved Ustinka to distraction, and that very year the aunt would surely pay them a visit in Zakup, in the province of Smolensk. A small but splendid country estate.

Wilhelm drank the cream eagerly.

He continued to write poetry as eagerly as he tutored Misha Glinka (a complete lazybones), and just as assiduously appeared without fail in all the salons, giving rise to knowing winks. To the nickname "Tapeworm," which had been given him once by Olosinka Illichevsky, was now added the salon nickname, "Sea Biscuit." The latter was even more offensive, because tapeworms were common to all nationalities, while sea biscuits were baked mainly by German bakers. But they were afraid to ruffle him because Sea Biscuit would flare up at once, his eyes would become bloodshot, and the careless offender would be in for trouble. This Sea Biscuit, among other things, was also a duellist. Even with his own friends he was quick-tempered to the point of distraction. So, for example, he once challenged a writer he had worshipped to a duel. This writer was a lively restless man, always on the boil, like a coffee pot. In the heat of conversation he forgot himself, and once, while topping up everyone's glasses, forgot to pour some for Küchlya, who was sitting at the table listening eagerly to him. Without a pause for thought, Küchlya stood up from the table and demanded satisfaction. The writer stared at him wide-eyed and took some time to understand why Küchlya had got so worked up. It took no small effort to settle the matter. Little by little, Wilhelm earned the reputation of a desperado, and the fops of the *monde* made fun of him behind his back, but cautiously.

Wilhelm lodged in two rooms with his Senka, who was now referred to as Semyon. Semyon was a cheerful chap. He would strum his balalaika in the vestibule, and Wilhelm, busy composing poetry, was too embarrassed to tell him that he was distracting him. Semyon's duties were relatively light because Wilhelm Karlovich would disappear in the morning, come back in the evening, and, putting on a dressing gown, sit at the desk—to gaze at the stars and write his ditties. Semyon once read these ditties when Wilhelm Karlovich was not at home and really liked them; they were long and plaintive, about love and stars, and deeply contemplative. Semyon had an extensive circle of friends. Once he even recited—in an amorous context—Wilhelm Karlovich's poems as his own;

they went down well and were greatly appreciated, even though he did not have time to recite them all. Semyon had been instructed by Ustinya Yakovlevna to look after Wilhelm Karlovich and in cases of emergency to report to her in writing. Semyon refrained from writing, but as far as looking after his master was concerned, he took good care of him: he had known Wilhelm from childhood and he saw that his master could not do without him and would be done for on the very first day.

Soon Wilhelm received an invitation to move to the premises of the University boarding house for noble youths, by the Kalinkin Bridge. He was offered lodgings in the mezzanine, in order to tutor Misha Glinka and Lev Pushkin, Aleksandr's younger brother, right there on the spot. Semyon moved with him.

II

Wilhelm rarely saw Aleksandr. Pushkin had thrown himself with abandon into the wild social whirl. By day he would be seen driving in a droshky in the company of some dubious beauties; in the evening he would infallibly visit the theaters, where he would stand near the first row of seats, joking and dropping waspish remarks right, left, and center; or else he would shuffle the decks with the hussars all through the night. His epigrams went round the city. Finally, as a result of such a merry life, he was taken ill and got down to finishing *Ruslan and Lyudmila*, a piece that, according to Wilhelm, would revolutionize Russian literature. Küchlya did not even think of judging his friend. He treated him as a man in love treats a girl, by turns flirtatious and shy, who eventually spins herself dizzy in an unstoppable waltz. While Pushkin was ill, Küchlya visited him every day. Pushkin, ugly, shaven, and pale, bit the quill and recited his poetry. Wilhelm listened, putting one hand to his ear (his hearing had been getting worse, which worried Aunt Breitkopf terribly but was of little concern to him). Eventually he could not restrain himself and jumped up wanting to kiss his friend. Pushkin would laugh, not entirely displeased.

No sooner had Pushkin recovered than they quarreled.

In fact, it was Zhukovsky who was to blame.

Küchlya was always inclined to respect Zhukovsky. He knew his "Svetlana" by heart and often quoted pensively from "Alina and Alsim":

Why, oh why have you ripped apart
The union of two loving hearts?
You each—you said to them—must live alone—
Now and forever on your own.

At that time Küchlya dedicated his poems to Zhukovsky and eagerly craved Zhukovsky's approval. For that reason he would visit him regularly, bringing a sheaf of his poems to read them at length to Zhukovsky.

Zhukovsky lived in a cozy bachelor apartment, wore a dressing gown, and smoked a long pipe. Only his servant Yakov shared his lodgings. Yakov was sedate and trim, of indefinite age, with gray mousy eyes; he paced the rooms silently in his soft shoes. Zhukovsky was not old yet but had already spread out into a pale roundness as a result of his sedentary life. The small coffee-colored eyes were half shut. He was sluggish, soft in his movements, wryly polite to everyone, and when he walked about the room, he looked like a well-fed cat.

He would give his approval not immediately, but after some thought. He could not put his finger on what it was in Küchlya that troubled him, and Zhukovsky did not like to be disturbed. For that reason, he was not too keen to see Küchlya.

Once Pushkin asked Zhukovsky: 'Vasily Andreyevich, why weren't you at the *soirée* last night? Everyone was looking forward to seeing you and it was such fun.'

Zhukovsky answered lazily: 'I had an upset stomach the day before.' He thought a little. 'And in addition, Küchelbecker looked in, so I stayed at home. Then Yakov locked me in by mistake and left.'

He uttered Küchelbecker's name especially meaningfully.

Pushkin burst out laughing and repeated several times:

'Upset stomach . . . Küchelbecker . . .'

In the evening at the ball Pushkin ran into Küchlya and said to him slyly:

'Fancy a new verse, Willie?'

Küchelbecker avidly put his hand to his ear.

And Pushkin chanted in his ear, taking his time:

At lunch I stuffed myself like sin,
Then Yakov went and locked me in!

And so, my friends, I felt unwell and feverish.
And worse than that, both sick and Küchelbeckerish!

Küchlya recoiled and turned pale. It was amazing: no one could mock him like his friends and no one made him as furious as his friends!

'For the ignoble distortion of my name,' he wheezed, rolling his eyes at Pushkin, 'I challenge you to a duel. With pistols. We shall meet tomorrow.'

'Ignoble?' Pushkin went white in his turn. 'Fine. My second is Pushchin.'

'And mine is Delvig.'

They immediately went looking for Pushchin and Delvig. Pushchin wanted nothing to do with a duel.

'Küchlya has gone out of his mind, he's up to his old tricks, he'll be throwing himself into the pond next. And you're the clever one too!' he said, but immediately added: "sick and Küchelbeckerish!" and laughed.

And Wilhelm was horrified to hear a young man, who was passing by without noticing him, say to another:

'I feel a trifle Küchelbeckerish today . . .'

A duel! He must fight a duel!

The duel was fought the following day. They went in a sleigh out of town, to Volkov Field, got out of the sleigh, and took up their positions.

One final time Pushchin said:

'Pushkin! Wilhelm! Stop this madness! You are guilty, Pushkin, ask for forgiveness—you've both gone out of your minds!'

'I am ready,' said Pushkin, with a little yawn. 'For the life of me, I don't see why Willie has got so furious.'

'Come on! Let's shoot!' cried out Küchlya.

Pushkin grinned, shook his head and took off his coat. Wilhelm threw his coat off too.

Delvig gave them a pistol each and they drew lots who was to shoot first.

The first shot went to Küchlya.

He raised his gun and took aim. Pushkin stood there nonchalantly, with raised eyebrows and looking at him with clear eyes.

Küchlya remembered "Küchelbeckerish," and again the blood rushed to his head. He slowly aimed at Pushkin's forehead. Then he saw his quick eyes and his hand began to sink. Suddenly, with a determined movement, he took aim a little bit to the left and fired.

Pushkin burst out laughing, tossed his gun in the air and rushed to Wilhelm. He pulled him about and tried to hug him.

Wilhelm grew furious again.

'Shoot!' he yelled. 'Shoot!'

Pushkin told him decisively: 'I am not going to shoot at you, Willie.'

'Why is that?' yelled Wilhelm.

'For the simple reason that the gun is out of order now—the barrel is full of snow.'

He ran quickly with small steps to the gun, picked it up, and pressed the trigger—no shot followed.

'Let's postpone it then,' said Wilhelm gloomily. 'You still owe me a shot.'

'All right,' Pushkin ran up to him, 'and for now come with us—we'll drink a bottle of champagne.'

He grabbed the resisting Wilhelm by the arm, Pushchin grabbed him on the other side, Delvig began to push him forward from behind—and finally Wilhelm burst out laughing:

'Why are you dragging me along like a sheep?'

At two o'clock in the morning Pushkin brought the woozy Wilhelm back to his lodgings and kept telling him that Wilhelm should dump all boarding schools for noble youths and dedicate himself exclusively to literature.

Wilhelm agreed and kept saying that Aleksandr alone was able to understand him.

III

And indeed, Wilhelm was beginning to get bored with teaching. He suddenly became fed up with the children, he would lock himself in his study more often, put on his robe and sit at the desk doing nothing and staring aimlessly out of the windows. This even began to worry Semyon, who was about to write to Ustinya Yakovlevna a letter of concern "in case something bad might happen to Wilhelm Karlovich."

On one of those evenings, he remembered that it was Thursday, and went to Grech's. He always visited Grech on Thursdays. Grech, a short burly man with horn-rimmed glasses, was an amiable host. At his Thursdays he treated all the Petersburg literati, and it just so happened that somehow one guest would give Nikolay Ivanovich poems (at a cheaper rate) and another one prose (also without asking a higher price). There were two centers in Grech's living room—one was Grech himself, all the time glancing vigilantly at the servants (when a servant caught such a look from Grech, he immediately raced with orangeade or champagne to the particular writer whom Nikolay Ivanovich wanted). The other center was Bulgarin. He was rotund, solidly built, bursting out of clothes that were rather too tight for him. His soft hands were sweaty, he rubbed them constantly, and with a chuckle hurried from one guest to another. When Wilhelm arrived, the gathering at Grech's was already quite large.

Two unfamiliar men were talking to Bulgarin. One was elegantly dressed, slender, his black hair was carefully smoothed down, his narrow face yellowish-pale and the small eyes behind his glasses as black as coal. He spoke quietly and slowly. The other one, ugly, with a poor physique, dark fluffy hair thickly whipped up on his temples, and with a cheeky quiff over his forehead and a carelessly knotted tie, was quick and impetuous and spoke loudly.

Grech led Küchlya up to them and said to the man with the quiff:

'Kondraty Fyodorovich, allow me to introduce Wilhelm. You asked about him the other day. (Küchlya signed his poems "Wilhelm.")

Kondraty Fyodorovich? The man who had written and published the epistle "To a Timeserver," in which he had said in print to Arakcheyev himself: "I care not for your attention, scoundrel!"

Küchlya dashed across toward Ryleyev and shook his hand.

The man with glasses, showing some perplexity and anxiety, immediately leaned back in his chair.

The host introduced him:

'Aleksandr Sergeyevich Griboyedov.'

Griboyedov shook Wilhelm's hand apprehensively and whispered softly into Grech's ear:

'I say, are you sure he isn't mad?'

Grech laughed:

'He is, if you like, but in a noble sense.'

Griboyedov looked at Küchelbecker over his glasses.

Ryleyev was speaking, his nostrils flared:

'And how long will it continue, this funereal wailing in literature? This attitudinizing? This non-stop crying for vanished youth? Just look what's happening in our literature, Wilhelm Karlovich.' Küchlya, who had no idea what was going on, was grabbed by the hands. 'Elegies, elegies without end, madrigals of some kind, *rondeaux*, damn them, all toys, knick-knacks—and all this while despotism grows stronger, the peasants are enslaved, and Arakcheyev and Metternich are lashing Europe with their horse-whips.'

'Yes,' Bulgarin rubbed his sweaty hands, 'that's all very true, my precious friend, all absolutely correct, but tell me, my dear friend,' Bulgarin pressed both hands to his chest and tilted his head to one side, 'tell me, what's the remedy? Oh yes, indeed, where is the cure for this?'

He looked with his clear, bulging eyes at Ryleyev; the eyes were cheerful, with a touch of elusive insolence.

Griboyedov said slowly:

'There is a remedy: what we need is a revolution in literature. What we need is to oust Zhukovsky with his palace Romanticism, with his parquet sighs. The spirit of the people, that's our stronghold. Language should be crude and unpretentious like life itself, only then will literature gain strength. Otherwise it will be forever lounging in bed.'

Wilhelm pricked up his ears. This was something new he was hearing. He jumped up, intending to say something, opened his mouth, then looked at Ryleyev and Griboyedov.

'Allow me to pay you a visit,' he said in his excitement. 'You, Kondraty Fyodorovich, and you, Aleksandr Sergeyevich. There is much I need to discuss with you.'

And without waiting for an answer, he bowed awkwardly and walked off. Ryleyev shrugged his shoulders and smiled. But Griboyedov, leaning forward, looked thoughtfully through his glasses at Wilhelm, who was huddled in the corner.

After this evening Wilhelm often went to Ryleyev's and Griboyedov's. In particular the latter, because Griboyedov was soon to leave for Persia. Within two months they became friends.

They were of the same age, but Wilhelm felt much younger. Gryboyedov's dry voice and gloomy smile were almost those of an old man. But sometimes, especially after too peevish a remark, he smiled at Wilhelm almost like a child. Wilhelm with enamoured eyes watched Griboyedov move unhurriedly around the room. Griboyedov had this habit—he always paced the room while talking, as if feeling for a secure place where he would be safer. His movements were elegant and light.

Once Wilhelm asked him about something that had been on his mind for a long time now: 'Aleksandr, why are you so friendly with Bulgarin? He is certainly an old hand at journalism, but he's a fool, a Falstaff, a lowly creature.'

'That's exactly why I am fond of him,' answered Griboyedov, smiling. 'I do not have much respect for people, my friend. And Faddey is just what he seems. He is Caliban, and that's all there is to it. Why shouldn't I be friends with him?'

Wilhelm shook his head.

With Ryleyev it was quite different. Ryleyev exploded every minute. He spat out words like bullets and, leaning forward nervously, inquired with shining eyes whether his interlocutor agreed, trying to provoke an argument. He did not like it when people agreed quickly and too easily. He came to life only in argument, but it was impossible to argue with him for long. The very sound of his voice persuaded his adversary.

There were names at the sound of which his face twitched—so, for example, he could not bear the name "Arakcheyev." It twitched in the same way when he spoke to Wilhelm about the peasants, who were ground down by the *barshchina*,[14] and about the soldiers who were flogged to death.

Griboyedov's quiet anger had an almost calming effect on Küchlya; Ryleyev's flashes disturbed him. He would leave Ryleyev in a whirl.

Once, at Ryleyev's, Küchlya ran into Pushchin. Pushchin was talking to Ryleyev slowly and weightily, in a low voice. Without taking his eyes off him, Ryleyev looked silently into Pushchin's eyes. Having noticed Küchlya, Pushchin immediately fell silent, and Ryleyev shook his head and said that both the *Son of the Fatherland* and the *Neva Spectator* were worthless and that a new journal must be founded. Wilhelm had the impression they were hiding something from him.

IV

For some time now, when Wilhelm came to see Aunt Breitkopf, she was not as happy as before. And although she still poured cream into his coffee in abundance, the sight of Wilhelm had begun to embarrass her. Wilhelm had changed—Aunt Breitkopf was clear about this. He was getting involved again, he appeared to be anxious. Placing her hands on the table and looking majestically at Wilhelm, Aunt Breitkopf racked her brains as to what was happening to him. Wilhelm drank her coffee absent-mindedly, equally absent-mindedly gobbled up the biscuits, and answered randomly. Finally, the aunt decided that Wilhelm was in love and that silliness was to be expected.

The aunt was right: Wilhelm was indeed in love, and one could really expect silly things from him.

He had fallen in love all at once, in the space of an evening, and as it seemed to him, forever.

Delvig had invited him to the salon of Sofya Dmitriyevna Ponomaryova.

Wilhelm had already heard about this lively salon and its beautiful hostess. The salon turned out to be a small and cozy parlor. At the round table littered with books, notebooks, and sheets of paper, the company sat in the dim lamplight. Küchlya immediately noticed Krylov's big face with its overhanging eyebrows, so immobile, as if in all his born days he had never uttered a word; Grech, whose horn-rimmed spectacles made him look like either a clerk or a professor, was there too; and there was a small man with a pink face and oily eyes, Vladimir Panayev, whose idylls Küchlya detested, the one-eyed Gnedich, and a blond man with a broad freckled face, the fabulist Izmaylov. They paid little attention to Küchlya and Delvig. In general, they did not stand on ceremony in the salon: people would come in, leave, and talk to whoever they wished. And the setting was simple and bare in order to allow freedom of movement. Küchlya immediately felt at ease, calm and cheerful. Delvig led him to the hostess. Sophie was sitting on a large sofa alongside four or five writers who brazenly paid court to her. She was only about twenty years old and very pretty—with dimples on her cheeks, small dark eyes with an oblique, almost Chinese cut, and a mole above the upper lip. She spoke rapidly, cheerfully, and laughed a lot. She immediately made an extraordinary impression on Küchlya. Without noticing, he stepped on the paw of a big dog sitting at Sophie's feet. The dog snarled, bared his teeth, and went for Wilhelm. Hearing the growl, a second dog went for Wilhelm from another corner of the room. Confusion ensued.

People were shouting: 'Hector! Malvina!'

Sophie could not utter a word for laughter. At last she somehow made an apology to Küchlya. Delvig sat down next to the hostess, he was apparently an insider. He sat very close to Sophie and, as Wilhelm noted, pressed himself to her quite immodestly. Wilhelm considered it somewhat strange, but Sophie, seemingly, thought it entirely natural. To his great displeasure, Küchlya caught sight of Olosinka Illichevsky, who was at that moment entering the drawing room and being joyfully greeted by the hostess. Within three years, Aleksey Damianovich Illichevsky had managed to acquire the appearance of a solid citizen; he had grown a belly and his face had taken on a greenish pallor like nearly all Petersburg officials.

Sophie tried to bring Küchlya out of himself with swift, sweet-sounding questions, to which he responded stiffly and timidly.

By the end of the evening, Küchlya was sitting in a stupor, scarcely speaking and looking morosely at Delvig and Illichevsky, who had been courting Sophie very indiscreetly. He paid no attention whatsoever to the others and even failed to show an interest in Krylov. He left with Izmaylov. Delvig and Illichevsky stayed. The fat and clumsy Izmaylov in a long blue frock coat and the tall thin Küchlya in black tails, retreating from the drawing room side by side, were an amusing sight. Sophie's laughter followed them out. Küchlya heard this laugh and winced. Izmaylov looked at him through his silver spectacles and gave him a sly wink.

In the vestibule they came upon a strange scene: two servants were refusing to admit a blind drunk man into the parlor. The clothes of the drunk were in disarray: his tie was undone, the collar of his shirt unbuttoned and splashed with wine. The drunk looked at Izmaylov and Wilhelm with blurred eyes.

'Ah, the quill-drivers,' he said, 'have you had enough of sitting about?'

And then, as though realizing something, he muttered with unexpected politeness:

'You are very welcome, very welcome indeed.'

Wilhelm opened his mouth but Izmaylov led him out.

'Sofya Dmitriyevna's husband,' he said smiling. 'She keeps him on a tight rein, so he drinks, poor fellow.'

Wilhelm shrugged his shoulders. Everything about this house was extraordinary.

He spent a sleepless night and next day sent Sophie some flowers. On the third day he went to see her. Sophie was alone. She saw Küchlya at once, went toward him, took him by the hand, and sat him beside her on the sofa. Then she looked at him sideways:

'I'm glad to see you, Wilhelm Karlovich.'

Wilhelm did not stir.

'Why are you so shy? They say you are a loner and a terrible misanthrope, an Alceste?'[15]

'Oh no,' muttered Küchlya.

'They say a thousand awful things about you—that you are a duellist, a menace. You seem to be a really terrible person!'

Küchlya looked into her dark eyes without saying a word, then he took her hand and kissed it.

Sophie gave him a quick glance, smiled, got up, and pulled him to the table. There she opened her album and said:

'Read it, Wilhelm Karlovich, and write something; I'll be watching you.'

Unaware of what he was doing, Wilhelm suddenly took her in his arms.

Sophie said in surprise:

'Oh, you don't seem to be as misanthropic as they say!'

She laughed, and Wilhelm's hand fell. He muttered:

'You are tormenting me.'

'The other day Delvig talked about you all evening,' Sophie said quickly, changing the subject.

'And what did he say?'

'He said that you are an extraordinary person. That one day you will be famous . . . and unhappy,' Sophie added in a softer tone.

'Not sure whether I'll be famous,' said Wilhelm sullenly, 'but I'm already unhappy.'

'Do write in the album, Wilhelm Karlovich: you are unhappy and you'll be famous in the future—that's very interesting for the album.'

Wilhelm began to leaf through it furiously.

On the first page was written in Grech's neat handwriting:

IV. Contemporary Russian Bibliography
New Books
1818

Sofia Dmitriyevna Ponomaryova, a comical, but tender novel with a brief Afterword. St. Petersburg, demi-octavo, in the printing house of Madame Blümer, 19 pages.

(I began to read this book and was about to lose patience: the author's thoughts scatter in all directions, one feeling runs into another, words fall like snowflakes in November, but all this is so pleasant and congenial that one can't help but carry on, and, having finished the book, one says: what a charming publication! Shame about some uncorrected misprints!)

'What's this?' Wilhelm asked indignantly. 'Has he been through this book already? And what is this "Afterword"?'

Sophie blushed:

'Dear misanthrope, you are becoming insolent. You have no patience at all.'

'The wit of Nikolay Ivanovich is that of a clerk,' muttered Wilhelm.

On the second page was written in an angular old-fashioned hand:

The prettier the flower,
The shorter its hour,
And for that hour alone
The loving Sylph will moan.
But let it once fall
And his ardor will pall,
No rapture at all.

Under the poem, as playful and clumsy as a dancing bear, was the name of a famous scholar.

Suddenly, Küchlya felt sick: the poetic confectioner, Vladimir Panayev, had written some immodest verse for Sophie:

Happy the man who dares at you to peek;
Thrice happier one little word to seek.
The one who truly reaches heavenly bliss

Is he who steals from you a loving kiss.
But the man who immortality has felt
Is he whose blest bold hand unties your belt.

'Why did you let this barber into your album?' Wilhelm asked crudely and turned pale.

'The album is open to everyone,' explained Sophie, looking away.

And finally, in the magnificent handwriting of Olosinka Illichevsky himself:

On seeing you, all men complain,
Sighing, they all agree:
The married wish they had no chain,
The others that you were free.

Küchlya slammed the album shut.

Sophie opened it stubbornly in the middle with her white fingers and said insistently:

'Write.'

Wilhelm looked at her and made up his mind.

He sat down and wrote in English:

"I was well, would be better, took physic, and died."

Then he stood up, took a step toward Sophie and put his arms around her.

V

The ground was shifting under Wilhelm's feet. Often at night he would jump up, sit on the bed and stare empty-eyed at Petersburg, which was sleeping the sleep of the dead. A cold hand would grip his heart and slowly—finger by finger—release it.

Was it Sophie? Or was it just spleen that drove him away from lessons, from Aunt Breitkopf, from the journals?

He did not know. And everything around him was beginning to totter. Shockwaves were going through everyday life, and Wilhelm felt them painfully.

Every day these shockwaves were felt throughout Europe, throughout the world.

The dagger of the student Karl Sand flashed out in 1819 and that dagger struck not only the spy Kotzebue;[16] all Europe knew that Sand had also dealt a blow to tsar Alexander and to Metternich. Kotzebue was a Russian spy to whom Alexander, with the blessing of the Holy Alliance, had entrusted the surveillance of the German universities, the only places where the Germans could still hide from Metternich, in whose long arms the Russian tsar danced like a cardboard clown.

Louvel's stiletto flashed out after Sand's dagger: the Duke of Berry was assassinated in February of that same year. The disquieting thing was not only that a duke had been murdered, the actual scene of the murder was striking in itself. People recounted the details of it in the drawing rooms: the entire French court was at the opera; near the exit, someone imperiously thrust his way into the crowd, calmly took the duke by the collar, and stabbed him once in the chest with a dagger, curved at the end. He was seized at once. His name was Louvel. Under interrogation he declared haughtily that his aim was to exterminate the entire Bourbon breed.

The royal thrones had been rocked once more. The heir to the throne had been slaughtered in the middle of a crowd, practically in front of Louis the Desired.

In Spain the situation was possibly even more serious: the king, cowardly and hunted down like a hare, yielded to the Cortes[17] step by step. At the demand of the people a former convict, sent to the galleys by the king, was made minister of justice. The people, led by their chiefs Quiroga and Riego,[18] were seething and demanded heads, and the king surrendered his former favorites one after another.

The details of Sand's execution became known in May 1820. He died looking death straight in the eye. The public dipped handkerchiefs in his blood and carried away fragments of wood from the scaffold as if they were relics. Karl Sand's execution was his second triumph: the government was afraid to execute him and did so at an earlier hour than usual, stealthily. Even so, a crowd of thousands swarmed in front of the scaffold, and when Sand calmly ascended the scaffold, the students bared their heads and sang a hymn to liberty as a parting farewell.

On September 15, 1820, a ship arriving in Petersburg from Lisbon brought news of a revolution in Portugal, where the Spanish constitution had been adopted.

A war of liberation from the Turkish yoke broke out in Greece. The spirit of ancient Hellas was resurrected in new secret societies, the *eterias*.

Such was the calendar of the earthquakes in Europe.

The earth had been shifting not only under Wilhelm's feet. Pushkin would hurl himself into his room like a bomb, pull Wilhelm about, proclaim that everyone should rush off to Greece, recite wicked songs about the tsar, give Wilhelm a kiss, and then leave for who knows where. He could not sit still. He went off to the theater or the hussars, went after women; looking at his friend, Wilhelm was astonished how Pushkin contrived to be everywhere, how he managed not to burst from this constant seething of energy. His forbidden poems circulated all over Russia, people could not have enough of them, ladies copied them avidly into their albums, they spread through the country faster than a newspaper.

And finally, Pushkin could stand it no longer. One day, sitting at the performance of an opera, he casually handed a man next to him a portrait of Louvel, on which was written clearly in his hand: "A Lesson to Kings." The portrait went all round the theater. When it reached a tall dark figure in a tattered coat, he slipped it into his pocket and whispered to the man sitting next to him:

'Who wrote this?'

His neighbor shrugged and answered with a smile:

'Must be Pushkin, the scribbler.'

The tall dark man waited until the end of the performance, before leaving quietly and unobserved. He was Vogel, the chief spy and right-hand man of the Petersburg Governor-General, Count Miloradovich.

Next day, Count Miloradovich had a lengthy confidential meeting with the tsar.

The tsar was taking a vacation at Tsarskoe Selo. After Miloradovich's report, he went out into the garden and ran into Engelhardt. The tsar had a cold look of disgust on his face. He beckoned to Engelhardt and told him:

'Pushkin must be exiled to Siberia: he has flooded the country with outrageous verses. All the young people recite them by heart. His behavior is brazen in the extreme.'

Engelhardt was horrified and wrote to Delvig and Küchlya at once, imploring them to break all ties with Pushkin. Engelhardt wrote:

"Discretion and judiciousness, my good Wilhelm." He was greatly afraid and did not quite know why: for the Lycée or for himself.

Pushkin was exiled in May—not to Siberia, but to the south.

And the good Wilhelm "reassured" Engelhardt. One day in June, Yegor Antonovich opened the latest issue of the *Champion of Enlightenment and Beneficence*, a respectable journal, and was delighted to find out that Küchlya kept working over the summer too: his poem "Poets" was published in a prominent place.

Yegor Antonovich put on his glasses and began to read. As he read, his mouth opened and his forehead covered in sweat.

Küchlya wrote:

O Delvig! Delvig! What is the reward
Of verse and of the hero's sword?
How can a talent ever rejoice
With fools and knaves as the only choice?
....
In Juvenal's unflinching hand
For villains a fierce horsewhip cracks;
It drains the color from their cheeks,
And tyrants' power is forced to bend.
....
My friend! Oppression's at the gate!
Eternity's the certain fate
Of every brave and dazzling deed
And each sweet song from oaten reed.
Likewise, our union, proud and high,
And full of bliss, will never die.
And the chosen ones of the holy Muse
Joy and grief together firmly fuse!

And finally, the unassuming *Champion of Enlightenment and Beneficence* ran this stanza in the most ordinary type:

And you—young leader of our band—
Singer of love and of "Ruslan!"
What is the hissing of snakes for you,
What is the cry of an owl or a crow?

'An owl or a crow,' repeated Engelhardt in a puzzled voice.

How had the censor missed this? How had the paper tolerated it? This was the end of Küchlya, God bless him! Ah, but the Lycée, the Lycée! A shadow had been cast over the whole Lycée. It would perish, the Lycée, without any doubt. And who were the villains of the piece? Those two chaotic creatures, those two madmen—Pushkin and Küchelbecker.

Engelhardt took off his glasses, placed them neatly on the table, pulled out of his pocket a huge handkerchief, buried his face in it, and sobbed.

VI

One day Pushchin came to see Wilhelm, stayed with him for a while, looked around with clear eyes and said, making a face:

'What a mess you have here, Wilhelm!'

Wilhelm gazed around absent-mindedly and noticed that the room was indeed in a terrible clutter: books were scattered all over the floor and on the couch, there were piles of manuscripts, and the desk was strewn with tobacco ash.

Pushchin looked at his friend carefully. He always managed to determine the true state of affairs at once, and to resolve matters very quickly. He brought order to everything he touched.

'My dear chap, you need something to do.'

Wilhelm, on whom Pushchin always had a soothing effect, said:

'I work a lot as it is.'

'That is not the point: what you need is not a job but a cause. It's time to take yourself in hand, Willie. Are you free tomorrow night?'

'I am.'

'Come to Nikolay Ivanovich Turgenev's, we'll talk there.'

He did not say anything more than that, smiled at Wilhelm, embraced him somewhat unexpectedly, and left.

The following day at Turgenev's, Wilhelm met people he knew: Kunitsyn, Pushchin, and a few other lycéens were already there.

Turgenev limped toward Wilhelm to greet him. He had fluffy blond hair and a large pink face with regular, almost antique features; the look in his gray eyes was unusually hard. He held out his hand to Wilhelm and said brusquely:

'Welcome, Wilhelm Karlovich, we were expecting you.'

Wilhelm apologized and immediately frowned. It seemed to him that Turgenev was dissatisfied with him for being late.

Pushchin nodded to him as they once did at the Lycée and Wilhelm gradually calmed down.

About fifteen people were sitting at the table. The small, thin face of Fyodor Glinka, with kind little eyes, was smiling affably at him. Chaadayev stood in the corner, one foot crossed over the other and his arms folded across his chest, his dazzling uniform conspicuous among the black and colored frock coats and tail coats. His pale eyes glided indifferently over Wilhelm. Everyone was waiting for Turgenev to speak.

Turgenev began with the gesture of an accustomed orator. He spoke coldly, and this gave his speech added strength.

'Correct me if I am wrong, gentlemen,' said Turgenev, 'when I say that all of us present are united by one thing: the desire for immediate change. Life is hard. All around us ignoramuses put obstacles in the way of education; surveillance is on the increase with every passing day. The fashionable world is immersed in its private, petty concerns; a good game of boston is the best opium for them, it has a more powerful effect than any other. We are all suffocating. And herein lies mainly what distinguishes us from the boston devotees: we hope to change society. Of course, a sensible person,' Turgenev declaimed ironically, 'might conclude that everything in this world shall pass. Both good and evil will leave almost no trace. Doesn't it seem obvious?' He looked around the gathering. 'What use is it now to the Greeks and Romans, that they were Republicans once? And should these considerations perhaps cause a man to remain apathetic?' And he looked half-inquiringly at Chaadayev.

Chaadayev stood with his arms crossed and not a single thought was reflected on his great shiny forehead.

'Man is a social being,' Turgenev rapped out his words. 'He must strive for the good of his neighbors, not just for his own good. He must always strive,' he repeated, 'even if he is not certain that he will achieve his goal,' and Turgenev made a defensive gesture, 'even indeed if he is certain that he will not achieve it. We live—therefore, we must act for the common good.'

And again, he turned to Chaadayev, as if he was not sure whether Chaadayev agreed with him:

'It's easy to convince oneself of the insignificance of human life,' he said, 'but this very insignificance forces us to despise all the threats and violence that we in-e-vi-tab-ly,' he drew out the word, emphasising each separate syllable, 'bring on ourselves, acting on the convictions both of the heart and of the reason.'

And, as though he had now said all he had to say, he ended sharply:

'In a nutshell, no matter how empty or insignificant the goals of our lives may be, we cannot disregard those goals unless we ourselves want to be disregarded.'

He looked around. His voice suddenly softened, he gave an unexpected smile:

'It may well be that what I have just said is superfluous... But the task I would propose for us is a difficult one, and it's better to state the obvious than not to express what is essential. Let me go on. Twenty-five years of struggle against despotism, a struggle that ended happily everywhere, led to an even worse despotism. Europe has been pushed back by its rulers into the backwoods of barbarism, in which it wandered for a long time and from which another escape will be all the more difficult. Here and everywhere tyrants are like the shepherds from the old fables.'

Chaadayev from the corner spoke through clenched teeth:

'Here in Russia they are also like shepherds in their limited education.'

Turgenev appeared to ignore this remark and continued:

'. . . Like shepherds driving sheep in whatever direction they choose. But when the sheep refuse to obey, the shepherds set the dogs on the sheep. What should the sheep do?' he smiled a haughty smile. 'The sheep must cease to be sheep. The despots who control the sheep through their henchmen are afraid of wolves. We shall resolutely oppose robbery, baseness, and greed. We shall stand firm or at least fearlessly, even if with little hope.'

He spoke stonily, as a monument would speak in a square, if it had acquired the gift of speech.

'I am coming to our ultimate goal. With each year that passes we are closer to the denouement. Autocracy is reeling. If *we* don't put an end to it, history will. But when will the denouement happen? Will we live to witness it? We do not know, though we all feel this is the beginning of the end. Let us not wait for our hour in dull torpor. Let us proceed at once to our most immediate goals.'

Turgenev's gray eyes darkened and his face turned pale. His voice sounded hollow and harsh.

'Our first goal is to eradicate our disgrace, the brand of the galley slave—the shameful slavery that exists in this country, where Russian peasants are bought and sold like cattle.'

Turgenev lifted himself slightly in his armchair.

'A disgrace, a disgrace in which all of us here are complicit!' he cried out and shook his crutch.

Everyone was silent. Turgenev drew breath and leaned back in his armchair. He looked around at the gathering.

'Our Russian peasants must be freed from their chains throughout the entire country, and at once.'

Suddenly, staring absent-mindedly, he spoke with a strange expression on his face, as if needing to dispel his own doubt:

'This matter takes precedence over all others to the extent that the entire form of government toward which we must strive depends on it. This is the heart of the matter. The benefits of the republican form of government are indisputable. Under it, the distinctive character of people and parties is much more prominent'—he said it in French: *plus prononcé*, 'and here a person chooses, without any . . . indecision, *duplicité*, his way of thinking and acting, his party, whereas in monarchical rule, he is always obliged, even against his will, to hold a candle to both the angel and the devil. A definite position is often harmful for him and always useless. The tsar always has been and always will be surrounded by worst kind of scoundrels. Infamy and the tsar are one and the same. The benefits of the republic are undeniable,' he mused, 'but on the other hand, it is dangerous to abolish autocratic power before slavery itself has been abolished.'

Again he looked around distractedly at everyone and ended ponderously:

'Because the fellow nobles, to whom the autocratic power will inevitably pass, will not only fail to limit it, but will even strengthen it.'

There was silence. Then Kunitsyn spoke as if continuing some long-standing dispute:

'All the same, I cannot agree with Nikolay Ivanovich. Class interests cannot be placed above state ones; a state system is reflected in every sphere of public life. In the republic, peasants will be free citizens.'

Turgenev spoke coldly:

'If the nobles who will have the power over the whole republic care to free them. In any case, we all seem to agree that serfdom, in other words, absence of rights, must be eradicated. And the only means for this, as I see it, is freedom of the press. I propose we publish a journal without the approval of the censorship committee. The purpose of the journal should be to fight serfdom and for civil liberties. Gentlemen, I welcome any suggestions in this regard.'

The first to speak was Fyodor Glinka, a small man with a meek and gloomy look:

'I believe, gentlemen, that first of all the journal should be affordable enough for the ordinary citizen and even the peasant to buy it.'

Turgenev nodded in agreement:

'And as an economist, I will suggest, dear Fyodor Nikolayevich, that in order to achieve this we'll need the largest possible circulation, twice, or even three times the usual.'

Pushchin added in his casual, rather homely manner:

'The printing press has to be set up somewhere remote, in the countryside, or somewhere like that, so that neither shepherds nor law officers can get a sniff of it.'

Everyone laughed. Wilhelm came in, stammering and anxious:

'A journal is difficult to handle, publication can be slow, it is hard to sell. It would be better to go to the masses, to the markets, and to circulate separate sheets. And to the army, too, and the provinces.'

Turgenev peered intently at Wilhelm:

'Brilliant idea. And we can circulate caricatures of the tsar and Arakcheyev. Laughter is more effective than scholarly analysis. I suggest we should elect the editors, gentlemen.'

'Turgenev,' said everyone.

Turgenev nodded slightly.

'Küchelbecker,' suggested Pushchin.

Wilhelm flushed, stood up, and bowed awkwardly.

'And why, Pyotr Yakovlevich, do you not cast a vote?' Turgenev said to Chaadayev, with a chuckle.

'I will be delighted to participate in the illegitimate journal, delighted,' Chaadayev said quietly.

Turgenev smiled.

When everyone was leaving, he addressed Wilhelm in a friendly and at the same time condescending manner:

'I treat the dreams of my youth with respect. Experience often puts an end to our striving for good. How lucky we are still to be inexperienced!'

VIII

But the venture stalled. Pushchin came to Wilhelm a couple of times, saying that the printing press had still not been set up, that it was hard to find a suitable place for it. Turgenev soon went abroad. The illegitimate magazine never saw the light of day.

And Wilhelm, not knowing what was wrong with him, pined. He did not even know for sure whether he loved Sophie. He did not know what it was: this longing at night, the suffocating desire to see her right now, this minute, the dark Chinese eyes, the mole on her cheek, and then, when he met her—the silence and the coldness. Was he pining because he was in love, or was he in love because he pined? He was prepared to die at any moment—for what or how, he himself could not yet say. The fate of Karl Sand stirred his imagination.

Sophie entered his soul as one enters a room and settled there with all her belongings and habits; it was a rather odd and uncomfortable room for her, interesting and strange. Wilhelm watched distractedly those Chinese eyes shift fleetingly from the pink Panayev to the pale Illichevsky and then to the languid Delvig and even to the one-eyed Gnedich.

Turgenev's journal never came to fruition; his service in the College of Foreign Affairs, his lessons at the University boarding school for noble youths, and all that fuss with children began to weary Wilhelm. He was even irritated by the view of the Kalinkin Bridge from his rooms (he lodged in a tiny mezzanine of the Boarding School building). Misha Glinka spent days playing the grand piano, and this entertained him. All the pieces played by this disheveled little boy with the sleepy eyes, even those that Wilhelm had heard before, came out in a new way. Lyova Pushkin, a white-toothed curly-headed boy, a desperate brawler and ne'er-do-well, never failed to touch Wilhelm's heart. But he was such a prankster, he caused him so much trouble and laughed so uncontrollably that Wilhelm looked at him dumbfounded. He began to regret that he had moved to the boarding school.

Once at his Aunt Breitkopf's Wilhelm met Dunya Pushkina. She had just graduated from the St. Catherine Institute and she was only fifteen. She was a distant relative of Aleksandr Pushkin, and Wilhelm was now fond of everything that reminded him of his exiled friend. Dunya was joyful, her movements were light and free. He began to visit his aunt more frequently—Dunya was often there. Once, when Wilhelm was particularly gloomy, she touched his hand and said timidly:

'Why are you so sad?'

When Wilhelm returned home and tiptoed to his room (the boys in the room next door had long since fallen asleep), he stood at the window for a long time looking at the sleeping Neva and remembered: "Why are you so sad?"

VII

Wilhelm stayed late at Ryleyev's one night. It was autumn outside, a very clear night. That day Ryleyev was quieter and gloomier than ever, he had some domestic troubles. But Wilhelm was reluctant to leave.

Suddenly beneath the window they heard some unfamiliar voices. Ryleyev quickly glanced out of the window and grabbed Wilhelm's arm: agitated groups of people were running along the street. Then came the steps of marching soldiers, the rumbling of cannon and of shell boxes, horses' hooves. An officer with an agitated face galloped past.

'Let's go and see what's going on.'

They left hurriedly and joined the running men, asking as they went:

'What's happened?'

Nobody really knew. A young officer replied grudgingly:

'Something's going on in the Semyonovsky Regiment.'

Ryleyev stopped and took a breath. He turned pale and his eyes flashed.

'Let's get over there,' he said to Wilhelm in a hollow voice.

They hurried to the Semyonovsky parade ground.

A black mass of soldiers in full combat equipment stood in front of the sick-bay. The bewildered, frightened company commanders were racing about in front of them, asking for something, waving their hands, running from one flank to the other—no one took any notice.

It was dark.

Wilhelm felt a quietness in the darkness and in this quietness a continuous buzzing and shouting. The shouting issued from a single spot, a solitary and not particularly loud shout, then it rippled over two or three ranks, intensifying, and finally became a roar:

'Company!'

'Bring back the company!

'Bring Schwarz!'

Things had not been going well in the Semyonovsky Regiment for a long time now. The regimental commander, Schwarz, was a disciple of Arakcheyev. He was a favorite of Grand Duke Mikhail Pavlovich. The grand duke was fond of martinets. He himself had a heavy hand. Schwarz was responsible for unprecedented penal servitude for his soldiers—endless drill from morning till night, rehearsals of parades almost every week. He wouldn't let the soldiers off to work, saying that their peasant labor interfered with their military discipline. But the soldiers had no money, and Arakcheyev's disciple demanded an impeccable turnout. In two months Company No.1 spent on brushes, chalk, and leather the cash assigned for beef. The soldiers looked exhausted. To top it all, Schwarz introduced his famous "tens." He ordered that every day each company in turn should send him ten men. He instructed them in the hall as a distraction from his daily labors. He had them strip naked and stand motionless for hours, their legs in wooden shackles, he tugged at their mustaches and spat in their faces if they made a mistake; he gave them commands lying on the floor and tapping it with his hands and feet. From the floor it was easier to inspect the toes in the lines of boots.

Particularly annoying was the fact that Schwarz was no ordinary brute: he mocked, clowned, and mimicked soldiers and officers; he had fits and screamed out shrill senseless curses in their faces. No, far from being an ordinary brute, he enjoyed his part. Perhaps he played the fool in an attempt to mimic Field Marshal Suvorov.

Between May 1 and October 3, 1820, Schwarz punished forty-four soldiers. He ordered them to be given from one hundred to five hundred lashes each. In total, this amounted to fourteen thousand two hundred and fifty lashes—three hundred and twenty-four per person.

Company No.1 lost its patience. They brought a petition. The company was fed up.

Then the corps commander Vasilchikov made an inspection.

Reining in his horse before them he yelled in a frenzy that he would make anyone who dared open his mouth run the gauntlet.

He demanded from the commander a list of the petitioners.

He concealed a battalion of Pavlovsk grenadiers with loaded rifles in the drill-hall. Then he sent an order to the regiment to send the company in fatigues and without officers to the drill-hall *for a check-up of ammunition.*

At the entrance to the drill-hall Vasilchikov met the company.

'Well, are you still unhappy with Schwarz?' he cried, almost trampling the soldiers underfoot with his white snorting stallion.

The company answered as if on parade:

'Yes, sir, Your Excellency!'

Vasilchikov yelled:

'You scum! Quick march to the fortress!'

And the company went to the fortress. That was at ten in the morning. The regiment did not know that the company had been taken to the fortress. There had been no news.

By noon there was still no company. The officers did not appear, preferring to wait at their quarters. The grumbling spread from barracks to barracks. Soldiers gathered everywhere in little groups, which melted away, and then re-formed.

Night fell, and the regiment became agitated.

The soldiers did not sleep that night. They threw things about, smashed the bunks, knocked out the windows, destroyed the barracks.

They came out into the square in full force. A feeling they had never experienced before took hold of them—a sense of freedom. They congratulated each other, they embraced. Their hour had arrived—rebellion. They demanded the return of the company and Schwarz to be handed over.

'Company!'

'Schwarz!'

'Death to Schwarz!'

They sent off a hundred and thirty men to execute Schwarz. The soldiers marched to his house. Schwarz was not in. They did not touch anything. Schwarz's coat with the Semyonovsky Regiment insignia was hanging on the wall; one of the soldiers tore off the collar; Schwarz was not worthy of the uniform. In the yard they stumbled upon Schwarz's son, a teenage boy, and arrested him. On the way back, they threw him into the water. A non-commissioned officer undressed with a groan and pulled him out in front of the company's eyes.

'He'll grow up and take after his father; we'll have time to deal with him then.'

There was no resentment in the company.

Ryleyev and Wilhelm were squeezing through the crowd while the detachment was coming back.

Spreading his hands, a young Guard said:

'He seems to have vanished from the face of the earth. We looked in the entrance hall, we looked in the closet, even got into his wardrobe—gone without a trace.'

An old Guard with a scar across his face said:

'Oi, you should have looked in the stables, sure thing he's dug himself into the dung in there, that's what he's done!'

Laughter all around. (And the soldier was right: as it turned out, Schwarz had indeed hidden himself in the manure in the stables.)

Wilhelm and Ryleyev asked the soldiers anxiously what had happened. The soldiers looked at them rather doubtfully but gave their answers.

A young general with a tall white plume had showed up on a horse. He was followed by mounted orderlies. He raised a white-gloved hand and shouted in a ringing voice:

'I'm ashamed to look at you!'

Then the same solider who had said that Schwartz had hidden in the stables, went up to the general and calmly said to him:

'And we are not ashamed to look at anyone.'

The general was about to protest but someone shouted to him from the ranks at the rear:

'Get the hell out of here!'

He turned his horse and rode away. A loud laugh rang out after him. Miloradovich and Grand Duke Mikhail Pavlovich rode up. Miloradovich looked gloomy.

'Have you taken it into your heads to rebel, chaps?'

He spoke loudly, in rough military voice, apparently trying to assume the tone of a soldier.

'We want to kill Schwarz, Your Excellency,' a young voice said cheerfully from the ranks.

Someone shouted shrilly:

'We've had enough of these tortures!'

Grand Duke Michael began to speak loudly and abruptly, bawling out the words. He was a squat young man with a thick neck and a broad round face.

The soldiers were silent.

Wilhelm suddenly felt furious and said:

'Arakcheyev *le petit*.'

The grand duke caught sight of Wilhelm and said something to Miloradovich, who shrugged his shoulders.

Prancing on the spot, the grand duke began to beseech the soldiers and even pressed his hand to his chest. His words could not be heard. The soldiers were silent. Then a hoarse voice called from behind.

'Tyrants! May you burn in hell!

Miloradovich said something quietly to the grand duke and the latter changed color. They turned their horses about and left.

An adjutant appeared holding a paper over his head. He shouted out:

'Colonel Schwarz is removed from his command, General Bistram is appointed in his place.'

A moment of silence, then a succession of separate voices, then a general roar:

'Hand over Schwarz!'

'Bring back the company!'

The gray-haired Bistram rode up and saluted the regiment. He said in a pleading voice:

'Let's get on with our duties, lads.'

The old Guard took a step forward:

'We can't get on, one company is missing. Nothing is going to happen until you tell us where the company is!'

Bistram lowered his head and looked at the soldiers.

'The company is at the fortress.'

The old Guard said calmly:

'You see, we can't go on duty without them. We shall go to the fortress too: the tail follows the head wherever it goes.'

The company commanders began to gather the companies together. The battalion commanders stood at the front of the battalions. They gave the command and the battalions marched off.

Wilhelm whispered to Ryleyev:

'Where are they going?'

The latter answered impatiently:

'Can't you hear—to the fortress.'

They followed the regiment. Not far from the fortress, Ryleyev stopped. Wilhelm looked at him thoughtfully and said:

'The first step is the hardest.'

Ryleyev was silent.

Wilhelm returned home toward morning. The sleepy Semyon told him:

'Some gentleman came to see you.'

'What gentleman?'

'He didn't say. He asked a lot of questions about you: who you mix with, who you visit.'

Wilhelm was perplexed:

'What for?'

Semyon suddenly sounded resolute:

'You see, Wilhelm Karlovich, it seems like you and I will have to leave. This gentleman even promised me a fair bit of money if I'd report to him about you every day. He's got to be a spy. He has this kind of blackish hair.'

'Idle chatter,' said Wilhelm after a moment's thought. 'Just some odd fellow. Go to bed.'

But he himself stayed up. He opened the notebook and began to write in it quickly in large calligraphic scrawls. He crossed things out, rewrote, sighed.

IX

One day Semyon silently handed Wilhelm a letter. Wilhelm glanced absent-mindedly at the envelope and turned pale: it was a mourning envelope, edged with black.

'Who brought it?' he asked.

Semyon shrugged:

'Some servant, he didn't say whose.'

On a sheet of English-made funeral paper was a message in delicate handwriting with curlicues (Wilhelm had already seen this hand somewhere):

> With deepest regret Ioakim Ivanovich Ponomaryov has the honor to inform you, Dear Sir, of the sudden death of his wife, Sophia Dmitriyevna, which happened in accordance with the will of God on November 1. The memorial service will be held on the 1st day of this month of November. The interment will take place on the 4th day of November.

Wilhelm wrung his hands. So this was what fate had in store for him! Tears burst from his eyes, his face was twisted, becoming at once comic, and terrible, and ugly. Frantically he threw off his dressing gown and put on new black clothes, finding it difficult to get his hands into the sleeves.

He remembered Sophie's Chinese eyes, her pink hands, and he cried out. The images of the drunken husband, of Illichevsky, and of Izmaylov, went out of his mind at once. He wanted to tell Semyon, who was looking at him dutifully and timorously, not to expect him back soon, but his teeth chattered, which frightened Semyon out of his wits. Wilhelm was unable to utter a word.

He arrived at the Ponomaryovs' staggering, oblivious to everything around him. The entrance vestibule was empty. He paid no attention to the chambermaid, who squealed at his appearance and dashed through a door. He entered the drawing room. It was teeming with people, but because of the tears in his eyes Wilhelm did not recognize the faces, except for the pink Panayev who for some reason was keeping a handkerchief at the ready. Seeing Wilhelm, those around him raised their handkerchiefs to their eyes as if on cue and sobbed loudly. Wilhelm shuddered: he seemed to hear some laughter among the general weeping.

He stared at the coffin.

Black and elegant, it stood on a platform. A flat lace-trimmed pillow appeared dazzlingly white against it. Wilhelm looked at the pillow through tears that screened everything else.

Sophie's face was entirely alive, as if she had just fallen asleep. It had a light glow on it; the black eyelashes seemed still to be fluttering.

Wilhelm rushed to the coffin with a loud cry, paying no attention to the others. He peered at Sophie's face, then touched her forehead and her hand with his lips. Suddenly his heart skipped a beat: when he was kissing her hand, he felt as if the deceased gave his lips a light flick. He wanted to rise from his knees but the deceased threw her arms round his neck. Wilhelm felt faint. Then Sophie jumped up from the coffin and began to ruffle him. He looked at her with blurred eyes. She laughed:

'This is how I test whether my friends really love me.'

The hall roared with laughter. The pink Panayev in particular was splitting his sides. He even crouched down and whistled through his nose. Wilhelm stood in the middle of the room and felt the floor swaying under his feet.

Then he stepped toward Panayev, grabbed him by the collar, lifted him a little, and croaked into his face:

'If you were not so detestable, I would shoot you like a rabbit.'

Suddenly afraid, Sophie grasped his hand:

'Wilhelm Karlovich, dear, it's entirely my fault, I just wanted a bit of fun, don't be angry, will you?'

Wilhelm leaned toward her, gazed crazily into her face, and walked out.

Panayev recovered and muttered contemptuously:

'*Monsieur, qui prend la mouche.*'[19]

X

In fact, Semyon was right. It was indeed time to leave. Life had been sweeping Wilhelm away, pushing him out from everywhere. With increasing ease and without noticing it he ceased to attend the College of Foreign Affairs, then after a little more thought he also gave up his work at the journals. Somehow, as if naturally, it turned out that he began to skip lessons at the boarding school, stopped paying any attention to Misha and Lyova—and soon he and Semyon moved out of the mezzanine. They embarked on a strange and aimless life. He would either be out of the house for days on end or be pacing his room without even taking off his dressing gown. He ceased to notice Semyon completely.

His mother wrote him gentle letters, which he had to force himself to answer. His health had been shattered: his chest ached and his right ear grew noticeably deaf. Once he went to see his Aunt Breitkopf. Solemnly she put a cup of coffee before him and gave him a long stare. Then she said:

'Willie, you must leave this city. Justine and I have had an idea. You must become a professor. Leave for Dorpat. Dorpat is a nice enough town. There you'll have some peace and quiet. Mr. Zhukovsky undoubtedly holds you in the highest possible regard and can arrange a post for you.'

Wilhelm listened closely.

'You may well be right about Dorpat.'

A professorship in Dorpat, a little green garden, windows with shutters and lectures on literature. Let the years pass by, what did it matter? Settle down. Settle down forever. He jumped up from his chair and thanked his aunt.

Dutifully he went to see Zhukovsky and found out all he needed to. Things were working out brilliantly: Dorpat University's Professor of Russian Language, Perevoshchikov, was about to retire.

Zhukovsky had a word with Count Lieven; Küchlya wrote a letter in German to His *Magnificenz* the Rector and began to pack.

At Sophie's *soirée*, he jotted in her album a farewell note, very sad but cold:

> This man has never been satisfied with the present situation, he has always sacrificed it to the future and he has foreseen nothing but trouble. Some people regarded him as an extraordinary person and were mistaken; others . . . Believe me that he was better and worse than the gossip and judgments of those who knew only by his outward appearance.
>
> W. K.

Next day, however, he called to say goodbye once again. He simply could not just leave. He entered unannounced, having pushed the servant aside. Sophie was sitting on the sofa. A pink pomaded Panayev was holding her in his arms.

Without saying a word to the dumbfounded hostess, Wilhelm turned around and left.

Sophie did not exist for him any more. Yet he was reluctant to go to Dorpat. Oh, to be quit forever of Russia, of Petersburg, of Aunt Breitkopf, to breathe in new air! Wilhelm longed for the sea.

He went to ask Delvig for advice. Delvig said serenely and even lazily:

'Piece of cake. I've been offered the post of secretary to that fat-bellied Naryshkin. He is going abroad for a few years. He's livid that his wife had been overlooked for the order of St. Catherine and wants to get out of Russia. I can't be bothered to go. I'll have a word with him tomorrow—and you can be on your way. We've been scattered all over the world: Pushkin's in exile, you're leaving. Funny, isn't it?'

Wilhelm sighed freely for the first time in six months.

The following day he and Naryshkin came to an agreement. Aleksandr Lvovich was very gracious. He scrutinized Küchlya with narrowed eyes. The odd figure of his future secretary appealed to him immensely. There was something unusual about it. One wouldn't get bored traveling with a man like this. They agreed on the day of departure. Wilhelm still had to resign his previous job, settle his affairs, and obtain a passport. The route was: Germany, Southern France ("the most scenic places," said Naryshkin, "better than Italy"), and Paris. There Aleksandr Lvovich was going to settle for a while.

As Wilhelm was walking back to his lodgings, a girl's voice called out to him, he looked up: a carriage with Dunya Pushkina was passing. She smiled at him happily. Wilhelm lifted his top hat and for a few moments watched her driving away.

For a long time that evening he paced up and down his room. He was thinking about Pushkin, about Sophie, about Ryleyev, and briefly he remembered Dunya's face. But he could already glimpse new fields and seas, all of Europe beyond them. Who was he leaving behind? His friends would soon forget him. There were no letters from Pushkin—well, he was far away . . . Mother? He brought her no joy. He remembered Pushkin's words: "Neither friend nor sweetheart will you ever know." He looked at Pushkin's portrait and started to pack.

Europe

I

Freedom, freedom!

As soon as the border barrier closed behind them, Wilhelm too put everything behind him: Sophie, Panayev, and even Aunt Breitkopf. He was twenty-three years old. What lay ahead of him was the homeland of Schiller, Goethe, and Karl Sand, and enigmatic, noisy, and affable Paris with the still smouldering shadow of the great revolution and the Latin Quarter, and Italy with her unparalleled skies and an air that would heal his chest. Onward, onward!

Squinting wryly at Wilhelm with his puffy little eyes, Aleksandr Lvovich Naryshkin was struck by his loquacity. The tall Sea Biscuit was definitely a curious conversationalist and, what was even more enjoyable for the old wit who had half lost the taste for everything, even for witticisms, he really was "a frightful eccentric." Aleksandr Lvovich had lived a long life. He had been a courtier (with the rank of Ober-Hoffmarshal), then Director of Theaters and a Petersburg host celebrated for his hospitality, who had somehow failed to stay for long either here or there, he had not settled anywhere—and was now traveling abroad to jest away his free time, of which, by the way, he had quite a lot. Why he was doing this was unclear to anybody, including, as a matter of fact, Aleksandr Lvovich himself, though it might indeed be because his wife, Maria Alekseyevna, had been overlooked for the Order of St. Catherine. Aleksandr Lvovich's mood changed a dozen times a day. A good helping of substantial witticisms and puns at breakfast, a discontented, self-important, and antagonistic mood toward evening, and in the intervals, a thousand unexpected decisions and startling actions. If Aleksandr Lvovich decided at breakfast time not to spend an hour too long in "this poky little town," it meant that he would get stuck in it for a week. If he was happy with all his employees in the morning, it was a sure sign he would scold everyone at lunchtime. His conversation was not only witty, he had an amazing memory and occasionally Wilhelm was surprised to uncover in his rotund patron a knowledge that he had not previously suspected him to have. Aleksandr Lvovich knew so many stories about the courts of two reigns that Wilhelm often asked him why he didn't write them down, it would have been a most entertaining book. Aleksandr Lvovich would wave him away and say:

'If I ever wrote such a book, they would say that I'd made it all up, so what's the point?'

Naryshkin was fabulously rich, and this, apparently, weighed on him because he managed to spend even when it seemed impossible to do so. While on the road he would buy pretty much everything: luxurious fabrics, carpets, vases, precious stones, and books, as long as they were all "original."

He was old, half-burnt-out, and Wilhelm could only guess what a firework this man must have been in his youth.

The old crank grew fond of the new-fangled eccentric. When Wilhelm jumped out of the carriage to pick a wild flower along the road, Aleksandr Lvovich regarded him with delight. The new eccentric's judgments intrigued him, like some fashionable knick-knack from a Leipzig bric-a-brac shop.

A bit of Livonian boredom on the road delighted Wilhelm. Huge spruces, dark green pines, impassable peat-bogs reminded him of those places in which he had spent his early childhood: the gloomy town of Ulvi, the estate of Avinurme, the sandy Nennaal, divided by streams. Wilhelm talked so much romantic Gothic rubbish about Livonian castles that Aleksandr Lvovich, superstitious like any other Russian follower of Voltaire, was even slightly embarrassed.

A fine carriage bore the two along. The roads, the miles, the dusty leaves of roadside trees were flashing by.

Onward!

And so Wilhelm arrived in Germany.

II

The road between Herzberg and Großenhain. October 27/15, 1820[20]

We have left Berlin and Prussia. In Berlin, I visited (among other places) a porcelain factory. Mechanical operations, machines, crucibles, and other objects, which are very entertaining for many, not only do not excite my curiosity in the least, I find them off-putting; the unclean and stuffy conditions prevailing in the factory are stifling, the banging is deafening, the dust plunges one into despair, and any comparison of such insignificant but intense human labor with the eternal energies of nature awakens in me a vague indignation.

I feel happy only when I can break free and run for protection beneath the free and lofty sky; I feel happy even with the howling of storms and peals of thunder; it deafens me, but the fullness of sound elevates the soul.

Dresden. October 30/18

Elisa von der Recke, née Countess Medem, a tall majestic woman, used to be one of the greatest beauties in Europe, and even now, in her sixty-fifth year, she still captivates with her kindness and imagination. Von der Recke was once a friend to illustrious people who immortalized the last years of Catherine the Great's age: she was held in high regard, because she knew how to combat the disastrous superstitions that Cagliostro and similar swindlers had begun to spread in the last two decades of the last century. These days even among men these superstitions do not encounter such enlightened opponents as this courageous female author of the eighteenth century; in our time they spread quickly, resurrecting the old, long forgotten tales of our late mothers and nannies, and finding patrons in high places! We all laugh at ghosts, house sprites, wizards, and prophecies; but how is it that we cannot recognize the power of those black and white magicians, who speak in the most convoluted and obscure language about the possibility of uniting with souls separated from their bodies, about the existence of primal spirits, about secret revelations and premonitions? But the Cagliostros of our time are dressed in the best English cloth, wear fob watches, they smell of perfume, their hands are adorned with rings and their pockets are lined with our money; they know everything, go everywhere, they know everybody, our ladies find them gracious and ingenious, and we think they are extremely astute! And what heights do these gentlemen sometimes achieve! But let us go back to the lady who tore the mask from their predecessor. When Cagliostro visited Mitau, he managed to fire the imaginations of the young Madame von der Recke and her sister, the Duchess of Courland. Elisa did not remain beguiled for long, however, and soon exposed the deceitfulness of the fraudster and made it her duty to sacrifice her own ego to save others from the webs of such monsters; she published an account of the life and deeds of Count Cagliostro in Mitau. I shall never forget this majestic but modest favorite of the Muses: the evening of her days is like a quiet, beautiful sunset. Everyone adores her.

III

The room was small, cluttered with bookcases, manuscripts scattered all over the desk.

Looking at Wilhelm with his deep, sunken eyes, Tieck was evidently bored. His swarthy face was grumpy and his darting Gypsy eyes were sad.

Wilhelm felt uncomfortable with this restless and jaded man. They talked about Tieck's friend, the extraordinary Novalis, who had died so early and so mysteriously and whose works Tieck had published.

'One cannot but regret,' said Wilhelm, 'that with his prodigious talent and remarkably fertile imagination, Novalis did not try harder to make himself clear and got completely bogged down in mystical abstractions. His extraordinary life and exquisite poetry have left no obvious trace. He is virtually unknown in Russia.'

'Novalis is perfectly clear,' replied Tieck dryly and after a pause asked Wilhelm:

'And which of us do they know in Russia?'

This "us" sounded almost hostile.

'Wieland, Klopstock, Goethe,' Wilhelm enumerated, somewhat embarrassed. 'Schiller in particular, he is the most translated one.'

Tieck paced the room nervously: 'Wieland, Klopstock,' he repeated mockingly: 'One is a lecherous old ape and the other is a writer with not a single elevated thought.'

'Which of them does not have an elevated thought?'

Tieck replied:

'Klopstock. A heavy-going, turgid writer, with a faded imagination. A dangerous writer, a sceptic.'

Wilhelm looked at him in amazement and muttered:

'But Schiller?'

'Schiller,' Tieck droned pensively, 'is the falsetto in whom there is always falsity. There is something ambiguous about his loftiness. He sets your teeth on edge like an unripe fruit. Writing about love all his life and falling for ugly women. Composing his most tear-jerking monologues when breathing in the smell of rotten apples. Don't trust a man with such clear blue eyes,' he said, stopping in front of Wilhelm. 'He's almost always a liar.'

Wilhelm suddenly remembered the tsar's blue eyes and felt uneasy.

Tieck paced the room and asked abruptly:

'Would you like me to read something to you?'

He picked up Shakespeare in his own translation and began reading *Macbeth*.

Almost instantly he had forgotten about Wilhelm.

In front of Wilhelm were three, then four people. The intense and guttural voice of Macbeth as opposed to the lustreless, terribly docile, somnolent voice of Lady Macbeth. She is walking with a candle—Tieck picked up a candle from the table. His gaze became fixed, like a lunatic's. Wilhelm flinched. Tieck looked at his outstretched yellowish hand. The words came out devoid of meaning, stark and terrible, like the sallow hand lit by the candle.

Tieck sank heavily into the armchair and again looked with a dull expression at Wilhelm, who was now pale.

'I will never forget your *Macbeth*. I will translate it into Russian.'

Tieck said indifferently:

'I am so pleased. I'm sure you will do a better job.'

Wilhelm took his leave and ran out into the street.

This was it then, that fearful Europe, the Europe of romantic visions, like the dreams of a drunk asleep in a dungeon.

Out into the fresh air!

IV

Dresden. November 3/October 22

I have met a young man I have become fond of since our first two meetings: his name is Odoyevsky, he is on military service and is now in Dresden accompanying his mother, whose health is somewhat delicate. You can well imagine, my friends, how often I visit Odoyevsky, you can imagine how we talk exclusively about Russia and cannot speak enough about her: the present state of our Fatherland, the measures that the government must take to eliminate abuses, the heartfelt conviction that holy Rus will one day achieve the highest level of prosperity, that it is not accidental that such wonderful abilities and such a language, the richest and sweetest in all Europe, are granted to the Russian people, that she is destined to be such a huge and positive presence in the moral world—that's what gives life and warmth to our conversations, which occasionally make me forget that I am not in the Fatherland. I have come across a few other Russians in the *Hôtel de Pologne*, where we are now staying; one told me about Pushkin, with whom he had dined in Kiev; and I was delighted to introduce them to Pushkin's latest narrative poem *Ruslan and Lyudmila.*

Dresden. November 9/October 28

I've seen miracles of various kinds here: two giants, wax effigies, and a sea lion, intelligent and good-mannered, who—miracle of miracles!—speaks German and, it is claimed, even the Lower Saxon dialect! I enjoy mingling with common people and observing the character, gestures, and passions of my brothers, who are separated from me by their position in society and by prejudices, but to whom I am bound by the common ties of humanity; they are nowhere to be seen more clearly than at the show; here their curiosity is aroused and this reveals their temperament in their speech; here they show all their knowledge, feelings, and ways of thinking. On such occasions a Saxon is generally reticent, thoughtful, and attentive; children and old men, men and women maintain a reverent silence; they seem genuinely to see before them the silent rulers of Europe who are being introduced to them in a rapid sibilant voice by the woman who owns their caricatured images; they look as if they want to rush at the "madman Karl Sand" who assassinated Kotzebue, and they look at Madame de Staël and at the sea lion, at the female giant and all those present knowingly, calmly, intently, and majestically.

Leipzig. November 20/8

We arrived here in Leipzig yesterday morning.

Leipzig is a neat, bright city; it seethes with life and activity; its residents are distinguished by a particular refinement and courtesy of manners; I noticed nothing in the way of provincial manners here; Leipzig rightly deserves the name of the German Athens. In the surrounding area, as in Saxony in general, there are almost no traces of the recent war; the inhabitants are well-off and talk about the past as a bad dream; I find it hard to believe that just a few years back, the fate of mankind was decided here, on the peaceful fields of Leipzig. Blessed is the land in which the power of hard work lives and supports its citizens and provides them with ways to efface the traces of destruction!

Here twice in our time the peoples fought for independence: here they were finally freed from their fetters.[21] Holy, memorable war! Strife did not yet divide the citizens and the rulers, as it does now; then there was still a common soul, one heart beat in all breasts! Was the blood of the Leipzig fields really spilled in vain?

Weimar. November 22/10

Last night we arrived in Weimar, Weimar, where the great men once used to live: Goethe, Schiller, Herder, Wieland; only Goethe has outlived his friends. And I have seen the immortal one. Goethe is of medium height, his black eyes are lively, full of fire and inspiration. I imagined him to be a giant even outwardly, but I was mistaken. He is unhurried in conversation; his voice is soft and pleasant. It took me a long time to realize that the giant Goethe was actually before me. Talking to him about his works, I even referred to him once by name in the third person. He appeared to be pleased that Zhukovsky had introduced the Russians to some of his shorter poems.

Weimar. November 24/12

I have also visited Dr. de Wette here, famous for his letter to Karl Sand's mother. There was none of the restless spirit and vanity of a demagogue about de Wette. He is quiet, modest, almost shy; and moderate and cautious in his manners and conversation. I received a letter of recommendation to de Wette from F., an old friend of mine; he knew me back in Werro; I was then just over twelve years old; and as a pupil at a county boarding school, looked at the schoolboy F. with great reverence whenever he came from Dorpat to visit our good kind teacher; we had not seen each other since. In Leipzig I found him an intelligent, thorough, and learned man. When those who were close in childhood and youth part, then meet again at another time and under different skies, their chance reunion takes them by surprise. Lucky are the ones who at least manage to see the companions of their springtime, but how often we are separated from our dear friends and do not even know when they bid goodbye to life!

V

Wilhelm walked back from Dr. de Wette's as if in a daze. The soft look from behind the spectacles and the long ashen-gray hair had an irresistible effect on him. A doctor's look! It was a look of understanding that Wilhelm had not yet seen. And in that look Wilhelm clearly felt some form of compassion for him. This worried him a bit, but the day was sunny, and the foreign street was noisy in a musical way, not like a Russian street. Wilhelm walked, looking at the blue winter sky, without a single thought in his head.

A young man touched his arm.

Wilhelm gave a start. It was Lenner, a student, whom he had met two days earlier, when buying books. He said to Wilhelm with a smile:

'Wonderful day, isn't it?'

And then immediately, changing the tone:

'Could you possibly come and see me tonight? I wouldn't dare trouble you, except for one circumstance, which I hope will be of interest to you.'

Wilhelm was slightly surprised but thanked him and promised to come.

Lenner lived on the edge of the town in a narrow lane, where tiled roofs almost met overhead.

'Nannerl!' shouted a stern voice somewhere in the distance.

Wilhelm climbed the rickety wooden stair to Lenner's room. The student was already waiting for him. The poverty of the room struck even Wilhelm. The entire furniture consisted of a skinny mattress in the corner, a round table with a lit candle, and a bookcase stacked with volumes.

There was another visitor at Lenner's—short, stocky, with thick lips and bulging black eyes. Both shook Wilhelm's hand very warmly and the short man stared at him intently.

The conversation was about literature, Russia, *Sibirien*, and *die Steppen*, of which the students had a rather vague idea. Then there was a pause in their talk. Wilhelm felt uncomfortable. The visit seemed pointless. Then the short, stocky one, looking at Wilhelm point blank, asked him:

'My friend Lenner told me that you are interested in our Karl?'

Lenner quietly opened the door and peeped out to see whether anyone was eavesdropping.

Wilhelm stared at him inquiringly.

'Karl, Karl Sand,' repeated the short one, and not waiting for an answer, he blurted out:

'We trust you implicitly. I know from Lenner which books you've inquired about. You were careless. Listen to me. Karl's cause has not perished. *Der Jugenbund* is growing in leaps and bounds. His blood was not shed in vain. The organisation has spread all over the country. But we are powerless against this great hydra—Metternich is still there and so is your emperor. Tell me one thing—when? Is there any hope?'

Wilhelm felt a little apprehensive. He spread his hands:

'Everything's on the boil, but it's unclear what it's leading to.'

'So, the situation is unclear, is it?' said the short, stocky one.

Wilhelm hesitated:

'Yes, unclear.'

He felt uneasy, he had the feeling that they were taking him for someone else.

The little man glanced at Lenner:

'We have faith, Friedrich, haven't we?'

He briefly said his goodbyes to Wilhelm and Lenner and rushed out.

Wilhelm asked Lenner:

'Who is this friend of yours?'

For some reason Lenner sounded reticent:

'He's our secretary; he was personally acquainted with Karl Sand.'

Shortly afterward he asked: 'May I ask you to accept a modest gift from a poor man such as I am?' His blue eyes darkened. 'Take it as a keepsake. God knows whether we shall meet again.'

He pulled out a desk drawer, looked around, and, making sure that they could not be seen, handed Wilhelm an oval portrait of Sand.

Wilhelm shook his hand and they threw themselves into each other's arms. It was a sudden friendship of the sort that is not struck by people over twenty-five years of age. It is as treacherous as a sunny day, it gets forgotten, and if it is occasionally remembered, one feels a sudden pang; and yet life would be incomplete without such friendships.

VI

The tsar was re-reading the note for the second time. The note had been passed over to him by the ever polite and ever beaming Benckendorff. The tsar did not like him very much; the young general had been climbing the ladder quickly and nimbly, he was already chief of staff of the Guards Corps, but his excessive diligence irritated the tsar. Benckendorff's blue eyes were singularly ingratiating. He was too close to Grand Duke Nicholas, and the tsar, jealous of power, could not stand this. They said that Benckendorff's face was reminiscent of the tsar's. The tsar had a perfect understanding of the type of good-heartedness that shone out of Benckendorff's blue eyes and captivated women (Benckendorff was a ladies' man).

And this note too depressed the tsar. It was early June. He had just returned to Tsarskoe Selo from Laibach and wanted only one thing—to rest. The Tsarskoe Selo lime trees, white female hands, regimental music, a small parade, and a review of the troops—that was all he needed now.

And for the second time he pored, with some vexation, over the note of the inordinately diligent Benckendorff, which could have waited.

And the note was extremely unpleasant.

There was no doubt that a very suspicious secret society had been formed in Russia. These were no longer just the Freemasons, who, of course, were also no good, disagreeable, and meddled in affairs that had nothing to do with them. But the society Benckendorff was writing about was openly rebellious and political, with some very dangerous features and some resemblance to the Carbonari: triads and tens and sessions . . .[22]

And yet Benckendorff was wrong. There was certainly a society, but not a revolutionary one. What was the point of using the word "revolutionary" in relation to Russia? Society might be blighted by the spirit of criticism but there was not and could not be any revolution in Russia. The tsar did not want to read the word "revolutionary." He was afraid of the word and was annoyed with Benckendorff: "A critical tendency, that's all, no revolution whatsoever."

A memory flashed through his head of the Semyonovsky Regiment, *his* regiment, *his* Life Guards, who had so shamelessly failed to live up to his expectations. He feared that memory like a personal insult. He had disbanded the Semyonovsky Regiment, he had destroyed them, erased their memory from the face of the earth. But had he really? Oh yes, they had been promptly transferred to the Sveaborg Fortress, apparently when a storm was raging, it was the time of year when ships don't put to sea—they nearly died—and indeed it would have been better if they had perished, it would have served them right, it might just have taught them not to rebel in future.

So much trouble! And how perfectly it would have worked out if the entire regiment had perished somewhere out there, on the way to Sveaborg! As it was he'd had to send them south, to join the second and third corps. And God alone knows what other trouble they could stir up over there. All this, of course, was the work of the smart alecks that Benckendorff was writing about, as the half-crazy Karazin used to do.

And yet Benckendorff was wrong: there could not be any revolution in Russia at the moment. The clever ones had just to be eliminated—and the critical movement would cease. He resumed reading. He did not read the general part of the note, just skimmed it through with a vague sense of fear, and the word "revolution" caught his eye once more, and again made him wince. The general had gone over the top. He shouldn't be promoted. Instead, the tsar noted the names with great precision, thought about them, and jotted them down in a notebook.

> . . . Nikolay Turgenev, who does nothing to hide his views, is proud to be called a Jacobin, a proponent of the guillotine, and, holding nothing sacred, is ready to sacrifice everything in the hope of winning all in the case of a coup . . .
>
> . . . together with Professor Kunitsyn endeavored to publish a journal, at the lowest price and for large circulation, funded by the society, and containing articles relating to the purposes of the society. All members were obliged to contribute. Also promising to contribute: Chaadayev (still on probation to join the society), Küchelbecker (a young hot-head, educated at the Lycée, at the moment abroad with Prince Naryshkin), and others . . .

What do you think of that then, may I ask you?

The tsar looked out of the window and fixed his eyes on the Lycée. He had warmed the vipers in his bosom, in his own bosom . . . The Lycée, Kunitsyn and this son of dear mama's maid of honor, the German. Right under his nose! Outrageous! Poems by Pushkin! And all this had been happening close to his very home. And it was he *himself* who had established the Lycée.

He went to the bureau with its secret lock and took out another piece of paper. It was a denunciation by Karazin. Yes, indeed—this one too was warning about the Lycée. The poet Pushkin . . . a portrait of Louvel . . . Pushkin nothing more than a convict, a *brigand* . . . And here were the verses of that outrageous German, Küchelbecker:

> *For villains a fierce horsewhip cracks;*
> *It drains the color from their cheeks,*
> *And tyrants' power is forced to bend...*

'What do you think of that then, may I ask?' asked the emperor aloud and made a gracious bow . . .

> . . . As the piece was read in the society immediately after Pushkin's exile had been announced, it is obvious that it was written for that occasion.
>
> No doubt about it . . .
>
> . . . All this is written and published brazenly not by some reprobates, condemned by public opinion, but by young people who have just left the imperial schools; consider the consequences of such an education!

Alexander looked involuntarily out of the window.

. . . Certainly, evil was brewing right in front of him. Denial of divine providence everywhere. And everywhere the critical spirit of opposition . . . He had to see Arakcheyev, something really needed to be done.

"And the powerful tyrants begin to quake."

He gave a laugh . . .

. . . Just a boy. Abroad now? He frowned. Shouldn't have been allowed.

And he wrote: "Küchelbecker: place under secret surveillance and submit monthly reports on his behavior."

VII

Lyon. December 21/9, 1820

The Germans have recently proved that they love freedom and are not born to be slaves, but some of their customs are bound to seem humiliating and slavish to anyone who is not used to them. The use of sedan chairs in particular belongs to this category. I admit that I was forced to use them a few times in Dresden, where there are no cabs, in bad weather or when I was feeling unwell; but when I saw myself riding or being carried on the shoulders of people just like me, I always felt inclined to jump out. Even less appealing is the custom of making orphans, who are being raised at the public expense, sing for money in the streets; it hurts to see these poor children in their long black robes and huge hats, like the ones our grave-diggers wear at funerals! In the evenings the children sing by the light of torches: their languid and lingering tunes sound terrifying in the silence, which reigns everywhere; just entering life, already they must be preachers of death, Doomsday, and destruction. I always came across this choir in the new square in Dresden; the singers looked like ghosts, or like the deceased, who had left their graves to remind the living of the vicissitudes of all earthly things.

When Aleksandr Lvovich and I were strolling over the bridge that connects Kehl and Strasbourg and separates Germany and France, the memory of my separation from my native land welled up in my heart: the green waters of the Rhine were lapping at our feet; the morning was clear, quiet, and warm. Delvig bade me remember him on the banks of the Rhine; along with him all my friends rose up in my imagination. I remembered our good old nightly conversations over Rhine wine, quiet, full of passions and dreams, when our hearts soared and were united in expressions that are understandable only in our circle, in our dear family of friends and brothers.

VIII

As soon as they arrived in Paris, Wilhelm abandoned his duties altogether and scarcely saw Aleksandr Lvovich. The truth was that Aleksandr Lvovich did not particularly burden him with assignments, and Wilhelm's secretarial duties were for the most part limited to talking and reflecting on the widest possible variety of subjects. Occasionally he would have to write letters, formal and rather odd ones. At the end of each letter, Aleksandr Lvovich never failed to inquire about the weather in Petersburg and what was being performed at the Petersburg theaters.

They spent all that winter in Paris. Wilhelm wandered about the city. He would stand for hours in the Louvre in front of the Venus de Milo, along with a dozen English tourists, or stroll aimlessly along the Boulevard of the Capuchins and drink cheap wine in the taverns of the Latin Quarter. He completely forgot about his poor health. His breathing came with great ease. But Paris was far from joyful.

Spies scurried about among the smartly dressed crowds: Louis XVIII feared conspiracies.

Recently an untidy little person, blond, with watery eyes, had been following in Wilhelm's footsteps wherever he went. The man was patient, he would shadow Wilhelm into the taverns, scrutinize Old Masters' paintings at the Louvre.

One day, as Wilhelm was wandering the boulevard, a man in a broad-brimmed hat looked back at him and stopped. Wilhelm's huge height, his strange appearance, and wandering eyes often caught the attention of Frenchmen and, what particularly hurt Wilhelm, of Frenchwomen too. He was well aware of his ugliness and was used to curious looks. But the man peered too intently. That was insolent. Wilhelm flushed and stepped toward him. A familiar pair of squinty eyes suddenly fixed on him and the man said in astonishment:

'*Guillaume*!'

Küchlya peered closely.

'Silver!'

My God! It was Broglio.

Broglio had matured, grown stout, and although cross-eyed, looked genuinely handsome. Since they'd graduated from the Lycée he seemed to have vanished off the face of the earth, nothing had been heard of him.

They went to a cafe. It was full of people. The blond man with the watery eyes, either a hairdresser or a shop assistant, was sitting in a corner.

Next to him was an empty table. The friends sat down, ordered a Veuve Clicquot, and started to reminisce.

'Do you remember my fight with Komovsky?' said Silver and laughed.

He laughed not because there was anything funny in his memory of Komovsky but simply because he was in good health, cheerful, handsome, and young, and because he had met an old friend—and they both laughed at every trifle they remembered.

Broglio prompted him:

'And the jester, Yakovlev, remember?'

With this fine, handsome, jolly man. Wilhelm too felt in rude health, forthright, and perhaps even handsome.

They sat over their Veuve Clicquot.

Growing tipsy and smartening himself up, which suited him very much, Borglio said:

'We're probably seeing each other for the last time, old boy. Let's drink to it, shall we?'

Wilhelm asked:

'Why are you so sad?'

Broglio sighed what seemed like a genuine sigh.

'All right, I'll tell you what it is. I'm a Philhellene, that is, I support the Greek struggle. All of us are for the Greeks, for their independence.'

Wilhelm asked:

'And who are "us"?'

Silver looked around and said meaningfully and rather loudly:

'The Naples Carbonari.'

Wilhelm peered at Broglio eagerly.

'Is this true, Silver? No joke?'

Silver replied, shaking his head:

'I'm not joking. I'm heading off to Greece soon, to lead a detachment.'

He grew a little gloomy but looked at his comrade with some superiority.

'Yes, and when you receive the news of my death you must remember me with Vieuve Clicquot, old boy.'

He was clearly posing: the Veuve was replaced by a cheering bottle of Aï. Wilhelm looked at his friend with surprise and even apprehension. As it turned out, of the two of them it was the carefree Broglio who was the greater benefactor of mankind.

Wilhelm began to lament:

'I'm so unlucky, Silver. Wherever I go I am enveloped by these heavy vapors. I am pushed out from everywhere. It's fate, Silver. There's so much I'd like to accomplish . . . I'm a poet, a real poet. And what do you think? Women steer clear of me; I've been kicked out of Russia . . .' (Wilhelm was drunk and he was slightly exaggerating, he felt both good and sad.) 'I don't know where and what to settle on . . .'

Silver caught only his last words.

'*Guillaume*,' he said very weightily and simply, 'you too must go to Greece.'

Wilhelm almost sobered up.

He gave Broglio a quick glance and fell into thought. How simple it was! Everything resolved with a single stroke. To go to Greece! To fight and to die there! He reached out his hand to Broglio.

'"Trattoria marina," Naples. When you get there, ask for "the younger one."'

Wilhelm scrutinized him anxiously and yet delightedly.

As they were leaving the cafe, the small man, a hairdresser or sales assistant, hurriedly left the nearby table and started walking a couple of steps behind the friends, barely moving his feet and humming under his breath so that passersby pointed at him and laughed. But when there were no passersby and the friends did not look back, he would suddenly straighten up and the humming would break off.

He was listening intently.

IX

In the morning, Wilhelm quickly got dressed and began to pace the room. The thought of Greece would not leave him. Naples, Greece. He knew that if he went there, he would not come back. To go to Greece meant to go to his death. Death did not frighten him. He had faced bullets, he could have died twenty times in all his silly duels. Something else was stopping him. So many unsettled scores, so many unfinished labors! To go to Greece was heroic, and at the same time it would look like running away. For some reason he remembered how Dunya looked at him that time at Aunt Breitkopf's. He paced the room. Too simple a solution for everything—both longing and failure, at one fell swoop. This was much too short a route. He remembered Pushchin. What would Pushchin do in his place? And he could not imagine Pushchin in Greece. The one who would certainly run off to Greece was Pushkin.

How terrible that he couldn't take anyone into his confidence; he needed Griboyedov so desperately right now.

There was a knock on the door.

A servant came in:

'Aleksandr Lvovich is asking you to come and see him.'

Wilhelm went to Aleksandr Lvovich's quarters. Naryshkin had rented himself an entire town house in Paris, large, preposterous, uncomfortable. Aleksandr Lvovich had a special talent—he could never settle comfortably in any one place. Perhaps, that was the reason why fate had sent him such a secretary as Wilhelm.

Aleksandr Lvovich had just received a furious letter from Marya Alekseyevna. Since angry letters from her were a frequent occurrence, Wilhelm guessed it at once from the old man's face. Marya Alekseyevna had been a beauty thirty years ago and she still could not forgive her husband for it. She had always been passed over for honors; her husband did not appreciate her enough either. She was a great schemer and a famous gossip, and she kept all of Petersburg society in fear of her. Marya Alekseyevna had in fact insisted on traveling abroad, but at the last moment had suddenly become obstinate and stayed in Petersburg on her own. Now she terrorized Aleksandr Lvovich with her letters.

Aleksandr Lvovich looked at Wilhelm plaintively.

'Wilhelm Karlovich, my dear,' he grumbled, 'I need you to write two or three letters, to Prince Ivan Alekseich and to someone else. I am sorry to trouble you.'

Wilhelm unfolded the papers and prepared to listen to Aleksandr Lvovich, but the latter was in no hurry to get down to business.

'Or we can postpone it,' he said suddenly, then hesitated, and finally made up his mind: 'Yes, let's postpone it.'

He looked at Wilhelm sadly and suddenly said:

'I am fond of you, Wilhelm Karlovich, bless your soul, I am very fond of you indeed.'

Wilhelm bowed in confusion and muttered:

'I am fond of you too, Aleksandr Lvovich.'

'And you know what?' said Naryshkin. 'I am dying to go back to Russia. I doubt if I'll stay here till spring. I'll go to my Kursk estate. I had enough of the French thirty years ago, old chap. If it hadn't been for Marya Alekseyevna, I wouldn't have moved an inch.'

Then he pondered and said:

'And you know what, my dear chap, let's go to my estate together. Once you've heard my horn orchestra, you'll be sick of the *Grand Opéra*.'

Wilhelm listened to him with a kind of secret pleasure. He knew that something had got into the crazy head of Aleksandr Lvovich, but that an hour later he would set off in an outlandish cavalcade for the Bois de Boulogne, would roll his r's like a natural Parisian, and by night-time he would safely forget Russia, Kursk, and the horn orchestra. But at such moments Aleksandr Lvovich had a huge appeal to him.

Aleksandr Lvovich bowed his great head and spoke impishly:

'And hand on heart, for the life of me I can't understand what the hell you and I are doing here in this rented house—I can't make any sense of it, everything is so chaotic, whereas in Russia things are both convenient and cozy, and, most importantly, they make sense.'

Wilhelm smiled inquiringly:

'Everything?'

The old courtier answered smilingly:

'Everything. What, for example, do they sing here: *Faridondaine*?'

And shaking his head, with a defiant liberalism, he hummed the tune of the new song by Béranger:

La faridondaine
Biribi . . . Biribi.

'Can you make it out: *biribi-biribi*?' he repeated, perfectly pronouncing the r's in the French manner and admiring the nonsensical word. 'Whereas in a Russian song it couldn't be clearer: *bayushki-bayu*.'

Wilhelm roared with laughter. Aleksandr Lvovich liked his own joke immensely and repeated it several times, gazing in triumph at Wilhelm:

'*Biribi-biribi*. There you have me.'

And then he added very quickly, in response to some other idea that was in his head (he had lost some money playing *biribi* the day before):

'One can come to Paris empty-headed, but there is no way one can come here empty-handed.'

When Wilhelm returned to his rooms, his determination was shaken. Greece beckoned him, but he recalled the handsome Broglio with a certain displeasure. Nothing was simple. The way to Greece was a roundabout one. It was impossible to go there "empty-handed." He remembered Aleksandr Lvovich's "*biribi*" and burst out laughing. He looked out of the window. Paris in spring was gray but cheerful. The streets teemed with strolling crowds, and women's laughter was heard from time to time. Where was Pushkin now? How did he like those dirty southern Russian towns? What was Delvig doing? And he sat down to write him a letter. He had an important visit the following day—to Benjamin Constant, who had undertaken to arrange for Wilhelm to deliver lectures on Russian literature.

X

Papa Fleury, the orator of mankind, a friend of Anacharsis Cloots, a lonely and gloomy mathematician, a leftover from the year 1793, had been working on a study of world revolution. Only the solidarity of all peoples could save the revolution from the decayed Monkey XVIII (so Papa Fleury called Louis "the Desired"). He had long been studying all the oppressed countries in which a conflagration could break out.

While a single tyrant remained alive, freedom couldn't be guaranteed to any nation. Naples—one, Spain—two, the States—three, Greece—four. In Germany, Karl Sand's head had just fallen; in France the spirit of murdered liberty had been stirring again.

What remained was England and Russia.

Russia was a conundrum, and Papa Fleury did not like conundrums; his study of world revolution was written in the form of axioms, lemmas, and theorems.

In Russia, tyrants were not killed by the people, but by one another. There was slavery in Russia. Two names had attracted Papa Fleury's attention: *Stefan Razin*, a terrifying Cossack who threatened to overthrow the despotic old order; and in particular *Emilian Pugatschef*, the slave leader, the Russian Spartacus, who impressed Papa Fleury with the directness of his military tactics. Slaves were the body of the revolution. The body needed a head. Papa Fleury could not see that head. His Russian theorem No. 5 in Section Two of his study was unfinished.

Papa Fleury kept a watchful eye on information from Russia. That was why when he learned that a young Russian professor and poet was giving lectures on Russian literature at the Athénée Royal, he did his best to attend them. The poet had a strange name, which Papa Fleury struggled to remember: something like either "Beaucouque" or "Kückelberg." As soon as he saw and heard the Russian poet, he was even more surprised.

A long, stooped figure, an elongated face, a lopsided mouth, huge hands with feverishly moving fingers, a thin and hoarse voice—all these reminded Papa Fleury of someone. He had heard that voice somewhere before.

He attended the lectures punctually. The Athénée auditorium was jam-packed, the literary celebrities sat in the front rows—Papa Fleury spotted the cold profile of the blond Constant, the pale face and burning eyes of Jullien, the thick, large face of de Jouy. An inconspicuous man with dull eyes sat beside him, diligently taking notes from the lectures and peering anxiously at all the faces, apparently a newsman, a journalist.

Papa Fleury enjoyed the first two lectures. The poet began with the history, going back centuries. Early Russia, with its simple customs, the courageous spirit of the common people, the scheming of the boyars and the failure to organize a single, sufficiently robust state, the development of private life, and the imperfection of the state machinery, all this was fascinating for Papa Fleury. Through these distant ancestors, he now had an opportunity to come closer to the solution of the Russian question. The entire audience also listened to the poet keenly, apparently stunned by his extraordinary appearance.

Who did this tall enthusiastic poet remind him of? Papa Fleury still struggled to remember.

And only third time round, during the third lecture of the strange poet, did he remember. The poet was speaking about early Russian folk poetry. He argued that the Russian people could be remarkably cheerful and witty in their fairy tales and proverbs. Those who heard and knew them were amazed by the kindness, cordiality, sharp wit, and lack of rancor of those anonymous old authors. The courage of Russian warriors was extraordinary. But the songs, the old Russian songs, their very melodies and lyrics were somewhat melancholy.

The poet asked: 'And why?' He stood there pale, his bulging eyes shone. His voice grew suddenly hoarse. He spoke breathlessly:

'Is it not a bad omen that from early on in Russian history there has been something that prevents her people from becoming blessed and great in the moral world, among all other peoples?'

'Slavery,' he said in a hollow voice, 'slavery that imbues the bread sown by a slave and the songs he sings. Oh, how vile is the picture of corruption spread by this slavery! What can compare with the daily bondage of the people, who have created those cheerful stories and composed those sad songs, and how can we bear to think that all this is being crushed, that all this is dying, that all this might disappear without bearing any fruit in the moral world? No, it will not!'

And, panting, no longer in control of himself, he staggered and, trying to keep his balance, brushed his hand against the decanter of water and the glass.

The decanter tumbled down and was smashed to smithereens.

In his exhaustion, Wilhelm fell into the chair, and his head rolled back.

The audience roared with enthusiasm.

And then Fleury realized that this head was thrown back just like the head of his friend, Anacharsis Cloots, the orator of the human race. Papa Fleury remembered how the executioner had lifted that head by its hair.

People crowded around Wilhelm. He had already recovered, and, still pale, was shaking their hands. Benjamin Constant spoke to him enthusiastically and deferentially. Wilhelm found it hard to concentrate on what he was saying.

Papa Fleury squeezed through the crowd to the speaker. He shook his hand and said, looking at him with a stern expression:

'Young man, take good care of yourself, your fatherland has need of you.'

Wilhelm was one of the last people to emerge from the auditorium of the Athénée. Two people walked with him: Papa Fleury and the small blond man with watery eyes. The latter darted sideways out of the door and at once disappeared.

Papa Fleury took Wilhelm by the hand:

'My young friend, I'd be happy if you'd join me at a small coffee house in the Latin Quarter. I need to say a few words on which much depends for me.'

Wilhelm bowed to him readily, and with some curiosity. His head was still burning in any case, and he was unable at this moment to go home.

An hour later Papa Fleury accompanied Wilhelm back to his house and watched him for a long time as he walked away. Then he muttered regretfully:

'No, not really. The head's not ready yet.'

He thought and added with surprise:

'But the heart's there.'

XI

No sooner had Wilhelm got dressed than there was a knock at the door; Aleksandr Lvovich was asking for him immediately.

Wilhelm found him greatly agitated and pacing the room with his small steps. He made a cool reply to Wilhelm's bow.

'Please sit down.' He frowned and continued to pace about the room. 'I regret to say I must speak to you frankly. You, my dear sir, are acting extremely rashly and putting yourself in harm's way. I have just received an invitation from the consulate to visit the consul without delay, to provide explanations regarding your behavior. And I surmise—I have grounds to surmise—that the reason for this is the public lecture that you gave yesterday in the Athénée. Apparently, the Prefect of Paris has already been informed about you.'

Wilhelm sat up in his armchair.

Aleksandr Lvovich paced the room without looking at Wilhelm. This time he spoke in a highly official tone:

'It goes without saying, good sir, that I have never dreamed of censuring your conduct in any way, but you know very well that while you are in my service, your behavior is causing difficulties and even danger for people who are completely innocent of any wrongdoing.'

Wilhelm looked pale and smiled at Aleksandr Lvovich:

'So, it's the parting of the ways then, Aleksandr Lvovich.'

Aleksandr Lvovich continued to dart about, saying nothing. Suddenly he stopped in front of Wilhelm.

'What on earth have you been up to, my friend?' he said. His expression was one of wistful apprehension. He had suddenly dropped all formality.

'I must have been careless in my choice of language. So permit me to thank you. I'll leave at once.'

Aleksandr Lvovich appeared visibly relieved:

'Well, now you see for yourself, my friend, the fruits of your carelessness.'

He went up to Wilhelm, shook his hand distractedly, embraced him, and said hastily:

'Godspeed! I've grown used to you, my friend, it's a pity we have to say good-bye.'

But as it turned out, Wilhelm had to leave their lodgings even sooner than he thought.

Two people with leaden faces were sitting in his room.

One of them handed him a dispatch.

The Prefect of the Paris Police was informing Collegiate Assessor Küchelbecker that, in accordance with the order of the Prefect of Paris, he, Küchelbecker, was to leave Paris within twenty-four hours, having notified the prefecture of his intended route.

The other man silently handed him a second paper, which authorized him to inspect Collegiate Assessor Küchelbecker's personal effects and papers and, if necessary, seize them.

They began to rummage through his papers.

One man pulled out a portrait of Karl Sand and inquired suspiciously:

'Who is this?'

Wilhelm replied:

'My late brother.'

An hour later, having turned Wilhelm's belongings upside down, both bowed and took their leave, requesting written details of the route that Mr. Küchelbecker was intending to follow. Wilhelm jotted down: Paris—Dijon—Villa Franca[23]—Nice—Warsaw.

He was about to write "Naples," but scribbled "Warsaw" instead. He had to be careful.

One of the prefect's messengers said: 'We shall come again to witness your departure.'

The following morning, Wilhelm took a stagecoach. There were not many passengers in the coach: a few Englishmen, two French merchants, and a small untidy man with little pale blue eyes.

Where had Wilhelm seen those eyes and that man? At the lecture? In the street? Odd, that by sheer accident their paths kept crossing like this all the time.

One of the Englishmen got off at Dijon. The little man took exactly the same route as Wilhelm, all the way to Villa Franca.

XII

Villa Franca was a little white-walled town, nestled against the cliffs. A large jetty protected it from storms; the Mont Albano fortress cut sharply through the blue air.

White houses were surrounded by gardens with weeping willows, almond, citrus, fig, and olive trees. The decrepit stones were covered with ivy, the yellow rocks overgrown with wild anemones, lilies, hyacinths, and thyme.

Wilhelm kept stumbling upon aloe plants sprouting out of the clefts.

In the distance, fishermen hauled their nets, puffed their short pipes, and chatted. Further along one could see and hear noisy shipyards.

Wilhelm went down to the bay and dropped in at the seaside trattoria for breakfast. His companion, the very same little man, came in, too, and sat down at a table, away from Wilhelm. He was unassuming but looked anxious and expectant.

Something held Wilhelm back from nodding to him and asking him to join him at his table.

Wilhelm was served some oysters and a bottle of the local wine, young and strong.

The night, as always in the south, fell suddenly, without warning, without twilight. The lantern was lit. A few boatmen were sitting at the tables, one of them a handsome fellow, with black eyes. Wilhelm beckoned him and began to bargain for a trip to Nice.

The boatman looked out of the window, then at the sky and said lazily:

'No, *signore*, a storm is coming.'

Wilhelm's companion looked at the boatman and slowly shut his right eye. The boatman thought for a second and suddenly agreed but set a very high price.

Wilhelm was staggered. His companion winked at the boatman again, the boatman pondered and coolly lowered the price.

Wilhelm said good-bye and left.

Only the fiery points of lanterns on the boats bobbed up and down across the water, they were no more than bright balls that did not illuminate the darkness. It was pitch black. The boatman waited a little bit longer at the trattoria. He went out without looking at Wilhelm and, pulling his cap over his head, headed for the shore.

He called quietly: 'Luigi.'

A child's voice answered: '*Ao*.'

The boat reached the shore, a boy jumped out and began speaking quickly, pointing to the sky. The boatman made an impatient gesture.

Hunched under the low roof of the boat, Wilhelm felt short of breath. The boat slid from wave to wave.

The boatman was silent. A thunderstorm broke. They were no longer gliding on the waves, but bouncing up and down, while the rain fell heavily and inside the boat it was as stuffy as if they were underground.

Wilhelm said to the boatman:

'Row to the shore, row to shore, dammit! Don't you have a second oar?'

'No, *signore*.'

The boat sped along the coast and with every moment it was carried further offshore.

A quarter of an hour passed like this. Finally, the storm stopped.

The stuffiness passed immediately. The boatman breathed heavily, put down his oar and rested.

A light loomed far ahead, then another one, probably fishing boats. The boatman stepped into the cabin and sat down next to Wilhelm. He said nothing. His quietness and his cautious movements were alarming.

Suddenly, the boatman seized Wilhelm by the throat and threw him down to the bottom of the boat. Wilhelm wrapped his enormous hands round the boatman's neck. Both men lay in the bottom of the boat. Wilhelm was gasping for air. He felt that he was weakening and gave the boatman's throat one last fierce squeeze. Instantly it became easier to breathe. He released his head, lifted himself a little, and pressed down on the boatman's chest with his knee. The man was breathing heavily, looking at Wilhelm with rolling eyes. Wilhelm frisked him and found a stiletto stuck in his belt. He threw the stiletto into the water. He was furious. He was burning to kill the boatman and hurl him overboard. But he only gasped in his face: 'Row.'

Suddenly, with an imperceptible movement of his foot, the boatman again threw Wilhelm down. Wilhelm shouted and hit his head on the side of the boat. Then it felt as if the boat was violently rocked. He came to and saw some fishermen holding on to the boatman, who was pale and confused, looking at them with a puzzled air.

'Why did you want to kill me?' Wilhelm asked him.

The boatman waved his hand in the direction of Villa Franca and muttered:

'For money.'

What money? Wilhelm did not understand a thing. Suddenly he remembered his companion with the watery eyes, who had kept crossing his path ever since Paris. He looked at the boatman curiously.

'Is the little fellow a spy?'

No answer. The fishermen still kept a tight hold of the man's arms. Wilhelm shrugged and said to the fishermen:

'Let him go and help me get to Nice, will you?'

Only when he had reached Nice, did Wilhelm discover that out of the three wads of banknotes Aleksandr Lvovich had slipped him during their farewell, only the lightest one was left. The other two had probably fallen out during the skirmish in the boat. Or the boatman had managed to pocket them after all.

He could kiss goodbye to any thoughts of Naples, Broglio, and Greece.

XIII

Rumors circulated widely. There were whisperings in the streets. In Piedmont the Carbonari, friends of liberty, had rebelled against the Jesuits and the judges, against the king. The king called on the hated Austrians. Rumor had it that Austrian troops were advancing in order to crush the people's liberties. The Austrians, the *tedeschi*, were universally hated.[24]

Wilhelm hated them along with everyone else and, walking through the streets, he felt like a Piedmontese.

XIV

". . . I left Italy in a gloomy mood.

". . . Rumors that spread in the last days of my stay in Nice about the movements of the Piedmontese Carbonari, the revolt in Alexandria, and the unrest in the army, the threat of war and devastation, all this doubled my despondency . . .

Thunder will rumble; each dull eye
Be dazzled as the bright dawn spills;
The dreaded tedeschi come from on high
Down from the awe-inspiring hills;

Death from a thousand guns will boom,
A thousand bayonets flash like morn;
Spring will wither in the womb,
Liberty die before it is born!

. . . Oh here I saw the promise they make
Of golden days free of all pain;
But here too suffering stays awake,
The Muse is alarmed by the rattle of chains."

XV

And here was Petersburg again.

Back in Petersburg, Wilhelm was once again in a turmoil.

First, he didn't have a penny. Ustinya Yakovlevna herself lived from hand to mouth, God only knew how, on crumbs from some pension. Meanwhile, Wilhelm felt that he was shunned by everybody. When they met him, two or three people pretended not to notice him at all. Modest Korf barely nodded to him. Ryleyev, on the contrary, embraced him, and kissed him hard.

'I've heard a lot about you, a lot, they speak wonders of you. Tell me about Germany, about France. Where is your lecture? Is it written down? And, tell me, what's the news of Greece over there?'

Wilhelm talked to him eagerly. The summaries of his lectures in Paris were snapped up by Vyazemsky, by Aleksandr Ivanovich Turgenev, and even by the chatterbox Bulgakov. Meanwhile, the wolf was at the door.

He attempted to go back to the university boarding school, but was received coldly there and told that he would have to wait. He began to consider publishing a journal, but that required money.

Finally, Vyazemsky and Aleksandr Ivanovich Turgenev undertook to intercede on his behalf.

While they were busy doing this, Wilhelm kept paying glum visits to Aunt Breitkopf. Dunya no longer went there; this year she was living with her mother in Moscow. He did not go to Sophie's either. Once he met her in the street—she was riding with someone in a chaise, laughing out loud. With a beating heart Wilhelm quickly turned into an alley. That night he did not sleep well. He received a letter from Sophie, a happy fragrant letter. Quite nonchalantly, she reprimanded him for coming back and not putting in a single appearance. Was it because he was too proud? These days he was the talk of the city . . . Wilhelm cringed. Sophie was treating him now as a curiosity to be exhibited in her salon. He tore up the letter, buried his face in the pillow, burst into tears, and did not go to her.

Instead he frequented his brother, Misha, whom he found increasingly fascinating. Thin, stern-faced, gloomy, and taciturn, now, as in their childhood, he was the complete opposite of Wilhelm—he had his father's nature, the blood of the old German, Karl Küchelbecker. He was very fond of his brother but made sure not to show it. Misha lived in the Marines' Barracks, in the officers' quarters, took the same food and drink as an ordinary sailor and had already begun to keep himself aloof from those around him. He had a slight limp: he had broken his leg during naval exercises. The able seamen were fond of him and Wilhelm would often find his brother in conversation with them when they came to receive orders. Wilhelm himself fell into talk with them. Able seaman Dorofeyev, a cheerful red-haired man with a snub nose, took to chatting to him—they had a lot to talk about concerning travel. Dorofeyev had been round the world, and he had visited Hamburg and Marseille.

Each time they met Wilhelm grew more convinced that he was justified in his devotion to the common people. This sailor with intelligent eyes and his comrade Kuroptev, a thickset gloomy fellow, knew a vast amount and, slowly rolling their cigarettes, they considered their answers. They were truly thoughtful people. More thoughtful than his Lycée friend, Modest Korf.

Misha, like Wilhelm, shunned high society, which was closed to both brothers—to one because of his temper, to the other because of his humble career. And, rejected by high society, seeking a crust of bread for the morrow, with a quagmire instead of firm soil underfoot—because the activities of the one and the service of the other depended every day and every hour on the whim of some general or policeman—the brothers could only withdraw, either into themselves or into some cause that would completely absorb them. And this brought them closer.

Aleksandr Ivanovich Turgenev was trying to help Küchelbecker. He dropped hints about him to his patron, Prince Golitsyn, who, against all expectations, reacted to the name of Küchelbecker with sympathy and quite surprised Turgenev with his readiness to find a post for the young man. A week later he told Turgenev that the only way out for Küchelbecker was to enlist under General Yermolov, who was now in Petersburg; he had just arrived from a congress and would soon be setting off for Georgia.

Turgenev spoke to Wilhelm about this.

'Ah, Griboyedov's in Georgia now. I agree, naturally. Right away if you like.'

And he suddenly asked Turgenev:

'Tell me, Aleksandr Ivanovich, wasn't Yermolov on his way to help Greece?'

Turgenev explained:

'It didn't work out. Metternich managed to placate the tsar.'

Wilhelm pondered and repeated:

'I agree and I am grateful.'

A new plan hatched in his head.

Yermolov was the only general who was "national," that is, popular among young people. He was the "general of youth." The government suspected him of "ambitious designs," the tsar was simply afraid that Yermolov would somehow oust him from the throne and, for the time being, had handed him the Caucasus—the blessing of which was that it was far away. From the Caucasus to Greece—just a step. What if. . .? What if Yermolov himself decided to advance to Greece? All young Russia would stand up for him.

Wilhelm's head spun.

This would mean going to Greece, but not "empty-handed." It was no longer Aleksandr Lvovich's "*biribi.*"

He firmly shook the hand of the slightly puzzled Aleksandr Ivanovich and ran out. Turgenev muttered:

'So delighted, poor fellow.'

Golitsyn's interest in Küchelbecker was not an idle one. He had heard the name and had reason to believe that it would also be of interest to someone else whom Prince Golitsyn treasured in the depths of his soul more than the name of the god to whom he prayed at least three times a day.

Yermolov's name too cropped up for a reason. Prince Golitsyn had dropped Wilhelm's name at a meeting with the Minister of Foreign affairs, Nesselrode. Nesselrode, a dry little German, pricked up his ears.

The following day he reported to the tsar:

'Your Majesty, Collegiate Assessor Küchelbecker has come back from abroad and is asking for your permission to join the service.'

The tsar looked at the minister inquiringly.

'Isn't he in Greece?'

'No, Sire, not yet.'

'The reports gave me the impression that he is in Greece.'

'Your Majesty, due to certain reasons that are known to you, in my opinion he should be kept at a distance for a while—like his friend Pushkin.'

The tsar was pleased to hear that.

'Just the other day Prince Golitsyn was telling me that somebody had been interceding for Küchelbecker. May I respectfully suggest the following: General Yermolov is currently here. How would Your Majesty like the idea of sending this troubled young man to an equally troubled country?'

The minister's clear eyes looked into the clear eyes of the tsar.

The tsar bowed his shiny bald head.

'Yes, only to Georgia—no further. Keep him in Georgia and don't let him leave. Kindly have a word with Aleksey Petrovich.'

On September 19, 1821 Collegiate Assessor Wilhelm Karlovich Küchelbecker was officially enlisted to serve in the office of the governor of the Caucasus. On August 31, without waiting for the appointment to be approved, he set off with Yermolov for the Caucasus.

Caucasus

I

In Vladikavkaz Wilhelm lagged behind Yermolov. He fell ill and spent a few weeks on a hard mattress in a squalid hotel. He arrived in Tiflis in October 1821.

The meeting with Griboyedov was a joyful one. The friends did not sleep all night and talked about everything all at once—Europe, the tsar, Yermolov, the Carbonari, Pushkin. Dressed in a flimsy *arkhaluk* thrown over his undergarments, with his hand in a sling (earlier it had been shot through in a duel, and on the way to Tiflis, he had broken it), Griboyedov asked his friend many questions, speaking slowly, looking at Wilhelm's tanned, emaciated face, and smiling at him.

'What's the news in Petersburg?'

'All the same, dear chap, city gossip, petty scoffers, I am ridiculed and despised by everyone—except you and Pushkin. I've come to stay with you for a good while; I'm tired, I can't settle anywhere.'

'By all means, my dear friend, join me. This is the ultimate extremity. The land of oblivion.' These last words Griboyedov uttered almost with pleasure. 'Once you've found your bearings here—you'll fall in love with this land.'

'Any interesting people around here? Who are you keeping company with?'

'All sorts, like everywhere else. I'm not particularly liked here. You'll see tomorrow. Interesting people? Aleksey Petrovich, you know, is a wonderful old man, though sly. Don't get too excited by his sweet talk. He's as courteous as an old lady. Yakubovich is still here, but as you know, I'm not friendly with him.'

Griboyedov glanced involuntarily at the wound on his hand. (The duel had been with Yakubovich.)

Finally, Wilhelm said with some hesitation:

'You know the plan I've hatched, Aleksandr? Aleksey Petrovich must be persuaded to go to Greece.'

Griboyedov asked in astonishment:

'To Greece? What for?'

'The tsar sold out the Greeks in Laibach.[25] They'll have to manage without him. If Aleksey Petrovich goes to Greece of his own accord, all Russia will be with him.'

Griboyedov was silent for a moment before replying with some displeasure:

'No, leave it. The situation in Europe is not good at all, and here it's even worse. Do you know what Metternich wrote after Laibach? "I enjoy the curses of the people whose toes I tread on." He has trodden on the feet of Naples, has been strangling the Carbonari, and will slaughter Greece. Besides, Aleksey Petrovich won't go there. It's not what he wants.'

Wilhelm jumped to his feet.

'Oh no, Aleksandr, how wrong you are! I've traveled all over Europe, and everything is in a state of flux. In Germany, the *Jugendbund* is growing. In Jena, Stuttgart, minds are seething. The Carbonari are in Paris. I met a wonderful old man there. They are ready for anything. What is this rotten lecher Metternich compared to liberty!'

Griboyedov stared at Wilhelm without taking his eyes off him. His swarthy, gaunt cheeks blushed. Suddenly, he leaned back against the pillows and said dryly:

'Popular outrage, my little friend, is not like a theater audience's anger at the management for a bad production.'

'Ah, Aleksandr, believe me . . .'

Wilhelm pressed his hands to his heart. He stood in the middle of the room in nothing but his undergarments.

'I believe,' Aleksandr said dispassionately, 'I believe you need to cool down a little. Or else, in spite of the Parisian Carbonari, they'll have time to put you in shackles. Sleep, my boy,' he laughed, looking at the awkward Küchlya who still stood there in his undergarments, aflame and affronted. 'The sun will wake us up early tomorrow.'

II

Next morning, after a breakfast served by Griboyedov's servant, who shuffled about with his shoes on bare feet (by a strange chance, he was called Aleksandr Gribov), the friends went to find Yermolov.

What a strange sight Tiflis (or Tbilisi) was: a pile of stones. Works were going on in the two or three main streets. Near the large new building of the arsenal, half-dressed soldiers were carrying bricks and flagstones up to the scaffolding, bending under the weight of the hods. The soldiers' heads were covered with wet sacks—the autumn sun was still scorching in Tiflis, which was a hot city. The sound of the pickaxe, smashing and levellng off bricks, was unusually sharp in the morning air.

'Are the soldiers doing construction work here?' Wilhelm asked.

'All the soldiers here are military workmen,' explained Griboyedov. 'Aleksey Petrovich has allowed our regimental commanders to use their soldiers as builders and soon all the commanders will have wonderful houses. The civilians can't keep up—where can they find a free work force?'

They passed the new headquarters that were being built. Next to the low houses, new ones were already looming so that the low houses seemed rather oppressed and affronted.

Wilhelm commented: 'He has a bold vision, building a new capital.'

"He" was Yermolov. When Küchlya was in love with someone, he did not call them by name. And he was always in love with someone. This time it was Yermolov.

'Yes, too bold, I daresay.' grinned Griboyedov. 'He spares neither people nor money, but there is no real plan, many of the novelties are quite unnecessary, they only annoy the residents, as they are neither practical nor elegant. For example, he refused to build a covered balcony around the whole house. Even though a canopy provides shade. And how can you live without shade in this hell? Here bricks melt in the heat without a canopy.'

'Why did he do that then?'

'No reason, he does everything without thinking.'

It was still too early to see Yermolov. They took a walk. The further from the fortress, the quieter it became. Winding, narrow streets ran into each other chaotically. The stench of sewage and garbage hung in the air. They began to come across empty houses.

Griboyedov said: 'Better not to go any further, it's all wasteland.'

Wilhelm felt a touch of fear: 'Why is that?'

'Fear of raids. People settle closer to the fortress; in an emergency it can protect them if they are within the range of its guns. Once the Chechens broke in. The slaughter was appalling. It's quieter now. Yermolov has put the fear of God into them. He gathers the local and Kabardian princes, brings his experienced interpreters, and no one dares utter a word. He threatens them with floggings, hangings, burnings, and executions.

'Assuages brutality with words,' said Wilhelm with satisfaction.

Griboyedov smiled crookedly and an unpleasant line appeared round his mouth:

'Well, not only with words—he really does hang and burn. Last week there was a major incident. Prince Kaikhosro Gurieli killed Colonel Puzyrevsky. So, the old man issued a decree: not to leave anything standing. And they didn't. Everyone in the village was slaughtered.'

Wilhelm felt awkward.

'What can you say?' Griboyedov added hastily in a different tone, looking at him obliquely. 'In the eyes of the law, his arbitrary actions are unjustifiable but remember that he is in Asia, where every child has a knife at the ready.'

Yermolov's house was behind the fortress wall. In the courtyard of the fortress everyday life went on—the cannons, which had recently returned from action, were being dragged into place, a company was lining up, and an orderly was giving orders on the porch.

Wilhelm noticed a bunch of half-naked boys between twelve and fifteen. Some were playing, chasing each other with guttural cries. The others sat downcast talking gravely among themselves.

'Who are they?' he asked.

'They are *amanats*, hostages. It is customary here to take child hostages, all from the best families.'

'Children as hostages?'

'This is war,' Griboyedov grinned grimly. 'The old man once captured some Chechens, married off the best female captives to the Imeretians,[26] and sold the rest for a ruble apiece to the mountain tribes.'

Wilhelm lowered his head. What Aleksandr was telling him about the "old man" frightened him. That amiable, witty, sardonic Yermolov, with whom he had fallen in love along the way, was apparently a different man here.

They entered the house. Yermolov occupied three small rooms. There were already a few people in the front room. The ceilings were low, the furniture was a jumble. There was a huge Turkish sofa by the wall. A tall, middle-aged officer, with a sharp fox-like face and black hair with consumptive bald patches on his temples, was talking to an impassive artillery captain in an excessively long great coat.

Aleksandr introduced them. The tall one was Voyeikov, the captain was Liszt.

A young man, pleasant and very slim, with smooth hair, entered from the adjacent room. He immediately dashed toward Griboyedov and bowed to him respectfully.

'Aleksandr Sergeyevich, Aleksey Petrovich has already inquired about you. Aleksey Petrovich is bored without you.'

Griboyedov introduced the young man to Wilhelm:

'Nikolay Nikolayevich Pokhvisnev.'

Pokhvisnev was enthusiastically shaking Küchlya's hand.

'Would Aleksey Petrovich be able to see us now?' asked Griboyedov.

'He will always find time to see you, Aleksandr Sergeyevich,' replied Pokhvisnev obligingly, 'give me a moment to inquire.'

And he disappeared again into the inner room.

'Who is he?' asked Wilhelm in a low voice.

'A secretary, a nobody,' grimaced Griboyedov.

A minute later Pokhvisnev took them through to Yermolov, who was at his desk. The desk was covered with reports, a map criss-crossed with pencil marks, an income-expenditure book, and, to one side, a kind of sketch.

A few maps hung on the walls; an infinite number of gray lines, condensed in places into dark circles; the mountains were intersected by blue and red lines.

At that moment Yermolov did not resemble his portrait by Dow. His bushy eyebrows were slightly raised, his broad face looked flabby, and his little elephant eyes seemed to be waiting for something and laughing in anticipation. He was wearing a thin *arkhaluk,* open on his bare chest with its curly gray hair. He looked a bit like Krylov.

Seeing friends, he got up and immediately turned out to be massively built. He shook Griboyedov's hand good-naturedly, embraced Wilhelm, and said in a subdued but pleasant voice:

'Welcome. Please take a seat.'

Then he asked Wilhelm: 'How was your journey over here, dear chap? How are you keeping?' and looked at him, obviously pleased. 'You didn't get scared in the Daryal Gorge, did you? A place to give you the creeps. The other day I was rummaging through my papers and found an old sketch of it—just take a look at my handiwork.'

Yermolov's drawing was remarkably accurate, there were almost no shadows in it, the mountains were just outlined.

'I had no idea you were an artist, Aleksey Petrovich,' Griboeydov said, smiling.

'Well, there you are, I had no idea myself at first.' Yermolov laughed. 'Everyone's full of surprises. You, Wilhelm Karlovich, probably think of Zhukovsky as a poet. So do I, of course, but what you don't know is that Zhukovsky used to write first-rate bulletins.'

Wilhelm was agape:

'What bulletins?'

'Skobelev's, in 1812. Excellent newsletters. Kept quiet about his authorship out of modesty while Skobelev enjoyed the undeserved fame. Well then, what about Greece?' he asked Wilhelm wryly, apparently teasing him and carrying on a long-standing conversation.

'That is something all of us should be asking *you*, Aleksey Petrovich.'

'Would you believe it,' said Yermolov playfully to Griboyedov, 'your friend tried to tempt me to Vladikavkaz. He begged me: "If you march your troops to Greece, Aleksey Petrovich, all of Russia will be with you." "Well, dear chap," I replied, "if I do that, they will make *me* march." But really, he almost had me tempted,' he laughed suddenly, openly. 'I only just got out of it. I said: "What are you talking about, dear chap? I have trouble enough in the Caucasus." That's poets for you!'

All three laughed. It was easy talking with Yermolov. Wilhelm was looking at him with enamoured eyes. Then Yermolov said with a sly look on his face:

'But what Wilhelm Karlovich really convinced me of in the end is the Russian folk spirit. Yes, apparently there are genuine poetic treasures hidden in the Russian native spirit, that is, the folk spirit. It's a fascinating thought, and I seem to remember that you too, Aleksandr Sergeyevich, said something along those lines.'

Griboyedov smiled:

'I see, Wilhelm Karlovich made you not only a Greek enthusiast along the way, but a poet too, Aleksey Petrovich.'

'No, I don't write verse, how could I? Suvorov wrote some feeble rhymes. I write communiqués. And how is your hand, Aleksandr Sergeyevich?' He was changing the subject.

'Still hurts, the doctor wants to break it again.'

'Then have it broken—good luck with it. We shan't let you go to Persia, unless you yourself are burning to go. I've already written to Nesselrode. Stay with us as foreign affairs secretary, that's it then, set up a school of eastern languages here. Are you still into all those Persian things?' he smiled again. 'By now your Persian must be better than the sheikhs', don't you think? We have a long-standing argument,' he explained to Küchelbecker. 'I am not fond of Persia, I don't care for their customs and I hate their language. And Aleksandr Sergeyevich defends them. The Persians want everything spelled out at length. We Europeans can put a few full stops in a row and they immediately acquire some hidden meaning, while they take ten pages to write a run-of-the-mill letter.'

Wilhelm pricked up his ears.

'How well you put it, Aleksey Petrovich. That's how Pushkin writes: lines of full stops.'

Almost gracefully Yermolov leaned back his shock of half-gray hair. His chest was heaving with laughter:

'Once I wrote a letter to the *sadrazam*[27]: "From the day of our separation," I wrote to him, "the sun has been dimmed, the roses have withered and smell of wormwood, the light in my eyes has gone hazy, and my eyes wish they were at the back of my head." And we couldn't even stand each other!'

The friends smiled.

'Do you know their arabesque paintings?' he asked, and again his chest heaved. 'They'll draw a man who has an oak tree growing out of his arse and grabs acorns from it with his teeth. Dear God, how stupid!'

Wilhelm laughed and said:

'No, Aleksey Petrovich, I do not agree with you on this point either. Persian poetry in Rückert's translations is beautiful.'

'That's in Rückert's translations! The unvarnished East with its dirt and stench is one thing, but what we make of it and how we understand it is quite another. Europeans adapt Asia to their own ways—both in poetry and in politics.'

Pokhvisnev came in with some business matters.

Wilhelm and Aleksandr bowed and took their leave.

'Well, for today, unfortunately, I'm not going to keep you. Business,' Yermolov said gravely and politely, 'but you're very welcome any time. I hope you're not going to be overburdened with service—no doubt we shall soon be hearing poems about the Caucasian countryside.'

He glanced out of the window. There was squealing in the courtyard: two of the *amanats* were fighting.

Wilhelm plucked up his courage and asked quietly:

'Aleksey Petrovich, where are the parents of these children?'

Yermolov quickly turned around and looked at Küchelbecker:

'Are you talking about the hostages? My friend, this business is not so much military as economic. Adult *amanats* used to be terribly expensive; some cost three silver rubles a day. I started to take kids. They play here and their parents come to visit them. I feed them gingerbread, and the parents seem to be delighted and clear roads in the forest.'

He grinned wickedly at Wilhelm, who gave an embarrassed smile in return. When the door closed behind the friends, Yermolov ceased to smile and sat down at the desk. Pokhvisnev was standing in front of him, looking expectantly into his eyes.

'What an odd man,' Yermolov said thoughtfully, 'Wilhelm Karlovich Küchelbecker, a Slavophile. Then he should be called a *khlebopekar*, not Küchelbecker.'[28] He grinned: '"Vasily Karpovich Khlebopekar." That would make more sense; as it is, there's a contradiction.'

Pokhvisnev was laughing dutifully by the desk and kept repeating in a thin delighted voice: 'Bread-baker!' And then he said cautiously: 'A package has arrived for you from the prince—Prince Volkonsky. Top secret.'

Yermolov took the package and answered absent-mindedly, with a frown:

'You may go, my friend.'

The chief of the General Staff had written him long reports on the transit trade and the establishment of oil fields in Baku, as well as on the progress of measures for pacifying the Abkhazian region, most respectfully informing His Excellency about the government's thoughts for the future.

'Oh yes, of course, you people know better.' Yermolov grumbled brusquely and barely read it to the end.

At the end of his letter, the chief of staff was inquiring about the young man, Wilhelm Karlovich Küchelbecker, whether His Excellency would deem it possible to employ this civilian official in the assignments most associated with risk, for the passionate nature of this young man was well-known to everyone.

Yermolov got up from the desk. He knew what this meant and remembered his conversation with Nesselrode. He paced the room, pondering, then went back to the desk. There he stood for a minute deep in thought. His eyebrows were knitted, his lower jaw thrust forward.

'Not a chance,' he said suddenly and pulled a face at someone. Then his face cleared. 'You think I'll send him into the line of fire? I've never been an executioner.'

And he sat down to write a reply in large but elegant handwriting.

Top secret.
Your Excellency,
Dear Prince,

In response to the received confidential directive No. 567 I hasten to inform you that I have devised a special plan for pacifying the Abkhazia region, the details of which I do not believe it possible to go into at present for lack of space and considerations of top secrecy . . .

. . . Development of oilfields as an enterprise of the first importance to the state . . .

. . . As far as Mr. Küchelbecker is concerned, owing to the ill health that he suffered in Vladikavkaz he has arrived only today. I believe that due to his current lack of experience this official cannot be engaged in those matters of importance, which require particular aplomb.

Yermolov looked at the letter and admired it:

'Work that one out, dear prince!'

And he signed it:

Your Excellency's faithful servant,

Yermolov

He put Volkonsky's paper in the "Top Secret" folder, then sighed, buttoned up his uniform, and left the room.

When Pokhvisnev returned half an hour later, the room was empty. He sneaked up to the desk, searched for the folder, read Volkonsky's letter and began to ponder.

III

Griboyedov and Wilhelm followed Yermolov's advice and did not particularly burden themselves with work. In the mornings they would go for a ride, in the evenings they would visit the Nobles' Club or sit on the balcony, looking at the Caucasian foothills and listening to the conversations of the Tiflis women down below, who spoke rapidly and with a burr, exchanging news of the Tiflis day. Griboyedov's servant, Aleksandr, shuffled around quietly in his shoes and hummed to himself as he pottered about. At nights Griboyedov would go up to the pianoforte and start tinkling something softly, and then would sit down properly and play Field for hours. It was a specially adapted piano, because of his right hand, which had been shot in the duel. Yakubovich had shot at it on purpose so that Griboyedov would no longer be able to play.

Once Griboyedov said to Wilhelm, rather self-consciously:

'It's too early to go to the Club; if you like, I can read you some of my new comedy.'

From the way Griboyedov had been musing for hours at the window, gnawing his quill impatiently over some mysterious papers, and from his insomnia, Wilhelm knew that Aleksandr had been writing. But this was first time he had mentioned it to Wilhelm.

'My comedy *Woe to Wit*[29] is a comedy of character. My protagonist is like us, he has a little bit of me in him, rather more of you. Imagine, he comes back, like you now, from foreign lands to discover that he has been cheated on and with whom? Well, imagine someone like Nikolay Nikolayevich Pokhvisnev, for example. Meticulous, obliging, and at the same time a common-or-garden rotter. Hence the catastrophe, a comic one, of course.'

He walked around the room as if dissatisfied with what he was saying.

'But that's not the point. The main thing is the characters. Portraits. It's time to shake up our style of comedy, where one little plot twist is hooked up to another, and there isn't a single real person—just soubrettes from French comedy.'

He stopped in front of Wilhelm:

'You see, the thing is that in a comedy I want not action but movement. I'm fed up with the expositions, the denouements, with all the machinery showing. Portraits, just portraits, that's the essence of comedy or tragedy. I'll set the protagonist against his opponents, I'll create a whole gallery of portraits and make them live in the theater.'

Wilhelm listened intently, then said:

'What a simple idea! What an easy way to revolutionize the theater! But how will you do it? I've been thinking long and hard about both our comedy and our lyric poetry. I'm tired too—tired of writing endlessly weepy elegies. I know everybody writes them in the same style. And how could we not see French soubrettes on stage, when the language of our plays is so coy that it's suitable only for a soubrette? I too would be glad to give up writing elegies. You can't sigh for lost youth for the rest of your life, but as soon as you start writing, what comes out is an elegy. The language itself prompts us to elegy.'

'And what about Krylov?' said Griboyedov suddenly.

Wilhelm was nonplussed.

Griboyedov repeated, his eyes burning:

'What about Krylov, Derzhavin? Do they speak a coy language? My friend, as long as we waste our time on this Karamzinian nonsense, nothing will come of it. Our language should be either rough and simple—from the street, from the hallway—or elevated. I can't bear half-measures in anything. I know that Aleksey Petrovich says that my poems set his teeth on edge. I'd rather his teeth suffer than our literature. Excessive precision in verse structure is an affectation too. One must write as one lives: free and easy.'

Wilhelm listened to him ecstatically: 'I'd already had the same idea, old boy,' he said quietly. 'Oh, yes, how I understand you! Our authors all write like foreigners, too correctly, too beautifully. In ancient Athens a merchant once recognized a foreigner only because he spoke too correctly.' He jumped to his feet and shouted: 'I've got it! Now I know how I should write my tragedy!'

Griboyedov asked intently: 'Are you writing a tragedy?'

'Yes, but not for publication. In my tragedy they kill a tyrant. One in the eye for the censor.'

'In my comedy I seem to be killing a tyrant too,' Griboyedov said slowly, 'my dear country, most precious Moscow, where my dearest uncle organizes balls and wishes for nothing more.'

He began to read.

Wilhelm sat glued to the spot. His cheeks were burning. A young man at a ball whom no one listened to, whose venom was wasted in the salons,—Küchlya saw in him now Aleksandr, now himself. Griboyedov read calmly and confidently, accompanying the verses with light gestures.

When reading Chatsky's lines, Griboyedov's voice grew deeper, tenser, he put all of himself into Chatsky and read the rest in a humdrum sort of way. Then he asked:

'What do you think?'

Moved and overwhelmed, Wilhelm rushed to embrace him.

Griboyedov was pleased. He went to the pianoforte and began to play softly. Then he took off his glasses and wiped his eyes.

When he turned round, his face was shining. He said:

'You see, Wilhelm, my original design was so much grander, and everything had a higher meaning: but what can you do if you love the theater with its gossip and bustle? I'm dying to see my *Woe* on stage—so I'm already spoiling the play here and there, adjusting it to the stage. And now, how about a ride?'

IV

When Wilhelm entered the Club, mocking glances followed him. This lanky German, hunched, with bulging, wandering eyes, sharp movements, and rapid, incoherent speech, was a mystery to Nikolay Nikolayevich Pokhvisnev.

Laughing at Wilhelm in his absence, Pokhvisnev behaved with particular wariness and courtesy when they met, and for some reason avoided looking him directly in the eye. The presence of the highly strung Griboyedov held everyone back.

At one point a tall stout major with big black mustaches showed up at the Club. His eyes, huge and motionless, and his entire face, yellowish, swarthy, like a mask, were extraordinary. He greeted Griboyedov politely and rather casually, and went quickly into the inner rooms, where they were playing cards.

'Who's that?' Wilhelm asked Aleksandr.

Griboyedov answered reluctantly: 'Yakubovich.'

So here he was, Yakubovich, the hero of Pushkin's imagination and of Wilhelm's, this insane duellist, this somber lionheart!

'A "hero of fate," you think?' Aleksandr smiled wryly. Do you want me to tell you his last heroic feat? Not far from here, at Baksan, the army was attacking the rear-guard of the mountain fighters and they had to go through a mountain cleft. They are extremely narrow here, so they walked in single file. Yakubovich went down and down and got stuck in the cleft. They had to pull him out by the legs. His uniform was in tatters and almost all the buttons were gone. Picture that.'

He laughed gleefully.

'Now that cleft is called "Yakubovich's hole."'

Wilhelm could not get used to Aleksandr's way of talking. Since childhood Wilhelm had had heroes of his imagination; he would "fall in love" with Derzhavin, then with Zhukovsky, and then Yermolov. And every time when Wilhelm, as it was fashionable to say, became "disenchanted" with the hero of his imagination, it was painful and hard for him. But as soon as Aleksandr noticed that Wilhelm was "in love," he immediately poured ridicule on him like cold water. Occasionally Wilhelm heard Aleksandr groaning in his sleep, he saw his dry, tearless eyes in the evenings—and forgave him everything, but he was saddened by each instance of his mockery. Griboyedov well knew the effect his icy speeches had on Wilhelm, but he did not and could not speak of people otherwise. He even derived a secret pleasure from gently tormenting his vulnerable friend. His feelings, as always, remained constant, and as always, his visible deeds contradicted them.

Yermolov arrived at the Nobles' Club accompanied by Pokhvisnev and two military men. In Yermolov's presence everyone braced themselves, the soldiers walked particularly nimbly, the civilians were especially witty. This time Yermolov was in a bad mood. Smiling politely, he shook hands left, right, and center, but this time his smile appeared to Wilhelm almost unpleasant and even forced. Yermolov quickly went to his room, a small room with a Turkish ottoman, wide armchairs, and a round table; here he played cards with young people.

He sat down and scowled. Pokhvisnev, pausing for a second in the next room, had already managed to whisper something about a not very gracious epistle from the tsar, which Aleksey Petrovich had just received. Then he immediately slipped in after Yermolov.

'Call Voyeikov and Griboyedov, my friend,' Yermolov said grumpily, 'and ask Khlebopekar to come in.'

And as they came in, he said with the same unpleasant smile he was wearing that day:

'Would you like to share my boredom, good sirs?'

He was a little edgy, and the joke fell flat. 'You win,' he addressed Griboyedov. 'I've received an order concerning Persia—to defend it more than Russia. Fine with me, I don't mind at all. Diebitsch and Paskevich are the advisers. Let's wait and see where Russia gets with the two Vankas.'[30]

The pun was a success, everyone laughed, and Yermolov cheered up. Both Paskevich and Diebitsch were called Ivan.

Griboyedov frowned. Paskevich was a relative of his and he enjoyed his patronage, albeit reluctantly.

'Do you really consider them equals, Aleksey Petrovich?' he asked fretfully.

'Ah, my friend,' Yermolov grew agitated, 'ever since my youth I've had no sense of smell: for me a rose and a primrose are all the same. No, really, what do they want from me?'—with Yermolov "they" stood for the government, the tsar, and Petersburg in general. 'I make no requests or demands, I have gone off into the wilderness, left everything for them to decide, and I ask for no reward as long as they leave me in peace.'

'When you write your memoirs, Nikolay Pavlovich,' he turned to Voyeikov, 'say this: he wanted nothing else but to be left in peace.'

Pokhvisnev dealt. Yermolov held his cards, screwing up his right eye: when he won a trick, he screwed it up even more. He loved to win. Suddenly, he turned with a sly expression to Griboyedov:

'It's a pity, God's my witness, such a pity, Aleksandr Sergeyevich, that they give me such orders. Really though, wouldn't it be nice to fight with Persia and Turkey and grab Khiva and India?'

He was teasing Griboyedov.

'Aleksey Petrovich,' responded Griboyedov, 'you should really be Pyotr Alekseyevich,[31] you've got his Greek strategy off to a "t."'

'Not a bad thought, old chap,' Yermolov answered almost indifferently. 'We need trade, we desperately need eastern trade, without it we're in trouble. Just look how Tiflis is swarming with Englishmen. They haven't come here just for me: Persia, Turkey, Khiva, and then India—we should go for it, dear chap—don't you think? We should go the whole hog.'

'Don't make us pay the price, Your Excellency, if one day you declare war on Persia,' said Griboyedov with an icy smile.

Yermolov shrugged:

'Don't worry, old chap, I can't imagine it will come to anything.'

'And what about "them"?' asked Griboyedov teasingly.

Yermolov stamped his foot:

'"They" are dreadful bores. In Tilsit, I was sitting opposite "him" and "he" said: "Aleksey Petrovich, you look as if you should be wearing imperial purple." I said that I should be—then I noticed that he had turned pale, so I ended by saying: ". . . under any other monarch."'

Yermolov loved making jokes like this in the presence of young people. The tsar's fear and hatred of him was their usual subject.

Voyeikov gazed at him intently:

'The eastern state is a tremendous idea; all of Asia will be ours then. But can you imagine, Aleksey Petrovich, "the collegiate assessor for foreign affairs" wearing the purple of an eastern tsar?'

"Collegiate assessor" was what Pushkin called the tsar. That *bon mot* had circulated all over Russia.

Yermolov narrowed his eyes: 'Why? You can make a purple uniform.' He suddenly changed the subject, turning to Küchelbecker: 'And you, Wilhelm Karlovich, why do you look so miserable?'

Wilhelm spoke quietly:

'Mankind is tired of wars, Aleksey Petrovich.'

'Well I never,' Yermolov spread his hands, 'wasn't it you who wanted me to march on Greece?'

'Greece is a different matter. The war for the liberation of Hellas is different from a war for trading benefits.'

Yermolov frowned: 'And I'm telling you,' he answered harshly, 'that the only worthwhile reason for fighting on Greece's side is to lay hands on Turkey. What are the Greeks? Sponge merchants. Hellas is in the past, Wilhelm Karlovich, Hellas is just a good rhyme. Hellas—Pallas, Hellas—alas.'

Wilhelm jumped to his feet:

'You may jest, Aleksey Petrovich. But the Greeks, fighting for their liberation, are not in the mood for jokes right now.'

Yermolov smiled:

'You're too hot-tempered, Wilhelm Karlovich. A man does what he can. I, for example, can laugh, so I am laughing, otherwise I would probably be crying my eyes out.'

They all fell silent and got down to a game of boston.

Wilhelm and Griboyedov walked home silently. Aleksandr said:

'I don't care for these three-star people. He's got it into his head to go to war with Persia—and we are all expected to pay for it.'

Wilhelm walked along wearily, thinking his own thoughts.

"Greece" had not worked out.

Voyeikov caught up with them: he was agitated: 'I'll walk you a little way home,' he spoke softly, as if embarrassed. 'You, Wilhelm Karlovich, have a plan for Greece. I too have a plan. Aleksey Petrovich has mentioned Khiva, Bukhara, India. Don't you think that's a splendid idea?'

'I don't,' responded Griboyedov sharply. 'State borders must be respected. One can't fight forever.'

Voyeikov spoke quietly, his consumptive face was pale:

'The East, the great Eastern state is Alexander the Great's idea. Not our Alexander of course, not Alexander I.' And he added anxiously: 'I believe I can trust you: what we need is an eastern state under Aleksey Petrovich's rule.'

Griboyedov stopped, astounded.

'The Yermolov dynasty?'

Voyeikov held out his gaze:

'Yes, the Yermolov dynasty.'

They walked a few steps in silence. Then Griboyedov said in a calm voice:

'And what about heirs then? We need to get Aleksey Petrovich married off as soon as we can!'

V

Wilhelm left off going to Yermolov's. His smile had begun to seem unpleasant to him, he was afraid to hear the pleasantly hollow "old chap."

There were very few business matters, and the friends went for walks and carriage-rides. Wilhelm struck up a friendship with Liszt. When the gray captain's intelligent eyes looked at him, Wilhelm had vague memories of his own father, also a tall German in a gray frock coat, stern and sad. The captain lived out of town, and Wilhelm would often ride over on the fiery stallion that the obliging Pokhvisnev had dutifully procured for him. Recently Pokhvisnev had never left Wilhelm's side, he sought his company, and tried to be of service to him. Griboyedov began to feel suspicious. He warned Wilhelm:

'Dear chap, don't go hobnobbing with this little man. He'll sell you out as soon as he gets a chance.'

But Wilhelm, though he was on his guard against mockery, was gullible with people. As he saw it, Pokhvisnev might be generally inclined to curry favor with people. Griboyedov thought about it and gave up warning him. He accompanied him on his visits to Liszt, who lived in a good, secluded area. On the Kura River, two or three miles downstream, there was a little island with a garden, huge and tangled, with labyrinthine paths through the vines. The garden belonged to an old drunkard, Jaffar. Jaffar would greet them with great dignity. In the mornings he was sober and pompous, like a crown prince. He pottered about in the garden, where his sons were employed, but more for the sake of appearance. He respected Griboyedov because Griboyedov spoke Arabic, he esteemed Liszt because he was a military man, and he paid scarcely any attention to Wilhelm. When the friends showed up, Jaffar invited them with a broad gesture to sit under a chestnut tree.

It was cool under the huge century-old chestnut, and nearby there was a monotonous murmur of running water.

Here it was, the true land of oblivion.

Here Liszt would forget about his tedious soldier's life, about the old mother who lived on Vasilyevsky Island in Petersburg; puffing on his eternal pipe, he would recount to his friends his various campaigns. He remembered Kaikhosro Gurieli fighting off ten people, until an officer cut off his right hand, and the old man killed himself with the left. Wilhelm listened to his sad stories with a shudder. The captain once told them how Yermolov had brought some German sectarians to their senses. They were originally from Württemberg and believed that the second coming was approaching, that God would come from Persia or Turkey via Georgia. They were exiled to Russia and settled in the Caucasus. Yermolov suggested that they choose a few men they trusted, send them to Persia and Turkey, and make sure that the second coming had begun. A month later, the deputies returned, exhausted, ragged, and hungry. After that, the German colony stopped believing in the second coming.

The captain could not spend long with his friends, he had a busy life in the army. Once, while sitting under the old chestnut, Griboyedov said to Wilhelm:

'I can't live like this any more, I am not much use in ordinary times, dear chap. You know, Yermolov says I'm like Derzhavin—in everything, in verse and in life. A back-handed compliment. He considers Derzhavin to have been the most restless and incapable person in all Russia. People are shallow, their actions are absurd, their souls are cold.'

This morning Griboyedov was anxious, irritable, with something on his mind.

'I feel the same, too,' replied Wilhelm, 'I can't sit still here. I have one impulse that has never misled me: a yearning for fellowship. What do you think, Aleksandr,' he whispered, looking anxiously at Griboyedov, 'might it be possible to flee to Greece from here? My dear fellow, remember Pushkin's line: "And burning with a thirst for death"? How well Pushkin understands all this.'

Griboyedov repeated in a flat voice:

'A thirst for death. And time flies, a flame burns in my soul, thoughts are born in my mind, and yet I can't get down to business, knowledge is always progressing, and I have no time even to learn, let alone to work. What kind of curse is over us, Wilhelm? It's as if the prophecy was made for me: thou shalt move from every place under the skies.'

'Let's go home,' said Wilhelm, 'let's go north, we'll all die here from inaction. You can't spend your life on the highways.'

Griboyedov paid no attention:

'Do you want me to tell you what is killing me? Dear fellow, I'm dying of boredom. That fat-bellied Shakhovskoy told me once: "Everything you write is excellent, old boy, but it's boredom that holds your pen." How tedious! What will we have achieved with our literary works by the end of the year, by the end of the century? What will we have done and what might we have done?'

Wilhelm jumped to his feet and started walking back and forth, then stopped abruptly in front of Griboyedov. There were tears in his eyes.

'I'm ready for a life of crime or vice, not for a life without meaning. But where can we run to?'

Griboyedov rose from the grass too.

'There's nowhere to run. The land of oblivion—we're lucky to have it. We'll live somehow. What's the point of going back to Moscow—to dance at the *soirées*? or work on journals—back to the gossip and all that literary nonsense?' He grinned. 'My dear uncle in Moscow is dreaming of my becoming a state councillor.'

VI

One day, Wilhelm and Aleksandr heard an unusual noise in the street. They looked out of the window. People were racing toward the fortress. Their host's boy, half-naked, with his heels kicking desperately in all directions, was running flat out. Griboyedov asked:

'What's happening?'

'Jambot,' shouted out an Armenian as he ran past.

'Jambot has arrived,' grinned another, baring his teeth.

Griboyedov began to button up his uniform silently and solemnly, then said to Wilhelm:

'Let's hurry, he means business.'

Kuchuk Dzhankhotov was the richest landowner in the region: his name resounded throughout Chechnya and Abkhazia. Old Kuchuk was a great diplomat, he did not want to risk his livestock and pastures. That was why he was friendly with Yermolov. When they met a detachment of Chechens, his *esirs*[32] would bow their heads and endure their derision. Kuchuk remembered perfectly well how Yermolov had thought nothing of driving away fifteen thousand head of cattle from the neighboring settlement, which had let men from beyond the Kuban River pass through their village. For the same reason he tried his best to build good relations between his son Dzhambulat and Yermolov. Dzhambulat, or, as all the Circassians called him, Jambot, was his only heir. But Jambot was not a chip off the old block. And even though he had taken part in Yermolov's Persian embassy, he behaved so secretively with the Persians, who had got involved in some kind of negotiations with him, that Yermolov had to recall him from Persia. And when the tribes from beyond the Kuban invaded again, Jambot turned out to be one of their leaders. That was big trouble. He was famous throughout Chechnya, throughout Abkhazia. While riding a horse at full speed he could shoot an eagle in the eye or hack off a young bull's head with a stroke of a saber. Jambot's notoriety was growing fast. All the Kabardian girls knew songs about him, and on his latest journey Yermolov had had the pleasure of hearing a slender girl in a *saklya*[33] sing a song, every second word of which was "Jambot." Ever since the hostile tribes from beyond the Kuban had been defeated, Jambot had been living at his father's.

A week ago, Yermolov had sent Kuchuk an encouraging letter, in which he asked Kuchuk himself and his son Jambot to visit him for talks on an extremely important matter and promised him peace. Everyone was eager to take a look at the young Dzhankhotov, which was why they were running.

The friends arrived just in time, at the moment when Kuchuk and his son were entering the fortress on horseback. A crowd swarmed at the fortress gates, not being allowed entry. Kuchuk and Jambot rode slowly. The old man had on a huge white turban—he had made pilgrimages to Mecca and Medina; other men, landowners of the lower nobility, rode at a distance, and the rank and file *uzdeni*[34] rode ahead. Jambot was by his father's side. He was dressed magnificently with a colored *tishli* over his chain-mail, a dagger and a sword on his side, a richly decorated saddle, and a quiverful of arrows on his back.

Wilhelm looked at him eagerly. Jambot's face was long, narrow, almost girlish, with lively brown eyes. He rode lightly and nonchalantly.

They dismounted before the gates and handed the horses over to the *uzdeni*. Wilhelm and Griboyedov squeezed into the courtyard. Yermolov was waiting by the porch with his retinue. He was scowling. He bowed his elephantine neck slightly and leaned with one arm on his sword. An interpreter, a timid man in a fur hat, stood before him. A company of serf soldiers were lined up to the right. Having spotted Kuchuk and Jambot, Yermolov took a step forward and stopped.

Kuchuk bowed deeply to him, pressing his hand in turn to his forehead, his lips, and his chest. Yermolov lowered his head. Greetings began. The interpreter translated diligently. Then Kuchuk stepped aside. Jambot took his place. His gait, too, was lithe as a girl's, he bowed slightly to Yermolov and uttered the usual greeting.

Yermolov stood immobile. He spoke to the interpreter:

'Tell him that I am pleased to see the son of my friend, Kuchuk Dzhankhotov, but I should have been even more pleased if I had seen him here two months ago when he was with the hostile tribes beyond the Kuban.'

The interpreter translated. Jambot said something casual and rapid, like all his actions. The interpreter said:

'He says that he hopes for the general's friendship.'

Yermolov frowned:

'I'm very happy with his repentance,' he said in a hollow voice, 'but there must be a reckoning for the past. Let him hand over his dagger and sword.'

The interpreter trembled all over and said something that was barely audible.

Jambot took half a step forward. His neck stretched out, his body leaned forward. His face began to color slowly and deeply.

Griboyedov, who was talking to Kuchuk, turned around adroitly and shielded him with his back from both Yermolov and Jambot. The old man was speaking slowly and ponderously, almost calmly, but his eyes, looking at Griboyedov, were half closed and his face had turned pale.

Wilhelm squeezed through the crowd and took up a place beside the retinue. Yakubovich stood nearby, as still as a statue, his black eyes gleaming.

Jambot made one sharp, short movement: he clasped the handle of his dagger. Voyeikov was standing next to Wilhelm. He pulled out a pistol and cocked it. At the same moment, two or three men in the retinue drew their sabers. Yermolov looked up at them and stopped them with a movement of his hand. He stood there heavily, his right hand leaning motionlessly on the long saber.

Jambot was leaning toward him like a snake poised to strike. His face was pale yellow, white teeth bared. His narrow brown eyes were fixed on the little cold gray ones of Yermolov.

Then suddenly, in one movement, he drew the dagger back and shouted out a single word. His voice was piercing but sounded choked.

And, stretching his thin hand toward the Caucasian foothills, he began to shout something in Yermolov's face.

Yermolov ordered the pale interpreter:

'Translate.'

The interpreter hesitated.

Yermolov bellowed: 'Translate!' and his nostrils flared. 'Everything, every word.'

'He is calling Your Excellency a jackal and a coward and speaks of Your Excellency's baseness,' mumbled the interpreter.

Jambot was shouting.

Without realizing what he was doing Kuchuk grabbed Griboyedov's hand and listened; his head was trembling.

'Look at the mountains,' shouted Jambot, 'remember that this is the place where our ancestors crushed Nader Shah to dust. And Nader Shah was not like you, jackal, not like you, you dog!'

The interpreter translated, stammering.

'He was not Russian trash like you, cowards and fire raisers!' shouted Jambot. 'With you the head man is the real coward, the basest one is the *pasha*. And the biggest coward and the basest man is your feeble master. We will scrape you off the mountains like dried mud.'

The interpreter hesitated.

'Translate.'

He interpreted as best as he dared, muttering, skipping words.

Yermolov frowned silently. Suddenly he nodded to the commanding officer, who detached himself from the company and stood to attention:

'Shoot him,' said Yermolov, 'for publicly insulting the supreme authority!'

Five soldiers with bayonets advanced toward Jambot.

A soft sigh swept over the retinue. Someone at the gate gave a piercing scream. Wilhelm shrieked. Yakubovich's immobile expression and fixed gaze flashed before him for a moment. Wilhelm threw himself between Jambot and the soldiers. He raised his hand and shouted something in a voice that did not sound like his own.

Then Yermolov, suddenly bristling, stepped closer to him, grabbed his arm, and hissed in his face:

'You're out of your mind. Get out of here.'

He wrapped his huge hand around Wilhelm's arm and led him quickly to the entrance. Voyeikov and Pokhvisnev followed. Yermolov closed the door behind him, pushed Wilhelm on to the sofa, quickly and deftly poured him some water, and raised it to his mouth. Wilhelm's teeth were chattering, his wildly bulging eyes were staring around. Yermolov spoke distinctly, looking point blank at Pokhvisnev and Voyeikov:

'Mr. Küchelbecker is prone to nervous fits.'

A salvo rang out in the courtyard.

Wilhelm pushed Yermolov aside and dashed out of the room. Griboyedov, white as a sheet and with a trembling jaw, was hugging Kuchuk. The old man was almost peaceful. His head hung down on his chest, he was whispering something softly, possibly praying.

The soldiers were busy with something in the corner of the courtyard. There wasn't a single person left in front of the fortress.

At night, a strange, yelping sound woke Griboyedov. Wilhelm was weeping, barking, and sobbing, clutching at the iron bed.

VII

Yermolov made no report concerning Wilhelm's behavior. He only bowed to him more briefly and gave a more forced smile. Pokhvisnev on the contrary was especially attentive. He couldn't do enough for him. He showed Wilhelm excellent places for walks—deserted, silent, inaccessible. Ah, when life is going haywire one just wants to let one's horse gallop at full speed and take flight, surrendering one's spirit to the storm—what joy!

At one point Liszt said to Wilhelm:

'You'd better not take that road, Wilhelm Karlovich.'

'Why is that?'

'Some Chechen might shoot at you.'

'I have my pistols.'

Liszt shook his head.

Going for a ride one day Wilhelm met Yakubovich. To Griboyedov's great displeasure Wilhelm had often met with Yakubovich recently. Yakubovich had come on a mission from Karagach and for whatever reason stayed in Tiflis. He often went out for rides too, and, huge and gloomy, on his black Karabakh stallion, he reminded Wilhelm of a monument he had seen in Paris. Yakubovich looked closely at Wilhelm and said abruptly:

'I'll go with you, where are you heading?'

'I've no idea.'

'How's your riding?'

They let the horses trot. Beneath their feet the mountain road came to an end, a valley lay below.

'I watched you at the fortress,' Yakubovich said slowly. 'They're talking about you. I love people who get talked about. But you are wrong. Wars and executions are not the worst things.'

Wilhelm looked up at him.

'What do you mean, Aleksandr Ivanovich?'

'In our society war is a holiday—one doesn't have to think about anything.'

He twisted his black mustaches and knitted his thick eyebrows.

'I can't live in Russia. I come alive only in life-and-death combat. Only the whistle of lead makes me forget about oppression. That's why I'm glad to have been exiled to the Caucasus. Does it matter to me where exactly the bullet gets me?'

Wilhelm said timidly:

'You are embittered, Aleksandr Ivanovich.'

Yakubovich turned abruptly in the saddle.

'Embittered, am I?' His eyes flashed. 'No, not embittered; I am thirsting for revenge. I always carry my order of demotion on me.'

He took a tattered sheet of paper from his side pocket and waved it in the air.

'If the tsar had known what he was letting himself in for with this paper, he would not have transferred me from the Guards as a major out here.'

He changed the subject, but still wore the same expression:

'Wilhelm Karlovich, I have a confession to make.'

Wilhelm was all ears.

'I'm writing a note that has a certain purpose. The only person to whom I could have shown it and who could have understood it is my enemy. I believe you know who I'm talking about.'

Wilhelm nodded. (Yakubovich meant Griboyedov).

'Only Voyeikov knows about it.' Yakubovich continued mysteriously. 'I am writing about the oppression of the peasantry, the depravity of officials, the ignorance of officers, and the deliberate demoralisation of soldiers prescribed at the highest level.'

Yakubovich's black eyes grew bloodshot, his wide nostrils flared. He suddenly let his horse gallop and they rode in silence for a while.

Wilhelm ventured to speak:

'Aleksandr Ivanovich, I have been thinking about this for a long time myself. I notice every tear on the face of the common folk but I can't see any way out.'

They were riding along a steep precipice. Yakubovich stopped his horse:

'I have to go back, Wilhelm Karlovich.' he said slowly. 'You want to know the way out?' His nostrils flared again. 'The treatment ought to start from the head. The other day Jambot spoke the truth about the weak-willed master. The immediate way out, as I see it, is the total eradication of the imperial family. Good afternoon.'

He turned his horse and trotted off.

Wilhelm watched him for a long time. Then, as if someone had whipped him, he spurred his horse and galloped forward, not looking, not thinking, drinking in the air with open mouth.

He rode for a long time. Already it was getting dark. The horse suddenly stumbled and then bolted off to the side. Wilhelm looked around. He saw unfamiliar terrain in front of him. There were dunes along the cliff. The barrel of a rifle flashed behind the shrubbery and a bullet whistled over his head.

Then he heard a hoarse voice, a man in a tall cap leapt into the road and aimed at him. Wilhelm pulled the gun from his belt.

VIII

Griboyedov was sitting on the balcony, the door to the room was open. Twilight was falling. The foothills faded before his eyes—the balcony faced north. He had no glasses on, his gaze was abstracted. Then he turned and looked back into the depths of the dark room. In the back of the room a servant was busying himself with the candles. Slowly and sluggishly he stuck the candles into the candlesticks, struck the flint, and lit them, shuffling his shoes. He showed no interest whatsoever in Griboyedov. He sang quietly:

If only you knew, dear brothers,
What bondage is, what it is like.

Griboyedov looked straight at him. Aleksandr Gribov was the son of his wet-nurse. For fifteen years this man had been living with him, and for fifteen years they had hardly noticed each other. But they knew each other inside out. Aleksandr Griboyedov knew, for example, that if Aleksandr Gribov sang about bondage, it meant that he would now dress up smartly and go to a party somewhere in Sololaki. But he would surely have been surprised to be told that Aleksandr Gribov knew what Aleksandr Griboyedov was about to do. On this particular day, Griboyedov had not gone riding, had not played the pianoforte, had not said a word. This meant that he would now ask for an ink-stand and some paper and tell him to sharpen up the quills. Gribov smartened himself up, went to the pianoforte, lifted the lid, and sat down on the stool. He began to play softly. Aleksandr Griboyedov stared at Aleksandr Gribov. He was slightly surprised.

'Do you know how to play the piano?' he asked crossly.

'I do,' replied Gribov impassively.

Griboyedov went over to the piano. Gribov stood up.

'And what can you play?'

'Various pieces.' Gribov answered reluctantly. '"Madame," for example.'

'Go on then, play it.'

Gribov sat down on the stool, looking bored, and began to play by ear.

Madame, madame,
Arch your leg.

Griboyedov listened attentively, then suddenly grimaced:

'You don't have a clue, you idiot. You can't play at all, all you do is ruin my pianoforte. Go and play knucklebones. Get up now. I'll show you how to play.'

He sat down and played.

Gribov seemed unimpressed and said cagily:

'That's what *you* think.'

Griboyedov looked at him in surprise:

'Very well, you idiot, then what is *your* opinion?'

Gribov made no answer.

His master paced the room. Ennui drove him from corner to corner, made him walk round the desk—ennui, the same old acquaintance who drove him from Petersburg to Georgia, from Georgia to Persia, forced him to play people off against one another, to fight duels, and to be insolent with women.

He asked Gribov:

'And where's Wilhelm Karlovich?'

'He's gone out for a ride.'

'So late? Do you know where to?'

'He didn't say.'

Griboyedov grew alarmed.

'He said don't worry, he'd be back later on today.'

Griboyedov sat down at the desk and wrote a note to Voyeikov:

> I'm dying of hypochondria, I can see myself spending the entire night in the grip of a fevered mind, so do me a favor, my dear Nikolay Pavlovich, send me all the numbers of last year's *Bulletin*, or just the latest issue, so I have something enjoyable to read.
>
> Ever yours,
>
> Griboyedov
>
> If this note does not find you in, then when you come back please send the *Bulletin* to me with your servant.

He handed it to Gribov:

'Take it to Voyeikov.'

Another half an hour passed and it became almost completely dark. Across the road, Pokhvisnev walked suavely along the street. Griboyedov recognized him by his gait. Now he was really alarmed.

'Where on earth is Wilhelm?'

He ran out, saddled his horse, and rode off.

IX

When the man took aim, Wilhelm quickly shot at him and dug the spurs into his horse. At a gallop, leaning in the saddle, he turned around. The man was pursuing him. He shot again without aiming.

'Damn, missed him.'

And immediately, a bullet whizzed right past his ear. The horse plunged to one side. Wilhelm was racing along the precipice on the straight line of the road, on the edge, over the void, clutching the reins firmly. The man ran behind him with surprising ease and speed. Another bullet. The horse suddenly whinnied, trembled and wheezed, then staggered, and collapsed. Wilhelm did not have time to pull his foot out of the stirrup and it got tangled. He fell, badly hurt.

He lay there for a minute like that, writhing in pain, trying to free his foot from under the horse.

In a couple of minutes the man in the tall cap would be on him. Wilhelm jerked his leg with all his strength and dragged his foot from under the horse. He attempted to get up, grunted, then crawled like a lizard, suddenly and quickly, dragging his aching leg and groaning rhythmically, as if on purpose.

Did it make sense to crawl any further?

The man would certainly not be going away.

But so far he hadn't heard any footsteps. He looked ahead. About five paces away was a huge oak tree. It grew on the very edge of the road, its lower branches on a level with the cliff.

A second later Wilhelm had made up his mind. He crawled quickly to the tree. It was exactly like the ones in the Tsarskoe Selo gardens. Wilhelm had always been good at tree-climbing. Writhing in pain, he clung on to the lowest branch.

He was almost fainting but squeezed the branch tightly, as he had held the reins. An effort took him to the second branch, another effort to the third one.

Further up there was a hollow, a huge one, the size of a man.

Wilhelm tried not to look down—beneath him was the precipice. He moved his foot, screamed in pain, and hurled himself into the hollow.

He immediately smelled coolness and rot.

For a second everything went dark as in a cold black river, a wave was spinning him round, a whirlpool sucked at his leg.

He opened his eyes. A hollow—dark, dry, cool; a mosquito singing overhead; a faint ringing up above—and then a branch flew past him.

Wilhelm looked out.

The Chechen was standing down below firing at the oak tree. He had spotted him. He was trying to pick him off the oak calmly and carefully, like a bird.

Wilhelm fumbled at his belt, there was still one pistol there.

He took aim.

His hand was shaking.

A shot—a miss, another shot—again a miss. He had to aim more carefully. He felt a sudden anguish.

He would have to sit in this hollow tree and wait for death!

He took aim and fired again. The Chechen screamed, clutched his leg, and quickly took aim. Wilhelm ducked. The bullet whistled into the hollow just above his head. He had only one bullet left.

X

Griboyedov had been riding for a long time. No one to be seen. He thought about it, turned the horse, and took the most dangerous road, along the cliff. By now it was pitch dark.

He was almost weeping:

"He's run away, run away, the crazy man! He wants to get to Greece—he'll be taken prisoner instead and he'll end up in a dungeon. Oh, Wilhelm, Don Quixote, dear chap . . ."

The horse snorted and bolted. The corpse of a horse was lying across the road. Griboyedov felt sudden fear. Involuntarily, he turned his horse and galloped back. His sallow face regained its color. He tugged angrily at the reins and galloped forward again. He reached the fallen horse, dismounted, and approached it. Pokhvisnev's stallion. So, Wilhelm . . . where was Wilhelm? He went to the cliff and looked down—had he been killed and thrown down the precipice? Mystified, he looked into the darkness but couldn't see a thing. A groan came from above his head.

'What's that? Who's there?' Griboyedov cried out, and again he felt afraid.

Someone groaned again. The groaning was coming from the tree. Griboyedov cocked the trigger and approached the oak.

'Who's there?' he shouted.

'Could you get me out of this hollow tree, please?' said a voice.

'What the hell is this? Is that you, Wilhelm?'

The voice in the hollow tree rejoiced:

'Aleksandr!'

Griboyedov burst out laughing. He just could not help himself.

'What have you got yourself into that hollow for, old boy?'

There was a chuckle in the hollow, a very weak one.

'I was in a gunfight.'

Then a little later:

'I believe my leg is broken.'

Griboyedov became serious. He climbed onto the branches and turned his back to the hollow.

'Get on my back.'

He dragged Wilhelm out, and saw how pale and weak he was. He helped him up onto his horse.

'Who shot at you? Where is he?'

Wilhelm pointed to the precipice.

XI

He had to spend almost three weeks in bed. Griboyedov cared for him devotedly. Yermolov visited him a couple of times but didn't stay long and kept frowning. Jokes fell flat, and Wilhelm suddenly felt that Yermolov had ceased to be the hero of his imagination.

One day Gribov announced:

'Nikolay Nikolayevich Pokhvisnev.'

Griboyedov turned his head calmly and said without getting up:

'Wilhelm Karlovich cannot receive Mr. Pokhvisnev at this moment.'

For all of those three weeks Griboyedov was in a black mood, he was out in the evenings and got home late. Wilhelm never found out where he went. Griboyedov could not forgive himself the fear he had experienced on that night when he was looking for Wilhelm. He would ride every day along the same road and stand for a long time by the oak tree, waiting to be attacked.

After Wilhelm recovered, life went on as before: Jaffar's garden, conversations with Liszt, the Nobles' Club.

Once, entering the Club, he remembered in the vestibule that he had left a book at home, which he had promised to Voyeikov. He heard someone talking and laughing in the anteroom. A voice crackling with laughter said:

'I can just picture our Bread-maker in the hollow of a tree!'

Wilhelm blushed and listened.

'Oh no, you don't know him,' said someone else. Wilhelm recognized Pokhvisnev's voice. 'Believe me, our Bread-maker knows what he's doing. He uses his simplicity to worm himself into the good books of whomsoever he needs to.'

'You don't say!' someone said incredulously.

Pokhvisnev droned, sounding somewhat offended:

'Of course. As he has wriggled into Aleksey Petrovich's favor. The other day, after the incident in the hollow tree, I even received a reprimand. Yermolov said to me: "Why do you egg him on to go to such places?" And I must tell you confidentially . . .'

The voice became a whisper; Wilhelm stopped listening.

He closed his eyes and leaned against the wall. The door opened and Pokhvisnev came out into the vestibule. Wilhelm stepped in front of him and, without even looking, slapped his face. Pokhvisnev clutched his cheek silently and ran out. Wilhelm went to his lodgings.

Griboyedov was there. Seeing Wilhelm, he quickly asked:

'What's happened?'

Wilhelm paused. Then he thumped his chest and began to tremble:

'That scoundrel said I worm myself into Yermolov's confidence with my simplicity. Would you agree to be my second?'

Aleksandr leaned back in his chair, obviously interested. His face took on a serious expression. He made Wilhelm tell all.

'My dear friend,' he said impressively, 'Pokhvisnev will not fight with you. You insulted him in private. He won't insist on satisfaction. He values his life too much.'

Wilhelm stared at him wide-eyed:

'Is he so base he might refuse?'

'Undoubtedly. I know him very well, the fop. He won't fight. He'll complain about you to Aleksey Petrovich, who will summon both of you, and do some play-acting—and that will be the end of the matter.'

Wilhelm said: 'No, I'll not have that!' and suddenly became terrible in his anger, foaming at the mouth. 'He won't get away with it. I'll slap him again.'

Griboyedov replied in a business-like manner:

'Just make sure to do it in public.'

Wilhelm waited for two days. There was no challenge from Pokhvisnev. Apparently, Yermolov was also unaware of what had happened. Two days later Wilhelm went to the Club. Aleksandr had told him that Pokhvisnev would be there. When he came in, the usual gambling was going on. The room was filled with smoke. Liszt was standing alone by the window: the gray artilleryman did not play cards. Pokhvisnev was sitting at the *hombre* table with Voyeikov and two other officers. When he saw Wilhelm, he turned pale and shrugged his shoulders. Wilhelm walked straight up to him.

'My dear sir, I demand an explanation,' he said in a sonorous voice and ran out of breath.

Pokhvisnev stood up, his eyes darting about. He was pale and trying not to look Wilhelm in the eye.

The room fell quiet.

Wilhelm said in an unnaturally thin voice:

'I am challenging you to repeat in front of everyone what you said about me two days ago at the Club.'

'I did not say anything,' Pokhisnev muttered, stepping back.

Wilhelm raised his voice:

'Then I'll have to remind you and those to whom it was said will surely be ready to confirm it. You said that I use my simplicity to worm myself into Aleksey Petrovich's confidence.'

The crowd drew closer round the two of them.

Then Wilhelm slapped Pokhvisnev's face with the back of his hand.

'This is my response.'

And he hit him again.

They were dragged away from each other. Pokhvisnev's teeth were chattering as he shouted:

'Id-d-iot . . .'

Then he burst into tears and laughter. Wilhelm stood breathing heavily. His bloodshot eyes were darting around.

Griboyedov, calm and purposeful, approached Liszt:

'Vasily Frantsevich, surely you will not refuse to act as a second for Wilhelm Karlovich?'

Liszt made a sad bow.

XII

Pokhvisnev was standing at the desk about to make his usual daily report.

Yermolov was out of sorts. He gripped his pipe tightly between his teeth and took a puff.

He barely glanced at a couple of documents.

Then he cast a sidelong glance at Pokhvisnev:

'Nothing else for me, Nikolay Nikolayevich?'

Pokhvisnev hesitated:

'I'd like to lodge a complaint, Aleksey Petrovich.'

'Concerning what?' Yermolov inquired in an innocent voice.

Pokhvisnev grew bolder:

'Concerning Mr. Küchelbecker. He has insulted me gravely, Aleksey Petrovich, without any provocation on my part.'

'How exactly did he offend you, Nikolay Nikolayevich?' Yermolov sounded surprised. 'What did he say his reason was?'

Pokhvisnev shrugged:

'Aleksey Petrovich, you yourself know his unbridled temper. He said his reason was that I had alleged that he used his simplicity to ingratiate himself with people.'

Yermolov asked gravely:

'Eh? And so? You said no such thing, did you?'

Pokhvisnev shifted from foot to foot.

'And where did the insult occur?' inquired Yermolov, clearly interested:

'The other day at the Club,' Pokhvisnev replied reluctantly.

'Damn it!' Yermolov suddenly became angry and knitted his eyebrows. 'I won't leave it like this.' He was genuinely annoyed. 'Right,' he went on, turning to Pokhvisnev, 'and what do you intend to do, Nikolay Nikolayevich?'

Pokhvisnev gave him a crooked grin:

'At first, Aleksey Petrovich, I definitely wanted to fight; but then I decided that as Mr. Küchelbecker is subject to fits, which you, Aleksey Petrovich, are also aware of, and can't be considered a man in good health, then perhaps it would be better to submit the matter to the consideration of the court.'

Yermolov nodded nonchalantly.

'Very well, you may go, my friend,' he said blankly.

After Pokhvisnev had left, Yermolov got up and walked around the room. Then he sat down, took a drag of his pipe, blew out the smoke, and smiled cheerlessly. He sat down at the desk and began a letter:

Dear Nikolay Nikolayevich:

It had completely slipped my mind to remind you, my friend, that the correspondence forwarded to us by the civilian units has to be registered by means of special numbering, designating the correspondence as received. Those wretched scribes muddle it up all the time, which makes paperwork very difficult. This is all I have to say. Forgive me for troubling you with it. As for the grave insult that Mr. Küchelbecker has flung at you, I don't believe that a court hearing will be sufficient to settle it, and you will certainly have to fight.

All good wishes,

Yermolov

He rang the bell. A random scribe came in: the duty officer was away. Yermolov told him to take the letter to Pokhvisnev. He looked at the clerk carefully and, when left alone, grumbled:

'Hmm, it's not just the auditors—even clerks imagine that they are specially created beings.'

XIII

The duel is tomorrow. Perhaps, when the uncertain light of the next day shines, he will be in his grave. Well, cold Lethe—it has its day too. Ustinka's face and his mother's flashed in front of his eyes; Wilhelm buried his face in his hands. They will get through it. He mentally kissed his mother's dry hand. He remembered Dunya and gave a start. Yes, if this chance villain murders him, everything will be resolved at a stroke, and there will be no need to bother about himself, or about the childish heart, which sets riddles for him.

He began to write letters. A short one in German—to his mother. Another one to Pushkin.

The other Aleksandr, Griboyedov, is here. He can tell people all they need to know; all petty scores have been settled. And this was where his life had been heading! Suddenly he remembered Papa Fleury. Greece? Or . . . or Petersburg? But what was there in Petersburg, except ridicule, ennui, Naryshkin's patronage, Yegor Antonovich's grumbling?

He listened. The sounds of a waltz were coming from the next room—note after note, at first uncertainly, then more confidently. Wilhelm hadn't heard it before. Griboyedov was composing.

Suddenly he realized: if he survived tomorrow, he would have to burn himself up, it didn't matter where, completely, at once, in the shortest possible time. He would have to perish, but in such a way that afterward life would at once become different, and his friends would remember him as long as they lived.

XIV

Five in the morning and the sun has risen. Four men in the green Artachilakhi Valley. One in a gray military coat, neat and solemn, has paced out ten steps and marked out the agreed barrier. Another, short one, is busying himself with the pistols.

A pale man with smoothly combed hair stands fifteen paces from Wilhelm, who has no interest in him. The man has lowered his eyes and is not looking at Wilhelm.

A green branch is close to Wilhelm's face. He studies it closely. If he is killed, his last memory will be the lush dark greenery of this branch.

The gray artilleryman stops in front of the duellists.

'Gentlemen, one last time: I suggest you end the quarrel and make it up.'

Silence.

Wilhelm shakes his head. Pokhvisnev waves his hand.

The first shot is of the one who has been insulted.

Pale and uncertain, Pokhvisnev takes one step forward. A small barrel is looking Wilhelm in the face. The trembling barrel is rising. He stands half-turned. Oh hell, it is aimed at his forehead. No, apparently, he has no intention of ruining his career. The barrel is coming down. And points at his leg.

The trigger clicks—a misfire. Pokhvisnev looks confused.

Now it's Wilhelm's shot.

Wilhelm looks around at the sky, the green trees, the mountains, slightly lit by the sun, gives a deep sigh, sees a pale man before him, and shoots in the air.

XV

Yermolov was smoking his pipe and writing a testimonial for Küchelbecker. He wrote a formal letter, frowning, and suddenly surprised himself by adding: "And he carried out his assignments with zeal and in a manner worthy of praise."

He leaned back in the chair and thought for a moment. His hand refused to write the truth to that old milksop, the minister, about this Bread-maker chap. He remembered, with a frown, the face with the bulging eyes and chattering teeth, remembered Küchelbecker's shriek, his Greece, frowned, and crossed out the last sentence. He thought for another second.

Then he quickly wrote: "Due to the brevity of his time here, he was not much used in the office, and his abilities for the service as such are therefore difficult to assess."

He waved with vexation either at Küchelbecker or at the testimonial.

'Off my hands.'

XVI

Looking distractedly at Wilhelm packing, Griboyedov suddenly said to Gribov:

'Aleksandr, pack up my things, I am leaving with Wilhelm Karlovich.'

Wilhelm quickly turned around toward him:

'Are you sure, Sasha?'

Gribov did not move.

'Did you hear what I've just told you?'

Gribov calmly left the room. A couple of minutes later he returned with an armful of fur coats.

'Why are you bringing the fur coats?' Griboyedov was amazed.

'It might still be cold in Russia,' said Gribov impassively.

Griboyedov suddenly shuddered and spoke rapidly to the dumbfounded Wilhelm.

'No, no. God be with you, my dear fellow, take care of yourself, off you go. I cannot pluck up the courage to return to our dear Fatherland.' And he waved his hand in horror at the fur coats.

'Corpses—foxes, jackals, wolves. The air is infected with their smell. You have to rip open a beast and wrap its skin around your own in order to enjoy the sweet air of the homeland.'

Wilhelm looked at him intently:

'Why not go together, Sasha, old chap?'

Griboyedov suddenly lifted a fur coat and pulled it on.

'So heavy,' he said with a bewildered smile. 'Pulls the shoulders down to the ground.' He dropped it with an incomprehensible loathing.

'Off you go, Wilhelm, off you go, old friend. I can't bring myself to,' he said, and embraced him.

'Aleksandr,' he said sternly to Gribov and pointed to the fur coats, 'take these away.'

Outside the window a little bell rang sadly: the mule was tired of waiting and kept shifting from foot to foot.

In The Country

I

"Dear brother and friend," wrote Ustinka, "I am begging you by all that's holy to leave Petersburg, which is really bad for your health, and come to stay with us at Zakup. Grigory too is pressing you to come. The children are anxious to see you, you won't be bored with us. They say that Mitya resembles you very much, if not in his talent, then in his soul. Your favorite grove is waiting for you at Zakup and the nightingales are already back. My dear brother, do not hesitate, come and stay with us, and not just for a day or a month, though I know how quickly you get bored with things. How is Misha doing?"

It had been carefully planned. Aunt Breitkopf had thought hard about what was to be done with Wilhelm, who could not settle anywhere for more than a month at a time. Alas, she no longer asked Wilhelm any questions—she had been told in confidence what they were saying about him. He had become a dangerous man. He had been ruined by his trip abroad and those ill-fated lectures. The Caucasus had done him no good either: the hot-headed Willie had slapped someone there and fought a duel—the aunt did not even want to know any of the details. And as a result, Willie was persona non grata and his career, which had begun so well, was put on hold.

The aunt could sense the fatal influence of some illicit passion—such a thing had to involve a woman. And she had written to Ustinka, who, thank goodness, was living peacefully with her husband Glinka on the Smolensk estate, that if she could not get Willie to come to her place, then her aunt couldn't vouch for anything—the poor boy didn't even have any loose change to his name.

Be that as it may, Wilhelm was being offered unexpected shelter, almost a home. He had time on his hands now. Three days later, he was in Smolensk, and by the night of the fourth day he reached the village of Zakup, in the Dukhovshchina district.

Ustinka led a quiet life. Zakup was a small estate, but with a flood-meadow, a grove, the one so loved by Wilhelm, which Ustinka had mentioned in her letter, and a thousand acres of arable land, even though it was not particularly fertile and rather loamy. The manor house stood on a hill, surrounded by ancient birches. The house was old, the wooden columns along the façade were peeling; the rooms had low ceilings. But they were spacious, cool in summer, and warm in winter, when the fire was roaring. The walls were covered with portraits of the Glinkas. One among them, which particularly attracted Wilhelm, dated from the time of tsarina Anna Ioanovna; the man in the picture was fat, heavy-jowled, with a predatory nose and particularly shrewd, unpleasant eyes. Wilhelm found it somewhat demonic. He was given a small room, very light and clean. There were colorful engravings on the walls—the story of Atala.[35] A young man carrying a languid girl across a stream was depicted in one of them, and in the other a dying girl with big eyes, somewhat crossed, from which were falling tears as large as beans.

The window faced a river, cheerful and meandering, if shallow, and the village itself, its log houses surrounded by little gardens with rowan trees.

Wilhelm was greeted by everyone with great joy. Grigory Andreyevich Glinka, Ustinka's husband, was a man remarkable in many respects. His career was somewhat unusual. In his youth he had been a highly successful page, then a Guards officer, he had lived in grand style and had quickly climbed up the career ladder. Then one day he went adrift, locked himself in, began to brood, then resigned and retreated to his estate. His friends were surprised to learn that the cheerful Guardsman was poring over books like a schoolboy, and after a while they heard even stranger news: Grigory Glinka had become a professor of Russian literature at the University of Dorpat, a position more suitable for a pen-pusher than for a real nobleman and a Guardsman to boot.

Then Grigory Andreyevich was invited by the Grand Dukes to become a tutor or a *chevalier*, and now he lived peacefully. He was rather taciturn, loved his garden, his flowerbeds, and, in particular, his quiet wife.

He watched Wilhelm with some curiosity; probably he did not agree with his literary opinions but he did not get involved in argument. Peace was what he loved most and enthusiasm always struck him as absurd. However, he loved Wilhelm in his own way, or rather, admired him, as he admired his children, his wife, the flowers, and the forest, with that broad-mindedness that is characteristic of people who have gone through a major turning point in their lives.

Of all the children, Mitya, a timid, shy boy with rapturous eyes and a thin neck, was the most happy to see Wilhelm. He revered his uncle and would not leave his side. This even upset Ustinka, who was afraid that he would be a nuisance to Wilhelm. But Wilhelm read *Scheherazade* to the nine-year-old Mitya, a book he loved to distraction, and he also made him excellent crossbows.

And one other person was delighted to see Wilhelm almost as much as Mitya: while Wilhelm had been wandering about Europe and the Caucasus, his servant Semyon had lived at Ustinka's. He was still the same cheerful and carefree fellow, though, he seemed very bored with his menial duties. On the very first evening he came to see Wilhelm and begged him to take him along with him when the time of his departure came round.

The Glinkas had many servants. The storekeeper Agrafena stood out among them both in height and importance. Wilhelm couldn't abide her.

Occasionally he heard singing coming from the chambermaids' room, then her voice: 'Girls!' and the singing stopped short, and all you could hear was the spindles whirring.

Once, irked by this, Wilhelm asked Ustinka:

'Why does she stop the poor girls singing?'

Ustinka opened her eyes wide.

'But Wilhelm, songs distract them from work. And besides, they are not unhappy at all.'

Wilhelm said nothing and did not raise the topic again.

He established a rigid routine: riding in the morning, then work, reading after lunch, in the evenings playing with Mitya and going for walks.

He was a good rider, but the roads were straight and flat, completely devoid of the fearsome Caucasian romanticism. Soon, however, Wilhelm found romanticism here too: the morning mist as thin as smoke (he set out early, about seven o'clock), the damp birch leaves with the dew still dripping from them, the clouds seeming frozen in the sky—all these were attractive to him in their own way.

Occasionally on the road he would come across an old woman with a jug of milk or a girl with a wicker basket who would bow to him timidly. Wilhelm suffered from these quick, low bows, as if these people had been lashed on the neck. He would politely raise his hat, which frightened the old women and girls even more. He did not visit the neighbors: once Ustinka suggested that he should drive ten *versts*[36] to their neighbors where everything was very jolly, and where there were young ladies who would be delighted to see him, but Wilhelm's face displayed fear and disgust, and Ustinka left him to live the life of a recluse.

There was work and reading. Wilhelm worked hard—on his tragedy. He made corrections, crossed things out, wrote another draft. The tragedy was intended to bring about a revolution in the Russian theater, if . . . if it were ever to be published. Wilhelm doubted this. The hero of the tragedy was Timoleon, a stern Republican, the murderer of his own tyrant brother.

He contrasted the straightforward Timoleon with the weak though generous tyrant. When writing about the leader of the uprising, an astute but unassuming Republican who would not baulk at assassination, Wilhelm recalled Turgenev's resolute eyes. Poring over Plutarch and Diodorus just like Timoleon, Wilhelm learned the same things he had learned from Turgenev and Ryleyev. He himself was surprised by his hero; and finally he imagined him so clearly that he even felt real anguish—if only Timoleon were alive!

And Wilhelm read Timoleon's monologues to Mitenka, who listened, still as a statue:

An ill-timed mutiny's a dreadful thing,
And if you, youths, truly wish to bring
Back to your homeland liberty and good,
Sparing the shedding of innocent blood,
Listen, young men, to those who decree
That you should accomplish this sacred deed.
They will speak to you when the time is right,
When the fateful hour has come—to fight.

Wilhelm was fond of ancient heroes almost as much as of Pushkin and Griboyedov. Breathless with excitement, he read Brutus's letters to Cicero, in which Brutus, determined to act against Octavius, reproached Cicero for his cowardice. And after reading them, Wilhelm would mount his horse and gallop like a madman.

Tears choked him: he was twenty-six years old—what had he done for his fatherland? And his heart would start feeling heavy even in Zakup, among his kind and caring family. Slavery surrounded him, real and degrading.

This dear sister of his, this learned husband of hers, they were wonderful people and without them Wilhelm would have been alone; they neither greatly oppressed the household servants nor particularly burdened their peasants. But once he saw the coachman leading an old menial to the stables. The old man's offense was serious: he had had too much to drink, had caught the eye of his masters, and had spoken rudely to them. He was walking, with his head lowered, frowning, not looking around. The coachman, a heavy-set man with a bowl hair-cut, was leading him along with an indifferent air.

He bowed to his mistress's brother. Wilhelm stopped them:

'Where are you heading?'

The coachman replied reluctantly:

'Lukich has to be punished for a misdemeanor.'

Wilhelm said firmly:

'Go home, both of you.'

The man scratched his head and muttered:

'I am not sure what I should do, your lordship, I have an order to carry out.'

'Who gave you the order?' Wilhelm asked without looking at the coachman.

'Grigory Andreyevich.'

Wilhelm yelled: 'Go home at once!' and advanced on the coachman in a frenzy. 'Let the old man go!' he shouted again in a shrill voice.

'What do I care?' muttered the coachman. 'I'll let him go if you like.'

At home Wilhelm did not go down for dinner. Having learned about the incident, Grigory Andreyevich had a serious word with Ustinya Karlovna.

'It won't do. Wilhelm should have come to me. This amounts to a fundamental undermining of all the power of the landowners.'

For two days their relations were strained and there was silence at dinner. Then things were smoothed over.

A week later Wilhelm called for Semyon. Semyon came in his skimpy, rather tight dark blue tail coat. Wilhelm scrutinized his clothes with disgust.

'Semyon, I have a request for you. Do me a favor, bring me the village tailor. He'll make some Russian clothes for you and me. You walk around dressed like a clown. And get hold of a pair of knee boots for me.'

Five days later Wilhelm and Semyon were sporting simple peasant shirts and trousers. They had *armiaks*[37] made for them too.

Grigory Andreyevich shrugged his shoulders and said nothing.

The chambermaids jeered at them in the servants' room:

'His lordship is making a fool of himself.'

Wilhelm was not embarrassed at all.

Soon he started to visit the village. The Glinkas owned two villages: a large and tidy one, Zagusino, which lay two *versts* from the manor house, and Dukhovshchina—five *versts* to the other side. Wilhelm would visit the nearest one, Zagusino. On seeing the mistress's brother, the headman, Foma Lukyanov, a tall and upright old peasant, would go out onto the porch and bow low. Foma was an intelligent, taciturn man. Ustinya Karlovna called him a diplomat. He treated Wilhelm with respect, but there was mockery in his small gray eyes. The village timidly steered clear of the master. Only one old man greeted him affectionately. This was Ivan Letoshnikov, an old village joker and a drunkard. Ivan was almost seventy years old and had a clear memory of Pugachev's rebellion and the division of Poland. He lived on his own, was desperately hard up, and was a poor worker. Wilhelm had long talks with him. The old man would sing him songs, and Wilhelm would write them down in a notebook. Looking out of the window, Ivan would start singing about whatever came into his mind. Once he sang to Wilhelm:

A hundred and fifty ships
Sail out on the dark blue sea.
Each ship has five hundred sailors:
All as one they row and sing.

And so the ships take wing,
The songs are bold,
The talk is told,
And they all curse Rakcheyev . . .

Ivan looked around, gave Wilhelm a sly wink and lowered his voice:

You son of a bitch, Rakcheyev,
You noble piece of scum.
You've kicked us up the bum!
Canals are here, canals are there
And birch trees everywhere . . .

Wilhelm was surprised:

'How did you come by this song?'

'I don't know,' responded Ivan, 'From a passing soldier. No idea who.'

Wilhelm thought: "So much for Turgenev's propaganda sheets for the peasants—they can manage without."

'Do you want me to tell you some verses about Arakcheyev?' he asked Ivan.

And he recited in a drawn-out voice:

An arrogant time-server, insidious, none slicker,
An ingrate to the tsar, a sly and base boot-licker,
A violent tyrant of his native land,
A villain promoted for his sleight-of-hand!

What is this cymbal sound of your passing glory,
Your illustrious rank and your terrible story?

Ivan liked the poem,

'Cymbal,' he repeated and shook his head. 'That's it. Did you write it yourself or just hear it somewhere?'

'My friend composed it,' said Wilhelm proudly. 'Ryleyev is his name.'

Ivan was extremely taken by the verse.

'Rakcheyev has grabbed all the power,' he confided quietly to Wilhelm. 'One day a traveling man told us that Rakcheyev poisoned the tsar and set up military settlements all over Russia, that the tsar has a decree buried in the ground somewhere, which will free all the peasants after his death, and Rakcheyev is the only one who knows where it is. It'll be lost anyway.'

'It's true that Arakcheyev has influence over the tsar,' said Wilhelm. 'He is his evil demon; but it's unlikely the tsar has written this testament.'

'We know nothing,' said Ivan, 'but there's been talk. No matter. Maybe there's no testament. I know you write about peasants,' Ivan winked at him slyly. 'What do you write it for?' he asked curiously, narrowing his eyes.

Wilhelm shrugged:

'I like the common people, Ivan, I envy you.'

'You don't say!' said Ivan and shook his head. 'Do you really? Why is that?'

Wilhelm, for the life of him, could not explain the reasons for his envy.

Ivan said sternly:

'You're a kind and decent master, but it's a bit of a joke to go envying peasants. Someone else, a soldier for example, might envy a peasant, or a convict. They don't have a thing to call their own. But why should *you* be envious of peasants? It's like envying a hunchback. A peasant's life isn't all cakes and ale. What's there to envy?'

'I didn't explain myself properly, Ivan,' said Wilhelm thoughtfully, 'I'm ashamed at the sight of your servitude.'

'You just wait, sir,' Ivan gave him another wink, 'it won't always be servitude. They executed Pugachev but there'll be another.'

Wilhelm shuddered involuntarily. He feared Pugachev possibly even more than Arakcheyev.

He frowned and asked Ivan:

'Do you remember Pugachev? Tell me about him.'

Ivan was reluctant:

'I don't. What's there to remember? We know nothing.'

II

One evening, Grigory Andreyevich looked at Wilhelm too intently, as though he was hesitating to begin an important conversation. Finally, he took him by the hand and said to him with that special courtesy from which Wilhelm could guess what a gracious Guardsman he had once been.

'*Mon cher Guillaume*, we need to talk.'

They went into a small office with portraits of writers and generals on the walls. A portrait of Karamzin was in a prominent place with his own handwritten inscription on it. A few books, a manuscript, and portraits of the grand dukes in military uniforms, with labels in childish handwriting, were arranged very precisely on the desk. Grigory Andreyevich sank into the armchair and thought for a couple of minutes. Then, looking awkwardly at Wilhelm, he said, with some trepidation:

'I've been watching you for a long time, *mon cher Guillaume*, and I've come to the conclusion that you are on the wrong track. I know as well as you do that things can't go on like this, but I find your behavior with the peasants quite embarrassing.'

Wilhelm frowned.

'Grigory Andreyevich, I see a source of rejuvenation for our life and literature in the Russian folk spirit. Where else has it survived in such a pure form as in our splendid people?'

Grigory Andryevich shook his head:

'No, you are mistaken, you are playing with fire. I know perfectly well that thrones are tottering and it's not this gentleman—he waved his hand at the portrait of Grand Duke Constantine on his desk—who will hold onto it after Alexander's death, not to mention the boys,' he pointed to the portraits of Nicholas and Michael. I see what you mean. The business with the Semyonovsky Regiment made it all clear to me. But don't deceive yourself, *mon cher*, in order to achieve the liberty your Timoleon is dreaming about, one has to rely not on the mob, but on the aristocracy.'

Wilhelm looked at Gregory Andreyevich in amazement. This quiet, taciturn, and withdrawn man, who loved flowers, suddenly appeared not at all as straightforward as Wilhelm had imagined. He muttered:

'But in my tragedy, I make no mention of the mob. I like peasants for their folk spirit and consider their serfdom our sin.'

Grigory Andreyevich smiled:

'I'm not talking about folk spirit, *mon cher frère*, but if people like you continue to associate with the mob,' Grigory Andreyevich's eyes took a steady expression, 'on some critical day that may not be so far away, hundreds of thousands of house servants will be sharpening their knives, and that will be the end of us all.'

All at once Wilhelm became pensive. He had no answer to Grigory Andreyevich, he had not imagined that freedom and folk spirit were somehow linked to the knives of domestic servants.

Looking pleased, Grigory Andreyevich then said:

'But that isn't what I have really invited you here for. I want to ask your opinion on literary matters.'

Wilhelm was even more astonished.

'I thought, Grigory Andryevich, that you had given up literary work long ago.'

Glinka waved his hand:

'To hell with it, literary work. I've made up my mind to write a memoir. Today I've looked through my old notes and found a lot of observations that might be useful for a future historian. They may slip my memory if I don't get them into shape.'

Wilhelm pricked up his ears:

'Grigory Andreyevich, I believe your memoir will be of interest not only to historians.'

Glinka smiled again.

'Yes, I've had a long life, thank God: I've known tsars, soldiers, and Russian writers. However, I think that every historian is most concerned with characters, and I'd like to ask your advice, *mon cher*: should I leave in the little details or should I omit them?'

Wilhelm said confidently:

'Details are the most precious thing in the depiction of character.'

'Thank you.' said Glinka. 'I'll leave all the details as they are. So, if now we go over to the characters of crown princes Nicholas and Michael, whom I tutored, I noticed first-hand how a person is revealed through these little details. I remember,' he said wistfully, 'that Nicholas, who was thirteen at the time, once behaved very affectionately, then suddenly bit me on the shoulder. I looked at him—he was trembling all over and, in some sort of frenzy, began treading on my feet. Isn't that a telling detail?'

Wilhelm replied slowly:

'Is Nikolay Pavlovich really like that? I knew he was a cruel commander but I didn't know that about him.'

'I observed him for years,' continued Glinka, 'his personality was frightening; he was rude in games; many's the time he hurt his play-fellows or swore at them. But the essential thing is this: not only was he quick-tempered but when he was angry, he was very much like his father, Emperor Paul. In fits of anger he used to hack at his drum with a hatchet and break his toys, all the time clowning around and pulling faces.' Glinka suddenly laughed. 'One time I was telling him about Socrates's life and death, and he said back to me: "What a fool."'

'And Konstantin Pavlovich? Were you close to him?' Wilhelm inquired, full of curiosity.

Grigory Andreyevich made an angry face and said blankly:

'Let's not talk about Constantine. It is frightening to think that a person, whose actions should be punished in law by penal servitude, will succeed to the throne.'

He suddenly fell silent, frowned and, as if displeased with what he had said, began to thank Wilhelm courteously. And no matter how much Wilhelm pressed him to tell him more, Grigory Andreyevich kept stubbornly silent.

III

Once, when he was out riding, Wilhelm overtook an expensive carriage with an elderly lady and a young girl. Seeing Wilhelm, the girl suddenly clapped her hands and laughed.

It was Dunya. She was accompanying her aunt on a visit to the Glinkas. Grigory Andreyevich was her cousin twice removed, and all the Glinkas loved their relatives and were friendly with each other.

With the arrival of Dunya, Wilhelm's entire timetable changed; both the village and his tragedy were kicked into the long grass. Wilhelm saw and heard no one but Dunya. She understood him like no one else. Strolling in the grove, they talked for hours about everything, and Wilhelm was amazed how well the seventeen-year-old Dunya understood people and, almost without hesitation, said of them what Wilhelm could only guess at. And even when she was wrong about people, she was extraordinarily entertaining and impish. She knew Pushkin well, had seen Griboyedov a couple of times, and was friendly with Delvig. At one point she said to Wilhelm about Pushkin:

'It seems to me that Aleksandr Sergeyevich has never loved anyone or anything in his life except his poems.'

Wilhelm was astonished.

'Funny but someone already told me this, either Engelhardt or Korf. Does it mean that you really don't like Pushkin?'

Dunya smiled and changed the subject. Six months before meeting Wilhelm, she had been in love with Pushkin and kept it secret. Another time, quite unexpectedly, she said about Grigory Andreyevich:

'*Oncle Grègoire* must have done something terrible in the past: that's why he loves *tante* so much.'

Wilhelm told her everything. He told her about Griboyedov and Yermolov and talked at length about Paris, which had left an indelible impression on him.

In the evenings, he read his tragedy to her, and her judgments were surprisingly astute. She said about Timoleon:

'I'm afraid that in your play the tyrant is more attractive than the hero who kills him. The person one falls in love with must have at least one failing.' And added impishly: '*You* have a lot.'

Everything became clear to Wilhelm in her presence. The most important decision, on which the whole of life depended, could be taken, without agonising, in half an hour, simply and without hesitation, like a hand at whist. The most terrible action was understandable and merely unpleasant. There was no need to torment oneself, it was easy to make up one's mind, and to live was sheer joy. She was seventeen years old. They went riding, and Dunya held herself in the saddle firmly and easily, and clearly loved to ride fast. She took off her hat. Her blond hair fluttered. A hunched, huge Wilhelm galloped by her side and saw neither sky, nor road, nor distant forest—only the blond hair.

A week later, a declaration of love took place in the grove. In fact, there was not even a declaration, they simply kissed. For Wilhelm the coolness of her lips was the line beyond which lay the start of a new life. They swore everlasting love to each other, eternal, till the grave. But then doubts began, which kept Wilhelm awake at night: he was dog-poor, and threadbare, and homeless, without a corner to call his own. The status of Russian writer was a curse rather than a title. Such a class did not even exist. What would Dunya do in his smoke-filled Petersburg cell? He had to take a decision. He did not mention any of this to Dunya.

When she was leaving, they said their goodbyes in the grove. They took their time, Dunya cried. Then he decided: he would work day and night, he would drag himself out of poverty, so as not to condemn Dunya to vagrancy and deprivation. He gave himself a year. One year later a new life would begin. Wilhelm didn't dare to think about that life, such a joy it would be. And he began to write letters. He wrote to Engelhardt, then he thought and wrote to Komovsky. Little Fox was still a good friend. He had been making his way in the service, he might help him in some way. Wilhelm wrote to him about his plans to publish a large magazine. Little Fox answered immediately. The letter was, in fact, amusing, but it sent Wilhelm into a fury. It suddenly reminded him of Petersburg, of the destitution and uncertainty of his position, and it disheartened him. Little Fox called Wilhelm a crazy fellow, advised him to enter the service, and ended by pointing out that Wilhelm himself was to blame for his misadventures. Why hadn't he stayed in St. Petersburg when it was in his interest, why had he given those lectures in Paris—he ought to have done that with the greatest caution, if at all—and finally, why had he not got along with Yermolov in the Caucasus, and even given offense to someone there? And in conclusion, Little Fox advised Wilhelm to marry, which would supposedly cleanse his soul immediately.

He listed Wilhelm's sins so gleefully that Wilhelm vividly remembered how Komovsky used to eavesdrop behind doors. He replied:

> Komovsky, what do you want from me?—you want to be right . . . Well, if it is any consolation, you *are* right. I'll let you call me crazy or whatever you like—you seem to like the expression.
>
> I had no wish to write any more in the heat of the moment: I am taking up my pen to prove that if I did not get along with people, it was not because I did not want to, but because I could not. It is brutal and inhuman to reproach an unfortunate man for his misfortune: but you were helpful to me in the past and they even say you care for me. I hope and believe that you do not understand what it means to talk to me like this in my circumstances. But let's put an end to this: I implore you by all that is sacred to me, do not make me fear your favors, if they give you the right to rub salt into my wounds. You, lucky people! You still don't know how painfully the wounded soul shudders at the slightest touch. As I said: let's put an end to this! Give me your hand: I'll forget all you have said,

but do not write to me like this, do not write things that are more painful than death.

Wilhelm

P.S. You mention marriage—believe me, I am sick of the rough and stormy life that I have been obliged to lead. All the more so as, to be honest with you, my heart is not free, for the first time in my life I am in love and the love is mutual. But do not mention this to your family, *je ne veux pas que cette nouvelle leur cause de nouvelles inquiétudes.*[38] I fear for my very happiness. My hair is turning gray in my twenty-sixth year; I entertain no hopes; I have had joy in my life, but who knows whether I will have any more? I wish you, my friend, every success—in society, in the service, and in family happiness. My sister sends her warm regards and says that you are a nice kind young man.

IV

Ustinka saw how worried Wilhelm was. She thought it over and decided to write to Griboyedov, whom she hardly knew personally, but was fond of from Wilhelm's stories.

She wrote to Griboyedov that she feared for her brother's future, not because he was pursued by adversity but because her brother's very character drew misfortunes on him.

Griboyedov took a long time to reply.

Finally, Ustinka received a letter from him. Griboyedov wrote:

My gracious lady, having lingered so long over my answer to your kind letter, I am at my wits' end how to come up with an excuse to justify myself, and you won't be fooled. Think about the distance that separates us, and my constant travels, which occupy five-sixths of my time in this country; the letters of those who remember me languish for ages in the mail until I manage to get hold of them. One thing that gives me comfort is that your worthy friend and mine is well aware of my character. He has probably warned you that my typical infringement of customs and decorum is not to be blamed either on my heart or any general disregard for feeling.

Counting on your understanding, I want to talk to you about a man who is in every respect better than me and who is equally dear to both of us. What is he doing, our good Wilhelm, experiencing misfortune before he has had time to take advantage of the few true pleasures provided to us by society, tortured and misunderstood, while he approaches every person he meets with the most sincere attachment, cordiality and love? . . . Should not all this make everyone well-disposed toward him? Always fearing to be a burden to others, he becomes a burden only to his own sensitivity! I presume he is with you now, surrounded by a caring family.

Who could have said six months ago that I would end up envying even his ill-fated star! Oh! If someone else's unhappiness can bring relief to another unfortunate being, then tell him that now I am a burden to myself and alone among people to whom I am completely indifferent; a few more days, and I shall leave this city, I leave behind the boredom and frustration, which haunt me here and which, perhaps, I will find again in another place.

Please persuade your brother to submit to fate and to look on our suffering as an ordeal, from which we will emerge less passionate, more cold-blooded, with a store of spiritual steadfastness that will awaken reverence in the inexperienced; it will no doubt seem to them that we have prospered all our lives, and if fate grants us a long life, a capricious decrepitude, a dry cough and an eternal repetition of the lessons of youth will be the refuge that each of us will attain in the end—Wilhelm and I and all our fortunate companions. I am sorry, my dear lady, that I have included in this letter these sad outpourings, which I might have spared you. Picking up my quill, my only intention was to salve my soul with a sincere admission that I owe you an apology.

Please accept my assurances of absolute respect,

Griboyedov

Ustinka pored over Griboyedov's letter and tears welled up in her eyes. Strangely, she felt even more sorry for him than for Wilhelm. Dear God, alone, far away, among those foreign semi-savages. What misfortune was looming over them all!

She wanted to see Aleksandr that very minute, to convince him that he was young, that he did not need, did not need (what he "did not need"—Ustinka could not really understand herself). Ah, if only they could all be reassured and comforted—Aleksandr and Wilhelm and the unhappy Pushkin. What had come to them all was a kind of madness. They were all homeless and wild.

Wilhelm came in. Ustinka quickly hid the letter in her bosom. She did not have the strength to show it to him, she was afraid of bursting into tears.

V

It was time to leave. Shortly afterward, an accident happened to Wilhelm, and, as a result, his departure from the countryside began to look like flight. One day, passing by the neighboring estate, he saw a bizarre picture. There was a strange object by the fence, black and shining in the sun. Flies were buzzing around it. A man in a green frock coat with a whip in his hand stood nearby.

Coming nearer, Wilhelm noticed that the black object was tied to the fence with ropes, and he heard a groan. The man in the frock coat looked at him calmly. Wilhelm stopped his horse. The black object stirred and said hoarsely:

'Water, for the love of Christ!'

Wilhelm shuddered and asked, uncomprehendingly:

'What's this?'

The man in the green frock coat grinned.

'Not what, but who, dear sir. May I ask to whom I have the honor of speaking?'

Wilhelm introduced himself, still totally uncomprehending.

'And I'm your neighbor, a landowner of the Dukhovshchina district,' the man said, quite pleasantly and gave his name. He was about fifty years old, portly, with a clean-shaven wholesome pink face. 'What fine weather we are having today. Are you out for a ride?'

Another groan. Wilhelm came out of his stupor and asked:

'What's a Negro doing here? Why is he tied up?'

'Forgive me, dear sir,' the landowner chuckled, 'where do you see a Negro? This is Vanka. Except, as you can see, he is being punished for a misdemeanor. With tar, you see . . . This will teach him a lesson.' The landowner's eyes began to dart about, then grew blood-shot, and he squeezed the whip.

Wilhelm finally understood. He rode up to the fence and dismounted. Silently, he took a knife from his pocket and cut the ropes.

'For God's sake! What the hell is this?' The landowner grew alarmed. 'What right have you?'

Wilhelm was clutching a metal whip, slender but very heavy. Not feeling the earth beneath his feet, he stepped toward the landowner. The black figure slowly crawled away across the grass. Wilhelm raised his whip high and lashed the smoothly shaven face with all his might.

'What right?!' he muttered plaintively, 'what right?!' and he lashed again and again.

The landowner screamed wildly—and immediately there was a noise of hooves, a whooping, and a barking of dogs.

'Tally-ho! Halloo!'

Wilhelm jumped onto his horse.

Two days later Grigory Andreyevich was visited by the district marshal of the nobility. He informed Grigory Andreyevich that the offended nobleman would not leave the matter like this, that he had powerful friends in St. Petersburg, and that no matter how regrettable the marshal of the nobility found it, he, for his part, must not only condemn the actions of Mr. Küchelbecker as unworthy of a gentleman but must take appropriate measures.

Glinka said icily:

'And can you tell me what measures you intend to take against the torture of human beings who are smeared with tar? I take it these actions too are unworthy of a gentleman?'

The visitor spread his hands:

'My work is done, Grigory Andreyevich. I have called to warn you out of respect. And permit me to offer Mr. Küchelbecker a piece of advice: he'd be better off leaving our province, at least for a while. Otherwise he could find himself in real trouble, and this is not only my opinion but the governor's too.'

'Allow Mr. Küchelbecker and myself to be the judges of that.'

On learning about this conversation, Wilhelm decided that there was no need for him to continue enjoying Grigory Andreyevich's hospitality.

The following day he packed his things and left. It was time to put his life back on track, the life that stubbornly did not want to get better. Semyon went with him.

Sons Of The Fatherland

I

How did it happen that he had not entered the service, had not advanced in literature, had not carved out a solid position for himself, and had finally sunk to doing hack work for Grech and Bulgarin's journal?

In the same way as everything else happened in Wilhelm's life—of its own accord. His miscellany, into which he had poured not only his talent but his heart and soul, brought him only journalistic invective, debt, and a conviction that one could not live by the pen. Wilhelm did not even have a clear idea of how and on what money he had lived for the last year and a half. For the first six months after his return from the countryside he had lived in Moscow. Because of Dunya. Encounters with Dunya were brief and somewhat sad: both her mother and her aunt immediately guessed the intentions of the dangerous young man who possessed nothing but an eccentric appearance and a bad reputation. They treated him with great courtesy but took care (fairly successfully) that the young man should not be left alone with Dunya. He could not find a position in Moscow. He paid visits to Prince Pyotr Andreyevich Vyazemsky, who found his extreme opinions quite striking. Vyazemsky looked with his clever eyes at the eccentric young man, put in a word on his behalf, wanted to arrange for him to publish a journal, but then gave up, and would say to his acquaintances:

'There's nothing for him in Moscow. He needs to earn a crust of bread and here they don't put bread in the mouths of men with his looks and his unfortunate character—bashful and neurotic.'

And he added regretfully:

'There is nothing congenial about him, though there is much that is worthy of compassion and respect.'

And Wilhelm moved to Petersburg.

He and Semyon settled with his brother Misha at the officers' barracks of the Guards Company. There was nowhere else to lodge. Misha, stern and taciturn, had a tender regard for Wilhelm. He did not blame him, he knew that life was not easy for him. Sailors often visited his brother and Wilhelm would talk to them—saying that life couldn't go on like this. Stern Arbuzov with his red, weather-beaten face spoke sharply to him:

'Just you wait. No sooner had Cagliostro turned up at Louis's court than the physician Guillotin invented his machine. Here in Russia instead of Cagliostro we have a dozen monks and Madame Krüdener, so we shall have a dozen Guillotins.'

Wilhelm listened to him with pleasure. Misha was often visited by two petty officers, Dorofeyev and Kuroptev; one was sharp and high-spirited, the other squat, smug, and precise in speech. Wilhelm spoke with them about village life, recalled Zakup—Kuroptev was from the Smolensk region; both sailors had been on long voyages but still could not forget country life.

Dunya wrote him short, cheerful letters and did not lose heart. But there was no money, there was no position, and unlikely to be one. He wanted to make his way to Pushkin in Odessa; kind Vera Vyazemskaya, the wife of Prince Pyotr Andreyevich, felt sorry for Wilhelm as a woman would and pestered the Odessa officials on his behalf, but they just shrugged their shoulders:

'What are you talking about? Is that the one who was abroad and had a scrap with someone at Yermolov's? We've enough trouble here with Pushkin.'

Poverty stared Wilhelm in the face. Ustinya Yakovlevna would occasionally come to see her son, stroke his head for a long time with her old silky hand and ask him no questions. Wilhelm knew that once again she would put on her old-fashioned dress and go to see Barclay de Tolly, and again talk about her son, and again get no response.

He was tired of all this. Sometimes the thought of Greece came back to him, but it all seemed so distant, as if some other person, not he, but his younger brother or friend, had once intended to run off there. Now it seemed so difficult.

In April 1824 Byron died in Missolonghi and with him, Wilhelm and Pushkin's youth. Wilhelm wrote an ode on his death. In that ode he remembered Pushkin and challenged him to respond in verse.

And in this holy hour, who is the one
Who has no thought of rest or sleep?
Alone in the night, soundless and deep,
Plunging in dusk's transparent dun,
Under the star-choir, above the sea
He wanders, gazing fervently.

The bard, beloved of the Russians
In the land of Ovid's lone exile,
Is gripped by wordless inspiration,
And dream-like visions fill his eyes.
On a steep cliff he sits alone and pores,
And far beneath his feet the Euxine roars.

At that time Pushkin was leaving his southern exile for a new confinement: his village near Pskov. He was saying good-bye to the sea and also writing verse in memory of the poet whose work evoked both the sea and their youth.

Wilhelm often thought of Pushkin. When he met with Delvig, they remembered the Lycée.

Delvig was currently in love with Sophie and composing sonnets to her. He was cheerful when she was kind to him, and if Wilhelm found him sad, it meant they had had a tiff. He talked a lot to Wilhelm about Sophie, using him as a confidant as in the old days.

Wilhelm no longer visited Sophie, did not see her, did not even think about her, but still could not help being vaguely annoyed with Delvig's stories. He could not put his finger on what exactly annoyed him but when Delvig left, Wilhelm would sit long at his desk, the tobacco ash piling up on his manuscripts.

Once Semyon handed Wilhelm a black envelope. The mourning letter informed him of the death of Sophia Dmitriyevna Ponomaryova, as once before.

And again, just as on the occasion when Sophie had played a trick on him, he dressed in black and went to her place. Again, as then, an ornate coffin was placed on a platform in the middle of the room and Sophie was lying in it; but her face was wax-like, surrounded by incense smoke, and the priest was praying for the soul of God's servant Sophia. How far off all that was. It was an unknown woman lying in the coffin. Pink Panayev stood next to Wilhelm, sobbing hard, and Gnedich, upright as a statue, stared with his one eye at the dead woman like a sad bird of prey. Someone groaned nearby. Wilhelm saw Delvig. He cried, sobbed, then stopped, took off his glasses, wiped them, wiped his eyes—and burst into tears again. Wilhelm embraced him and quietly led him away. Delvig glanced at him distractedly and said, for some reason smiling:

'Well, Wilhelm? Life has passed, it's gone. Funny, isn't it?'

II

That was when Nikolay Ivanovich Grech and Faddey Venediktovich Bulgarin got their claws into him. Since they had started publishing a journal together, they had become inseparable. The two showed up everywhere—Grech, small and wary, dry, with a yellowish face, and Bulgarin, burly, red-faced, with plump lips. They did not trust each other. Bulgarin was obviously afraid of Grech and would say, bowing his head to one side and pressing his hand to his heart:

'He's a real blackguard, is Nikolay Ivanovich! Sell me out for a farthing, he would!'

As for Grech, when there were troubles at the journal, he would say, mysteriously taking the person he was speaking to by a button:

'It's all Faddey's fault. How can he in his ignorance understand literary subtleties? But what can I do? We are colleagues. And I have a family to feed.'

Grech's eyes looked sharply from behind his glasses. This father of a family had a good understanding of people. He saw into a man at once and either let him go or took him under his wing, and after a while the man would find himself obliged to him. And Nikolay Ivanovich would say with a magnanimous gesture:

'Don't mention it, it's a trifle!'

The trifles, however, were rarely forgotten. A year later, the person in question was up to his eyes in debt to Nikolay Ivanovich, and Nikolay Ivanovich had noticed that such people would work day and night.

Nikolay Ivanovich was a zealous liberal. He often said to Wilhelm, looking enigmatically through his horn-rimmed spectacles:

'Is *Son of the Fatherland* really the kind of magazine that is needed right now? I realize, dear Wilhelm Karlovich, that it is not what we currently need. But when things change,'—Nikolay Ivanovich lowered his voice mysteriously—'and there is no longer any censorship, *Son of the Fatherland* will be as it should be.'

Nikolay Ivanovich had influential acquaintances, but he did not like to talk about all of them. So, out of modesty, he was tight-lipped about his friendship with the highly esteemed Maksim Yakovlevich von Fock. As a matter of fact, Maksim Yakovlevich was the director of the special chancellery of the Ministry of Internal Affairs, which was a "department" in name only, being essentially the secret police. Maksim Yakovlevich was not now in favor, secret affairs being conducted by Vogel, the chief spy of the military Governor-General Miloradovich. All this was due to the machinations of Arakcheyev. But Maksim Yakovlevich was biding his time and did not give up. He did not abandon his operations. Vogel was a simple man, with narrow horizons. Maksim Yakovlevich was waiting for his hour to come, meticulously conducting operations off his own bat, just in case.

Maksim Yakovlevich had a great appreciation of Russian literature. Russian writers were essentially splendid people. In addition, Nikolay Ivanovich Grech was, among other things, a brilliant conversationalist. State officials would often lock themselves in his office with the fascinating Nikolay Ivanovich and waste their time talking to him. The main quality that the good-natured Maksim Yakovlevich valued in the irritable Nikolay Ivanovich was the subtlety of his literary observations. How many curious, air-borne threads became tangible in talk between the two friends! And after Nikolay Ivanovich had left, Maksim Yakovlevich would sit pondering for a long time, and a new report under a special number would be added to his neat folders. Collegiate Assessor Wilhelm Karlovich Küchelbecker was not overlooked in those reports.

But *Son of the Fatherland* could not have existed without Faddey Venediktovich. Nikolay Ivanovich was far too irritable. Faddey

Venediktovich was the opposite. He even came across as sincere. Red-faced, wheezing, forever wiping sweat from his forehead, Faddey was a good sort. He complained so amusingly about his "*tante*," the famous mother-in-law, that you had to laugh. He slapped his companion on the knee, giggled, wheezed, and chattered incessantly. His stories were full of lies, and he admitted it himself, but he lied so much that he often happened to hit on the truth. In some people Bulgarin aroused a feeling of almost physical disgust, as if they had stumbled upon some kind of slime, some kind of a sticky jellyfish. Bulgarin was afraid of such people, squinted at them with his moist blue eyes, and behaved particularly obsequiously. So it was with Pushkin. But others were drawn to Bulgarin. This slovenly, fat man, once a traitor (Bulgarin had served in Napoleon's army), who had been destitute in his youth (Bulgarin liked telling the story of his begging alms on the streets), attracted people, as a big, old frayed sofa, tattered and swarming with bugs but still soft, attracts a tired traveler at a coaching-inn. Everything was mixed in him in equal measure: sincerity and lies, complete lack of dignity and good nature, but his main trait was thoughtlessness. Bulgarin's irresponsibility was boundless. To betray a friend and steal from him was not a problem for him, because an hour later he would quite genuinely forget about it. On occasion he happened to do good deeds out of sheer thoughtlessness. His good-naturedness drew Griboyedov and Ryleyev to him; his thoughtlessness attracted Wilhelm.

And there was a strange thing—Wilhelm was a duellist; death did not scare him; he had the reputation of a madman and had proved it many times over; the slightest, even apparent insult drove him into a rage; but a secret weakness took hold of him when Grech pierced him with his tiny eyes and smiled at him, or the spluttering Bulgarin began to pat him on the knee. Before them he was defenseless.

When Wilhelm had reached the brink of destitution, Grech paid him a visit. He chided him for failing to reveal his situation to his friends, promised to get him a job, some tutoring, and fulfilled his promise. He modestly refused any thanks. Bulgarin patted Wilhelm on the knee, wheezed, laughed, and eventually it turned out that Wilhelm had to put a lot of work into Grech and Bulgarin's journal while still remaining short of money. He spent days on end writing reviews, correcting proofs, and editing. Finally, Nikolay Ivanovich suggested that Wilhelm move to his place. Wilhelm thought, looked around his unappealing "monk's cell," as he called his room (Grech called it a "lair"), checked with Semyon, and agreed. He moved to Grech's in Bolshaya Morskaya Street.

Nikolay Ivanovich called his apartment a "family ark." The ark might have been luxuriously refurbished, but the back rooms, in which the seven pairs of "clean animals" were mainly huddled, were untidy and uncomfortable. Nikolay Ivanovich had a passion for luxury, and yet his apartment was that of an average clerk's. One could say that Nikolay Ivanovich had a passion for money too, but he was not good at spending it. And his family was more that of a clerk than that of a man of letters: two daughters—the elder, Sofochka, caustic, canny, and sneering, with cold little eyes, and the younger, Susannochka, scrawny and quiet.

Susannochka avoided Wilhelm and watched him apprehensively as, carried away by the conversation, he tried absent-mindedly to scoop up his soup with a fork and cut the meat with a spoon. But Sofochka watched eagerly: she was enjoying herself. If Wilhelm fell into a reverie over his tea, she would quietly move the mustard toward him instead of the butter, and the short-sighted Wilhelm would spread his slice of bread with it. Wilhelm would flare up, Sofochka would be reprimanded and retire to her room. There she would bury her face in the pillows and burst into silent laughter for minutes on end. In the evening she would take out the little notebook in which she wrote her diary. Her records usually began with pious reflections on the past day, followed by harsh criticism of her female friends, details of the quarrels between father and mother, and astute observations on their strange tenant.

III

There was no money, no position, but, most importantly, there was no air. Everyone was living in a kind of vacuum, waiting for something. Russia was ruled by ignorant monks who fought each other like dogs, the censorship turned down verses where women's smiles were referred to as "heavenly." Arakcheyev's whitish eyes were on the lookout: who is going to cause a disturbance? Can't we straighten the streets, cut down the trees? Can't we turn a slovenly waddling *muzhik* into a soldier dressed in a uniform and marching in step? The military settlements were the new *oprichnina*,[39] which, according to Arakcheyev's thinking, was to replace the old Guard: after the Semyonovsky Regiment's revolt the Guard could no longer be relied upon. In the meantime, these new *oprichniki* were starved, lashed to death, and forced to march until they dropped. There was no conversation, except about riding boots, leather belts, and the correct way of marching. The number of steps per minute in the ceremonial march was strictly determined: no fewer than one hundred and five and no more than one hundred and ten. An ideal order of punishment was introduced.

One morning when passing a parade ground, Wilhelm observed corporal punishment. Twenty soldiers were being punished for some misconduct.

The main thing about the punishment was how orderly it was.

Two half-battalions of soldiers, each with seven hundred men, were drawn up in two parallel lines, face to face. Each soldier held his rifle in his left hand against his foot, and in his right hand a smooth flexible lash, seven feet in length. Seven exactly, neither more nor less. The motionless ranks with lashes in their hands looked like a gray rock formation with a young and leafless willow grove growing out of it. An officer stood in the middle, holding a paper and calling out names—he shouted out how many rounds each offender had to go through. His voice sounded wooden in the morning air. The first five offenders had been stripped to the waist; their heads were bare. They were put in single file, one behind the other; the hands of each of them were tied to a bayonet attached to a rifle; the bayonet was level with his belly, so that the offender could not run forward. Two non-commissioned officers dragged him along by the butt of the rifle so he could not go backward.

There was a sharp drum beat, and then the resonant and clear sound of a flute. Wilhelm felt that he was about to faint. The flute pierced the inhuman silence, the only other sound being the drumming.

And the offenders began to move like the automata under magnetism that Wilhelm had seen in the Leipzig *Kunstkammer*. They moved in a circle, one by one, to the sound of the drum and the clear voice of the flute. Each soldier took a right step forward from the ranks—the lash flew and fell on the offender's back—the soldier took a step back. All the movements were precise and measured, as if a lever were being pulled out of a machine and then going back in. From both sides, in time to the music, the lashes whistled melodiously and simultaneously struck the offenders' backs. Just the voices of the flute, the lashes, and the drumming. And the next five men moving along the green line and crying out before each blow:

'Mercy, brothers, have mercy!'

The officer began to call out names again . . .

. . . Wilhelm came to. He was half-lying under a tree at the edge of the street. The drums were still drumming. A black-haired little man was leaning over him, thin, sallow-faced, with a hawkish nose—Italian? Greek? Swiss? The dirty collar of his shirt caught Wilhelm's eye. There were hundreds of such people—at auctions, in theaters and taverns, on boulevards.

He threw some water in Wilhelm's face and said hoarsely, in French with a German accent:

'Now everything is all right. It'll pass. Nothing serious.'

And vanished.

When Wilhelm rubbed his eyes, the man was gone. And he immediately forgot about him. There were hundreds of such people—in theaters and taverns, on boulevards. Later, remembering the punishment, he forgot about the black-haired man. He recalled him only afterward, a long time later, and even then only for a moment.

What shocked Wilhelm about the punishment was the order, the refinement, the calculation in each movement.

Thinking about it, he would cry out, as if in physical pain.

He could not hate a landlord who smeared a man with tar—he could only beat him up or kill him.

But he hated the beautiful, flexible lashes, the sonorous whistle of the flute, and the measured movements—because he was afraid of them to the point of trembling in his shoes, to the point of utter repugnance.

IV

Only two people could calm Wilhelm down and dispel his gloom: Ryleyev and Sasha Odoyevsky. Each in his own way.

Sasha Odoyevsky was related to Griboyedov; he was a very young Guardsman, blue-eyed and rosy-cheeked. He wore a dapper uniform, and was a smart dresser. He was bursting with energy, unable to sit still for a minute. His thoughts, like those of a child, flew about in complete disarray. He laughed like a child too, with his mouth open, showing his white teeth, and when he laughed the dimples appeared on his cheeks.

He admired pretty much everything: fine weather, good poetry (he himself wrote verse), beautiful women, and noble thoughts. He tried to win Wilhelm's affection, as a calf does his mother's.

Jangling his spurs, he would run in to Grech's, hastily greet his host, who did not like excessive noise and laughter, and begin to pester Wilhelm.

To Wilhelm he confided the secrets of his heart, all of them happy ones. Women liked him.

He would say to Wilhelm:

'And her parents won't say no to me' (Sasha was going to marry every girl he had a fling with). 'I'll visit her family, talk lots, really lots, jangle my spurs—my dear chap, they won't be able to resist me.'

Sasha was fooling about—and he himself knew it: a week later he would forget about his intention to propose and discuss his literary plans with Wilhelm.

His head was clear and he had a good ear. He responded to poems as if they were women and loved them in the same way. And, listening to Pushkin's poetry, he would suddenly become quiet and sad.

He brought bucketfuls of fresh air into Wilhelm's room.

As for Ryleyev, Wilhelm often went to see him in his house by the Blue Bridge, a house belonging to the Russian-American trading company, of which he was secretary. Once at his place Wilhelm came across a merchant, Prokofyev, the director of the company. Prokofyev was an elderly and important person, who looked more like an official than a merchant. Looking at Wilhelm with his quick, darting eyes, Prokofyev said:

'It's high time Mother Russia followed America's example. We are a hundred years behind; we've grown lazy. And why?—just look,' and he nodded toward the window.

Wilhelm looked out. Some soldiers were marching across the Blue Bridge. Their step was measured and precise, their movements mechanical.

Prokofyev said:

'That's why. Instead of a military machine, we need American-style machines.'

Ryleyev shifted from foot to foot, displeased about something. Prokofyev cast him a quick glance and looked embarrassed.

'I do beg your forgiveness,' he said in a merchant's way. Perplexed, Wilhelm glanced quickly at Ryleyev.

'That's how merchants talk these days.'

But Ryleyev immediately changed the subject to literature, to his miscellany, the *Polar Star*. Together with Aleksandr Bestuzhev he was busy publishing miscellanies, which were a great success. Work was in full swing and he never put a foot wrong.

Ryleyev said:

'You have to understand, Küchelbecker, that our miscellanies are a commercial enterprise. You work for Grech and enrich Grech. Writers should join forces and reap the benefits of their work.'

Wilhelm could only gesture helplessly, he had no business skills, his miscellany, *Mnemosyne*, had brought him only losses and debts. He had produced it clumsily, the illustrations were crude, it was full of philosophical articles, while the public loved pocket editions, easy and entertaining verses, and novels with rapidly-moving plots. No, he was no publisher of miscellanies.

Ryleyev was fond of Wilhelm. Probably because of Wilhelm being treated high-handedly by Bestuzhev, because of his wild extravagance, his desperation, his homelessness and his vulnerability. Ryleyev was fond of people who had nowhere to go.

Impatient with self-possessed people, he was calm and affectionate with Wilhelm.

Various people visited Ryleyev. Aleksandr Bestuzhev would come, a black-moustachioed officer and writer with heavy fiery eyes; he was the Duke of Württemberg's adjutant. He wore his dandyish uniform with particular nonchalance and would unbutton his jacket when among friends. He remained aloof and alert, and then cracked jokes, loudly and wittily.

Grech, Bulgarin, and Pushchin were frequent visitors.

Once Ryleyev took Wilhelm to see Pletnyov, a timid writer and a friend of Pushkin. That evening Lev Pushkin was to read Aleksandr's new poem *The Gypsies*. Pushkin's friends adored Lev, or Lyovushka; in

Aleksandr's absence he reminded them of him. But up close the similarity disappeared, except for the abrupt laughter, white teeth, and curly hair, which were similar in both brothers.

Lyovushka recited beautifully, expressively, albeit without declamation, not wailing like Griboyedov or "singing" like Pushkin. In order to persuade him to recite, champagne was required; there was a reason why Lev Pushkin was called Spew by his friends. He was a hopeless drunkard.

After a bottle of champagne had been polished off, Lyovushka looked around at the gathering and began the recitation. Everyone was silent. Lyovushka read the first half. Pushchin was smiling: quite apart from the meaning, Aleksandr's poems gave him an almost physical pleasure. Wilhelm listened eagerly with his hand to his ear. Before the second half, Lyovushka had more champagne.

Deep in your wilderness, disaster
For wandering tents in ambush waits;
Grim passion everywhere is master,
And no one can elude the Fates.[40]

Wilhelm, weeping and laughing, rushed awkwardly toward Lyovushka and hugged him. 'My dear chap,' he muttered, 'you've no idea what you've just read.'

Ryleyev laughed and said quickly:

'It's worthy of Pushkin, naturally. But I've no idea why Pushkin has made such an elevated character as Aleko go around with a bear and beg money. This is base and unworthy of the main character. It degrades him. Better to make Aleko a blacksmith—at least there's something poetic in the blows of a hammer.'

'But it's not Aleko who is the hero here, it's the old Gypsy,' said Bestuzhev pompously, with a grin. 'But what verses! what lyricism! And what a murder scene!'

Ryleyev objected:

'The verses are magnificent, but the beginning is a bit slapdash.'

Wilhelm was beside himself:

'What are you talking about? It's the most simple and sublime work that Aleksandr has ever written.'

He stood in the middle of the room with tears in his eyes, awkward, confused, with twitching lips, and repeated:

> *Grim passion everywhere is master,*
> *And no one can elude the Fates.*

Looking at him, Ryleyev laughed again, softly and tenderly:

'What a delight you are, Wilhelm Karlovich, so young and fresh!'

Küchlya rushed toward him and suddenly embraced him.

Bulgarin hastily scribbled something in his notebook, looking alternately at Ryleyev, Bestuzhev, and Küchelbecker.

V

THE JOURNAL OF SOFOCHKA GRECH
(Excerpts relating to Wilhelm)

April 7, 1825

Konstantin Pavlovich[41] is terribly funny, he pinches my cheek. Krivtsov is a terrible rake and a flatterer. He keeps asking me to elope with him, clearly having a bit of fun at my expense. The other day Papa locked himself in his study for a very long time. In the evening, various people came along, literary men. They all speak very loudly. Ryleyev was the leader; he got so heated in the conversation that it was impossible to listen to him. The freak[42] jumped up and knocked his chair over. It became very noisy, everyone was laughing, but he just stared and kept yelling something, unaware of what was happening.

April 8, 1825

The freak read his poems. Papa made scary eyes at us but he didn't notice and kept on reading. Papa hardly listened to him but when he had finished, he said: 'Oh, that one has come out wonderfully.' He was delighted but Papa hadn't listened at all. At dinner he was pondering over something; I said to him: 'Monsieur Küchelbecker, why are you distracted today?'; he replied: 'Merci, madame, I'm quite full.' I split my sides laughing . . .

July 10, 1825

We have moved to the country. Great fun, there will be music every day. The freak and his servant have dragged themselves along here, too. He ran like mad along the paths, picked a bouquet of maple leaves and put it in water. He wandered all day in the park, talking to himself and waving his hands. Papa looked out of the window, marvelling. I do not understand why he is staying with us. Papa says he is useful.

July 15, 1825

The freak and his servant have left for a week on business to Petersburg. I've been to his room and read his fiancée's letters, some of them very interesting.

July 17, 1825

Serge has become too cocky. He shouldn't think, though, that I can't see through him. I decided to ignore him completely. The freak caused something of a row in the house. He said to Konstantin Pavlovich that at best officials take bribes. K. P. asked: 'And at worst?' 'And at worst,—they take bribes and sell the people out.' K. P. took offense and rose from the table. The freak behaved as if nothing had happened. Papa will scare off all our visitors with his journal. Insufferable!

July 18, 1825

A few entertaining guests came to visit the freak: Baron Delvig and Odoyevsky—I can't find the words to convey how charming he is! They talked and talked, endlessly. Finally they went out for a walk. How Odoyevsky laughs! I think I've fallen in love with him today. Ah, *Alexandre, Alexandre*!

July 20, 1825

The freak, as it turns out, still doesn't recognize me. Yesterday he called me Susanna, and she is ten years old! Today, when he met me in the park, he asked whether I had been long back from Petersburg. I said: 'Long enough.' He said: 'How strange, Maria Aleksandrovna, that we haven't met until now.' Then he bowed and marched past me. What a total oaf! I wonder who Maria Aleksandrovna is?

August 15, 1825

We would like to move back to the city. The weather is foul and it rains all the time. At last Papa has quarreled with the freak! Over literature. They were talking about Katenin and Griboyedov. Papa criticized them very harshly. The freak turned pale and began to shake, said that Papa had no understanding of literature beyond grammar and Karamzin. Papa took offense and said that he might not understand beyond Karamzin but that the freak had not gone far beyond Derzhavin. The freak said that he couldn't wish for any higher praise but papa was extremely affronted, and today he said that it was impossible to get on with the freak any more and even that he is a dangerous person. *Tante* Elise said that papa would get himself into trouble with people like the freak: just the other day she was told that the freak has been followed on orders from St. Pbg. What on earth is happening in this house!

August 18, 1825

All day yesterday the freak read Hoffmann's *Sandman* to us. Very scary. He reads well, even though he stumbles and drawls. I was too frightened to sleep all night. When the freak is in a good humor, he entertains the whole household; he was telling us a lot about his travels today. *Tante* Elise even said that he seems a decent person though he is mad as a hatter.

August 20, 1825

We are moving soon. The weather is awful, Papa has a lot to do in the city. The freak made everyone laugh. He bought a huge bouquet of flowers, presented it to me, and showered me with compliments. He was very courteous and kind to me. I even felt sorry for him . . .

August 27, 1825

One row after another. *Tante* Elise told Papa that she would stay with us no longer, if it went on like this. All because of the freak. Rows with Faddey Venediktovich. Faddey is terribly amusing, though rather *mauvais genre*. He sits all the time with a tankard of porter, puffs his pipe, and cracks jokes. He took it into his head to play a trick on the freak. And the freak is very touchy. He said to the freak: 'You, Wilhelm Karlovich, have not changed in ten years, you scolded me last year, and now you are scolding me again. You are full of youthful ardor.' And he patted him on the knee. The freak stared at him and said: 'Changing and cheating are not my business.' Faddey even dropped his pipe and wheezed at him: 'What are you hinting at?' And he blushed and said: 'I'm not hinting but saying straight out that changing one's opinions and being a turncoat are both a bad business.' Faddey even started crying, there were tears in his eyes, and he said: 'Do you really believe I am a traitor, W. K.?' The freak seemed to feel sorry for him and said: 'I'm talking about changing one's opinions, not betraying one's homeland.' And the other got even more offended, jumped up, went all red, and said: 'Well, don't forget your words, W. K., one day we'll have a reckoning. You've forgotten what I did for you.' And the other got angry again and said: 'I forget nothing, F. V., and I have gone so far as to mention you in my review of current writing.' When the freak left, Faddey said to Papa: 'As you wish, Nikolay Ivanovich, but I won't let this mad idiot work on the journal any more.' Papa tried this and that and just managed to persuade him in the end.

VI

After the rainy summer came a very fine autumn. Wilhelm was tired of living at Grech's; he was once again nursing the plan of a journal. One day he ran into Sasha Odoyevsky on Nevsky Prospekt, and Sasha suggested straight away:

'Wilhelm, you are alone and I am alone. Heart speaks to heart, let's lodge together. What is there for you to do at that grammarian Grech's?[43] And if it were only Grech alone, but there are the Grechess and the Grechlings as well. Make your escape!'

He laughed loudly.

'Move in with me, I have a good place. Two empty rooms. And you know what?' Sasha seized Wilhelm's hand ecstatically, 'let's get on with it. Move in tomorrow. I'm assuming you don't have too many possessions.'

Wilhelm had no time to think as the cabman drove them to Grech's, where Sasha took charge of getting his belongings packed up. Next day Wilhelm moved into his place.

Sasha's rooms were spacious and bright, though not richly furnished. He lived at the corner of Pochtamtskaya Street and St. Isaac's Square. They had a full view of the square. It was spoiled by the scaffolding, building materials, and stones piled up untidily for the construction of St. Isaac's Cathedral.

Sasha spent little time at home; he was, as usual, in love, or spent his days paying visits. Coming back at night, he would get Wilhelm out of bed and talk to him, arguing endlessly, with such a look on his face as if the world order would suffer if he waited until morning. He was barely twenty-two and had about two hundred years of life ready to be lived. He was a poet and wrote melodious light lyrics, which came to him quite easily, whereas Wilhelm sometimes spent whole nights composing. Sasha would reflect, his eyes would darken, he would pace from corner to corner, smoothly conducting with his right hand, then he would sit down for half an hour, and run to read Wilhelm his new poem. Their affection for Griboyedov brought Wilhelm and Sasha closer together. Griboyedov was related to Sasha, and Sasha loved him and from childhood had always been rather in awe of him.

He said to Wilhelm:

'He is breathtakingly insolent, you know. Once at the theater I heard him practically calling the chief of police an idiot. And so gracefully that the latter couldn't say a single word in reply.'

Wilhelm told him, regretfully but condescendingly:

'You judge him superficially, dear chap.'

His friends from the Guards often gathered at Sasha's. He was a good sort, well-liked in the regiment. Punch and champagne put in an appearance; there was a lot of noise. Sasha loved singing and they sang a lot at his place. They would begin with 'The Nightingale':

Nightingale, my nightingale,
Sweetly singing nightingale!
Whither, whither do you fly?
Where will you sing all night?

Wilhelm loved the song—Delvig had written the lyrics with Pushkin in mind. The sweetly singing nightingale was Pushkin. Wilhelm tried to sing along, though not quite in tune. Then they would switch to more cheerful songs:

All gendarmes are scratchers of backs,
All the schools are bloody barracks . . .

And Sasha stamped his foot:

Prince Volkonsky, chief of staff,
Is a pansy—what a laugh!

Cards would appear, but Odoyevsky was not a serious gambler, he soon became bored, and the moustachioed Shchepin-Rostovsky, a tough and experienced player, would get annoyed with him:

'Hold on, old man, why go right, when you need to go left? It's no fun playing with you.'

By the morning they would be tired and gloomy, and Sasha, serious and pale, would blare out a hymn like the *Marseillaise*, the one for which Katenin, after composing it, had been exiled to his village for the last four years:

O villain, our homeland groans,
Beneath your shameful yoke.
If tyranny oppresses folk,
We shall topple tsars and thrones.

And at the end everyone bellowed together with Wilhelm doing his best to be the loudest of all:

To be unfettered, to be free
That is how we wish to be!
Rather die than live as slaves
That's the oath for you and me.

Living at Sasha's was so much more fun than at Grech's.

VII

Wilhelm was penniless, his clothes grew tattered, and he would often spend a long time sighing at nights. Sasha knew what made Wilhelm sigh, as the sighing sessions coincided with the arrival of letters from Moscow: Wilhelm had a fiancée whom he did not wish to condemn to poverty. Sasha had money, but Wilhelm would not borrow from him and on one occasion had already quarreled with him seriously about it. Meanwhile, relations between Wilhelm and Grech had recently deteriorated. As for Bulgarin, he did everything he could to hound Wilhelm out of the journal, publishing him only at the insistence of his friends, and Wilhelm was left without even pocket money, living on breadcrumbs. The situation was desperate.

One morning, Wilhelm and Sasha were drinking tea. The door-bell rang. Semyon announced:

'Wilhelm Karlovich, there's a man to see you.'

An elderly servant came in, bowed, asked if Collegiate Assessor Wilhelm Karlovich Küchelbecker lived here, and proffered him a package:

'From Pyotr Vasilyevich Grigoryev.'

Wilhelm asked:

'From whom?'

The man repeated the message.

Wilhelm said: 'Never heard of him,' and opened the package.

A bunch of banknotes flew out. Wilhelm stared at them open-mouthed.

He began to read the note, and an expression of amazement appeared on his face.

Sasha asked:

'What is it?'

'I don't understand a thing,' Wilhelm turned his staring eyes at him. 'Read this.'

The letter, written in an old-fashioned script by a trembling hand, apparently belonging to an old man, went like this:

Dear Wilhelm Karlovich:

Your late father was my benefactor, and for a very long time I have owed him a thousand rubles. Various circumstances deprived me of the opportunity to repay the debt. Now I am paying back to you the aforementioned one thousand rubles and most humbly implore you, Wilhelm Karlovich, my dear sir, to accept the assurances of true respect with which I have the honor to be faithfully yours,

Your humble servant Pyotr Grigoryev

St. Petersburg
September 20, 1825

Sasha said cheerfully:

'I say, what a terribly noble act!'

Wilhelm shrugged:

'I have no knowledge of any Grigoryev.'

'So what if *you* don't know him, your father must have.'

'Never heard the name mentioned in the family.'

Wilhelm thought, looked at the elderly servant with suspicion, and said to him:

'I cannot take this money. I don't have the honor of knowing Pyotr Vasilyevich.'

The servant calmly replied:

'I've been ordered to leave the money with you. That's all I know about it.'

Wilhelm looked around restlessly, still pondering the matter.

'No,' he protested suspiciously, 'no, it must be a misunderstanding.'

Sasha objected:

'What misunderstanding? The package is quite clearly addressed to you.'

'I don't understand,' murmured Wilhelm.

Sasha looked at him with innocent eyes:

'I would advise you, Wilhelm, not to offend the person who's done this noble deed by refusing, but to accept.'

Wilhelm looked at him intently:

'You're right, Sasha, thank you so much. He would certainly be offended. I should visit him and give my reasons.'

'Where does your master live?' he asked the servant.

'At Chikhachev's house in Serpukhov Street,' said the servant, avoiding his gaze.

'And when is he usually in?'

'Every morning till nine o'clock,' the servant replied, after a little thought.

Wilhelm said:

'Thank your master, my dear chap, and tell him that I shall call on him first thing tomorrow.'

The servant made a low bow and left.

The very next day Wilhelm set off to visit Grigoryev.

He returned home late, totally baffled.

'I couldn't find him,' he said to Sasha, confused.

'Really?' Sasha sounded surprised.

Wilhelm waved his hand desperately:

'I went the entire length of Serpukhov Street, there's no Chikhachev's house in it. I called a policeman and went around the entire quarter with him, and the Izmaylovsky quarter too. No luck.'

Sasha, a little perplexed, said 'Fancy that!' or words to that effect.

Wilhelm paused and shrugged:

'A hell of business this is. I've no idea what to do with the money. I can't consider it mine. I've decided to place a notice in the *Journal*.'

Two days later a notice from Collegiate Assessor Wilhelm Karlovich Küchelbecker appeared in the *St. Petersburg Journal*, in which the mysterious incident of the thousand rubles in banknotes was described in detail. Mr. Grigoryev's act was described as honorable and honest, but at the same time Grigoryev was informed that if he really wanted Küchelbecker to consider the money his, he had to notify him at once of his whereabouts and explain himself personally to him.

Pyotr Vasilyevich did pay him a visit.

He looked like some kind of scribe with a foxy face and pale eyes, and Wilhelm even thought that he smelt slightly of vodka, but immediately dismissed this unworthy thought.

Pyotr Vasilyevich referred to him affectionately as a benefactor and the son of a benefactor and took Wilhelm by surprise with his repeated attempts to kiss him on the shoulder.

He was a minor nobleman and thirty years back had been facing a severe punishment for a frivolous act committed by him at a very young age,—Pyotr Vasilyevich shed a tear,—and Karl Karlovich, his late benefactor—Pyotr Vasilyevich lifted his hands in the air, palms upward—had come to his rescue. For thirty years he had owed the sacred debt, and only this year had he been able to repay it.

Wilhelm was deeply touched.

'Except not Karl Karlovich, but Karl Ivanovich,' he corrected the old man. 'Why didn't you supply your true address, Pyotr Vasilyevich?' he asked softly.

Pyotr Vasilyevich pressed his hand to his heart: 'Simply out of shyness, simply because I did not wish to be utterly distressed by remembering my benefactor and my past youth.' And Pyotr Vasilyevich again shed a few tears.

Sasha said nonchalantly:

'When this conversation is over, Wilhelm, I have something important to tell you.'

Pyotr Vasilyevich bowed and left. Wilhelm walked him to the door and shook his hand warmly.

'What an old-fashioned sense of decency,' he said to Sasha, returning. There were tears in his eyes. 'What did you want to tell me, Sasha?'

Sasha's news, however, turned out to be nothing at all.

Wilhelm ordered a dark olive greatcoat with a beaver collar and a silver clasp, had some clothes bought for Semyon, and began to trust more in the goodness of life: one could still live in a world where there were such honest people as this funny old man, this ancient Pyotr Vasilyevich.

To the end of his life he never learned that Pyotr Vasilyevich was not Pyotr Vasilyevich at all, but a mere Stepan Yakovlevich, an old clerk; that Karl Ivanovich had lent him no money, nor had he known him at all; that Stepan Yakovlevich had sent no money whatsoever to Wilhelm; that he was tearful on account of his propensity to hard liquor and had been hired for the small sum of two rubles by Odoyevsky to play a small part, which he successfully performed; that the servant was not Grigoryev's but belonged to Pushchin's brother, Misha, and that the real Pyotr Grigoryev was made up of three persons: Odoyevsky, Pushchin, and Delvig, who relished the entire romantic farce and had a good long laugh when Odoyevsky impersonated Pyotr Vasilyevich attempting to kiss Wilhelm on the shoulder.

Sasha Odoyevsky once asked Wilhelm:

'By the way, do you ever visit Griboyedov's enemy?'

'What enemy?'

Sasha answered solemnly:

'Yakubovich. They fought a duel, you know. He's the enemy of another Alexander too' (Sasha was referring to the tsar). 'A frightening man.'

Sasha enjoyed and respected everything frightening.

Wilhelm became agitated:

'Is Yakubovich here then? I thought he was in the Caucasus.'

'He should be in the Caucasus but has been delayed here. He has some very interesting visitors and it's always fun there. Let's go and see him tonight.'

Yakubovich lived by the Red Bridge on the corner of the Moyka in a spacious, luxurious apartment. The furniture was well-padded, the tables spacious, the sofas comfortable.

He was still the same as ever: tall, with a grim expression on his swarthy face, with the eyebrows meeting on the bridge of his nose, and a huge mustache. A smile hovered over his lips—a sardonic one. His forehead was covered with a black bandage, a Caucasian bullet was lodged there. He welcomed Wilhelm very politely, and all those sitting in the drawing room were delighted to see him. The visitors included Ryleyev, Bestuzhev, several other Guards officers, among them a tall one with a red face, Shchepin-Rostovsky, and even Vasya and Petya Karatygin, Katenin's disciples. Vasya was already a rising star of the Bolshoy Theater, and Petya, with his quick wit and merry sense of humor, promised to be a good vaudeville actor, if not a character one. Grech and Bulgarin were also present. Everyone was in high spirits. There was wine and fruit on the table. Bestuzhev and Shchepin sat in unbuttoned uniforms and smoked long pipes. Ryleyev asked Vasya and Petya Karatygin to recite from some tragedy.

Vasya got up, took the pose of a tragic actor, and began to recite a soliloquy of Vitellius[44] from *The Clemency of Titus*[45] by Knyazhnin. Petya stood opposite his brother—in the same pose. Vasya declaimed in a singing voice, raising it toward the end of the lines and gesticulating at the end of the stanzas:

Oh friends, who took a part in my great vengeance
And put an end to Rome's humiliation,
  Let us strike off our bonds!
Ah! tell me citizens, did you have life
Through many centuries of constant strife,
  With exploits worthy of the gods
Making the kings your subjects outside Rome
Only to bow to tyrants here at home?

Petya immediately folded his arms gloomily on his chest and responded with Lentulus's monologue:

Those who are slaves may kiss his hand,
But he who has a soul
Of true nobility
And is not deaf to heaven's call,
That man, impetuously
And not enduring bondage,
Will tremble in his rage
And hurl his thunderbolt at Titus.

Suddenly he grabbed Sasha's foil standing in the corner and, having deftly drawn it from its scabbard, plunged forward with it:

This sword will make our fellows free,
Our country's savior it will be,
All tyrants to subdue!
If one remains who sheds a timid tear,
Whose heart misgives, depressed by shock and fear,
Who does not feel sufficient burning rage
To brave the irksome glory of the age,
Let him be banished from us at this hour,
And in the tyrant's presence let him cower,
Where this abhorrent traitor will relate
How we have struggled to be great.

Ryleyev was looking at the young men with satisfaction. Yakubovich was puffing his pipe, frowning gloomily. Sasha, agape, was listening to the elevated voices. Petya finished, lowering his voice to a furious whisper:

But he who feels that slavery can't be borne
And views all tyrants with a bitter scorn,
Who'd come with us to glory's shrine,
Let him display before our eyes
The fierce eruption of his sword
And terrify the tyrant lord.

Everybody clapped. Vasya and Petya, suddenly overcome, sat down on the sofa and got up awkwardly, bowing to the applause. Ryleyev paced the room and ran his hand through his hair.

He repeated:

Those who are slaves may kiss his hand.

Bulgarin suddenly said, his lips pouting:

'Plato is my friend, but a greater friend is truth. I do not find much taste here, gentlemen, "fierce eruption"—what kind of expression is that?'

Ryleyev went up to him and said suddenly, coloring up:

'And you, Faddey, have recently found a taste for something else—for kissing the hand. Just you wait, if there's a revolution, we'll chop off your head right on your *Northern Bee*.'

Bulgarin cringed and gave a hoarse laugh:

'Robespierre Fyodorovich, I beg you for one thing only: allow me a mug of porter at the hour of my death.'

They all laughed. Ryleyev forgot about Bulgarin and paced swiftly about the room, thinking something over before turning to Bestuzhev:

'Shall we leave singing to singers? Zhukovsky will manage on his own. We must write satirical songs and circulate them among the people. Tragedy for us, comedy for the people. Neither is a laughing matter. The time for light verse has passed.'

Bestuzhev spoke through clenched teeth, holding a cigar in his hand:

'You won't lure Zhukovsky out of the palace for love or money. He's too busy entertaining the maids of honor with palace Romanticism. Let me recite you something . . .'

He struck a pose, his spurs jangled, and he recited, imitating Zhukovsky, slightly wailing, and lifting his eyes upward:

He changed his shroud for a flunkey's rig,
His laurel wreath for a powdered wig,
And wormed his way as tutor to the palace.
There, bowing to the nobs—alas!
He shakes a lackey's hand so hard . . .
Poor bard!

Grech laughed and clapped his hands:

'Bravo, bravo! It would be great to see this in print. It's alright to publish Khvostov, but anything like this is out of the question.'

Wilhelm asked Yakubovich:

'Will you be staying here for long, Aleksandr Ivanovich?'

Yakubovich shrugged gloomily:

'I'm not the master of my destiny, Wilhelm Karlovich.'

A servant came in and handed Yakubovich a package. Yakubovich raised his black eyebrows, opened it, skimmed the paper, and turned purple.

'Just look at this! An official inquiry as to why I'm not leaving for duty in the Caucasus. They know perfectly well that I'm being treated here for my wound.' He touched his black headband. 'I put my head in the line of fire to serve the tyrant, and my reward is persecution and disgrace.'

He pulled out a crumpled paper from his side pocket: an order of transfer, demoting him from the Guards.

'Only Tsar Alexander and his servant Arakcheyev believe that the Carbonari spring up from nowhere. The tsar creates them himself—with bitter pills like this.'

Ryleyev went up to Wilhelm.

'Wilhelm Karlovich, I have business with you regarding the *Polar Star*. I need to see you tomorrow. Do you have any poems for the journal? We need verses badly.'

December

I

Alexander I died in Taganrog on November 19, 1825.

The surgeon Tarasov performed an autopsy on the body, emptied it, filled it with embalming herbs and aromatic spirits, placed special little cushions filled with ice in the leaden coffin, pulled a dress uniform onto the corpse, and white gloves onto its hands. In this way the emperor could be preserved for a fortnight or even a month.

For several weeks, couriers from Diebitsch and Prince Volkonsky in Taganrog had been relaying one another to Warsaw and Petersburg. Grand Dukes Constantine and Michael were in Warsaw, the old tsarina and Grand Duke Nicholas in Petersburg.

Constantine had not left Warsaw for nine years; he was lieutenant general of the Kingdom of Poland. He had been esconced in Warsaw for good reason. He was the fear and shame of the entire family. Even ten years ago Alexander had been horrified at the thought that the throne would pass to Constantine. The murder of a beautiful Frenchwoman had taken place practically in full view. A carriage arrived for her, a man jumped out and told her that her friend was dying. The Frenchwoman got into the carriage and was taken to the Marble Palace—Constantine's residence. She was dragged up the stairs. Guardsmen protected the entrances. Three hours later, the same windowless carriage rushed the Frenchwoman back to her house. Two *hajduks*[46] carried her out in their arms. Her husband ran out to meet them. The carriage raced off. The Frenchwoman said to her husband: 'I've been dishonored, I am dying.' She was covered in blood. She died on the spot, outside their home. A crowd gathered. The next day the French consul visited the minister of Foreign Affairs. Prince Constantine's adjutant, who was obviously innocent, was arrested. Alexander was tearing his hair out. Crown Prince Constantine, heir to the imperial throne, a hunched ungainly man with a broad pink face and his father's upturned nose, was clearly the murderer.

One day, a young Guards colonel was found murdered at the window of Empress Elizabeth's palace. Rumor had it that the colonel was Elizabeth's lover and that it was the very same Constantine who had killed him. Everyone shunned him. Alexander spoke to his brother with dread and revulsion. And Constantine was sent to Warsaw. His mother addressed him in letters as "dear Konstantin Pavlovich." Soon he started divorce proceedings—a scandal unheard of in the imperial house. His mother took a long time to give her permission. Finally, she agreed to the divorce so that dear Konstantin Pavlovich could marry one of the German princesses. Constantine stayed in Warsaw, whistling and composing an obscene song in which he equated his marriage to a German princess to fire and flood. He openly mocked the family to which he belonged. This frightening man also had a sense of humor. In the end he did divorce and immediately married a Polish woman, Jeanette Grudzinska. He got into an open carriage with her, took the reins in his hands, and, whipping the horses, drove with her first to the Orthodox church and then to the Polish Catholic one. The scandal was again public.

Years went by. He quietened a little, his gaze grew empty and uncertain, he was even more hunched. In Warsaw, he lived in the sulky solitude of a prodigal son. Bestuzhev and Ryleyev nicknamed him "the sorcerer." Maria Fyodorovna and Alexander were even happy about his marriage. It was a pretext to take away the throne from a murderer of whom everyone was terrified. Constantine agreed to abdicate. He remembered his father's death well enough. 'They made a real mess of it, didn't they?' he used to say about it. But his abdication and Alexander's order for the succession to the throne were not made public. The tsar gave the original of the document to Metropolitan bishop Filaret, Filaret put it in a little casket in the Moscow Cathedral of the Assumption, and three copies were kept rather carelessly by the State Council, the Senate, and the Synod. When Alexander was asked about the heir to the throne, he would spread his hands and look up to the sky. He would not publish the manifesto. The document concerning Constantine's abdication was the tsar's testament. He was bequeathing Russia to his youngest brother, Nicholas, as any landlord could bequeath his estate to the younger brother, bypassing the elder one. Why did he delay publication? No one knew. It might well be because Nicholas was detested even more than Constantine.

Nicholas spent two years on campaigns abroad; in the third year he rode all over Europe and Russia and, on his return, assumed command of the Izmaylovsky Regiment. He was stern, cold and withdrawn. His face was pale and inexplicably harsh. In his childhood he had been cowardly and scared of gunfire: he would hide in the summer-house instead of attending shooting lessons. He was always eager to be on top, to be the first on parade, in billiards, in practical jokes and puns. Alexander kept saying to all and sundry that he found the throne a burden, but he feared rivals. He made Nicholas play the pathetic and hollow part of brigade and divisional commander, but Nicholas performed it with unusual zeal. He was a demanding commander and an insufferable head of brigade. As far as he was concerned, military order was the only acceptable order. In his early youth, he was asked to write an essay: "Prove that military service is not the only service appropriate for a nobleman, but that there are other activities equally respectable and useful for him." Nicholas did not write a word and handed in a blank sheet. He treated reviews and parades as welcome relaxation. He would say: 'You have order, strict and unconditional rules, no debates, no know-alls.' For the rest of his life he remembered how once he had come across an officer wearing civilian clothes under a military cloak—which was totally incomprehensible to Nicholas: everything civilian seemed to him suspicious. Sometimes, on the parade ground, he would pick up a rifle and perform the drill so well that the best corporal was hardly likely to equal him. Or he would show the drummers how to drum. And yet he secretly envied his brother Michael and would say that compared to Michael he knew nothing. And the officers wondered among themselves what this brother was like then.

The youngest brother, Michael, had a different approach to drill and witticisms. He liked to play with words and toy soldiers; his puns were a success. Unlike Nicholas, he had no aspirations to be always the best, he simply enjoyed practical jokes and military parades. A steady frontline of marching soldiers would send him into a joyful frenzy. He had the highest notion of hierarchy. The rank of commander of a regiment, of a brigade, and even more so of an army corps, flattered his vanity considerably more than that of Grand Duke. He could not comprehend why everyone in Russia did not do military service. He was a real Guardsman. On parade he was merciless, inspiring awe with a mere glance, but outside the service he liked to be a regular fellow, to make jokes, and to court maids of honor. Nicholas, who lost sleep over Michael's profound knowledge of drill and his puns, gradually distanced himself from him. As for Constantine, he frankly hated Nicholas and taunted him. When Nicholas traveled through Warsaw, Constantine would treat him as emperor. And when Nicholas lost his temper and pointed out to him that it was inappropriate, Constantine would laugh and say: 'It's because you are Saint Nicholas of Myra.'[47] All three brothers were keen on witticisms, puns, and practical jokes.

Nicholas knew about Constantine's abdication and that Alexander had made Nicholas his heir as far back as 1819; Michael learned of it in 1821.

Now Michael was living in Warsaw at Constantine's Belweder Palace. Just one room separated his chambers from the master's quarters. For the last few weeks something had been amiss with Constantine. He was preoccupied, his gray cheeks flashed red, and he paced the rooms for hours, all hunched up. Then, as though swatting away an annoying fly, he would jump to his feet, ruffle his hair, and make a quick exit. Often he did not even join his brother at table for meals. Michael sometimes asked:

'What's the matter with you?'

Constantine would answer reluctantly and abruptly:

'I'm under the weather.'

Michael began to notice that his brother was receiving couriers from Taganrog.

'What does that mean?' he would ask his brother, puzzled.

Constantine answered impassively:

'Nothing of any importance. The tsar has approved the award I requested for various palace officials here.'

In conversation Constantine always referred to Alexander as "the tsar."

On November 25, as night began to fall, Constantine locked himself in his study with the courier who had just arrived. Then the door opened quickly, with a bang, and Constantine cried out hoarsely:

'*Michel*!'

Michael hastily threw on his frock coat and ran to see his brother, who stood hunched and dull-eyed in the middle of the room. There was even a blush on his gray face.

'*Maman*?' asked Michael thinking that his mother had died.

'Thank the Lord, no,' said Constantine, coming to his senses, 'the tsar is dead.'

The brothers locked themselves in the room.

Constantine, pacing the room with large, stiff steps, spoke tersely and looked grimly at his brother.

He had got used to the idea that he was not to inherit the throne, but at the last moment he was still sorry to relinquish it. Power both frightened and attracted him.

Scrutinizing Michael closely and carefully with his dull eyes, Constantine said quietly:

'I have to give it up though. I am not popular. The Guards are in a ferment. I have some reports here. Otherwise I'll have the same fate as my father. I'd better stay in Warsaw, at least it's quieter here. Besides, mama has always been against me.'

Michael replied cautiously, narrowing his eyes:

'And what about the abdication you agreed to some time ago?'

Constantine stopped abruptly in front of him.

'It's unofficial,' he said quickly and rudely. 'The manifesto hasn't been published.'

Michael gave it some thought and asked:

'What makes you think you are unpopular? They've forgotten about you in Petersburg.'

Constantine was pacing the room. Then, as though regaining consciousness, not looking at Michael, he said with a sigh the words he had learned:

'No, I've abdicated and nothing has changed in my intentions. My will is to renounce the throne.'

Michael was weighing things up, pondering, trying to understand. The night passed like that. It was five o'clock. Constantine sat down to write letters to his mother and Nicholas. Two official and two informal, private ones: a long one to mother, a short note to Nicholas. He wrote, crossed out, searching for the most discreet choice of words and expressions. Michael helped him. At the top of the official letter to Nicholas,

Constantine wrote: "To His Imperial Majesty." The letter was evasive. Constantine was *requesting that he remain in the post and rank previously occupied*. And one could remain in the rank of Inspector General of all the cavalry (such was Constantine's rank) even while being tsar. Then, looking at Michael, Constantine said:

'When all's said and done, you'd better take these letters yourself. Get ready to go today.'

He looked up at his brother and said, somewhat vaguely:

'Have a look around.' Then he corrected himself: 'Deliver the letters.'

The morning came. In the morning it was necessary to announce the death of the tsar. Constantine said to Michael hesitantly:

'The people should not know about what has happened. The retinue ought to be informed.'

He called his closest subordinates, who had been in the know for quite a time. The crafty Novosiltsev said in a business-like manner and, as if in error:

'We are here, Your Majesty.'

Constantine pretended not to hear. Without looking at the retinue, hunched up, with red cheeks from a sleepless night, he spoke falteringly:

'The Emperor has passed away. I have lost a friend and a benefactor. Russia has lost her father.'

Constantine never referred to Alexander as his brother.

Then he got carried away. He began to shout out phrases one by one, as if not understanding the meaning of the words:

'Who will lead us to victories now? No one. Russia is lost! Russia is lost!' He got stuck on the last phrase and repeated it mechanically several times.

One of the generals from the retinue tried to curry favor.

He stepped forward and said with a deep bow:

'Your Imperial Majesty, Russia is not lost but, on the contrary, is welcoming . . .'

Constantine began to shake and turned purple. He was utterly terrified. He rushed to the stunned general, grabbed his chest, and shouted furiously:

'Shut up, will you! . . . How dare you say those words!! Who gave you the right to prejudge matters that don't concern you?'

And, stepping back, he grabbed his own head and muttered:

'Do you know what you are exposing yourself to? Do you know that people are put in shackles and sent to Siberia for that?' And having drawn his breath: 'Kindly place yourself under arrest and hand over your sword.'

Michael looked at his brother meaningfully. Constantine suddenly scrutinized them all, bowed his head, and went into his study. Michael followed him.

Count Kuruta, a cunning Greek courtier who was very close to Constantine, said to the bewildered general:

'What does it have to do with you, *mon cher*? If Russia is lost, well, good riddance. Let her be lost! Talk's cheap, but what was there to object to?'

They all laughed.

The same day Michael left for Petersburg.

II

Ryleyev was lying in bed, pale and gloomy, with a compress on his throat. He had just woken up. Yakubovich ran into the room. He did not look himself; his eyebrows were knitted, his expression was wild.

'Ah,' he cried, 'still sleeping? Well, rejoice—the tsar is dead. It was you that robbed me of him!'

Ryleyev jumped up from his bed and asked quietly:

'Who told you?'

'Bestuzhev, he heard from the prince.'

Yakubovich pulled from his side pocket the tattered order demoting him from the Guards.

'I've been wearing this on my chest for eight years, eight years I've been longing for revenge. And now it's all in vain. He is dead.'

He tore up the paper and ran out.

Ryleyev paced the room.

Their entire plan had collapsed.

March 12, 1826 was to have been the twenty-fifth anniversary of Alexander's reign. They had already begun to prepare for that day, the day the imperial review of the third corps had been expected to take place. In 1820 Alexander had transferred the Semyonovsky Regiment to the third corps. The third corps was entirely in Pestel's hands. Alexander was to have been killed on the day of the review. Two proclamations had already been prepared, one for the army, the other for the people. The plan had been for the third corps to advance to Kiev and Moscow. Along the way all the troops seething with indignation would join them. In Moscow, the insurgent troops would demand that the Senate reform the state. The rest of the southern corps would establish itself in Kiev. Simultaneously, Ryleyev and Trubetskoy would lead the Guards and the fleet in revolt, put an end to the whole imperial family and, together with the third corps, would present the Senate in Petersburg with the same demands. Alexander's death had turned everything upside down.

Somebody knocked cautiously at the door.

Trubetskoy entered, slowly and warily.

He was quiet and discreet—two qualities lacking in Ryleyev—as a result Ryleyev thought him strong.

'Well, it's over, His Majesty is no more. They have just sung a liturgy for him: the Guards chief of staff went up to Nicholas and whispered something in his ear. Nicholas crept out and everyone followed him to the palace. They are swearing allegiance to Constantine. All without a hitch so far.'

Ryleyev was still pacing the room, his hand pressed to his forehead.

He did not say a thing.

Trubetskoy continued slowly:

'It doesn't matter, though. One main force is the Southern Society. They will rise up; we can expect this any day. From all this you can see that the circumstances are exceptional and critical for our plans. We must be ready.'

He left shortly afterward.

Ryleyev sat on the bed, leaning his elbows on his knees and resting his head between his hands.

Another knock at the door. Nikolay Bestuzhev came in.

Rapidly and breathlessly, he said to Ryleyev:

'Don't you know the tsar is dead?'

Ryleyev struggled to speak:

'I know, Yakubovich and Trubetskoy have just been here.'

Bestuzhev walked around the room, wringing his hands:

'Well done, all of us, well done! The tsar has died and we learn about it almost from the manifesto.' He put his hands to his head. 'We're doing nothing! No one knows anything, no one cares.'

Ryleyev was still silent. Then he said slowly, swaying as if in physical pain:

'Yes, this just shows us our powerlessness. I got things wrong. There is no plan in place, no measures taken, and very few Society members in Petersburg.'

Then, biting his lip and wrinkling his forehead, he began to think.

Finally, he got up and stood up straight.

'We must act. We can't afford to miss such an opportunity. I'm going out fact-finding.'

He ran his hand over his forehead and looked intently, almost calmly at Bestuzhev:

'Return immediately to your units. Assess the state of mind in the army and among the people.'

Another knock at the door. Aleksandr Beshuzhev came in.

'Proclamations, we must write proclamations to the troops,' he said, panting, barely nodding, and not greeting anyone.

They sat down to write the proclamations.

On the same day Trubetskoy was elected dictator.

From that morning on, the door to Ryleyev's apartment was never shut. It was the main headquarters of the uprising.

III

Miloradovich, the Governor-General of Petersburg, was a Serb, stocky, gray-haired, with quick little black eyes and a hoarse military way of talking. These days there were two people in charge of the imperial throne: Maria Fyodorovna and himself. Since the day when Emperor Paul had been strangled, Maria Fyodorovna had considered herself the guardian of the throne. She continued to reject Constantine and believed that the general opinion was that Russia rightly belonged to her third son, Nicholas. It was a domestic matter. According to the late tsar's will, Russia belonged to the one whom the family considered appropriate. Miloradovich thought differently. He went to see Nicholas and said, looking him calmly in the face:

'Your Highness, the Guards are not with you. If you become emperor, I cannot vouch for anything.'

Nicholas turned pale.

'Are you familiar with the order of the deceased sovereign?'

Miloradovich answered calmly:

'The Emperor's order is a domestic matter. Russia cannot be bequeathed. The Guard has already been instructed to swear allegiance to the legitimate heir to the throne.'

An emergency meeting of the State Council was held at two o'clock in the afternoon of November 27. Prince Golitsyn demanded that Alexander's will should be executed. He insisted. He knew that if Alexander's will was not executed, the fate of those close to the deceased tsar was uncertain. Hence his insistence that failure to execute the tsar's will amounted to a state crime. Prince Lobanov-Rostovsky said haughtily:

'*Les morts n'ont point de volontè.*'[48]

Looking with his inflamed eyes at those present and shaking his huge aged head with its shock of gray hair, Admiral Shishkov mumbled:

'Take the oath immediately. The empire cannot be without an emperor for a single instant.'

Miloradovich stood up and shouted hoarsely:

'Nikolay Pavlovich has solemnly renounced the right bestowed on him by the testament. The Russian sovereign cannot dispose of the throne by inheritance.'

Everyone fell silent. A man who had sixty thousand bayonets in his pocket could not be argued with.

Nicholas swore allegiance to Constantine. The government swore allegiance. From that time onward Miloradovich never left Nicholas's side. He followed him doggedly. Nicholas looked at him with hatred, but Miloradovich was his usual self: he dropped little jokes, laughed hoarsely, and did not move a step away from His Imperial Highness. He was unable to see his mistress, a dancer, for a few days and was incredibly absent-minded. He relied too much on the sixty thousand bayonets. They might not, after all, be in his pocket. His secret police were inactive. A very efficient man, Fyodor Glinka, was in charge of secret affairs. He spent his days on Miloradovich's secret papers, and in the evening he went to a familiar apartment near the Blue Bridge—the house of the Russian-American trading company...

IV

Michael galloped furiously. He rushed through Kovno and Siaulie[49] without stopping. Until Mitau,[50] no one knew about Alexander's death. In Olai, while the horses were being harnessed, the aide-de-camp told him:

'Your Imperial Highness, a traveler from Petersburg told me that his Imperial Highness Nikolay Pavlovich, all the troops, the government and the city have sworn an oath of allegiance to Constantine.'

Michael's jaw dropped. Instinctively he clutched the briefcase containing Constantine's letters: "What will happen now? Will a second oath be needed—to another person?"

Michael made the entire journey in four days.

On December 1, at six o'clock in the morning he was already in the palace. He went through hastily to his mother. Nicholas already knew about his brother's arrival and ran out to meet him, but the doors to his mother's chamber were slammed in his face. He clenched his teeth and waited in the hall.

'Well, well, well, *mon cher frère*.'

Michael took a long time to come out; he looked worried. The brothers embraced hurriedly and Nicholas led him to his office. The unshakable Miloradovich went after them.

The courtiers bowed before them one after another, the glances they cast at Michael were quick and keen—they wanted to guess by the expression on his face what news he had brought. Michael assumed a stony expression.

'Is *His Majesty the Emperor* well?' asked Baron Albedyll suavely.

Michael's response was quick enough

'*My brother* is well.'

'How soon can we expect *His Majesty*?' said Benckendorff, peering into his face.

Michael retorted, without looking at him:

'I have heard nothing about a trip.'

'Where is *His Majesty* now?' prattled Count Bludov with a gracious lisp.

Michael said dryly:

'I left *my brother* in Warsaw.'

They went into the office. Miloradovich accompanied them, jangling his spurs, and took a seat in an armchair.

Michael also sat down, shrugged, and frowned.

'What sort of a position have you put me in? Everyone's talking about Constantine as emperor. What am I to do? I've no idea.'

He looked sullenly at Miloradovich and, still frowning, took a letter from Constantine out of the briefcase and handed it to Nicholas.

Seeing the inscription: "To His Imperial Majesty," Nicholas turned pale. He paced the room silently. Then he stopped in front of Michael, stony-faced, and asked flatly:

'How is Constantine?'

Michael glanced sideways at Miloradovich.

'He is sad but steadfast,' he said, emphasizing the last word.

Throwing his head back Miloradovich asked:

'Steadfast in what, Your Imperial Highness?'

Michael was evasive:

'In his resolution.'

At that moment Miloradovich's adjutant stuck his head into the room.

'Your Excellency,' he said to Miloradovich, 'there is a big fire in the Nevsky Monastery, threatening to spread.'

Miloradovich grunted with vexation, jangled his spurs in front of the two brothers, and left.

Michael looked at Nicholas:

'I do not understand you. Does the document exist or does it not?'

'It does,' replied Nicholas slowly.

'Then, having submitted to the Guard, *mon cher frère*, you have formally committed a *coup d'état*. Yes, indeed, without any doubt.'

Nicholas smiled and said nothing for a while.

Then he turned to Michael and lowered his voice:

'Has Constantine definitely decided to abdicate?'

His gray eyes were searching his brother's face.

Michael answered with a question:

'Do you really think that Constantine could succeed to the throne, in spite of the testament?'

Nicholas did not say anything in response, and peered out of the window. Snow was falling, whirling round the square, and sticking to the panes. It was a very quiet, sluggish winter morning.

Michael spread his hands, wondering:

'What will a second oath mean, once the previous one has been canceled? How will it all end? When a captain is promoted to major—it is in the order of things and no one is surprised; but this is quite a different matter,' Michael lifted his finger impressively, 'to skip a rank and promote a lieutenant to a major.'

Translated into military language, the fact seemed to him clearer and more significant.

Nicholas was scrutinizing his brother closely:

'Are you still sure that Constantine seriously doesn't want to?'

Michael shrugged:

'He is not popular.'

Nicholas said hesitantly, without looking at his brother:

'Why are you so worried about the second oath? In the end, it's not that bad. In essence, it's just a family transaction.'

Michel spread his hands purposefully:

'It's hard to explain to everyone, to the army and to the mob, that this is a family transaction, and why it's like this and not otherwise.'

Nicholas thought for a moment.

'This is the crux of the matter,' he said quietly, 'this is the thing. The Guards do not like me.'

'What wretches!' mumbled Michael. 'They like you—they like you not! They like nobody.'

Looking at Michael point blank, Nicholas asked again, in French (when the brothers wanted to be frank, they spoke French, Russian for them was the official language):

'Do you think that Constantine is seriously considering abdicating?'

Looking away, Michael gave a vague gesture.

'How would I know? He has told me nothing. You'll see it in his letters.'

Nicholas sighed and frowned:

'I can't see anything in the letters.'

Michael sat for a while, drumming his fingers, then thought about his own position and spoke heatedly:

'Bloody hell, what a position you've put *me* in! I can't swear the oath to Constantine, or to you either, everyone keeps asking me questions. It's a bloody mess!'

Nicholas did not answer. He was writing a letter to Constantine.

A day passed.

The courtiers were indeed starting to whisper: neither Michael nor his retinue had sworn the oath to Constantine. Something was not right here, even rather sinister. These whispers spread from Michael's entourage to the courtiers and then onward—from one palace to another. And they were threatening to spread from the palaces to the squares.

A courier with a letter from Nicholas was already riding to Warsaw, to Constantine.

Nicholas pleaded with his Imperial Majesty Emperor Constantine to come to Petersburg. His mother wrote to his Imperial Majesty somewhat differently: she requested an official statement either on his accession to the throne or on his abdication. There was no reply from Constantine.

On the morning of December 5, Nicholas spoke anxiously to Michael (he had just had a conversation with Benckendorff):

'Your staying here is becoming really difficult. Constantine is keeping silent. We can't wait a minute longer, or there will be trouble. *Maman* is asking you to go and see Constantine. Yes or no—either he comes here to ascend the throne or—he sends an official manifesto concerning his abdication. It can't go on like this. Leave today. Stop the couriers on the way and open the dispatches—so as not to miss the reply. And now *maman* is asking to see you.'

Michael winced and went to his mother. Maria Fyodorovna's secretary issued him with a certificate:

> The presenter of this open order, His Imperial Highness Grand Duke Michael Pavlovich, my dearest son, is authorized by me to accept in my name and to open all letters, packages, etc. from the Emperor Konstantin Pavlovich that are addressed to me.
>
> Maria

Maman had a long conversation with Michael. Then she embraced him and spoke insistently, raising her index finger:

'*Quand vous verrez Constantin, dites et répétez-lui bien, que si l'on en agit ainsi c'est parce qu'autrement le sang aurait coulé*.'[51]

Michael shrugged sulkily and muttered:

'Il n'a pas coulé encore, mais il coulera.'[52]

The very same day he was on his way back. Just before the barriers, he suddenly stopped the carriage and ordered the two generals from his retinue who had been traveling with him to go no further. He thought:

'Should I go back?'

Then he made an impatient gesture and drove on.

V

As Wilhelm was leaving Ryleyev's, he felt a sudden joy. His heart was beating differently, the snow underfoot looked different. Some people were walking toward him, cabs were driving about. The sunlight poured down on the snow. The chimes rang out at the Admiralty—noon. Half an hour ago Ryleyev had admitted him into the secret society.

People stood crowded by the windows of Smirdin's bookshop. Wilhelm went up to the windows. In one of them two portraits were displayed: one showed a man with a hooked nose and deep-set black eyes, the other one was of a young man with his head thrown back.

"Riego and Quiroga," Wilhelm whispered in surprise. "What a strange coincidence." And in the other shop-window, which was the main attraction for the public, there was a large portrait of Constantine. A ruddy broad face with high cheek-bones, prominent blond side-whiskers, and unfathomable light eyes looked out from the portrait, offensively cheerful. The inscription on the portrait read: "His Imperial Majesty, the autocrat of all the Russias, Emperor Constantine I."

'Looks just like his dear papa,' said a commoner wearing a dark blue coat. 'Same snub nose, same way of looking up at the sky.'

'Never mind the nose, old chap,' said a young merchant. 'You can rule without a nose. It's not a nose you need, my friend.'

An officer in a fur coat glanced at them, smiled, and asked Wilhelm quickly in French:

'Not bad talk for the start of a new reign, don't you think?'

Wilhelm laughed, sighed deeply, and went on his way. Everything was strange that day.

A tall Guardsman walked by, wrapped in a greatcoat and rattling his spurs. He was speaking quickly to a man in a coat with a beaver fur collar. "Maybe they are in it too?" Wilhelm smiled blissfully.

He was dying to see Griboyedov this very moment.

'Oh, Aleksandr, Aleksandr,' he said out loud, not noticing the tears running down his face.

Why was there no Griboyedov, Pushkin, or Dunya at this time on the Nevsky Prospekt?

Wilhelm took a cab and went to see his brother Misha. He had just learned from Ryleyev that Misha had long been a member of the secret society.

He found him sitting there gloomy, silent, business-like, a distant memory of their father flashed through his mind, he dropped his great-coat, ran up, tripping over himself, hugged his brother, and burst into tears.

'Misha, brother, we are together to the end,' he muttered.

Misha glanced at him and smiled shyly. He seemed somewhat ashamed; he avoided his brother's gaze and asked him briefly, without spelling it out, as they had in childhood:

'How long have you been . . . ?'

'Since just now,' said Wilhelm, smiling senselessly.

They were silent for a while. To speak was difficult and seemed unnecessary. They felt happy and just a little self-conscious.

Misha asked his brother with a smile:

'Would you like some breakfast?'

They raised their glasses high and clinked them silently. Wilhelm suddenly remembered:

'I've come on an errand. Ryleyev sent me to ask how things are going.'

Misha became purposeful:

'You can rely on the Company. Dorofeyev and Kuroptev should be here any minute. They are well informed, have a word with them.'

Dorofeyev and Kuroptev were the main agitators among the sailors. They were Wilhelm's old acquaintances. They arrived shortly afterward. Misha asked them cheerfully:

'Well, how's it going?'

Dorofeyev was shifting from foot to foot, Kuroptev looked suspicious.

'You can speak openly,' said Misha, 'my brother's in the know.'

Dorofeyev smiled broadly and said to Wilhelm:

'Really and truly, Your Honor, wherever I look, all the folk are aggrieved. Not to mention us. You know yourself what they say about us: fatherland's guard, wallop him hard; fatherland's pleasure, kick him at leisure, give a sailor a thump, up the ranks you'll jump' (Dorofeyev spoke the ditty quickly and was pleased that he managed to bring it off so casually). 'All the sailors are aggrieved, of course. And the others don't have it so good either. Everyone wants a change.'

Wilhelm rushed up to him and shook his hand. Dorofeyev grew embarrassed and offered his hand woodenly. The hand was hard and calloused.

Kuroptev spoke to Misha with the self-satisfaction of the old seaman:

'Don't worry. I know my battalion like the palm of my hand. We'll all come out if anything happens. Just come and give the order: this is it, lads, quick march to the square—and we'll all do our bit.'

VI

On getting back to his place, Wilhelm found Lyovushka Pushkin there. Spew was sleeping peacefully, curled up on the couch. Odoyevsky was not in. Wilhelm shook him and laughed at his sleepy look.

'Lyovushka, dear friend.' He embraced Lyovushka.

What a wonderful person Lyovushka was!

Lyovushka looked around in wonderment: he had been waiting for Wilhelm, he had been in his cups the previous night, and had fallen asleep on the couch.

Then he remembered why he had come and impassively took a paper out of his pocket:

'Wilhelm Karlovich, Aleksandr has sent a few poems—there is one about you. He asked me to pass them on.'

Six weeks earlier, Wilhelm, Yakovlev, Delvig, Illichevsky, Komovsky, and Korf had celebrated the Lycée anniversary, and everyone drank Pushkin's health.

Yakovlev, the man of two hundred tricks, remembered his old pranks and buffooned—great fun.

The sheet of paper that Lyovushka now handed to Wilhelm was Pushkin's poem on the Lycée anniversary.

Lyovushka had long since left, but Wilhelm was still poring over the sheet.

He read slowly and quietly:

To serve the Muse we must have peace
And beauty lives in majesty;

But youth gives us such sly advice,
And we seek joy in noisy dreams.
We wake, but it's all gone! Down-hearted,
We look behind, but it's too late.
Wilhelm, is that not how we started,
Dear brother in the Muse and fate?

He noticed his voice turning into a whisper and his lips twisting; he was struggling to read and by now was scarcely understanding the words:

It's time, it's time! We waste our labor
On the world's business. Let it end!
Let's hide our lives in deep seclusion!
I'm waiting for you, tardy friend . . .

He burst into sudden tears, like a child, immediately wiped them away, and paced the room. No, no, and this too had already passed. There would be no seclusion, no rest. They had settled the scores with their youth—it had passed, disappeared, disintegrated, and only Pushkin was left of it. And him Wilhelm would never forget. It was over.

Evening came. Semyon entered and lit the candles.

VII

Letter from Wilhelm to Dunya

My Dear Beloved,

You write that you are going to Zakup at Christmas. What pleasure this news gives me! Oh, what I would give to be with you again, to walk in the grove and ride past Zagusino! But enough. Until recently I have been a plaything of fate, only now comes a decisive hour for me.

We shall be happy. My head is turning gray, my heart is full of you, and in everyone's life there comes a time when he must say in the words of old Luther: here I stand and I can do no other.

I'm closer to happiness than ever before. You are my joy.

Your Wilhelm

Everything before you was just a delusion.

VIII

Nikolay Ivanovich was greatly surprised to find Wilhelm out of hours at his print works. When he spotted Nikolay Ivanovich, Wilhelm quickly hid some proofs in his side pocket. The typesetter looked nervous.

Wilhelm muttered:

'Funny thing, Nikolay Ivanovich, I've misplaced my article of last year, I need it now, and I've been looking for a proof.'

Nikolay Ivanovich shrugged:

'Wasn't it printed?'

'It wasn't, actually,' said Wilhelm quickly.

Nikolay Ivanovich glanced sideways at the typesetter, then at Wilhelm, took Wilhelm aside, and said in a whisper:

'I saw nothing, I know nothing, I guess nothing.'

Wilhelm shook his head and ran out.

With piercing eyes Nikolay Ivanovich watched him leave. Not merely the proof of the article but the actual proclamation was in Wilhelm's pocket. Grech had frightened him off, and he had had no time to reach an agreement with the typesetter.

Wilhelm was spending his nights in an unusual way now. Ryleyev, and Aleksandr and Nikolay Bestuzhev had told him one day of their plan: to talk to soldiers at night, to stir them up. They had already been walking about the city for three nights. They stopped every soldier they met, talked to every sentry. Wilhelm began to do the same. On the first night he was timid, not because he was afraid of running into an informer, but because it was not easy to stop strangers and even more difficult to talk to them.

The first soldier he came across was a tall Guardsman, of the Moscow Regiment, to judge by the uniform. Wilhelm stopped him:

'Where are you going, my dear fellow?'

They were walking through the part of the city where the Izmaylovsky Regiment was quartered.

'To the barracks by the Semyonovsky Bridge. I'm a bit late,' the soldier said anxiously. 'I don't want to get into trouble.'

'That's fine, I'm going that way,' said Wilhelm, 'we'll go together. How are you?'

The soldier looked into Wilhelm's face.

'Not great.' He shook his head and sighed. 'May be better now, under the new emperor.'

Wilhelm shook his head.

'It won't be.'

'How do you know?' asked the Guard and cast a sidelong glance at Wilhelm.

'They're not allowing the new emperor to come to Petersburg. The will of the late tsar is being kept hidden. And in that will the term of your service is reduced by ten years.'

The soldier listened eagerly:

'Could be.'

For five minutes they walked in silence.

'They won't get away with this,' said the soldier, suddenly stopping. 'Can you credit it, hiding a paper like that from the soldiers?'

He was as red as a beetroot.

Wilhelm said:

'Tell your mates. The truth'll be out soon, I daresay.'

'Well, thank you,' said the soldier. 'We just want what is fair. They can't hide that paper from the soldiers.' He stood for a while and quickly disappeared into the darkness.

They were passing the armoury. Wilhelm waited till the soldier was out of sight, then went up to the sentry, asked for a light, and talked to him too.

So for three winter nights soldiers would meet strange gentlemen here and there, one of them was tall and awkward and, by the look of him, a holy fool, but they all knew some truth that was being hidden from the soldiers.

IX

Sunday, December 13, midnight.

In Taganrog, the tsar's physician, Tarasov, raises the heavy cover of the lead coffin with the help of two Guards sentries. He looks closely at the empty corpse. He looks at the yellow face with the dark blue eyelids and black lips.

'Damn it, another stain! I can't vouch for more than another fortnight.'

He takes a sponge, wets it in an aromatic essence, and gently applies it to the temple, on which a little black spot has appeared. Then he looks carefully at the gloves.

'They've turned yellow again!'

He pulls the dusty yellowish gloves off the dead hands, and slowly, unhurriedly, pulls white kid gloves onto the stony fingers. The hand falls back into the coffin with a wooden knocking sound.

The dead man is calm, he can afford to wait another two weeks or even three. He will wait.

At midnight Michael, together with General Toll, his retinue, and Nicholas's couriers they have detained on their way, ride from Nennaal Station to Petersburg.

Michael spent a week at Nennaal, a miserable, remote, log-built station. He intercepted the couriers, opened the messages, and sent them under escort to Petersburg. But there was no decisive message from Constantine. Perhaps he had missed the courier?

Instead of a courier from Constantine, the Petersburg and Moscow messengers came to Nennaal Station, having been sent back empty-handed by Constantine. On the ninth day, the War Minister's adjutant arrived. Constantine had refused the papers addressed to "His Majesty"; he said the adjutant had come to the wrong person; he was not the monarch.

On the night of the 11th to the 12th the ambassador from the Prince of Württemberg arrived with the same message. Constantine had come to see the envoys, given them a dull stare, and got rid of them with a joke. To Demidov, an inveterate gambler sent to him by Prince Golitsyn, Constantine had said, narrowing his eyes: 'Why are you here? I stopped playing dice long ago.'

All of them were detained at Nennaal Station by Michael. He, General Toll, and the adjutants wined and dined well from the traveling cellar. In the end, why not sit it out in this tiny Estonian town far from both brothers, from the courtiers' questions and the agonisingly empty Petersburg squares?

On December 13, just before dinnertime, a courier from Petersburg arrived and delivered a belated order: to appear immediately, at eight o'clock in the evening, at a meeting of the State Council, which would proclaim Nicholas emperor. Nicholas wrote to his brother:

"Finally it's decided: I must assume the burden of being the tsar. Our brother Constantine Pavlovich has written me a most friendly letter: hurry here with General Toll, everything is calm and quiet."

"Friendly letter" meant that Constantine had still not abdicated.

It was 270 *versts* between Petersburg and Nennaal, the courier had left after six o'clock the previous day, the road was bad, and the order was late. They sat down to dinner. Michael talked briefly with General Toll. Toll was serious and taciturn. Looking at Michael almost with compassion, he said:

'Congratulations on an important day for the dynasty.'

'Important or trying, Karl Fyodorovich?' asked Michael. They were speaking French.

Toll shrugged:

'There was only one legal solution. The Senate had proclaimed Konstantin Pavlovich sovereign. He was to come to Petersburg, to state by a formal act that the Senate had acted wrongly, to read the spiritual testament of the deceased sovereign, and to declare Nikolay Pavlovich tsar. Otherwise no one can understand a thing: the sovereign is not abdicating; the Senate is silent.'

Wearing bearskin coats, with heads muffled, they both climbed into a sleigh. The *troika* bells rang out and the horses dashed off. Michael hid his frozen face from the frosty air and shivered. He had failed to sit it out. Constantine had outsmarted everyone—he had stayed put in his Belweder Palace and did not give a damn. And why the hell had Michael undertaken to carry Constantine's letter to Petersburg. What was he—some kind of a courier for his brothers?

Michael was musing:

"I failed to sit it out, I need to recoup my position."

He tried to doze, but the road was bad, they were jolted, and he could not sleep.

At twelve o'clock in the morning the Anichkov Palace in Petersburg is full of people. Nobody is sleeping. The inner chambers give the impression of a domestic bivouac. Wrapped in a shawl, with a pillow under her head, the old empress is dozing on a couch in Nicholas's study. Dressed in a magnificent white silk dress, Nicholas's wife Alexandra Fyodorovna sits in the armchair next to her, motionless, stiff as a soldier—in half an hour she will be empress. In the next room little groups of courtiers, Albedyll, Samarin, Novosiltsev, Friderici, Dr. Ruhl, and Villamov doze, roam around, sit alone, or talk quietly—friends and family act similarly when they wait in an adjoining room for the death of a patient who has been sick for a long time and is dying a difficult death. Nicholas is at the State Council, which at this time must already have proclaimed him emperor. At a quarter to one he returns. He is wearing a tight dress uniform, which makes him look taller, with a sash over his shoulder. His face is lifeless and gray. Yesterday a courier from Diebitsch arrived and brought a warning report intended for the late Alexander: there is a powerful secret society in Russia; it will not miss the opportunity to act on the day of his ascension to the throne. The Guards, too, are infected. And today an officer by the name of Rostovtsev came to see him and handed in a letter in which he warned Nicholas that the next day there would be an uprising. Nicholas is in two minds tonight. On the one hand he feels like a general about to fight a decisive battle tomorrow, which will leave him either dead or an emperor. The other feeling is one of a strange awkwardness and fear, as if before a military review. That's why he is wearing a tight uniform, moving awkwardly, and, above all, making sure that not a single muscle twitches on his face, that his jacket is buttoned up, that everything is in order. A few minutes later, he and his wife go out to meet the courtiers. His mother, the old empress, walks ahead of him. They stand unnaturally straight before the gray, bald, sleek, and curled heads that are bowed before them.

Congratulations and greetings begin.

The mother responds to them. Nicholas stands as if he had forgotten who he is. At last, with an effort, he looks around.

'There is no cause for congratulation,' he says in a wooden voice, 'I should be pitied.'

At the building of the American company on the Moyka at midnight they are not asleep either.

Thick smoke is hanging in the room. The faces are unclear in the light of the lamps, the voices have grown hoarse, the uniforms and frock-coats are unbuttoned. They speak all at once, someone comes in, others leave.

Ryleyev is a formidable presence, and even Yakubovich cannot bear the stare of his black eyes. He frowns when Ryleyev addresses him.

Ryleyev walks quickly, with an unfamiliar light gait, from one group of men to the next. He gives instructions, asks questions, or simply shakes hands and says a few words. His face appears fleetingly, now and then, like a moon among black waves. No one greets the newly entered Wilhelm and Odoyevsky. Here people come and go, not noticing each other, paying no attention to each other.

Wilhelm hears how Evgeny Obolensky speaks to Aleksandr Bestuzhev, looking at him with his frank blue eyes:

'If we fail it won't be the end of the road: we shall withdraw the troops toward the military settlements, people there will all join us, and we shall advance again on Petersburg.'

Ryleyev walks past Wilhelm, who, oblivious to everything around him, is holding Odoyevsky by the hand, and, in passing, he quietly touches his hand. Wilhelm shudders at this mark of affection. Ryleyev shakes hands with Misha Bestuzhev, who silently stands to one side with the young Guards Lieutenant Sutgof:

'Blessed are you, people not of words but of deeds.'

Looking serious and gloomy, staff captain Misha Bestuzhev addresses Ryleyev:

'I don't like the look of Yakubovich. He is supposed to bring the artillery and the Izmaylovsky Regiment to me, and then we are to advance together to the square. Will he bring them?'

Ryleyev answers with a question:

'How many companies, do you think?'

Misha shrugs gravely, he feels as if he was going into battle for the first time.

'The soldiers are raring to fight, and the company commanders have given me their word of honor not to stop them.'

'And what about you?' Ryleyev asks Sutgof, leaning quickly forward.

'I can vouch for my company,' the lieutenant replies respectfully, 'others might join us too.'

Trubetskoy is overexcited, he rubs his hands, cracks his fingers, listens to what Yakubovich is telling him, looking somewhere above himself and everyone else, and says, gathering his thoughts:

'So, you and Arbuzov volunteer to occupy the palace?

Yakubovich interrupts him with a gesture. He screams hoarsely at Trubetskoy:

'Come on, let's draw the lots who's to kill the tyrant!'

'Chop their heads off!' cries Shchepin, turning purple.

Ryleyev rushes over to Kakhovsky and embraces him impetuously.

'My dear friend,' he says and looks with incomprehensible melancholy at Kakhovsky's calm yellow face. 'You are an orphan on this earth, you must sacrifice yourself for the Society.'

They all understand what this means and rush toward Kakhovsky. Wilhelm shakes the hand that is to kill Nicholas tomorrow. He looks around at everyone. Through the tobacco smoke, in the flickering light, the eyes are looking at him, only the eyes. He does not see the faces. And he raises his hand:

'Me! Me too. Here is my hand!'

Someone puts a hand on his shoulder. He turns around: a flushed Pushchin is staring at him grimly.

He had arrived from Moscow only on the 8th. Ryleyev had accepted Wilhelm into the society without him.

'Yes, *Jeannot*,' says Wilhelm quietly, 'me too.'

Odoyevsky looks at them both with tears in his eyes. He smiles, and dimples show on his cheeks.

Pushchin shrugs his shoulders angrily. He is listening to the conversation at the table.

'Who can we count on, then?' asks Trubetskoy with an effort for the second time, and it is unclear who he is trying to get an answer from.

Kornilovich, who has just arrived from the south, waves his hands at him:

'A hundred thousand men are ready in the first army.'

Pushchin turns to Trubetskoy:

'Moscow will join in at once.'

Aleksandr Bestuzhev is laughing loudly in another corner. Arbuzov and three other officers unfamiliar to Wilhelm come in.

Bestuzhev laughs: 'The plan of the Winter Palace? The royal family isn't a needle in a haystack, they can't hide when we come to arrest them.'

Ryleyev looks around for Shteingel and sees him sitting silently, his head buried in his arms.

Ryleyev touches his shoulder with one hand. Shteingel raises an old, exhausted face and tells Ryleyev flatly:

'God, our forces are too limited. Do you really think we should act?'

Everyone hears this and quietens down.

Ryleyev replies: 'Yes, act, act, act without fail,' and his nostrils flare.

A pair of wandering greenish eyes are fixing themselves on Ryleyev, Trubetskoy's eyes, and his lips are trembling.

'Maybe we should wait? They have artillery and they will shoot.'

Ryleyev turns white and speaks slowly, looking straight into the darting eyes:

'We are doomed to death in any case. It is imperative to act.'

He takes a paper from the table, a copy of Rostovtsev's denunciation, and, flaring his nostrils, says to Trubetskoy:

'Do you forget that we've been betrayed? The court already knows a lot, but not everything, and we are still quite strong.'

His gaze falls on the calm Misha Bestuzhev, and he suddenly speaks calmly, firmly, almost quietly:

'Our swords are drawn. There is no turning back, just the same we shall die. To the Senate tomorrow, then: they are gathering at seven for the oath. We will make them submit.'

Everything has been said.

Time to disperse—until tomorrow.

Wilhelm and Sasha walk quietly home. Before going back to Pochtamtskaya Street, they go to Peter's Square and past the Senate toward the embankment. An uneasy feeling draws them to the square.

The Senate's columns are white, its windows are dull in the dark, it is silent. The square is empty. In the dark air the monument to Peter the Great looks like a flat, black, cardboard cut-out. In the night sky, the needle-like spire of the Peter and Paul Fortress can hardly be seen in the distance.

The night is warm. The snow has melted a little.

The iron sleeps, the stones sleep. Spare beams lie quietly in the Peter and Paul Fortress; out of them in one night any ten carpenters could make a scaffold.

Peter's Square

I

Petersburg was never afraid of empty spaces. Moscow grew by houses naturally linking up, sprouting more houses, until finally the Moscow streets appeared. Moscow squares are not always distinguishable from streets, from which they differ only in width, not in the spirit of space; the same is true of the small winding Moscow rivers, which match the streets. The basic Moscow unit is the house, that is why there are so many lanes and cul-de-sacs in Moscow.

In Petersburg there are no cul-de-sacs, and each alleyway strives to be a *prospekt*. There are streets too, about which it is not known for certain whether they are *prospekts* or alleys. Such is Grechesky Prospekt, which Moscovites persist in calling an alley. The streets in Petersburg were formed before the houses, the houses merely filled in their outlines. And the squares were designed before the streets. That is why they are completely self-sufficient, they are unconstrained by the houses and streets that form them. The Petersburg unit is the square.

The river in Petersburg flows by itself like an independent *prospekt* of water. Petersburg residents today, just like those of a century ago, do not acknowledge any other rivers than the Neva, although there are also the Neva tributaries. These are called by the same name, the Neva. The independence of the river encourages it to revolt at least once a century.

Petersburg revolutions took place in the squares: December 1825 and February 1917 occurred in two squares. Both in December 1825 and in October 1917 the Neva took part in the uprisings; in December the rebels ran across the ice, in October the cruiser *Aurora* threatened the palace from the Neva.

The alliance of river and squares comes naturally to Petersburg; and any war within the city must inevitably turn into a war of the squares.

By December 1825 this alliance was as follows:

Peter's Square (not yet Senate Square), St. Isaac's Square, Admiralty Square (where there are now the trees of the Aleksandrovsky Gardens), Liftbridge Square[53] (not yet Palace Square), and the Neva.

Catherine the Great had erected Falconet's monument to Peter the Great in the square in front of the Senate, hence this square was called Peter's. Another monument intended for the square, Rastrelli's Peter the Great, had been scrapped, and the Emperor Paul had brought it back as he brought home from exile people banished by his mother. But the site was already occupied, so he put up the statue in front of his castle, in honorable exile.

A wide boulevard stretches around the Admiralty building, along Admiralty Square, Peter's Square, and Liftbridge Square. Before the October Revolution it was known as the Horse Guards Boulevard, and in 1825 it was a canal, called the Admiralty Canal, with a bridge over it.

St. Isaac's Square was named after the church, which was under construction but remained unfinished. The construction had begun at the same time as the Marble Palace and was also of marble. When the walls were built halfway up, Catherine "did not fancy the appearance" of the church and ordered it to "be left as it was." Her son Paul, after he had come to the throne, ordered it to be completed immediately with bricks, which led to the following satirical verses about the church:

Two reigns have passed, the church stands slick —
Its base is marble, above it's brick.

Alexander I did not care for the church and ordered it to be pulled down and a new one built. As a result, the material, brought from overseas, was lying on the embankment of Peter's Square, and the construction itself cluttered the whole of St. Isaac's Square, so that the rubble, flagstone, slabs of marble, and boards were lying about well outside the scaffolding. And another rhyme was soon written about the church:

Now three reigns seen in this construction:
One brick, one granite—one destruction.

Thus, Peter's Square, which represented the power of autocracy, adjoined St. Isaac's Square, which signified its weakness.

The uprising of December 14 was a war of the squares.

Through the canals of the streets the people flowed to Admiralty Square and St. Isaac's Square, first the insurgent regiments and then the ones loyal to the government.

Tsar Nicholas rode from Liftbridge Square to Admiralty Square as far as the lions of the Lobanov house.

Liftbridge and St. Isaac's Squares, where the government regiments were stationed, silently pressed on Admiralty Square, where the people were agitating, and Peter's Square, where the revolutionaries were. They blocked Peter's on three sides, and forced the revolutionaries into the river, shoving some of them through the gates of narrow Galernaya Street.

The day of December 14, in fact, consisted of a circulation of blood through the city; along the arteries of the streets the people and the insurgent regiments flowed into the vessels of the squares, and then the arteries were blocked, and like corks, the regiments were popped out of the vessels with a single push. But for the city this meant a rupture of the heart in which genuine blood was spilled.

Certain individual heroes of the day just darted around the streets, driving the blood of the city and Russia—the regiments—to the squares, but for the most part merely marking time. The whole day was a wearisome oscillation of the squares, which lay like pans on the scales, until the rough thrust of Nicholas's artillery knocked them out of balance. The squares decided the outcome, not the streets, and there were no heroes of the day. Ryleyev, who could have been a hero, understood that oscillation better than anyone else and in an incomprehensible gloom went off in an unknown direction. As for Trubetskoy, he simply marked time somewhere near the General Staff building.

They could not prevent the sinister, stupefied stasis of the squares like balancing pans in sets of scales.

The old autocracy, Emperor Paul's broken brick, was being weighed. If the fresh clay of the mob in Admiralty Square could have merged with Peter's Square, where the wind was driving the combustible sand of the aristocratic *intelligentsia*, they would have prevailed.

But the brick prevailed and pretended to be granite.

II

Grand Duke Michael was making his way from the city barrier to Liftbridge Square.

Sleepy and pale, he passed through the barrier at eight in the morning. It was not yet dawn, the morning was gloomy. He drove past the suburban shops, looking curiously at the windows. The candles were still burning there; in one shop a fat Baltic man wearing spectacles was scribbling at a desk: he was jotting something down, remembering, scratching his nose.

Michael looked at the windows with a vague anxiety—either he wanted to look at people and distract himself from the feeling of heaviness and dread (he never admitted to himself this fear of his), or he wanted to make sure that everything was still in its place.

Everything was still in its place. The shops were being opened. A few pedestrians walked the streets, which were quiet and dark. He crossed the empty Theater Square, passing a sentry box in which an old sentry was asleep with his halberd propped against the wall. Michael wanted to hail him and give him a good telling off but changed his mind. Across the Potseluev Bridge he drove into Bolshaya Morskaya Street. Dawn had now broken, but the streets were almost deserted. This started to frighten him.

What did it mean, this calm, this silence?

Was it really that everything was fine and there was nothing to worry about? The uncertainty scared him even more than any obvious danger. He looked dubiously at the silent houses, the smooth pavements.

'We'll see what happens next,' he muttered.

At the Winter Palace, he barely squeezed through the crowd of courtiers. Dignitaries dressed in uniforms with gold embroidery, young bucks, maids of honor, and generals stuck to him like treacle; congratulations, wishes, greetings showered on him like *petits pois*. Michael answered the men abruptly, almost rudely, and bowed stiffly to the ladies. Finally, he went through to Nicholas.

Nicholas embraced him, touching him with a cold cheek.

'Well, you see, everything is going well. The troops have been swearing allegiance and there are no riots.'

He talked to his brother rather condescendingly, not as he had on his first visit, because Michael had sat out in Nennaal twiddling his thumbs to no purpose all this terrible week, and Nicholas no longer relied on him: these three days had taught him to act alone. Besides, he was deluding himself with an uncertain hope: perhaps nothing would happen, and his brother reminded him of all the fuss with Constantine and was therefore disagreeable. Michael sensed it and droned through set teeth:

'Thank Heaven, but the day is not over yet.'

He almost wished now that something would happen.

The sight of Nicholas irritated him.

Suddenly they heard the beating of drums under the window.

Nicholas quickly ran to the window. He peered out closely, and Michael was delighted to see that Nicholas had turned pale. Only then did he collect himself and run to the window too. A company of soldiers was marching past, carrying a banner, the drumming went to the beat of the standard-bearers' march.

Nicholas took a deep breath.

'They are from the Semyonovsky Regiment,' he said casually, avoiding looking at his brother, 'they have sworn the oath, the banner is returning.' Then he seemed to remember, 'Oh yes, I forgot to see about something.' And he left.

Michael stood by the window for a while, looking at the square, at the retreating banner, and grinned:

'You don't need me, my little friend, and that's fine with me, I can live with that.'

In the corridor, he ran into Nicholas. Nicholas's face was as gray as a dead man's, and his thin lips were light brown. He gripped Michael tightly:

'The Horse Guards Artillery are refusing to swear the oath—get over there, will you?'

III

Since the morning, Wilhelm had been taken over by unbridled insanity. His head was heavy, his legs light and empty, and every muscle was part of a whole, the center of which was outside him. He moved as if by the arbitrary will of some terrible and alluring power, and every step, each of his movements, which from the outside seemed ridiculous and strange, was not his, he was not responsible. Everything was going as it should.

Semyon lit a candle. Wilhelm noticed him for the first time in many months.

'Well, Semyon, life goes on?' he said, smiling uneasily.

Semyon nodded.

'It does indeed, Wilhelm Karlovich. We're going to die, but let's live while we're waiting.'

'Aleksandr Ivanovich hasn't come yet?'

'No, he never comes before ten on Mondays.'

Wilhelm quickly got dressed.

He had to finish some calculations, arrange the manuscripts. Or else they might perish in case of . . . (and he did not want to finish thinking in case of what). Should he take everything to Delvig's?

He put on clean undergarments, a black frock coat, a new dark olive greatcoat with a beaver collar and a smart silver clasp, and took a round hat in his hands.

'Wilhelm Karlovich, Ryleyev's servant is asking for you.'

Wilhelm immediately forgot about the manuscripts. He stopped in the doorway.

'Semyon, don't wait for me today. If you should hear about me, don't get scared.' He paused. 'If something happens, go to Ustinya Karlovna.'

Semyon looked at him with understanding eyes. Seeing his eyes, Wilhelm suddenly stepped toward him and gave him a hug. Semyon said quietly:

'I'll wait for you, master, I will. We'll see. It's more fun together.'

Wilhelm ran down the stairs, took a cab, and drove swiftly to the Blue Bridge. Approaching the house of the American company, his driver almost bumped into another one: Kakhovsky was sitting in the sleigh, his face sallow from insomnia. He looked at Wilhelm with eyes as black and dull as olives, and did not recognize him.

Pushchin and Shteingel were already at Ryleyev's. Nothing had begun yet, and this hour before the battle was the most frightening of all, because no one knew how things would unfold and how it would all start. The threads of rebellion, which the previous night seemed to have been in Ryleyev's fervent hands, eluded him now, they were acquiring a power independent of his will or Pushchin's or anybody else's. The threads were in the barracks where the soldiers were now being armed, in the still silent squares, and the men who gathered this morning in Ryleyev's room looked like travelers who had only five minutes left before they departed for an unknown country, from which there is unlikely to be any return. Everyone was coping with this hour in his own way.

Shteingel was pacing up and down, sullen and concentrated; the fear that had attacked him the previous night was gradually dissipating. Pushchin sat at the desk like a sailor over his maps, marking something on the plan of the city. And Ryleyev stood by the window looking at the black railing of the canal, like a captain who had already silently and mysteriously determined the outcome.

'Many are refusing to be sworn in,' said Shteingel with satisfaction, apparently wanting to reassure himself, 'but who exactly and in what numbers is still unknown.'

Pushchin spoke to Wilhelm briskly:

'Get hold at once of the manifesto with Constantine's long-standing abdication, it must be shown to the soldiers. They must be told that it was forced and falsified. I've got only the one copy. Get it from Grech, he must have one too. And then go to the square. When the troops come, talk to the soldiers, shout hurrah for the constitution.'

Shteingel objected:

'But the first thing is to go to the barracks. We are counting on two officers in the cavalry artillery. And then the Guards Company, we have no news from them yet.'

Kakhovsky came in silently and nodded to everyone. He did not offer his hand to anyone and came in like a stranger.

Then Ryleyev moved away from the window and waved his hand:

'Go to the Company, will you?'

The square was empty, as it always was in the mornings. An elderly official passed hurriedly, hiding his nose in the collar of his thin overcoat, turned into Galernaya Street, shuffling along through the icy snow with knee-high boots, then two workmen passed and a merchant's wife in a bulky coat. Nobody, nothing. Even the doors of the Senate were closed and the doorman was not standing by the door.

Was it really credible that in an hour or two troops would flood this deserted square, so peaceful and ordinary, and that it would all happen here? It seemed almost impossible. On the ugly scaffolding of St. Isaac's Square hammers and pickaxes were already at work, masons went about their work slowly and smoothly, carrying up lime on hods, a carpenter was trimming some boards and squabbling with another—everyday work was going on. He went to Grech's house.

Grech was holding something like a family meeting—it was a special day: an oath of allegiance to the new tsar. Guests were already drinking tea round the table: Bulgarin in a dolman jacket, puffing his pipe, a lieutenant, a broker, and some family members.

Wilhelm entered, pale, waving his arms. Bulgarin dug the lieutenant in the ribs and said in a low voice:

'Top-notch theatrical bandit.'

Pompous Nikolay Ivanovich Grech, with knitted brows and gleaming spectacles, was reading aloud some decree.

Without greeting anyone Wilhelm asked him:

'*Qu'est ce que vous lisez là? Je crois que c'est le manifeste*?'

'*Oui, c'est le manifeste*,' answered Nikolay Ivanovich grumpily and continued reading.

Wilhelm interrupted again:

'May I ask what is the date of Konstantin Pavlovich's abdication?'

Grech gave him a searching look:

'Twenty-sixth of November.'

'Twenty-sixth.' Wilhelm smiled. 'Very well, three weeks ago.'

Grech exchanged glances with Bulgarin:

'Yes, sir, they have been silent for three weeks, what are they going to say now, I wonder.'

He winked at Wilhelm:

'I believe that it is not their turn to speak now.'

'Can I borrow the manifesto for half an hour?' asked Wilhelm, pulling the paper from Grech's hand and rushing from the room.

Bulgarin hastily ran after him.

'Good morning, Wilhelm Karlovich!' He grabbed his arm. 'Just look at him—he doesn't want to talk. What's being planned for today then?'

'Good morning and goodbye,' replied Wilhelm, pushed him away, and ran out.

'What's the matter with him?' asked the stunned Bulgarin. 'Has he gone out of his mind?'

Nikolay Ivanovich looked at his companion with narrowed eyes:

'No, there's something else going on, something fishy.'

Leaving Grech's, Wilhelm stumbled into Odoyevsky. Cheerful, elegant, with cheeks red from the frost, Sasha was returning from the palace guard—he had spent the night at the palace.

Two pistols in his belt bulged beneath his greatcoat.

They embraced like brothers, without asking each other any questions. Wilhelm merely nodded at the pistols:

'Could you give me one?'—and Sasha readily handed him a long sentry pistol with a ramrod, wrapped in green cloth. Wilhelm thrust it into his pocket with the handle of the gun sticking out.

And he rushed to the Company, to the officers' barracks, to Misha, while Odoyevsky went to Ryleyev's. In the Guards Company, Misha told him that a big riot had started in the Moscow Regiment, that General Shenshin and two others—the battalion and regimental commanders—had been killed, and he immediately sent his brother to the Moscow Regiment to find out whether they had marched out yet. As soon as the Moscow Regiment arrived, Misha and Arbuzov would order the Company to march.

Going hastily down the entrance steps of the officer's barracks, Wilhelm sees Kakhovsky running through the barracks courtyard and getting tangled up in his greatcoat. He is running steadily, blindly, pursued by some petty officers. They grab his greatcoat. Without looking back, Kakhovsky throws it off and keeps on running. He runs as if in a dream, and Wilhelm begins to feel that he is delirious and that any moment everything can crumble, slip through his fingers.

'Your Excellency, would you like to get in?' says a voice behind his back.

Wilhelm gets into the hired sleigh:

'Hurry, hurry!'

The cabby sets off. He is rather young, fair-haired, with a curly beard, his sleigh is shabby with jagged runners, the cover is tattered, and the horse is a clapped-out old nag.

Driving past the square, Wilhelm looks toward it again, vaguely fearful. The square is empty.

'Dear chap, drive faster, use your whip.'

The cabby gives him a sly glance:

'The road's terrible, Your Excellency, and my horse isn't so young, to be honest. We'll get there in the end.'

Wilhelm shouts in a wild voice:

'Drive! Drive at full speed!'

The cabby and the nag both get a fright. The driver cracks his whip, the nag races off, shaking its hind legs absurdly, and huddling down on its hindquarters. The spindly, hunched Wilhelm, with burning eyes, is jolted with every bump. In Voznesenskaya Street, just at the Blue Bridge, the nag makes a desperate sideways leap and dumps the passenger in a snowdrift. Snow sticks to his mouth and eyes—cold, quickly melting. Wilhelm hears a worried voice above him:

'Well now! I told you—he's not so young, no speed left in him.'

The pistol stands out black against the snowdrift. The barrel is choked with snow. Wilhelm tries to shake it out, but it is packed tightly. Then he climbs back in, the cabby shakes his head, pulls the impossibly tattered rug over him, and the clapped-out old nag rushes on.

'Drive, drive at full speed!'

IV

There is noise and movement at the Moscow Regiment; the soldiers are lining up, some are picking up live ammunition, others are loading rifles or pulling banners along. Shchepin-Rostovsky is among the soldiers, with an unfamiliar officer standing to one side. All around there is commotion, talking, yelling, and, it seems, a real scuffle in the yard.

"Ah ha, so it's starting, this is it!"

Wilhelm climbs out of the sleigh, getting his legs tangled, runs to the unfamiliar officer, and mutters unusually quickly:

'What do you want me to tell your brothers at the Guards Company?'

The officer says nothing. Wilhelm, thinking that he takes him for a spy, introduces himself. But the officer silently points to the soldiers and shrugs. Apparently, he does not want to talk.

At this moment Shchepin sees Wilhelm and screams in a gravelly voice:

'We are leaving now! Mikhail Bestuzhev has already gone off with his company. Have the Guards left?'

'Not yet.'

'Get across there then, we'll be in the square in ten minutes.'

The nag carries Wilhelm along the same streets to the Guards Company. The cabby whips it without saying anything, then turns to Wilhelm:

'Listen to me, your lordship. You'll get yourself into trouble. Are you military or what? Can't you see what's going on here?'

'I'll let you go at the Guards Company.'

The cabby cheers up instantly and pulls on the reins obediently.

'I understand that gentlemen drive around on all kinds of business, it all depends.'

The streets they travel along are agitated. People gather in little groups; timid solitary figures stand freezing on the pavements. Three workmen are running somewhere at breakneck speed, they have had no time to throw off their aprons yet.

'Senya, where are you going?' shouts a workman, having recognized a friend.

'To the square, to fight the tsar,' replies the other cheerfully, and gives a loud whistle.

'Shut up, you pipsqueak,' an old man in a cap shouts after him, 'not been beaten enough at home, have you?'

A sound is heard in the distance, the meaning of which at first Wilhelm does not understand; it is similar to the sound at low tide, when a wave ebbs from the shore dragging pebbles with it, or to the lively chatter of a thousand small hammers. He guesses what it is: the cavalry is coming.

At that moment a state councillor with a white plume dashes by in a beautiful sleigh, and, peering at Wilhelm, gives him a deep bow. Wilhelm does not recognize him but returns the bow courteously.

Thus on this day many people race around in their sleighs, gallop on their poor hired nags, or in service wagons, or run on foot, panting. Odoyevsky, Bestuzhev, and now this unfamiliar state counsellor are all carried by the same icy wind from the canals of the streets toward the square.

And the same wind has already been driving into the square the blood of the city—its troops, so that the squares could be filled to the brim with the blood that has been stagnant in recent years, but now rushes into the vessels.

The same wind whirls Wilhelm round the streets.

V

He was not allowed to enter the Guards Company.

There was a sound of footsteps in the courtyard, as if someone with a thousand feet was trampling the ground. Bolts were clicking, and there was a sharp command:

'Fall in!'

The sentry barred his way with a bayonet:

'The order is not to let anyone in.'

'What's in there?'

The sentry stayed silent. Then, looking at Wilhelm wild-eyed, he shouted:

'I'll let you have it!'

And it begins to seem to Wilhelm that he is some kind of a ball, which is thrown from one player to another—he has raced from the Company to the Moscow Regiment, from there to the Company, and then bounced back: the gates are shut. He is surrounded by a crowd of curious boys. The eyes of the sentry are darting about, he doesn't seem to understand either; in any case, it is impossible to pass through the gates.

Wilhelm asks the sentry: 'I am here to see my brother, my dear fellow, can I come in?'

Still no answer. Wilhelm suddenly stoops down and steps through the low gate.

The courtyard. Dark figures are dragging weapons and running around. One company has lined up.

Wilhelm hardly sees the people. He climbs onto some box. He screams in a shrill voice:

'Brothers!'

All around him there are the dark figures, the guns, the fluttering banner.

Wilhelm shouts:

'The Moscow Regiment has advanced! Ten minutes! . . .'

The men shout back at him, raising their guns.

'Hoorah!' they shout.

'To the square!' shouts Wilhelm and sways around on a flimsy box. They lift him up. Someone kisses him. He looks around.

Misha.

'You'd better go, get out of here,' says Misha in a low voice, breathing heavily. 'We are just leaving.'

He pushes Wilhelm along.

Wilhelm runs out of the gate obediently and races toward the sleigh.

Where now? To the square? Instead he is being rushed through the streets.

'To the Finnish Regiment.'

"The Finnish Regiment" slipped out accidentally—he had remembered someone's words: "We have Rosen and Tsebrikov at the Finnish Regiment."

At the regimental gate he is hailed by an officer sitting in a sleigh, flushed, excited, getting ready to go somewhere, and shouting to another one without a greatcoat, just in his uniform:

'*Enflammez! Enflammez*!'

Seeing Wilhelm, he hails him. It is Tsebrikov.

'I'll give you a lift,' he says, gazing around with wandering eyes. 'Dammit, there's no way through, the horses are stumbling.'

'How is your Finnish regiment?'

'God knows.' Tsebrikov catches Wilhelm by the clasps of his coat. 'Can't you get it into your head that this isn't the way to do it? I told him: just lead out the men and take the ammunition. And he replies: "I can't, without a clear account."' (Tsebrikov is starting to mix up his words.) 'Get in, I'll give you a lift. Are you going to the square?' He does not wait for the answer.

'Ivan!' he shouts desperately to the soldier on the coachbox. 'To the Senate! Get moving, for Christ's sake!'

Wilhelm looks anxiously at Tsebrikov who is rambling incoherently.

'I'll pick up a saber and I'll fight. I don't get it, how's it possible.'

Wilhelm's heart pounds—he has gone to the wrong place—like in a dream—God, why has he come to the Finnish Regiment? Everything is going to pieces, slipping away from him. Quick, to the square, this can go on all day!

At the Blue Bridge, Tsebrikov takes off his overcoat. He mutters:

'Take my greatcoat. It's a military one. You'll be more comfortable.'

Wilhelm does not understand a thing.

'I'm hot,' says Tsebrikov, throwing his greatcoat in the snow.

Wilhelm silently climbs out of the sleigh and runs.

Something is wrong with Tsebrikov.

On the Blue Bridge Wilhelm is hailed by Vasya Karatygin.

'Where are you heading, for God's sake? There's a riot in the square, you have no idea what's going on!'

"Ah ha, there's a riot in the square! That's it."

And Wilhelm shouts as he runs, grinning crazily and ecstatically:

'I know! We've done it!'

He glimpses some dark figures in the square. For some reason, workmen and masons are tearing off planks from the scaffolding of St. Isaac's Church. A dense, disorderly crowd of soldiers from the Moscow Regiment stands facing the monument of Peter the Great by the Senate; they are surrounded by people. Wilhelm passes between the crowd and the soldiers. The soldiers' faces are calm, and he hears an old gray-haired Guard telling a young Guard who is putting his gun to his shoulder:

'Put your rifle down, there'll be plenty of time for shooting.'

A black-bandaged Yakubovich and Aleksandr Bestuzhev, flushed and erect as if on parade, are walking up and down in front of the Moscow Regiment. Yakubovich does not look at Wilhelm, greets him absent-mindedly, then winces, raising his hand to the bandage:

'Dammit, my head is sore.'

Bestuzhev commands:

'Guns at the ready!'

Wilhelm joyfully repeats after him:

'Guns at the ready!'

Bestuzhev turns around, red with anger, sees Wilhelm, and says to him sternly:

'Don't get in the way.'

Odoyevsky runs by, waving to him:

'I'm going over to the sappers. Did you hear, General Fredericks has been killed?'

Not waiting for an answer, he runs off.

Tall, lean Kakhovsky, in a tail coat, has run by with a pistol in his hands and joined the crowd at the monument.

Wilhelm makes his way there too. Ryleyev, Pushchin, and the huge impassive state councillor with the white plume, who recently bowed to Wilhelm, are right by the monument.

Ryleyev hastily fastens on a soldier's belt and throws a bag over his shoulder. He is staring relentlessly ahead toward St. Isaac's Square, over people's heads.

'When will the Company be here?'

'They're up in arms, but the gates are locked.'

Pushchin shrugs and turns to Ryleyev:

'It can't go on like this, where on earth is Trubetskoy? We can't act without a leader.'

Yakubovich approaches them, dull-faced, holding on to his bandage. Gloomily and briefly he says to Ryleyev:

'I'll do it.'

And disappears in the crowd.

Wilhelm looks in fascination at the impassive man with the white plume. The man suddenly throws off his greatcoat and with long steady strides heads for the crowd; the white plume mingles with the caps and hats; he begins to give orders to the crowd, and they huddle round him. All the time, artisans and laborers are dashing over to the warehouse and emerging with logs and fragments of paving stones.

A little man in black runs from them to the square. His shirt collar is dirty. He is fast and nimble in his movements, his nose looks predatory, his restless eyes are darting wildly about. Where has Wilhelm come across him? There are hundreds of faces like that at auctions, on boulevards, in theaters. The little man quickly says something to the soldiers and runs back to the crowd. He stands next to the man with the white plume. Wilhelm pulls the pistol out of his pocket, then puts it away, then takes it out again.

'Where on earth is Trubetskoy?'

Wilhelm looks at Pushchin, makes a desperate gesture, and rushes off to the embankment, to Trubetskoy's lodgings at Laval's house. Along the way, he stumbles. Pushchin watches him leave and shouts:

'Hide the bloody pistol!'

He looks at the lanky Küchlya, who is waving the gun about, momentarily remembers the Lycée, and smiles.

VI

A clean-shaven doorman lets in the man with crazy eyes who is panting for breath, looks at him incredulously, then grimly helps him to remove his greatcoat. Wilhelm remembers that he has a gun in his hand and puts it in his pocket. He goes up a winding staircase with white marble statues on the landings and green plants. The uproar seems to be coming from far off, though the house is no distance from the square. The old aristocratic house lives its own life and does not care to listen to street cries or a few shots from the square. It has solid walls.

'How should I announce you?'

For a moment Wilhelm does not understand: "announce?"

The Winter Palace can be occupied by soldiers. The Senate can be destroyed. But as long as this house exists, the footman must announce a guest to the master, even if this guest has arrived from hell to tell the host that he is being summoned to the Last Judgment.

Wilhelm rummages in his pockets, takes out a pencil, and writes on a scrap of paper:

"*Guillaume Küchelbecker*. To be seen immediately."

The footman comes back after a while:

'The princess will receive you.'

The rooms are quiet, with pictures of Old Masters on the walls and porcelain on the marble tables. Wilhelm passes by a picture of a semi-nude girl with a grape vine, looks at her in bewilderment, and squeezes the pistol in his pocket. The old house with its immaculate order begins to frighten him. Is there really a riot in the square? Right at this moment Trubetskoy may come out, look at him in surprise, shrug his shoulders, smile, and say that all this is just his imagination.

The princess comes out. And Wilhelm gives a sigh of relief: the princess's face is pale, her lips are trembling. No, there *is* a riot in the square, there *are* soldiers out there, and, damn it, there will be blood.

'He's not in,' the princess says graciously and stares in wide-eyed horror at Wilhelm's hand.

Only then does Wilhelm notice that his hand is clutching the pistol again. He is embarrassed and puts it away in his pocket.

'Where is the prince?' asks Wilhelm. 'They are expecting him, princess.'

'I do not know,' the princess says almost inaudibly, 'he left very early.'

Wilhelm looks at her and, baffled, asks:

'How do you mean: left? He's not in the square.'

The princess lowers her head. Wilhelm understands everything, he rushes away, and without looking back, races down the wide, cool staircase, tripping over his own feet.

"Trubetskoy will not come to the square, he is either a traitor or a coward."

VII

A dense black square formation of the Guards Company is already positioned by the Admiralty Canal next to the Moscow Regiment. Ahead is a line of marksmen under Misha's command. The Company and the Moscow Regiment are divided by a small alley—the Senate Gate, leaving free the entrance to Galernaya Street. The Moscow Regiment have also formed a square. No one is commanding them.

Wilhelm has never seen so many people. They are everywhere—black ranks of people even fill the spaces between the columns of the Senate, or stand on the roofs of the neighboring buildings. Everything is black around the monument and further on in Admiralty Square.

Two workmen have grabbed an officer in the crowd and are holding him tightly.

'Are you trying to persuade us to disperse? Are you saying they are deceiving us? Come on, say it again, say it.'

Wilhelm intervenes and says imploringly:

'Let him go.'

At that moment, he notices Kakhovsky's unmoving eyes behind the officer. Kakhovsky is calm, his right hand is stuck into the left side of his coat. He pulls out a dagger and stabs the officer hard in the head. The officer gives a muffled moan and sinks down. A trickle of blood appears by his pink ear, creeps, spreads, floods the head, the eyes. The officer claws at the ground with his hands, mutters something, then falls.

'Serve him right, brothers, let 'em have it, boys!'

The lean Kakhovsky runs on, lightly and nimbly.

'Shoot the spies and informers!' Pushchin shouts from the foot of the monument.

A jovial workman has taken away a policeman's sword and is beating him on the head with it:

'Where are you going? Where d'you think you're off to, you swine?'

And Wilhelm makes an involuntary movement (he cannot stand seeing a man beaten). The workman looks at him, smiling and winking:

'Your Honor, why are you walking around with nothing but a pistol? Take the sword, it might come in handy,' and he puts the sword in Wilhelm's hands.

The strange little man comes up to them, dark shabby clothes, swarthy face, hooked nose. There are hundreds of faces like his—in theaters, taverns, on boulevards. He speaks hoarsely, in French, with a German accent:

'I am the leader of the crowd, we need to unite. We need to get the crowd organized and hand out weapons.'

'Who are you?' Wilhelm asks quietly, trying to remember where he has seen this man.

'Captain Rautenfeld, retired. Cavalry captain. If you want them, I have enough sabers and everything else. Who is your leader? The crowd is raring to go.'

Suddenly, Wilhelm recalls the early morning, the naked backs of the soldiers, the echoing sound of a flute, and the whistling of the whips. He looks blankly at the little man and immediately forgets about him, because he sees in front of him a familiar curly head with a mischievous smile.

'Well I never! Lyovushka!'

Lev Pushkin has come to the square—to gawp. Wilhelm takes him by the hands, thrusts his sword joyfully into them, and drags him to the monument, forgetting about what's his name?—Rautenfeld, Rosenthal, or Rosenberg? He leads Lyovushka up to Pushchin.

'Take this young soldier, will you?'

And immediately runs away across the square.

Lyovushka stands for a while and quietly lays the sword on the ground. Then he mingles with the crowd and disappears.

VIII

At this moment, a strange coach drives into the alley between the square formed by the Moscow Regiment and the Company. Pairs of horses, postilion in front. There is a young man sitting in the carriage, heavily powdered, wearing stockings and a smart velvet jacket, glasses on his nose. He looks blithely at the soldiers, at the people running, at the noisy mob.

His face at the coach window expresses curiosity and pleasure. Passing by the Company's square formation, he spots Wilhelm, looks at him for a few seconds, straightens his glasses, and then shouts cheerfully:

'Is that you, Küchelbecker?'

Wilhelm turns around abruptly, sees the outlandish coach, the young man in it, and instantly loses the sense of where he is. He approaches the carriage and peers at the young man:

'Gorchakov?'

The young man in the powdered wig is Prince Gorchakov, Wilhelm's Lycée friend. He has just arrived from London and is hurrying to the palace to take the oath.

'Very crowded here these days,' he says absent-mindedly, 'just like in London. I got used to the mob over there, you know, but here it's positively swarming.'

He casts a distracted eye over the Moscow Regiment and the Company and adds condescendingly:

'The troops are already mustering then. I'm rather late, you know.'

He squints and peers short-sightedly at Wilhelm, nods to him condescendingly, then suddenly notices the long pistol in Wilhelm's hand.

'What's this?' he adjusts his glasses.

'This?' asks Wilhelm, also distractedly, and glances at his hand. 'It's a pistol.'

Gorchakov thinks, looks around, and says to the postilion:

'Drive on, dear chap.'

He bows politely to Wilhelm and drives off, not having understood a thing.

IX

General Orlov is leading squadrons of Horse Guards to attack the rebels. The order is: to charge right into them and cut them to pieces.

Not being shod with sharp spikes, the horses slither and stumble on the icy roadway and fall down. Dark figures run through the crowd toward the arsenal and back, bending to pick up rocks; the crowd is commanded by the man with the white plume who waves his arms, and the other one, the short one, dressed in black. The Moscow Regiment fires.

Logs and rocks fly from the crowd into the Horse Guards. The Horse Guards haven't drawn their sabers. Wilhelm sees the divisional commander clutch his chest—he is wounded. There's the sound of horseshoes scraping over the ice, the thumping sound of horses falling heavily—and the Horse Guards turn their mounts. A young Guard flies past head down, comically, like a coat stand. In the distance there are screams, curses, and the noise of receding hooves, minute, disparate sounds.

Odoyevsky shouts:

'Brothers, don't shoot at the men, aim at the horses!'

Wilhelm nods:

'Yes, yes. Aim at the horses' muzzles, brothers,—shame to kill the riders.' He smiles.

'What's all this nonsense?' grumbles an old gray-haired Guard, 'Wasting ammunition, shooting horses in the muzzle. We're not fighting the horses.'

The attack has been repulsed.

And a silent stand-off begins—silent, despite the bustle, although there are shouts and the occasional command in the air. Because the outcome is decided now by the frosty, icy squares, not by the will of individuals.

X

Nicholas ran out of the palace oblivious to the cold, without his entourage, wearing only a uniform with a sash over his shoulder.

The crowd was noisy, but Nicholas did not know that the people in the square were merely splashes from the human river flowing unceasingly to Admiralty, St. Isaac's and Peter's Squares.

Nicholas's face was gray, maybe from cold. He puffed out his chest and looked around vigilantly. The military review had begun. He listened. In one group they were shouting:

'Get Constantine here!'

Nicholas turned and looked desperately at the two courtiers standing next to him. Benckendorff handed him a paper and he understood: he needed to read the manifesto. He made a gesture and began to read in a low, drawn-out voice.

Those standing nearby quietened down and listened, but Nicholas read monotonously, the manifesto was long, the square kept buzzing, and nobody could hear him.

A drunken clerk squeezed his way toward him and tried to kiss his hand. The situation was becoming awkward.

A quarter of an hour passed like this. Nicholas stood looking at the crowd, and the crowd looked at him. They were gradually getting accustomed to him, and he began to feel like a tedious actor who knows that the audience are bored with him. Benckendorff leaned toward him.

'Your Majesty, please, order them to disperse.'

Nicholas shrugged his shoulders. From far off, through the humming of the crowd, the noise of marching troops was coming from Millionnaya Street, sporadic but distinct.

He looked at the crowd, then at Benckendorff.

'Disperse,' he said softly, more to the bunch of courtiers than to the crowd.

Nobody was listening to him. The drunken clerk, his hands clasped in tender emotion, babbled:

'How can we? Thank goodness, we understand, Your Majesty . . . Permit me, your hand . . .'

At that moment, Nicholas saw a battalion marching along Bolshaya Millionnaya, and assumed a dignified air. The Preobrazhensky Regiment approached the palace and lined up.

'Well now, good fellows!' he said not very confidently ("will they answer or won't they?").

'Good health to Your Majesty!' the Preobrazhensky Regiment responded quietly, and Nicholas noticed that not everyone was answering.

He ordered the commander:

'Left turn.'

Miloradovich came running into view. The collar of his greatcoat was half torn off, his uniform partially unbuttoned, there were bruises under his eyes, and his hooked nose was swollen.

Miloradovich had been calmly breakfasting with his ballerina when someone rushed in to report the uprising. Such a message came just in time for the Governor-General of the capital, since he could have completely missed the whole thing, sitting there with pretty Teleshova. He raced to Peter's Square, which was seething with people, and shouted to them threateningly:

'Go home!'

The general was pulled off his horse and beaten up, two soldiers dragged him by the scruff of the neck as far as the corner of the General Staff building and dumped him there. Seeing Nicholas, he ran up to him. He threw off his torn greatcoat before the tsar and stood there wearing just his uniform, with the blue sash over his shoulder. He screamed at Nicholas:

'We must open fire—now!'

He looked at his half-unbuttoned uniform, did it up hastily, with trembling old man's fingers, and muttered plaintively:

'Look what they've done to me, Your Majesty.'

Nicholas gritted his teeth and looked at him. This was the man who had intended to deprive him of the throne. And this was how he was talking now, a commander with sixty thousand soldiers in his pocket. He stepped toward Miloradovich:

'You, as Governor-General of the capital, will bear full responsibility for everything. Go to the square.'

Miloradovich lowered his head.

'Hurry!' said Nicholas, looking with revulsion at the battered face.

Miloradovich gave a confused salute and staggered away.

The company moved off, jostling the mob, which slowly retreated, the soldiers marching with scowling faces. In this way they skirted the corner of the General Staff building. Just at the corner, Nicholas noticed a strange man in General Staff uniform, standing aloof from the crowd; on seeing Nicholas, he turned abruptly. Nicholas recognized him by his stooped back.

"Colonel Trubetskoy . . . Odd."

An advancing adjutant, seeing the tsar on foot, jumped out of his saddle and brought him his horse. Nicholas now had a company of the Preobrazhensky Regiment soldiers and a horse. The rebels had the Moscow Regiment.

Passing Gorokhovaya Street, he halts the company on the corner at the entrance to the Lobanov house with the lions. Too risky to go any further—the Moscow Regiment is standing in a diagonal line across the streets and the square. All around them swarms a motley, irreverent, almost hostile crowd. He catches oblique glances that feign indifference. The rabble is also on the scaffolding round St. Isaac's Church, and for whatever reason the workmen are tearing away the wooden planks from the scaffolding and picking up rocks. Which means that the mob, too, has rebelled. There are screams, ahead, in the square:

'Hoorah!'

'Constantine!'

A shot, another, a third one. He suddenly feels cold. He notices that he is not wearing his greatcoat.

At this moment a very tall officer with a black bandage on his forehead, unpleasant eyes, and a black mustache comes up to him. He has one hand stuck under his lapel. Nicholas peers at him: judging by the uniform the officer is from the Nizhny Novgorod Dragoons.

'What do you want?' Nicholas looks expectantly at the sallow-swarthy face.

'I was with them,' the officer says flatly, 'but when I heard that they were for Constantine, I left them and came to you.'

Nicholas holds out his hand to him:

'Thank you, you know your duty.'

Black eyes have an unpleasant effect on him and he is eager to appease the officer.

'Sire, I suggest we negotiate with the Moscow Regiment.' And the officer again sticks his hand under his lapel.

Nicholas makes a polite face:

'I would be grateful. It's high time we put an end to this misunderstanding.'

The hand beneath the coat is trembling. Noticing this, Nicholas reins in his horse slightly. Yakubovich turns abruptly and disappears. What a suspicious looking person, how uncertain everything is! A brick falls at the horse's feet and the horse rears up: a young mason is standing on the scaffolding, his torso still leaning forward. Nicholas bends toward the saddle, pulls hard on the reins and rides to Admiralty Square. He is overtaken by the adjutant:

'Your Majesty, General Miloradovich has been killed. General Voinov had been badly beaten up by the mob, beaten with logs.'

Nicholas shrugs and turns his horse.

He calls Adlerberg and asks him quietly:

'General, what's to be done about the palace? It's unprotected.'

'Sire, I have prepared the carriages for travel across country and if the worst comes to the worst I shall send Their Majesties to Tsarskoe Selo under the protection of the Horse Guards.'

Firing is heard again from the square. Von Toll, who has just arrived from Nennaal, approaches. (Michael had overtaken him.) Von Toll sits firmly in the saddle and frowns:

'Sire, the second cavalry attack has been repulsed. I have sent for the artillery.'

Seeing Nicholas's empty eyes, he thinks for a second, then makes up his mind:

'Sire, allow me to give orders to the artillery.'

Nicholas nods, not listening closely.

What is happening to the palace?

Adlerberg prompts him in a whisper:

'Your Majesty, go with the company to the palace.'

And he obediently takes charge. By the General Staff building he hears an extraordinary noise from Liftbridge Square. Raising himself anxiously in the saddle, he peers: a dense, disorderly crowd of grenadiers with rifles at the ready is running from Millionnaya Street right to the palace. Ahead of them is a young bandy-legged officer with his sword unsheathed. They are let into the palace courtyard and disappear there. Nicholas's heart is pounding loudly under his thin uniform. They have occupied the palace, it's over. A few minutes pass like this. But the crowd of grenadiers appears at the gate again. The grenadiers approach. The small bandy-legged officer is ahead of them all. Nicholas sees the first rows, makes out the gray stubble on the unshaven cheeks of the old soldiers, the ammunition at the ready, sees clearly now the red, excited face of the small officer, and does not understand a thing. Where are they heading? Why have they left the palace?

The grenadiers have reached Nicholas.

'Good day!'

Silence.

'Stop!'

Silence.

The jolly young officer passes by without saluting.

'Where are you going, lieutenant?'

'To join the Moscow Regiment,' the lieutenant answers cheerfully.

Nicholas feels at a loss and is horrified to hear himself suddenly say mechanically to the lieutenant:

'Then you need to head for Peter's Square,' and he waves in the direction of the Senate.

The lieutenant laughs:

'That's exactly where we are going.'

(Disgraceful, disgraceful, crush the grenadiers immediately!)

And the grenadiers are already being let through by his soldiers. As they pass, a few soldiers brush against his spurs. Nicholas assumes an impenetrable look and commands his bewildered soldiers:

'Let them through.'

Four insurgent companies of the Grenadier Guards head for Peter's Square.

XI

Nicholas's troops slowly draw together and gradually close down Peter's Square.

The Horse Guards have arrived—from the barracks, which are in Admiralty Square.

Grand Duke Michael, like Wilhelm, has been jolting in a sleigh along the ice-bound streets, from the artillery barracks at the Tauride Palace to the Preobrazhensky Regiment and on to the very same Moscow Regiment. He has brought the three other companies of the Moscow Regiment, and they have been ordered to line up opposite the Admiralty building. The Semyonovsky Regiment approaches, and Michael is sent to meet them. The Semyonovsky Regiment men are positioned to the left of St. Isaac's Church, directly opposite the Guards Company, on the heaps of marble rubble.

The second battalion of the Preobrazhensky Regiment and the three companies of the first battalion join up on the right flank with the mounted Life Guards and stand facing the Senate.

The Pavlovsk Regiment occupies Galernaya Street.

And the Moscow Regiment shoots, and the Guards Company stands in a dense black square. And the Grenadier Guards are on the right flank of the insurgents. But who understands anything in this strangely oscillating stand-off of the squares?

Ryleyev—unable to stand the noise, because behind the noise he heard the silence of the balancing scales—has left the square with his head bowed.

General von Toll, who has sent for the artillery, knows nothing of scales and pans and understands one thing: that cannonballs flatten people.

Nothing is certain about the relation between the opposing forces (as General von Toll well knows). Some soldiers separate themselves from the Preobrazhensky Regiment and quickly mingle with the crowd. Nicholas pretends not to notice, but he too knows that these are the truce envoys from the soldiers. And that is why he prefers to send his own envoys. Voinov was met with logs; the bishop may have better luck: he is decrepit and helpless, and therefore quite suitable to play the part of truce envoy.

XII

And now a sleigh approaches the Guards Company. In the sleigh, alongside a fat and pale-faced priest, there is a decrepit bishop with a mitre on his head. Getting tangled in his cassock, the bishop struggles to climb out of the sleigh while the priest supports him by the hand. The bishop says something with his thin, old lips. Wilhelm sees Misha, who is standing in front of the Company with a line of riflemen, whisper something to the nearest soldiers, and several young junior officers immediately surround the bishop. The bishop says in a shaky voice:

'His Imperial Highness Konstantin Pavlovich is alive, thank God.'

Wilhelm shouts:

'Then bring him here!'

Several soldiers repeat after him: 'Bring Constantine here!' But the bishop, as if not hearing, goes on:

'His Imperial Highness is alive, thank God!'

The priest, standing next to the bishop, begins in a treacly voice:

'Gracious brothers, remember the covenants of our Lord . . .'

Then Misha approaches the two priests with a measured soldier's step. He leans toward the decrepit bishop and yells:

'Get out of here, Father, it's not the right place for you!'

The bishop shakes his head, looks with his white geriatric eyes at the young officer, and hurriedly pulls his cassock together. The stout priest helps him into the sleigh.

Misha yells loudly to the bewildered bishop:

'Send Michael here for the talks! We won't shoot.'

A bullet whistles past.

The bishop shudders, grabs the priest with both hands, and the driver rushes off with them.

Wilhelm looks at Misha with horror:

'Why have you sent for Michael? Why have you vouched for his security? Who gave you the order?'

Misha stubbornly jerks his head and grins wickedly. He knows what he is doing, and his elder brother is not going to give him orders.

A voice is heard from behind:

'It's a great opportunity, we mustn't miss it.'

Wilhelm turns round and sees Kakhovsky's dull eyes.

Odoyevsky instinctively grabs Wilhelm's hand:

'Don't get so worked up.'

And Pushchin speaks quietly in a mocking voice:

'Godspeed, Your Imperial Highness.'

They stand in the middle of a living alley—between the square formation of the Moscow Regiment and that of the Company. In Wilhelm's hands is the same pistol, the splendid pistol that Odoyevsky gave him that morning, and which, thanks to the cabman, lay for at least two minutes in the snow by the Blue Bridge. Such pistols shoot splendidly, particularly if the powder in the pan is dry.

XIII

Things are unsettled where Nicholas stands: tradesmen, artisans, and workers are throwing stones from the scaffolding round St. Isaac's Church, the Moscow Regiment's bullets can also reach Nicholas—they know where he is. He must move to another location, under Michael's cover; keeping his head down, Nicholas rides over to the Semyonovsky Regiment.

Michael is fully aware of his significance. He feels a surge of military complacency.

'Let me talk to them myself. I've been told that the officers of the Company want to talk to me.'

Nicholas squints at his brother. He finds Michael's complacency disagreeable.

'We have already sent so many envoys,' he says with a dismissive gesture. 'Even the bishop was no use.'

Michael protests:

'Yes, but they've passed the message to me through the bishop.'

As in childhood, the brothers compete with each other. Michael is extremely reluctant to let Nicholas have his way.

'Do as you will,' answers Nicholas dryly.

Michael rides to the Guards Company with a general from his retinue by his side. Michael's black plume bobs up and down; he reins in his horse. At he reaches the square formation he suddenly realizes that it's quite true: he shouldn't have come to negotiate. The front ranks have quietened down: a few gray-haired soldiers stare at him sullenly. It looks as if the soldiers cannot be relied on; he needs to talk to the officers.

He asks Misha politely:

'May I talk to the troops?'

Misha shrugs.

Michael speaks loudly, so that his words lose any expressiveness:

'Look here, chaps. My brother Constantine has abdicated. Now you have no reason to refuse to be sworn in to Nikolay Pavlovich.'

Michael presses his hand to his chest:

'I beg you to return to barracks.'

'Bring Constantine here!' cries a squat sailor (it is Kuroptev, who is standing in the alley along with Dorofeyev, next to Wilhelm).

'Bring him here!' they shout from the ranks.

An inaudible conversation and some quiet movements are taking place right in the middle of the alleyway. Michael begins to watch the men surreptitiously.

A tall thin man takes off his overcoat and drops it on the snow, as if not noticing it. He has a black tailcoat on, and he holds a pistol. Beside him is a man in a long coat, thick-set, fair-haired, with calm clear eyes and flushed cheeks.

Michael tries to shout something to the soldiers, but at that moment the soldiers start shouting:

'Hurrah for the constitution!'

They drown his voice.

And at the same time Pushchin says in a somewhat embarrassed voice to Wilhelm:

'*Voulez vous faire descendre Michel*?'[54]

He has lowered his eyes slightly and is not looking at Wilhelm, squinting to one side.

And Wilhelm answers barely audibly:

'*Oui, Jeannot*.'

He moves forward slightly.

Michael catches sight of the thin lanky man again. He feels that he has seen that oddball somewhere before, his face looks familiar.

Sasha Odoyevsky asks Wilhelm:

'Do you have enough powder in the pan?'

He looks at the long pistol, tightly clutched in Wilhelm's long fingers.

'I have enough,' Wilhelm answers soundlessly.

("What the hell, the tall fellow is taking aim. At the general next to me. I must ride away, ride away at once." Michael gestures to the general and is horrified to see the black muzzle of the pistol creeping to the right and staring him in the eye.)

A quiet conversation in the alleyway:

'I'm short-sighted. Which of them is Michael?'

'The one with the black plume,' answers Aleksandr Bestuzhev.

Dorofeyev, who is standing on the left, gently touches Wilhelm's sleeve and shakes his head:

'Don't be too hard on yourself, sir.'

Wilhelm smiles at Dorofeyev without looking at him and answers so quietly that he does not hear:

'Dear chap, we must all die.'

And he aims at the black plume.

The trigger is pressed, but instead of a shot, there is a kind of clicking sound. Michael's and the general's horses prance on the spot, turn around, and gallop off. Wilhelm stares in bewilderment at the gun, then at the retiring black plume. He shoots downward.

Clicking.

'What the hell?'

He looks up at Pushchin. He does not understand. He has a feeling of almost physical pain—as if he had tried to throw a stone, but the stone had got away, spun from his hand, and fallen, and his arm was now hurting from the effort.

Someone is throwing an overcoat over his shoulders from behind—Dorofeyev. He is hot and choking with sobs. He throws off the overcoat and presses his ice-cold left hand to his burning forehead. (The right one clutches the pistol tightly.) Pushchin addresses Dorofeyev and Kuroptev, his voice full of regret:

'Oh, if only we could get this over with.'

And the haze, the haze before his eyes. Swaying, he looks at the ground, his left hand pulls a handkerchief from his pocket (the right one is as if lifeless, the pistol is in it), and he presses the handkerchief to his head. Oh, if only he could tie it round his head. And Wilhelm looks up. The white plume is facing the square formation.

Voices around him:

'Voinov, General Voinov.'

(Voinov has managed to make his way to the Company to have a word with them.)

'Which one is Voinov?' Wilhelm asks, struggling to speak.

'The one with the white plume,' answers a strange voice from inside the mist, 'in general's uniform.'

Another calm voice nearby says:

'Give me the pistol, it needs fresh powder, yours is damp.'

Wilhelm sees Kakhovsky pouring powder into the pan and says courteously:

'*Merci.*'

Struggling for consciousness, he steps out of the ranks and aims at the white plume, which in the approaching twilight stands out more clearly than the dark figure of Michael.

The powder in the pan flares up but no shot follows. Misfire.

Horrified—this is fate! fate!—he shoots again, not feeling his fingers.

Misfire.

He staggers; they take him by the arms—he can't see who. His overcoat is thrown over his shoulders and he is led out of the Company's ranks. The overcoat is heavy and he drops it; for a moment he feels cold.

And someone throws the coat over him again. And again he drops it in the snow.

He turns around.

Pushchin, Odoyevsky, and Kakhovsky are standing behind him.

Pushchin says disgustedly:

'God, three misfires.'

Odoyevsky looks sadly at Wilhelm and for a moment Wilhelm smiles a pale smile. Pretty much everyone is looking at him reproachfully.

"Well, then, so be it." Wilhelm takes a few steps.

A strange figure appears in front of Wilhelm. Yakubovich has straightened up, lifting his unsheathed sword. A handkerchief dangles from the sword. Yakubovich stands stock still with his sword in front of Wilhelm. Then quickly, as if coming to himself, he lowers the sword, tears off the handkerchief, and flushes deeply.

'It's a disguise,' he mutters. 'I have volunteered as an envoy.'

Wilhelm looks at him almost calmly.

Yakubovich says hoarsely: 'Keep it up,' and knits his eyebrows meaningfully. 'They are scared stiff of you.'

And he leaves the square with determined steps, holding the bare sword in his hand.

The delusion slowly fades. His throat is dry. He picks up a fistful of snow with his left hand and swallows it greedily. So pleasant, so cold. He eats more snow. And the haze lifts slightly. He looks around. He sees a general rushing from the Moscow Regiment followed by whistling and shouting. Riding at full speed, the general pulls the plume out of his hat and for some reason waves it in the air. Wilhelm rubs his eyes. Everything is clear again, his legs are light again, every muscle is again part of a whole, whose center is outside Wilhelm. And the first thing that he again sees clearly and distinctly is that the government regiments stationed opposite him have parted on two sides and a battery stands between them, yawning mouths of cannon, dimly lit by twilight.

And there comes a moment of silence, gray and translucent.

XIV

The battery of the Guards artillery brigade was brought to the square by General Sukhozanet. It was set up across Admiralty Square; the muzzles of the cannon on the right flank of the battery face the Senate, with Nevsky Prospekt on the left so that two guns can fire along the street.

There are no charges for the cannon, they haven't been brought along.

An adjutant rides back to the arsenal to fetch at least a few charges, but Sukhozanet is already giving orders:

'Battery! Prepare the charges, load the cannon!'

He is trying to frighten the crowd. But the crowd stands motionless, laughing. The Moscow Regiment is shooting, spraying them with bullets, and the Grenadiers and the Company stand as if rooted to the spot.

There are no charges.

General Sukhozanet catches up with Nicholas, who is riding about aimlessly, and says:

'Your Imperial Highness, order the guns to clear Peter's Square.'

He desperately wants to curry favor, but today he has fallen behind. He is late. Nicholas might not know that there are no charges. After all, the charges will soon be delivered.

But Nicholas stops his horse and glares fiercely at the general. His Majesty's teeth chatter violently and, without saying a word, he rides away to the left.

In a fit of official zeal, General Sukhozanet has forgotten himself and called him "Your Imperial Highness."

The general is in despair. He clutches his head, slowly follows the tsar, lies in wait for him, tries to catch him. Twilight falls.

It is nearly four o'clock.

And the Moscow Regiment shoots, and the Guards Company is standing in a black dense square. And four cavalry attacks are repulsed with some losses, and the Grenadier Guards are on the rioters' right flank. And Nicholas sees the mob running singly and in groups over to Peter's Square—to join the rebels.

If this drags on until night-time, victory is uncertain.

Who knows what will happen if all the mob join the rioters? Who can understand what is in people's minds—for example, the Izmaylovsky Regiment's? There is unrest in the Finnish Regiment too. It has stopped on the bridge, on Vasilyevsky Island. Things are dark at night.

General von Toll approaches Nicholas:

'Sire, I think we should put an end to this muddle by using the guns.'

Nicholas nods sullenly at von Toll, as he did before.

Things are dark at night, things are doubtful. General Sukhozanet is eager to distinguish himself. Not many charges have been delivered, they can be counted on the fingers of one hand.

The general does not lose hope of currying favor. He hears what von Toll says, approaches Nicholas and, lowering his voice, leans toward him:

'Sire' (that's safer), 'it's getting dark, the rebels' forces are increasing, in this situation darkness is dangerous.'

Nicholas is silent.

'Are you sure of your artillery?' he asks, frowning, and, without waiting for an answer: 'Try again to negotiate.'

General Sukhozanet rides up to the Moscow Regiment and shouts:

'Put down your guns, lads, or I'll have to use grapeshot.'

Whistling and laughter fly in his face.

Aleksandr Bestuzhev shouts back:

'Sukhozanet, you'd better send someone a bit cleaner!'

A young Guardsman aims at the general. Behind the Guardsman's back there are shouts:

'Don't bother with this nobody, he's not worth the bullet!'

And the cry rises all over the square:

'Hurrah for Constantine!'

'Hurrah for the constitution!'

Sukhozanet, purple with anger, turns his horse. Whistling and hooting follow him. Everybody has spat on him today—this rabble of soldiers, and the tsar himself.

While riding back he jerks the plume out of his hat and waves it in the air. (This was the first thing that Wilhelm saw when he came out of his stupor.) This is the signal for the first salvo.

The first salvo from the cannon is blanks.

The Moscow Regiment keep standing, the Grenadier Guards keep standing, the crowd huddles tightly round the troops.

General Sukhozanet receives an order from General von Toll: regular cannon fire.

XV

First salvo.

The grapeshot sings out shrilly—pe-oo!—and crashes down: it flies in all directions; some shots strike the roadway, ricochet, and kick up snow, others shriek overhead and hit people who have clung to the Senate columns and the roofs of the neighboring buildings—and others, stray shots, rake the frontline. When the snow settles, screams and groans rise in the air. One scream is particularly terrible—like the howling of an animal.

The troops stand firm.

Obolensky's clear voice:

'Fire!'

And in response to the shrill singing of the grapeshot—the dry chattering of rifles.

And the shrill singing again—pe-oo!—and again the crash—the broken windows of the Senate are ringing, the shots slam into the stone, and plaster dust pours down.

People fall in heaps. They fall like sheaves of grain and remain lying.

And still the troops are standing there, and in response to the singing of shrapnel there is the dry chatter of the rifles; but spasmodic now—the rifles stutter—the firing is erratic.

Third salvo—a delicate singing and crackling, and in response—isolated dry cracks of rifles: tra-ta-ta, like funeral drums.

Fourth salvo—and now the rifles fall silent.

Wilhelm sees everything with a terrible, intense clarity: how the front column has flinched and the sailors have run, how an old sailor with a pockmarked face drops his rifle, how a young soldier seems to slip on the ice, falls, and lies—and then comes the big push—and Wilhelm is jostled and carried forward by the running crowd—past the Manège—and his feet stumble over the corpses and the wounded. Once he feels the cracking of bones beneath his feet—and lets himself go with the crowd. As he runs, he sees two soldiers hiding between the niches at the base of the wall by the Manège.

The crowd carries him past Sasha—Sasha Odoyevsky is removing the white plume from his hat—he too is just about to be overwhelmed.

'Sasha! Sasha!'

But Sasha does not hear.

The grapeshot is singing.

And rage sweeps over Wilhelm. He is being pushed, carried along like a speck of dust, and the mad singing of the grapeshot mows everyone down like sheep. Humiliation, humiliation and anger, no fear at all. He clutches the pistol tightly in his hand.

'Stop!' he cries in a wild voice.

The screech of the grapeshot overwhelms his scream.

The crowd has flung him into a narrow courtyard next to the Manège.

The same mad, lucid anger keeps him in its grip. He understands everything clearly, notices the minutest details—the place, the number of people, whether they have weapons. The last wave of the crowd throws his brother Misha into the yard. He has no greatcoat on, the collar of his uniform is unbuttoned, and his eyebrows are knitted in perplexity. Wilhelm is not relieved to see his brother—he doesn't care any more.

He screams:

'Stop!'

And everyone straightens up obediently.

Wilhelm commands in the semi-darkness.

'Fall in!'

And this tall thin man with a twisted face, clutching a long-muzzled pistol, acquires power over people. His voice is obeyed. He gets people into line, and the soldiers frown and follow him.

Misha comes up and says to Wilhelm:

'Get away from here,' but he cannot go on and just moves his lips, looking at his brother with horror.

Wilhelm forcefully pushes him away.

Wilhelm's hour has struck—and he is the master of this hour. He will pay for it later.

'Fix bayonets!'

He leads the people out of the gate into the street, he will lead them in a bayonet charge—against the enemies, against the grapeshot.

'Don't do it,' the squat sailor says to him calmly, 'where are you taking them? They're giving us a pounding with the cannon.'

Wilhelm recognizes Kuroptev.

And in response, the singing of the grapeshot, the hateful delicate squealing, and a moment later—the cracking explosions of bullets.

Wilhelm stands with his head down, clutching the pistol. Everyone has got down. He alone stands.

Kuroptev whispers to him from below: 'Get down!'—and Wilhelm obediently lies down.

They crawl on a bit and Kuroptev tells him:

'Now let's crawl to the middle.'

St. Isaac's Square is enveloped in darkness. And Wilhelm obeys Kuroptev. They crawl to the middle of the square.

And at this moment an incomprehensible change takes place in Wilhelm—his consciousness remains intense, but there is no more anger, there is only acute caution, the insane cunning of the pursued beast. Now they must get past the Semyonovsky Regiment. He takes note of everything as before. He realizes in an instant that he has no greatcoat on, just his tailcoat, and that the pistol is still clutched in his hand, and that they must pass right in front of the Semyonovsky Regiment. And he leans down and silently drops the pistol in the snow. His hand is numb and releases it reluctantly: in the course of the day the gun has fused with the hand. And they pass the Semyonovsky Regiment.

In the twilight two soldiers look sullenly after him. Wilhelm walks straight, without hunching his shoulders.

The last thing he sees in the twilight is the officers of the Guards Company approaching the commander and one by one surrendering to him.

Then he walks lightly and cheerfully, his body is empty, and his heart, free of all care, beats mechanically in an empty breast.

A light figure by the Blue Bridge. Wilhelm overtakes Kakhovsky. They walk side by side. Wilhelm asks him quietly:

'Where's Odoyevsky, Ryleyev, Pushchin?'

Kakhovsky looks at him sideways with his calm, lifeless eyes and does not answer.

And in the dark they part company.

Half an hour later it is evening. Winter evening of December 14, thick, dark, frosty. An evening like night.

On the square there are lights, smoke, shouts of sentries, the cannon turned with their barrels facing in all directions, the cordon chains, the patrols, the rows of Cossacks' lances the dull sheen of the Horse Guards' naked swords, the red crackling of burning firewood by which the soldiers warm themselves, the rifles stacked in pyramids.

Night.

Walls riddled with bullets, smashed window frames all along Galernaya Street, whispering and quiet bustling in the ground floors of the surrounding houses, rifle butts bludgeoning bodies, the quiet, stifled moans of the arrested.

Night.

Fan-shaped splatterings of blood on the walls of the Senate. Corpses—in heaps, singly, black and bloodied. Carts covered with matting, dripping with blood. On the Neva River—from St. Isaac's Bridge to the Academy of Arts—surreptitious stirrings: corpses are being lowered into the narrow ice-holes. Sometimes groans are heard among the corpses—the wounded being pushed down into the narrow holes together with the dead. A quiet fuss and shuffling; the police undressing the dead and wounded, ripping off the rings, fumbling in the pockets.

The dead and the wounded will freeze to the ice. Later that winter, when people are hacking the ice, they will find human heads, arms, and legs in the clear bluish ice floes.

And it will be like this till spring.

The ice will float down to the sea in spring.

And the water will carry the dead to the sea.

Peter's Square is like a ploughed, harrowed, and abandoned field. Strangers wander about it, like dark birds.

Escape

I

Nikolay Ivanovich Grech had spent an anxious day. Who would win? If it was Ryleyev, Nikolay Ivanovich would have to pay for his friendship with Maksim Yakovlevich von Fock. If the tsar,—oh, Nikolay Ivanovich could get into trouble for his reckless liberalism: what speeches he had made at the meetings, what had been printed at his printing press in December!

'They are here, Nikolay Ivanovich, the dragoons have come, the gendarmes.'

Nikolay Ivanovich went out into the drawing-room.

In the drawing room stood Shulgin, the Petersburg chief of police, a man of enormous stature and with magnificent whiskers; with him was a whole detachment of policemen, gendarmes, and dragoons—the whole of the Santa Hermandad[55] in Grech's drawing room.

Nikolay Ivanovich shuffled his feet. Shulgin said:

'Answer these questions.'

He handed Nikolay Ivanovich a sheet of paper. On the sheet of paper, written in pencil in a slanting, clear hand he read: "Where does Küchelbecker stay? What is Kakhovsky's address?" Beside the name of Kakhovsky was written in brackets in a different, trembling hand: "The *Naples* hotel, owned by Mr. Moussar, by the Ascension Bridge."

Nikolay Ivanovich was well aware of Wilhelm's address. But he wrinkled his forehead, raised his right hand to his chin with a Ciceronian gesture, thought for a moment, and answered slowly and thoughtfully:

'As far as I know, Küchelbecker lives not far away, at Bulatov's house. Kakhovsky's address is written here, but whether it's the correct one, I do not know.'

'Is that so?' Shulgin asked.

'It is.'

Shulgin came up close to Nikolay Ivanovich:

'Look here, do you know who wrote this? His Majesty himself. You'll answer with your head for the accuracy of the information.'

Nikolay Ivanovich bowed respectfully:

'I confirm the absolute accuracy of the information.'

Shulgin said to the gendarmes:

'To Bulatov's house.'

The gendarmes left. Nikolay Ivanovich quietly returned to his bedchamber.

II

By the end of the day Faddey Venediktovich Bulgarin was completely at a loss. He took a cab and paid visits to his friends. The driver that Faddey Venediktovich hired was a taciturn chap. The city was deserted and quiet. In the distance, the Hermitage Bridge was black with army uniforms. To his own surprise, Faddey Venediktovich asked the driver:

'Tell me, dear fellow, can we go to Peter's Square?'

He spoke, then bit his tongue. The driver shook his head.

'We can't, sir, there's cleaning up going on over there, guns and soldiers all around.'

Faddey gave a silly giggle:

'What kind of cleaning up?'

'They wash off the blood, sprinkle the stains with fresh snow, then smooth it out.'

'And was there a lot of blood?' asked Faddey in a trembling voice.

The cab driver was silent for a moment.

'Must've been a lot, if they are dropping the bodies under the ice.'

Faddey looked round.

'Could you go to the Blue Bridge, dear fellow?' he said pleadingly, as if the driver might refuse him.

At the house of the Russian-American Company he got out, quickly settled the fare, and trotted up the familiar staircase.

“Go in or not?” he thought, “God help me, not worth even thinking about, back, better go back. Why on earth have I come here at all?’

He tugged at the doorbell.

A servant, pale, with frightened eyes, opened the door. Faddey entered the dining room hesitantly and, for some reason, rubbing his hands. Ryleyev, Shteingel, and three or four more people were sitting at the table. They were talking quietly among themselves, drinking tea. Nodding his head and smiling a guilty smile, Faddey approached the table. He did not greet anyone but had already spotted a vacant chair and was about to sit on the edge of it.

Then Ryleyev got up lazily, left the table, went up to Faddey, and took him by the arm above the elbow.

‘You, Faddey, have nothing to do here,’ he said slowly. He looked at Faddey and grinned. ‘You will be safe.’

Then, still holding his arm, he led him out of the room and shut the door.

Finding himself in the street, Faddey thought sadly:

“I’m done for. By God, I’m done for.”

He ran along the street, then stopped.

“No, no running. Home as fast as possible . . .”

Somehow, he reached home, wrapped himself in a dressing-gown, lay down, warmed up, and dozed off.

At two in the morning Faddey was still asleep. When he woke up, he saw an unknown moustachioed head above him.

‘Bulgarin, the journalist?’

Faddey sat up in bed. A gendarme stood before him. In the doorway he caught a glimpse of his mother-in-law, *tante*, looking at him majestically: he had finally got his just deserts.

“This is the end,” thought Faddey.

‘Get dressed now. You are going with me to the chief of police.’

Faddey muttered:

‘Right away. One moment. I’ll be with you in no time at all.’

His hands were shaking.

Police-chief Shulgin was sitting at the desk in an unbuttoned uniform. Before him stood two gendarme officers, to whom he was giving orders.

Faddey bowed in the most respectful manner. Shulgin did not respond.

"I'm done for," thought Faddey.

Having dismissed the officers, Shulgin peered at Faddey intently. Then he grinned and nodded at the chair: 'Sit down. Why are you so nervous?' He laughed. Faddey noticed that he was slightly tipsy.

'Not at all, Your Excellency,' he said, growing a little bit more daring.

'Do you happen to know Collegiate Assessor Wilhelm Karlovich Küchelbecker?' Shulgin suddenly looked at him point blank.

'Me? Küchelbecker?' babbled Faddey ("I'm sunk," he thought quickly), 'only through literary business, nothing else. I've had no other relations with this person, and one might say that our relations are distinctly unfriendly.'

'Literary business it may well be,' said Shulgin, 'but do you know him by sight?'

Faddey began to guess the drift.

'I do know him by sight.'

'Can you describe his appearance?'

'I can, sir.'

'Write it down,' Shulgin pushed a pen, an ink-stand, and a sheet of paper across to Faddey. 'Describe his features in detail.'

"Küchelbecker Wilhelm Karlovich, Collegiate Assessor," wrote Faddey, "tall, lean, with protuberant eyes and brown hair." Faddey thought about it, he remembered how Wilhelm had spoken this morning at Grech's. "His mouth twists when he speaks." Faddey looked at Shulgin's magnificent side-whiskers. "His side-whiskers are scant, he has a skimpy little beard, he is somewhat stooped and walks slightly bent." Faddey remembered Wilhelm's drawn out voice. "He speaks slowly, he is hot-headed, short-tempered, and of unbridled temperament."

He handed the paper to Shulgin.

Shulgin glanced at the sheet of paper, read it carefully, and smiled at the end:

'"Hot-headed and short-tempered" has nothing to do with how he looks. How old is he?'

'About thirty,' said Faddey, 'no more than thirty.' He spoke rather confidently.

Shulgin wrote it down.

'You'll answer with your head for the accuracy of the reported features,' he said hoarsely, staring hard at Faddey.

Faddey pressed his hand to his heart.

'Don't worry, Your Excellency,' he said, almost cheerfully, 'those features are enough to distinguish him among a hundred people. To be honest, this description is a real work of art.'

'You may go.'

Faddey got up. Feeling an influx of special, servile joy, he asked, unexpectedly for himself:

'Could you tell me, please, whether His Imperial Majesty is in good health?'

Shulgin looked at him with some surprise.

'He is well,' he nodded. 'You may go.'

Faddey stepped out and in his relief put out his tongue at himself.

"The Bread-maker must have got away then, if they are asking about his features," he thought later, with a kind of satisfaction.

III

A sort of rumbling in the distance, fractured yet sustained, as if they were pouring dried peas from one sack into another—the cavalry was returning, unhurriedly. Wilhelm walked further and further from the square. Then he stopped, looked, and thought for a moment. He turned back—he had noticed that he had just gone past the St. Catherine Institute. And he rang the doorbell. The gatekeeper unlocked the gate and looked at Wilhelm, somewhat taken aback. Then she recognized him. Wilhelm went through to his Aunt Breitkopf's. Dirty, in a ragged tailcoat, he stood in the middle of the room, water dripping from him. His aunt was standing by the table motionless, like a monument, and her face was paler than usual. Then she took Wilhelm by the hand and led him off to wash. Wilhelm followed her obediently. When he returned to the dining room, his aunt was composed. She put a cup of coffee in front of him, pushed the cream jug toward him, and looked at him intently, propping her head on her hands. Wilhelm was silent. He drank the hot coffee, warmed himself up, and stood up quietly, but almost with a show of energy. He said goodbye to his aunt. She replied quietly:

'Willie, my poor boy.'

She pressed Wilhelm to her majestic chest and burst into tears. Then she saw him off at the gate.

Wilhelm walked the streets stealthily. The streets were silent. Before reaching the Blue Bridge, he stopped for a moment.

He thought he saw a light in Ryleyev's windows. Suddenly, he heard the rattling of sabers and a few gendarmes walked by.

Wilhelm walked on with straight, quick strides, without looking back. Campfires were burning in the distance, in the square. He quickly turned into an alley and climbed the stair to his rooms.

Semyon opened the door.

'Is Odoyevsky not in?' asked Wilhelm.

'He isn't,' Semyon answered hoarsely.

Wilhelm sat down at the desk and thought for a minute. He gazed at his desk absent-mindedly, glanced out of the window. The desk, and the window, and the chair on which he sat, all looked like somebody else's. His room was no longer his. What was he to do? Sit and wait? Waiting was the worst. Wilhelm almost wanted the door to open and the gendarmes to come in. If only it would happen quickly. He sat at the desk for five minutes like this, though it seemed like an hour. They were not coming. Then he got up from behind the desk.

'Semyon,' he said hesitantly, 'pack my things.'

Without saying anything and not looking at Wilhelm, Semyon opened the wardrobe and began to pack.

'Oh, no, no,' Wilhelm said suddenly. 'That's far too much! Just give me two shirts.'

He took the bundle, looked around and saw his manuscripts and books, then his eyes fell on Semyon, and he nodded to him absent-mindedly:

'Goodbye. Leave the apartment this very night. Go to Zakup. Borrow some money. Say nothing to anybody.'

He put on an old sheepskin coat, threw an overcoat on top of it, and moved toward the door.

At this point Semyon grabbed his arm.

'How are you going to travel on your own, Wilhelm Karlovich? We've lived together, we shall leave together.'

Wilhelm looked at Semyon, then embraced him, thought for a second, and said quickly:

'Well, get ready quickly then. Take two shirts for yourself.'

They went on foot as far as the Blue Bridge. Wilhelm hid his face in his collar as he walked. He cast a last glance at the house of the Russian-American Trading Company, then they took a cab and drove to Obukhov Bridge.

At Obukhov Bridge, they got out. Turning his face away, Wilhelm paid and they walked up a dim street.

Not far from the barrier, in a dark alley, Wilhelm suddenly stopped, ripped off his white fluffy hat, and passed his hand across his forehead.

"Manuscripts . . . What will happen to my manuscripts, with all my work? They'll all perish." He threw up his hands. "Should I go back? See Odoyevsky too, I can't just leave everyone, everything."

Semyon stood and waited; the light of a street lamp flickered in a frozen puddle.

"No, it's over. Gone, gone, perished, and won't come back. Must move on."

'Wilhelm Karlovich,' said Semyon suddenly, 'how could we abandon the apartment? We've left all our stuff unguarded. It will be looted.'

Wilhelm told him:

'Be quiet. Life matters more than possessions.'

They went round the barrier and reached the highway leading to Tsarskoe Selo. They walked five *versts*. The road was quiet, dark. Occasionally a belated Baltic peasant rumbled by on a cart or a wary pedestrian passed by with a stick, looking back at the two silent figures.

In the German village they hired a German who, for five rubles, drove them past Tsarskoe Selo to Rozhestvino. As he was passing Tsarskoe Selo, Wilhelm looked into the darkness, trying to determine the whereabouts of the Lycée, but nothing could be seen in the gloom. He closed his eyes and dozed off, no longer thinking, feeling, or remembering anything.

IV

Top Secret

To His Excellency
Inspector General of all Cavalry,
Commander-in-Chief of the Lithuanian Separate Corps,
Viceroy of the Kingdom of Poland,
His Imperial Highness the Crown Prince
from the Minister for War

His Majesty the Emperor has graciously decreed the promulgation of a general announcement, that all possible measures be undertaken to locate Collegiate Assessor Küchelbecker, and that if anyone is found to be harboring him, then the laws against concealment of state criminals are to be enforced. I have the honor to inform Your Highness of the Emperor's will and to add that Küchelbecker is tall and thin, with protuberant eyes, brown hair, the mouth is inclined to twitch during speech, scant side-whiskers skimpy beard, he stoops and walks a little bent, speaks slowly, and he is approximately thirty years of age.

Minister for War Count A. I. Tatishchev

January 4, 1826, No. 76

Top Secret

To His Excellency
The Minister for War
from the Governor-General of Riga

Having respectfully received the dispatch from Your Excellency of January 4, regarding the measures to be undertaken in order to locate the whereabouts of Collegiate Assessor Küchelbecker, I consider it my duty to respond by informing you that, having learned of the escape of the aforementioned Küchelbecker, I have ordered his immediate detention, as soon as he appears anywhere in the provinces that are under my immediate jurisdiction. Subsequently the Military Governor-General of St. Petersburg informed me of His Imperial Majesty's will regarding the detection of Küchelbecker, in view of which I did not hesitate to confirm to the civil governors subordinated to me the exact execution of the Highest Command in this respect. In notifying you of this, permit me to assure Your Excellency that I never fail to pay due attention and to exercise strict personal supervision both in the undertaking of the measures aimed at pursuing important state criminals, and in general prompt and precise compliance with the orders of the Highest Command.

Governor-General
General Paulucci

January 12, 1826, No. 22

Top Secret

To the Chief of the 25th Infantry Division,
Lieutenant-General
and Cavalier Goguel 2nd,
From the Inspector-General of all Cavalry,
Commander-in-Chief of the Lithuanian Separate Corps,
Viceroy of the Kingdom of Poland,
His Imperial Highness the Crown Prince.

On January 4, the Minister for War Infantry General Tatishchev notified me that the Emperor had decreed the issue of a general announcement to the effect that measures be undertaken to locate Collegiate Assessor Küchelbecker, and that if anyone is found to be hiding him, they will be dealt with in accordance with all the strictness of the law against those harboring state criminals; appending that Küchelbecker is tall and thin, with protuberant eyes, brown hair, his mouth is inclined to twitch during speech, he stoops and walks a little bent, speaks slowly, and is about thirty years old. In fulfilment of His Imperial Majesty's present will, I request Your Excellency to announce this in the Highest Division entrusted to you and to undertake strict measures to determine whether the specified Küchelbecker is somewhere in the disposition of the troops of that division and if so to arrange his immediate arrest and report to me by a messenger.

Inspector-General of all Cavalry
Constantine

Warsaw
January 11, 1826, No. 77

Additional Note:
On January 14, the brigade and regimental commanders are ordered to take the strictest measures to find the criminal.

Lieutenant-General Goguel 2nd.

V

A tall, lean man with protuberant eyes was sitting at a separate table in a country tavern. He looked around and muttered:

'What shall I do? What shall I do now?'

Then he lowered his head on to his hands and burst into sobs. It was noisy and festive in the tavern, a Gypsy woman was singing, and a gloomy male Gypsy with big black mustaches plucking a guitar. A small, well-dressed man in the uniform of a retired colonel appeared as if from nowhere at the neighboring table. He scrutinized the tall man at length, then quickly pulled a paper from his pocket and glanced over it. He read it and gave a low whistle. Then he called the servant, paid, and went out. Half an hour later, when the tall, lean young man came out, staggering, he was immediately seized by two men, thrown into a sleigh, and hurried away. The tall man cried in an ear-splitting voice:

'Stop thief!'

Then one of the wordless individuals, who held him tightly by the arms, gagged him swiftly with a handkerchief, and the other one just as swiftly tied his hands with a rope. The tall man stared at them with his protuberant eyes.

He was driven to the police station. Three policemen on duty led him to a room, threw him in, and locked the door securely. The people who had brought in the tall man massaged their hands wearily.

'Got him,' said one of them contentedly.

Chief of police Shulgin immediately appeared, swaying. He had the tall man's hands untied and began the interrogation:

'Name, surname, rank?'

'Protasov Ivan Aleksandrovich,' muttered the tall man.

'Don't lie,' said Shulgin sternly. 'You are Küchelbecker.'

The tall man was silent, then said:

'Who?'

'Küchelbecker Wilhelm Karlovich, rebel, collegiate assessor,' Shulgin said loudly, 'not, as you say, Protasov!'

'What do you want from me?' muttered the tall man.

'Do you admit that you are the wanted state criminal Küchelbecker?'

'Why Küchelbecker?' the tall man was really surprised. 'I don't understand. First my fiancée, Anna Ivanovna, turned me down, then they grabbed me, and now you're saying I am a Küchelbecker. What's all this about?'

'Stop your play-acting,' said Shulgin. 'The description matches.'

He took out a sheet and began to mutter:

'Of tall height, protuberant eyes, brown hair, hm, *brown* hair,' he repeated.

The tall man's hair was jet black.

'What the hell is this?' asked Shulgin, puzzled.

The tall man dozed off on the chair.

'"No side-whiskers."'

Shulgin looked again at the tall man. The tall man definitely had no side-whiskers.

'Ah!' he slapped his forehead. 'I've got it. He's dyed his hair! He's changed the color!'

He called the gendarmes and said to them sternly:

'Wash this man's hair as well as you can, until it turns brown. This is a dyed Küchelbecker.'

The tall man was awakened and taken to the cell. There his hair was washed and scrubbed for an hour. The hair remained black. The chief of police dyed his side-whiskers, and at home he had a special spirit from a German apothecary, which washed off the dye perfectly. When his side-whiskers began to lose their color, Shulgin would wash them with it, and the dye would come off. He wrote a note to his wife:

"*Mon ange*, send the spirit that I have in the cupboard with this person immediately. It's very important, dear heart, so don't make a mistake. A little faceted bottle."

The tall man's hair was washed with the spirit.

Shulgin kept repeating:

'It'll come off, you'll see, it'll come off with the spirit.'

The tall man's hair did not lose its color.

Then Shulgin, somewhat puzzled, sent the gendarme to Nikolay Ivanovich Grech. Nikolay Ivanovich was quickly becoming an expert on Küchelbecker.

When Grech entered the room of the chief of police, the latter, who had just had a little glass of rum, said to him rather politely:

'I demand an explanation on a certain point, you must tell the whole truth as a matter of honor and loyalty.'

'Your Excellency will hear nothing but truth from me,' said Nikolay Ivanovich and made a slight bow.

'Do you know Küchelbecker?'

'Alas!' sighed Nikolay Ivanovich, 'I had dealings with him on literary matters.'

'Right. And do you remember his appearance?'

'I do indeed, Your Excellency.'

Shulgin led Nikolay Ivanovich into the other room.

A tall young man lay on the sofa staring with a wild expression at the ceiling. Shulgin looked regretfully at his black hair and muttered:

'They washed it and washed it but it wouldn't come off.'

'They washed what?' Nikolay Ivanovich was somewhat amazed.

Shulgin waved his hand.

'Is this Küchelbecker?'

'No!'

'Who is it then?'

'No idea.'

Then the young man jumped up and shouted plaintively:

'Nikolay Ivanovich, I am Protasov; we met at Vasily Andreyevich Zhukovsky's.'

Grech peered and said, crossly:

'Ah, Ivan Aleksandrovich.'

Shulgin looked at the tall man with disgust:

'So why didn't you say at once that you were not Küchelbecker?'

He waved his hand and went off to finish his rum.

On the same night, five more Küchelbeckers were arrested: the manager and a waiter at Naryshkin's, the son of State Councillor Islenev, and two young German bakers.

They did not have their hair washed, instead, Shulgin sent straight for Nikolay Ivanovich, who within a week had become accustomed to these summonses.

VI

A little *muzhik* sat in the Valuev tavern drinking tea, cup after cup. He had put his huge sheepskin hat with its black top on the table. He was pouring with sweat, he was on his third pot, but was still biting on sugar lumps and blowing at the saucer into which he poured the tea, all the while winking at the fat girl in a bright-colored *sarafan*[56] who bustled around between the tables. There were not many people in the tavern, and the *muzhik* was bored. Some travelers were sitting in the corner: a tall, thin man in a white Astrakhan hat and another one—young and blond. They were drinking and eating greedily. The peasant looked at the tall man with curiosity, then decided:

"Either a master or a menial. Could be a steward though."

The tall traveler also looked at the *muzhik* closely, not so much at him as at his hat. The *muzhik* noticed this, took the hat off the table, and, embarrassed, pulled it on. It was uncomfortable to sit there in a hat and he soon put it back on the table. The tall man nudged the blond man, and he went up to the *muzhik*.

'Hey, uncle,' he said cheerfully. The *muzhik* put his cup down.

'Uncle, do you want to swap hats? I'll give you this white one in exchange for your black one.'

The peasant looked at the white hat mistrustfully.

'Why should I?' he said calmly. 'I like my hat. I don't need yours.'

'Don't be ridiculous, uncle,' the blond man said. 'This hat is expensive, a real city hat, you can wear it on feast days in the country . . .'

'On feast days,' the *muzhik* said, wavering. 'And what will I do with it on weekdays? I'll be a laughing stock.'

'You won't,' said the confident blond man, picked up the sheepskin hat from the table, and gave it to the tall man.

The tall man put it on, smiled, patted it down on his head, settled the bill, and they both left.

The travelers had been dashing along the bumpy road in a canvas-topped wagon for a long time, while the peasant was still trying on the white hat, examining it, putting it on the table, and trying to understand why the tall man needed to swap a ruble for a kopeck—the white Astrakhan hat for a black sheepskin peasant one.

VII

Just before New Year's Eve, Wilhelm drove up to Zakup. It was the same road where he used to ride with Dunya, but now it was snowed under and all around there were desolate fields. There were only two or three more *versts* before Zakup and they had to drive through the large village of Zagusino. All Zagusino knew Wilhelm. Here lived his old friend, Ivan

Letoshnikov. Wilhelm stopped in Zagusino for a short rest, some tea, and to inquire about what they knew in Zakup.

The village head, Foma Lukyanov, a huge old gray-haired man, met Wilhelm outside his wooden house, gave him a low bow, and looked at him intently with his gray intelligent eyes. And Wilhelm felt at once that something was wrong. He jumped out of the wagon and entered the hut. Foma followed him unhurriedly. In the hut, an old woman was bustling by the stove, kneading dough in a bowl. Foma gestured to her sternly to get out.

'Heartily welcome, sir,' he said, pointing to Wilhelm to take a seat on the bench under the icons.

'Is everyone well?' asked Wilhelm, not looking at the village head.

'Thank heaven, yes,' said the village head, stroking his beard, 'both your sister and your mama are here, and Avdotya Timofeyevna is visiting. All in order.'

Wilhelm ran his hand across his forehead: Dunya was here and so was his mother. He immediately forgot all his fears.

'Well, thank you, Foma,' he rose energetically to his feet. 'I'd better see my family. Where on earth is Semyon?' And he moved out of the hut.

Foma looked at him sullenly from under his brows:

'What's the hurry, your lordship? Please sit down. Listen to what I have to tell you.'

Wilhelm stopped in his tracks.

'A courier came for you from Petersburg with two soldiers. They stayed in Zakup and waited for almost three days. They left only three days ago.'

Wilhelm turned pale and paced the hut hurriedly.

'They didn't wait long enough, obviously,' the village head went on, casting glances at Wilhelm, 'and her ladyship gave us the order: "If Wilhelm Karlovich comes, tell him that a courier came for him."'

'Has he left?' asked Wilhelm. 'For good?'

'The lads say they are still waiting for you in Dukhovshchina.'

Wilhelm looked around like a hunted beast. Dukhovshchina was a roadside village through which he would have to travel further along the road.

'Look here, sir,' said Foma, 'take your sheepskin off, have a meal with us, call in Semyon, he's spent enough time with the horses, and then we'll have a think. I've already sent my boy to Zakup. He'll tell them you're here.'

A bald old man with a round beard entered the hut. Wilhelm peered: Ivan Letoshnikov. As usual, Ivan was a little drunk. His coat was torn.

'Welcome, your lordship,' he greeted Wilhelm. 'How have you get so thin?' He glanced at Wilhelm's face.

Then he saw Wilhelm's sheepskin, his peasant hat, and wondered for a moment.

'Still got a soft spot for your Russian folk clothes?' he asked, shaking his head.

He remembered how three years ago Wilhelm had walked around Zakup in Russian clothes. Wilhelm smiled:

'How are you doing, Ivan?'

'Not really living, just living out my time,' Ivan said. 'I'm neither for this world, nor the next. And I hear it was hot with you there, in Petersburg?' He winked at Wilhelm.

'Yes, it was,' Wilhelm drawled absent-mindedly and said to no one in particular: 'How can I see my mother?' (He was thinking about Dunya.)

Foma said confidently:

'That can be arranged. They will go for a ride to the grove, so will you, and you'll meet there. You can even go with Ivan. But you know what, master, change your clothes for peasant ones.'

He shouted for the old woman to come in and gave her strict orders:

'Find whatever clothes we have for the master: a sheepskin, some bast shoes, a shirt, and a pair of trousers. Be quick,' he said, looking at the old woman's bewildered face.

Wilhelm changed.

Five minutes later he and Ivan were riding to the grove along a desolate side road.

'My dear man,' said Ivan, 'even the wolves don't know this road, let alone people. Rest assured, you'll be safe and sound. We'll outwit the courier.' (Foma had let the cat out of the bag.)

Dunya and Ustinka were already waiting in the grove. They had decided not to upset their mother and had left her at home. Dunya hugged Wilhelm simply and openly and touched his lips with hers, both cold from the frost.

Wringing her hands, Ustinka looked at her brother. Then she whispered anxiously:

'Do you have a passport?'

Wilhelm came to with a start.

'Passport?' he asked. 'No, no passport.'

'Is Semyon with you?' she asked.

'He is. He didn't want to let me go on my own.'

'Good man,' Ustinka said quickly, and a tear ran down her cheek. She did not notice it. Then she straightened the shawl on her head and said hurriedly: 'Wait here with Dunya. I'll bring you a passport and get together some things for the road. You can't travel so lightly.'

'Don't pack anything, for God's sake,' Wilhelm said quickly. 'What for? I won't take anything,' and he smiled to his sister.

Ustinka left. He stayed alone with Dunya.

Half an hour later, Ustinka returned with a passport for Wilhelm and furlough papers for Semyon.

'Go to Warsaw,' she whispered, 'from there it's not far to the border. And remember this name, Wilhelm: Baron Mohrenheim, mama's cousin. He lives in Warsaw. He's an influential man and won't leave you in the lurch. Remember?'

Wilhelm repeated obediently.

'Baron Mohrenheim,'

Dunya looked at him, smiling, but tears rolled down her cheeks.

He would remember her like this forever, rosy-cheeked with frost, with cold lips, laughing and crying at once.

'Master,' said Ivan on the way back, 'master, listen to what I'm saying: your Semyon is a townie. He doesn't know the roads down here. I'm a famous driver. I drove between Smolensk and Warsaw for nearly twenty years. Take me with you.'

'Impossible, Ivan,' said Wilhelm and smiled wearily, 'how would you manage at your age?'

VIII

The white road was monotonous with mileposts.

Wilhelm slept, huddled in the corner of a canvas wagon, stretching out his long legs. Semyon stared long at the snowfields, nodded drowsily, from time to time turned around from his coachbox, and peeped under the canopy of the wagon: Wilhelm's immobile face was rolling about there. Semyon shook his head, hummed quietly under his breath, and whipped the horses. Ustinya Karlovna had given them good horses. The roan one with the bald spot on her forehead was quiet and strong, the second one, a gray, was lazier. Semyon lashed the gray one. On the morning of January 6, dazed by their journey, they reached the city barrier, beyond which lay the outskirts of Minsk.

Huddling up against the cold, Wilhelm went into the guard house and immediately threw off his coat. The sentry at the desk could hardly read the tattered papers, tracing them with his finger. Another man sat next to him, a short man in a military overcoat with a small thin-lipped mouth and a cross expression, either a low-ranking gendarme or a police officer. Wilhelm threw his passport and Semyon's leave papers on to the desk and sat down on the bench. He stretched out his legs and waited. His body was weary all over, his shoulders ached. He was sleepy and hardly cared that now the soldier would read his passport and ask him questions, and again he would have to say something absurd, to give somebody else's name. "Semyon is still busy with the horse," he thought, "he must be hungry."

He suddenly opened his eyes and saw that the short military man was standing behind the sentry, peering carefully at his passport, making an effort to read it, and moving his lips. The soldier entered Wilhelm's passport in the travelers' register, muttering every word under his breath.

'Served in the Kexholm Musketeer Regiment as a private . . . Matvey Prokofyevich Zakrevsky . . . of the White Russian province . . . a nobleman,' muttered the soldier.

'Zakrevsky,' whispered the military man, moving his lips, and quickly glanced at Wilhelm. Wilhelm felt that this was not the first time he had looked at him that way. His heart suddenly began pounding so violently that he was frightened that its beating might betray him. He lowered his eyelids at the very moment when the military man was about to look him in the eyes and immediately became convinced that all the details of his face and clothes had been scrutinized, checked, accounted for.

The military man asked the soldier quietly: 'Age?' The soldier began to flick through the passport.

'"The present passport is issued to Matvey Zakrevsky, twenty-six years of age, in St. Petersburg on November 4 of the year 1812 . . ."'

'So, in eighteen hundred and twelve you were twenty-six,' muttered the military man, He thought for a moment. 'Which makes you thirty-nine now,' he said and cast a sidelong glance at Wilhelm. Wilhelm closed his eyes and pretended to be dozing. He was not worried about his age: at twenty-eight his head was already looking gray.

The soldier finally wrote down the name and rank of the former private of the Kexholm Musketeer Regiment, who had no campaigns, leaves, or detentions, and said to Wilhelm:

'That's all.'

Wilhelm put his passport under his coat and stood up. The short military man was writing something at the desk, from time to time glancing at the window where Semyon was busy adjusting the linchpin of the wagon. Wilhelm came out and, still feeling the ferreting eyes on him, bent over and climbed into the wagon. The sentry raised the barrier.

'Full speed!' said Wilhelm to Semyon softly.

The sentry watched them go and went back to the guard house.

The short military man was waiting for him on the threshold.

'Get me horses!' he shouted and waved his small yellow hand furiously. 'Right now!' he shouted, stuck his hand into his side pocket, and skimmed the paper, which was covered with writing on both sides.

Five minutes later he was driving at breakneck speed to the city. The paper he was carrying bore a record of the traveler's distinctive features.

IX

In the evening of the same day, Semyon awoke Wilhelm, who was dozing heavily in the wagon, with a loud whisper:

'Wake up, Wilhelm Karlovich! Something's wrong, there are horsemen behind us!'

Wilhelm did not immediately wake up. He was dreaming fragmented dreams, incoherent movements, faces, a small dark man with a predatory nose, and Captain Rautenfeld or Rosenberg talking about something with the man with the white plume. Wilhelm sensed that they were talking about him.

'Horsemen,' the captain seemed to say, 'wake up!'

The wagon hit a bump, Wilhelm started and woke up.

'Where?' he asked, still unconscious of what was going on.

Semyon pointed with his whip back to the left. Wilhelm poked his head out of the wagon and woke up completely. In the distance, at a turn of the road, three or four horsemen were riding fast. They were still far away; their faces and clothes were impossible to make out.

'Give it all you've got!' said Wilhelm quietly.

Semyon began to yell and whoop and lash the horses, and the wagon rushed on, bouncing in the potholes. The edge of the forest flashed by, then a roadside log-hut. The horses raced on.

In the autumn of 1825 they had begun to repair the Minsk Road; for a long time the old road from Minsk to Vilna had been inadequate: the ground was water-logged and a swamp had formed along the middle of the road. A road was temporarily laid out two hundred yards to one side. But then came winter, and work was abandoned. At this juncture the Minsk Road bifurcated; there were actually two roads, and one was impassable—it led into the swamp.

Wilhelm stuck his head out of the wagon:

'What have you stopped for? Keep going, Semyon!'

'Which way?' said Semyon, without turning around, 'left or right?'

Wilhelm looked round: the horsemen were not to be seen, they had disappeared behind a bend in the road. To the left? To the right? How can you tell which turn the pursuers will take?

He shouted:

'To the left!'

The wagon dashed off to the left. Ahead lay the swamp.

Less than ten minutes later, the three horsemen reached the place where the Minsk Road forked.

'Which way now?' asked one, a thick-set man, in a police uniform, who sat awkwardly in the saddle. 'They couldn't have gone by the old road, could they?'

'Who knows,' the small one with a thin mouth and bilious eyes answered dryly. He thought for a moment. 'Zykin!' he shouted, reining in his hot-tempered horse. The young soldier sat to attention on his horse in front of him. 'Zykin, go left! Do you have a weapon on you?'

'Yes, Your Honor,' the soldier said cheerfully and turned his horse in that direction.

X

The road came to an end. An impenetrable swamp covered with thin ice lay ahead. The exhausted horses snorted heavily, walked slowly, and barely flinched at the whip.

'If only we could hide them behind the trees,' said Semyon grimly.

'What trees?' asked Wilhelm, turned his head, and saw two lines of black, bare trees over on one side, to the right of the route the wagon had been following.

He jumped out of the wagon. Semyon got down from the driver's seat, led the horses by the bridle, while Wilhelm pushed the wagon from behind. Somehow they got to the trees, chose a denser spot, pushed the wagon over on its side, and waited. The trees were about two hundred paces from where any signs of the road disappeared.

Ten minutes later, there was a sound of hooves and a young soldier appeared on a horse. He looked hard at the wagon tracks and dismounted. Wilhelm could see his face clearly: lean, with blue eyes. The soldier stopped, pulled out his tobacco pouch, and began to light a cigarette. Having lit up, he once again looked into the distance, at the crushed snow, as if wondering what to do with it. Wilhelm lay hidden behind the wagon. He heard Semyon's loud breath beside him and thought: "God, let's hope the horses don't neigh." The horses stood still. Semyon looked at the soldier over the wagon.

The soldier was still standing in the same place, not knowing whether to go any further along the unknown road or to turn back.

At last he looked around, made a nonchalant gesture, spat out his finished cigarette, trampled it into the snow, and spat again. Then he mounted his horse and cantered back.

XI

From the Lithuanian Military Governor,
Infantry General Rimsky-Korsakov,
to His Excellency
the Minister of War

In response to Your Excellency's communication No. 78 of January 4, following His Imperial Majesty's highest decree, on the 12th of this month I ordered the Civil Governors of Vilna and Grodno to conduct a thorough search in their provinces with a view to the immediate location and apprehension, with the assistance of the description attached below of his distinctive features, of the escaped insurgent, Collegiate Assessor Küchelbecker, who participated in the event that occurred in St. Petersburg on the 14th day of December 1825, and to make a public announcement, that if it transpires that there is anyone concealing him, they will be dealt with to the fullest extent of the laws against harboring state criminals. Yesterday, on January 16, at 6 pm, I received by the messenger from Minsk communication No. 466 of January 15 from the Civil Governor, in which he informs me that two people closely resembling Küchelbecker have recently passed close to Minsk along the Vilna Road. Therefore, the Governor sent a Minsk police officer, Mr. Bobrovich, in pursuit of them to Vilna and, if necessary, further, and has forwarded to me the description of the two men with regard to their apparel, footwear, horses, and wagon, and requested to offer assistance to the said official. Upon his arrival in Vilna, the aforementioned police officer, Bobrovich, reported to me that he could detect no trace of the men's movement along the Minsk-Vilna route. Consequently, on January 16, the Civil Governor of Vilna issued an order circulated by the police officer, concerning the apprehension of these two individuals on any road from Vilna to the border, should they turn up or be found; of which the chief of the Kovno Customs District was informed by him; on the same day I sent to the Grodno Civil Governor by relay a description of their mode of transport, their two horses, apparel, and footwear (reported to me by the Minsk governor) and instructed him to alert immediately via a courier all the police chiefs of the province, in particular, of the border districts, and also the Governor of Brest, so that in the event of the two men appearing anywhere in the district or on the border in Grodno province, according to the existing descriptions and the new features described, they should be immediately seized and taken into custody in shackles; should any information be received of their heading to Volyn province, then the police officer should immediately go in pursuit of them and, having apprehended them, keep them shackled in custody. The head of the Kovno and Grodno customs districts has conducted a review of the appropriate action on the border and at the customs. On the same date, the Vilna Chief of Police submitted a note, attached here in the original, on the receipt of which a police official has been sent to Palanga and upon his return I will have the honor to notify Your Excellency of subsequent developments.

Infantry General Rimsky-Korsakov

Vilna
January 17, 1826, No. 146

According to the information on the insurgent, Collegiate Assessor Küchelbecker, wanted by highest decree, it is established that his sister is married to Smolensk landowner, Glinka, whom he, Küchelbecker, has visited and has taken two horses and one man, heading for Minsk; on the 6th or 7th he drove through the station of Yukhnovka, on the road from Smolensk to Minsk; and on the 10th two people with similar features were seen passing through the city of Minsk where their tracks were lost. It is safe to assume that the said criminal has the intention of escaping abroad, though it is possible that he is heading for Palanga where he can cross the border with ease due to the fact that Glinka, a relative of his sister, is in charge of it. The features under which this criminal conceals himself are as follows: *horses*: two peasant ones, a chestnut-roan, with a bald spot on her forehead, and a gray one; a canvas wagon, damaged on one side, and intact on the other; *persons*: the first (presumably Küchelbecker)—tall of height, lean, with protuberant eyes and brown hair, his mouth twists during speech, thin side-whiskers and beard, stooped, walks slightly bent; drawn-out manner of speaking, thirty years of age, wearing a simple peasant short coat, with a sheepskin on top covered with ribbed or similar fabric—of a yellowish-green color, tied with a large yellow kerchief, peasant hat made of black sheepskin, round, with a black top; the second man is of average height and the clothes on him are: a shabby jacket covered by a greatcoat of blue fabric and a light gray peaked cap. Both of them wear either knee-high boots or bast shoes.

Vilna Chief of Police Shlykov

XII

The canvas wagon pulled by a pair of horses, a roan one with a white bald spot on the forehead and a gray one, jolted along from Minsk to Slonim, from Slonim to Wegrow, from Wegrow to Liw, from Liw to Okuniew, past the noisy little towns, Jewish shtetls, and Lithuanian villages.

The gray one grew tired on the way, in Ruzany Wilhelm sold it to a Gypsy horse-dealer. Near Ciechanowiec they spent the night at a village inn. No sooner had they gone to bed, than they heard a cautious knock on the window. Wilhelm jumped off the bed and sat on the bench.

'Somebody's knocking,' he said quietly to Semyon.

The tavern-keeper came past.

'Don't worry, gentlemen,' he said calmly.

Three young Jews entered the room. An older Jew followed behind. They settled on the bench and began to speak softly among themselves. Wilhelm understood their conversation. To his surprise, they spoke melodiously in a dialect close to old High German. They were smugglers. Wilhelm cautiously approached them and spoke in German, trying to pronounce the words as close as possible to the dialect they used:

'Can you take me across the border?'

The smugglers looked hard at him, then at each other, and the older one said:

'It will cost you two thousand *zloty*.'

Wilhelm stepped away and sat down on the bench. He only had the two hundred rubles that Ustinka had given him. They waited till the morning and drove on.

Another tavern. Sitting there waiting, Wilhelm became thoughtful. To travel any further together with Semyon in the canvas wagon was impossible. He would have to try to cross the border on his own. Wilhelm looked at Semyon and said to him:

'Well, Semyon, we've done enough traveling.'

Wilhelm was terribly tired that day, and Semyon thought that he wanted to stay overnight at the tavern.

'Doesn't matter, we can wait. It's not long till nightfall,' he said.

'That's not what I mean,' said Wilhelm. 'Go back home. You've fussed over me quite enough. There is no way we can go together any further.'

Wilhelm asked the tavern-keeper for some paper and ink, sat down at the table, and began to write a letter to Ustinka. He said goodbye to her, asked her to pray for him and to grant freedom to his friend, Semyon Balashev. Semyon looked at him sullenly and suddenly said, almost crossly:

'How come, master, we've been together all the way and now we part?'

Wilhelm laughed unhappily.

'That's how it is, dear chap,' he said to Semyon. 'First together, then apart. Look here,' he remembered, 'have you got your documents?'

Semyon fumbled in his clothes and said in confusion:

'No, I haven't. No documents. I must have dropped them somewhere.'

Wilhelm threw up his hands:

'How will you travel home then?'

He thought about it, then pulled out his own passport, and handed it to Semyon.

'Take my passport. Doesn't matter, I'll get there one way or another.'

Semyon took the passport, leafed through it with a gloomy look, and then said hesitantly:

'This says I am thirty-nine years old; the horse-dealers put me at no more than twenty. It looks like you need this passport more.'

Semyon was twenty-five and very young-looking.

'Then throw it away,' said Wilhelm indifferently. Probably it's no good anyway: in any case exact copies of it have been made long ago, and by now, it's probably widely known. Get ready and God be with you,' he said to Semyon. 'Give my love to everyone at home; don't lose the letter. Deliver it to Ustinya Karlovna.'

He walked Semyon out to the yard. Semyon climbed into the wagon, then sobbed, jumped out, embraced Wilhelm tightly, got back in, and lashed the roan horse.

XIII

Semyon reached Ruzany. It was a market day. He wandered through the market-place. He had no money and decided to sell the roan horse and the wagon. Two Gypsies stopped in front of him. They bargained for a long time, examined the horse's teeth, felt its legs, and checked the wagon.

Finally, they agreed on a price and handed Semyon twenty *karbovanets.*[57] But when he wanted to use them to pay at the inn, the owner tried the coins on his tooth and said impassively:

'These are forged, I won't take them.'

Semyon was livid. He rushed back to the fair, found the Gypsies, and started shouting that they should either give him the horse and the wagon back or pay with real money. The young Gypsy screamed shrilly:

'That's forged money!'

Semyon hit him on the side of the head. The three Gypsies pinioned him and a fight began; when it petered out, the Gypsies released him. Semyon rubbed his eyes and saw two gendarmes in front of him.

XIV

On January 19, Wilhelm entered Warsaw on foot. He walked along the fringes of the outlying area called Little Prague, looking for a tavern. There was a great crowd in front of one tavern reading a notice.

'"The-re-fore it is ob-li-ga-to-ry . . . ,' a fat man in a blue jacket, apparently a shopkeeper, was reading it out by syllables, '. . . li-ga-to-ry . . .' He could not read any further. '". . . Obligatory,"' he finally read all at once and grunted contentedly.

'Can't you read?' said a commoner with a sharp beard. '"Obligatory for all home owners."'

The shop-keeper glanced sourly at him.

'You're not the only reader here,' he said and walked away.

The commoner read through the notice smoothly and solemnly:

'"December 30, 1825. St. Petersburg Police Chief Shulgin 1st,"' he concluded, admiring the formality of the official language.

Wilhelm could see them from far off. Head down, he went round the corner of the tavern and waited for everyone to disperse. Then he went up to the pillar and read:

Notice

Collegiate Assessor Küchelbecker is wanted here by order of the Police. His distinctive features are: of tall height, lean, with protuberant eyes and brown hair, the mouth twisting during speech, thin side-whiskers and beard, stooped and walking slightly bent; speaks in a drawn-out manner, and is about thirty years of age. Therefore, it is obligatory for all homeowners and housekeepers that, should such a person be residing or staying for a night, they immediately report him to the Police; otherwise, those harboring the criminal will be dealt with to the fullest extent of the law.

December 30, 1825
St. Petersburg Police Chief
Shulgin 1st

Wilhelm looked at the poster. His name, printed clearly on grayish paper, seemed strange to him, and only by the pounding of his heart did he realize that it was he, Wilhelm, who was wanted and pursued.

And he kept walking through Little Prague.

He knew what he had to do—he had to go and find Yesakov, his Lycée friend, or Baron Mohrenheim, mentioned by Ustinka. It was not a difficult task. But a strange feeling overcame him. Everything seemed to him unusually complicated. He had covered a thousand *versts* with Semyon, and now, with only fifteen to go, he began to waver. He was not frightened by the fact that a notice about him had been posted and he could be arrested—every time he approached any village or inn, he was mentally prepared for capture. No. He was alarmed at the thought that in two or three hours he might be free forever. When he was pursued, he would run off and hide. Now the hunt for him had become less intense, but it was in the very air, in these notices, posted on every pole. He did not know what to do about it, like a chess player with too wide a field of possibilities opening up in front of him.

Yet another notice on the wall of a house.

The house looked peaceful with its curtained windows. In one of them a boy was playing with a lazy cat, tickling it; the cat lay on its back, screwed up its eyes, and occasionally, for decency's sake, tapped the boy's hand with its paw. Wilhelm was unable to take his eyes off them.

What nonsense these clownish "distinctive features" were, how senseless that there was someone else's name—some chief of police, "Shulgin 1st," next to his name. He shrugged.

Unthinkingly, he went further and further away from the two notices, as if the gray sheets were the last remaining pursuers.

And after half an hour he became confused. Little Prague, with its non-Russian streets and houses, began to seem like a foreign town. He had exhausted his store of fears during the journey. He looked curiously at the few passers-by and read the shop signs. He was thinking now as if from afar about what was threatening him, remembering how close he had come to the abyss, but the abyss was already far behind, it had all passed long ago. "Wilhelm Küchelbecker" on the poster was just a name, it was not him, just as this Shulgin was just a name. Occasionally he would come to, forcing himself to be afraid, making himself realize that he was still in Russia, that he had not yet crossed the border, that it was yet to be crossed. He forced himself to think about it, thought, but could still not understand it. The thought became too much for him. Any literate person could earn Shulgin the 1st's gratitude with one look at this tall, thin man with protuberant eyes and a pensive gaze, wandering aimlessly through Little Prague.

Before getting to the Gorokhovsky Gate, in the square, he met two soldiers. One of them, stocky, red-haired, and freckled, was, judging by his insignia, a non-commissioned officer of the Guards Regiment, the other one was a rank and file soldier. The officer was carrying a folder of casefiles. On seeing Wilhelm, he looked at him sharply.

"Run for it, get away," thought Wilhelm and approached the officer.

'Would you be so kind,' he said, bowing slightly, 'as to tell me whether the Guards mounted artillery is stationed here?'

The red-haired officer looked hard at him. This man, dressed in a padded sheepskin coat on top of an unpadded coat with a belt and a Russian hat, was expressing himself with unusual courtesy.

'No,' said the officer, peering at Wilhelm, 'the horse artillery is in the city, and this is a suburb. Why do you need them?'

'I need to call on an officer here. He's the commander of the artillery company. His name is Yesakov,' said Wilhelm and was surprised by his own readiness of speech.

'We can take you there,' said the officer, frowning.

'Thank you very much,' replied Wilhelm, looking into his small gray eyes.

"Run for it, this minute."

He walked away with quick steps.

"Don't look back, just don't look back." And he looked back.

The red-moustachioed officer was still standing there with the soldier watching the stooping man intently as he crossed the square. Then he quickly said a few words to the soldier and, seeing Wilhelm staring, shouted:

'Stop!'

Wilhelm walked quickly along the street.

The officer gave the folder to the soldier and ran after him. He grabbed Wilhelm's hand.

'Stop,' he told Wilhelm sternly. 'Who are you?'

Wilhelm stopped. He looked at the officer and calmly, almost wearily, answered with the first thing that came into his head:

'I am a serf of Baron Mohrenheim.'

'You say you need to find the horse artillery?' said the officer, bringing his freckled face close up to Wilhelm's. 'Come with me, I'll take you to the horse artillery right now.'

Wilhelm looked at the officer and grinned.

'Is it worth your while worrying about trifles?' he said, 'I'll find my own way to the city.'

He said this and immediately heard his own voice: it was flat and drawn-out.

'No worry at all,' said the officer sternly, and Wilhelm saw him make a beckoning sign to the soldier.

He did not feel fear, only boredom, a terrible weight, a longing in his body, and perhaps a secret desire for everything to end soon. He had thought so often about being caught that everything that was happening seemed a repetition, and the repetition was awkward and crude.

He began to walk away, with confident strides, in the knowledge that this was necessary.

'Stop!' yelled the officer and grabbed his arm.

'What do you want with me?' Wilhelm asked quietly, feeling disgusted by the touch of someone's calloused hand. 'Go away.'

'A twisting mouth!' shouted the officer, pulling his sword from its scabbard.

'Get your hands off me!' said Wilhelm furiously, without noticing it, in French.

'Vaska, hold him,' said the officer purposefully to the soldier, 'he's the one we were told about in the regiment just the other day.'

Wilhelm squinted vaguely at the freckled face.

"How simple and how quick."

Half an hour later he was sitting in a windowless bare cell in the fortress. The door opened—they had come to put him in shackles.

Fortress

I

Küchlya's travels were of many kinds.

He traveled in carriages, on ships, in a little boat, in a jolting peasant cart.

He traveled from Petersburg to Berlin and to Weimar, to Lyon and to Marseille, to Paris and Nice, and back to Petersburg. He traveled from Petersburg to Usvyat, Vitebsk, Orsha, Minsk, Slonim, Wegrow, Lviv, Warsaw—and back to Petersburg. He did not make this last return alone: he was closely guarded; and though the journey with Semyon had not been particularly comfortable, this one was a hundred times worse: the hand and foot shackles were dreadfully heavy, they rubbed off the skin, ate away the flesh, and rattled at every step.

And then came Küchlya's penultimate wanderings: the Peter and Paul Fortress—Shlisselburg—Dinaburg Fortress—Reval Citadel—Sveaborg. These were the happiest ones for him.

Because when a person travels at will, it means that at any time, if there is money and desire, he can board a ship, hire a carriage or a rowing boat—and go to Berlin, and to Weimar, and to Lyon. When a person travels not of his own choosing, but in order to avoid the will of a stranger, he does everything he can to escape it.

And then he does not look at the sky, the sun, the clouds, the passing mileposts, the dusty green leaves of the roadside trees—or just glances at them in passing. This is because his mind has gone ahead of him, striving to leave behind these very clouds and roadside trees and passing mileposts.

But when the person is incarcerated in cell number sixteen—and the width of the cell is three steps, and the length is five and a half, and there are twenty years ahead of him in this room, and the window is tiny and cloudy and high above the ground—then the journey is joyful in itself.

In fact, does it matter where you are being taken, to which stone coffin, a little better or a little worse, damper or dryer? The main thing is that there is absolutely nowhere to go, absolutely nothing to look forward to, and therefore you can indulge yourself and enjoy the journey—and you look at the clouds, at the sun, at the dusty green leaves of the roadside trees and you do not want anything else—they are dear to you for their own sake.

And if you see only two or three human faces for several months on end, and even those only through the square hole cut in the door, from behind the lifted dark blind, and that face is the watchful-eyed face of the sentry or warder, you begin to treat trees and clouds and even roadside mileposts as people—each tree has its own strange, unique face, sometimes even showing sympathy for you.

And you drink in the air deeply, even though it is not always the life-giving air of the fields, but more often an air filled with the dust raised by your rattling wagon. Because in your cell the air is even worse.

And if there is not even a road or trees or the faint smell of manure through the road dust, if you are sitting in the smoothly rocking cabin of a prison ship, stifling and dark, not much different from a simple board coffin, you still experience joy, because your coffin is seaborne, because you feel the movement and occasionally hear the shouting of the crew above, especially if they are taking you away from the Peter and Paul Fortress, and if only twelve days previously two of your friends and three soulmates have been hanged in front of your eyes.

You can close your eyes, you can abandon yourself to the soothing movement of the ship, for it always keeps time with the movement of human blood. You can try to doze off—even for half an hour, even for ten minutes—and not to see the semi-corpse in a bag fall from the gallows shouting with the voice of your comrade, a noble poet and a friend who used to stroke your hand:

'You, General, must have come to watch us dying in torment.'

And for half an hour—or ten minutes—you can forget the coarse yell:

'Hang them again—now!'

All this you can forget in the dull, seemingly subterranean lurches of the ceaselessly moving ship.

And, if you manage to fall asleep, you will be able to forget the face of your fiancée, your mother, and friends; but you must really sleep and forget, because you have been condemned to death and are now sentenced to life—and decades of solitary confinement are ahead of you, all granted you out of mercy.

And your cabin is better than the cell three steps wide and five and a half steps long, even if you were taken half asleep out of your bed and blindfolded and put in this dark floating coffin, and even if you do not know where you are being taken—or even if you know they are taking you to Shlisselburg. Because below you there is movement and the gentle splashing of water lapping at the sides of the ship, murmuring non-stop, moving in time with the blood circulating in your veins!

II

Two widows lived on the same estate in Zakup: Ustinya Yakovlenva and Ustinya Karlovna. Ustinya Yakovlevna was now very old but took things as they came. Ustinka had also aged noticeably.

The children grew. Mitenka was a capable boy, but his character rather put Ustinya Yakovlevna in mind of his uncle Willie. Ustinya Yakovlevna did not mention this to Ustinka, and secretly spoiled Mitenka.

The village was still the same. Only Ivan Letoshnikov, an old friend of Wilhelm, had died: he had frozen to death on the road when drunk.

Semyon would sometimes come on foot for a visit on holidays; he now lived as a free man in the city and remained the same happy chap, a joker, at whose jests the chambermaids snorted with laughter. He had developed a little limp—the shackles had eaten away the flesh on his left foot: he had spent two years in the Grodno fortress. Ustinya Yakovlevna talked with Semyon for days on end—neither Wilhelm nor Mishenka were there, and Semyon talked to her about them. Shaking her old woman's bespectacled head, Ustinya Yakovlevna would listen to stories of Wilhelm Karlovich's childhood pranks, and would smile. Then she would let Semyon go and would sit down to write letters to the "boys"; her letters were long, and she wrote in tiny, crabbed handwriting.

Letters from the "boys" would arrive—from Wilhelm and Mishenka. Mishenka was doing hard labor in Siberia; Wilhelm . . . Neither mother nor sister knew where Wilhelm was. On his letters each time someone would have carefully scraped out the name of the place where the letter was posted, and blacked out the postmark carrying the place and the date with thick paint.

Then both widows would shut themselves in for a whole day—away from the children. The children ran, jumped, capered. Mitenka would stand for a long time at the door trying to hear what his granny and mother were talking about. But they spoke softly; and he soon tired of standing at the door.

Where was Wilhelm?

No one knew. There was news of all the others: where and how they were—and only of Wilhelm and one other person, Batenkov, was nothing known.

His letters came as if from the seabed.

Ustinaya Yakovlevna went to see "Herself," the emperor's mother, Maria Fyodorovna, but Maria Fyodorovna wouldn't even talk about Wilhelm—she kept silent and then, at the end of the audience, said coldly:

'I am deeply sorry for you, *ma chère* Justine, that you have such a son.'

And Ustinya Yakovlevna stopped visiting Maria Fyodorovna.

Ustinka would also visit St. Petersburg—to petition.

On such days Ustinya Yakovlevna would be especially affable and calm; she would not scold the children, she would read a book. She knew that if her Ustinka had made up her mind, she would have her way. Ustinka was an irrepressible petitioner, and for Wilhelm's sake nothing was too much trouble for her.

Ustinka stayed in Petersburg for a month, and all the time Ustinya Yakovlevna was calm and even-tempered. Ustinka came back: her mother looked at her face, asked no questions, and retired to her room. She sat there until dusk, then came out as if nothing had happened and as if Ustinka had never left, and began chatting with her about the housekeeping.

His mother knew that his friends had not abandoned Wilhelm, that Sasha Griboyedov, who occupied a very important post in the East, had long been soliciting for him to be transferred to the Caucasus; that

Sasha Pushkin, who was now at court, intended to talk to the tsar about Wilhelm and was only awaiting a convenient opportunity, and she gladly believed every rumor that Wilhelm was about to be transferred to the Caucasus—or even here, to the countryside.

Once she even began to tidy up the room in which Wilhelm used to stay, rearranging some furniture in it, and putting his books in order.

But she did not say anything to her daughter at the time and Ustinka never asked.

One day Dunya came to Zakup.

Both mother and daughter knew that Dunya loved Wilhelm. She was no longer, as before, a cheerful young girl, but her quick and confident gait remained the same and her decisions were just as quick and easy. When she was present, everything seemed remarkably simple and clear.

She left Zakup two days later, and on the last day both mother and daughter talked to her quietly about something, making sure the children did not hear—the children knew that when their mother and granny talked quietly together, they were talking about the uncles.

Then Dunya kissed the children hard and left, and both widows began to wait.

Dunya went to the tsar to ask permission to join Wilhelm and to marry him.

She had high connections; Benckendorff had personally promised that the tsar would see her.

And the tsar did receive her.

Dunya curtseyed deeply before him.

Nicholas politely got up from his chair and gestured her to take a seat.

'I am at your service,' he said, his cold eyes sliding over her face, bosom, and arms.

Dunya blushed but said calmly:

'Your Majesty, I have a request to you, the granting of which can make me happy for the rest of my life, while its failure can only make me very unhappy.'

'To make women happy is a duty as pleasing as it is unprofitable,' Nicholas smiled with his lips only, his glance never ceasing to glide all over the girl.

'I have a fiancé, Your Majesty,' said Dunya softly, 'and it depends on you whether I can be reunited with him.'

'Although the fulfilment of your desire might require a certain amount of self-sacrifice,' Nicholas looked into Dunya's eyes, 'I'm listening: how can I be of help?'

'The name of my fiancé is Wilhelm Küchelbecker,' said Dunya softly, enduring the tsar's stare.

Nicholas's lips puckered in disgust, he leaned back in his armchair, and smiled:

'I feel sorry for you.'

'Your Majesty,' said Dunya imploringly, 'I am prepared to follow my fiancé wherever necessary.'

'It's impossible,' Nicholas protested coldly, never ceasing to stare at her.

Dunya repeated:

'Your Majesty, I'm ready to go to places of hard labor, to Siberia, anywhere.'

'And what would you find there? Wouldn't you rather abandon such a fiancé?' Nicholas frowned again. Dunya pressed her hands together:

'If you agreed to this, you would be seen as a savior.'

Nicholas stood up. Dunya rose hastily. He gave her a little smile:

'It's out of the question.'

'Why, Your Majesty?

Nicholas winced.

'When I say it's impossible, it's unnecessary to inquire as to the reasons. But if you wish to know the reasons,' he added, smiling again, 'here you are: your fiancé is in the fortress and to marry while in solitary confinement is rather awkward, don't you agree?'

III

Wilhelm wrote to his mother that he was well and feeling calm.

And it was true, at least half true. He had indeed calmed down.

The colonel himself locked the door behind him. The key was big and heavy, similar to the one with which the Zakup watchman locked the gates at night.

Grech had his printing press, Bulgarin had a journal. Ustinka had a house and an estate, and the colonel had the keys.

Only Wilhelm had nothing, ever.

Grech made him do the proofs, Bulgarin paid him to write articles, and now this old colonel with drooping mustaches put him under lock and key.

All of them were people of order. Wilhelm never understood people of order, he suspected miracles, cunning devices in the simplest things, he puzzled over how a person pays money, or has a house, or has power. And he never had a house, or money, or power. All he had was his literary craft, which brought him ridicule, disparagement, and debts. He always felt that the day would come when the people of order would turn their attention to him, they would cut him down to size, put him in his place.

His friends, in fact, had wanted to find a place for him. But nothing had worked—everywhere he was rejected and every affair that seemed about to succeed fell to pieces at the last moment: even his shot had been a failure.

And now the people of order had found the right place for him, and it was a quiet place. For his own peace of mind, in the first year he was allowed no ink, paper, or quills. Wilhelm paced the cell composing poems and committing them to memory.

His memory let him down though, and after a few months the poems would escape him.

When he used to stay at Grech's and worked for Bulgarin, Wilhelm felt like a Gulliver among the Lilliputians. Now he himself was a Lilliputian and things around him were the Gullivers. His vast field of observation was now a little window high up, covered in bars. It was a cause for celebration when a March tomcat accidentally appeared outside the window.

Oh, if only it had meowed! If only it had arched its back!

Wilhelm studied the topography of his cell bit by bit, so as not to exhaust it too quickly. Today one wall—just a few inches, of course; tomorrow—another wall.

On the walls there were inscriptions, pictures in profile, female for the most part, and some verses.

"Brother, I've decided to take my own life. Farewell, my loved ones." (With an iron nail, long letters, uneven, but deep—they had survived a later scraping.) "*Hier stehe ich. Ich kann nicht anders.* F. S." (Extremely neat and precise letters, very well formed—probably with a fingernail.) "8 years 10 months left. I am ill." (Thick letters—probably done with a nail head.)

One inscription scared Wilhelm:

"Torturers, may you rot in hell! Napoleon, Emperor of Russia." (Very deep letters, but since the plaster at the edges was not damaged, probably with a fingernail.) Someone had gone insane in here.

Wilhelm arranged his memories too. When you were doing time in a fortress you needed to be frugal with your memories. They were all you were left with. And Wilhelm was only thirty years old.

Falling asleep, he made a note of what to remember tomorrow.

Lycée, Pushkin and Delvig.—Aleksandr Griboyedov.—Mother and sister.—Paris.—Brother.—And only sometimes: Dunya.

Only sometimes. Because if in the morning prisoner No. 16 began to remember Dunya, the steps of the warder outside cell No. 16 became more frequent.

A human eye looked through the square opening, and a human voice said:

'No running in the cell.'

Two hours would pass—and again the eye, and again the voice:

'No talking.'

And twice Wilhelm happened to hear strange injunctions:

'No smashing your head against the wall.'

'Really?' Wilhelm asked absent-mindedly.

And the voice added, almost good-naturedly:

'No crying too loud.'

'Really?' asked the bewildered Wilhelm and was frightened by his own shrill, screeching voice. 'Then I won't.'

That is why Wilhelm only occasionally made a note to remember Dunya.

And in the same way as he had once lined up men to lead them into a bayonet attack against the grapeshot, so now he managed to arrange his memories. On his own, Willie, Küchlya—was a poor, poor man; he had never succeeded in completing anything; and now this poor man hopped about the cage and counted the years left to be spent in it, not even knowing, in fact, how many he had to serve; he had been sentenced to twenty years of hard labor, instead he found himself in solitary confinement.

And another person inside him, his superior, controlled him from morning till night, walked around the cell, composed poems and arranged Willie and Küchlya's memories and celebrations.

Wilhelm also had days to celebrate: name-days of his friends, Lycée anniversaries.

In particular the name-day of Aleksandr, August 30: the name-day of Pushkin, Griboeydov, Sasha Odoyevsky. Küchlya spent that day talking to them in his imagination.

'Well, Aleksandr?' he would say to Griboyedov. 'You see—I'm alive against all the odds. Dear chap, what have you been writing? You've been transforming the entire Russian theater. You take Russian speech from the streets, not from the salons. You and Krylov. How is Aleksey Petrovich Yermolov doing? Are you two still arguing as you used to? How is your heart—still on fire? Do tell me, old chap.'

Wilhelm could not remember voices, but he remembered gestures: Griboyedov would shrug his shoulders, nod slowly, and to the question about his heart, raise and spread his hands with slender fingers in a gesture of bewilderment.

'Congratulations, Sasha,' Wilhelm pressed his cheek to Pushkin's. 'My dear chap, do send me everything, absolutely everything you've written; imagine, I remember your *Gypsies* from cover to cover:

Grim passion everywhere is master,
And no one can elude the Fates.

As you rightly said, Sasha, although I tread my own path in literature and consider Derzhavin the greatest poet, yet a part of my heart is always in your poems.'

Pushkin smiled in the darkness and in his confusion began to ruffle up his friend.

A whole day would pass like this.

More than once the screen on the opening in the door to cell No.16 would go up and an anxious voice with a Ukrainian accent would say:

'No talking in the cell.'

But at night the superior Wilhelm would disappear and only the solitary Wilhelm remain. Prisoner No. 16 was unable to control his dreams. He woke up, his entire body convulsed by an imaginary knocking (they had been woken up in the Peter and Paul Fortress with a sharp knocking several times a night—to stop them sleeping). In his dream he would again have the confrontation with Jeannot Pushchin, his old friend, and, crying and bowing, keep saying that it was Pushchin who had said to him on December 14: "Take *Michel* down."

And again, looking regretfully into Küchlya's crazy face, Pushchin shook his head in denial.

And again he kept writing witness statements—endless, senseless statements in a strange, alien hand—and was horrified to realize that he was not writing what he wanted to—and went on writing.

And once—only once—he dreamt of the morning of the execution—and fortunately he never had that dream again.

The door slams—somewhere on the side—there is a rattle of chains. And he hears Ryleyev's drawn-out voice: "Forgive me, forgive me, brothers"—and, rattling his chains, Ryleyev passes his cell, and Wilhelm cannot move his hand or his tongue to say goodbye.

The chains rattle and music seems to blare out. Sweetly and evenly.

Military music on the battlements of the Peter and Paul Fortress; in the thin morning air the trumpets sing out strong and resonant—beautiful, calm music.

The doors, the clicking of a key in the lock.

He is taken out and thrust into the square formation.

He embraces Pushchin and Odoyevsky.

It's very easy to breathe.

"Hush." (Someone seems to be ordering them to be quiet).

And, yes, how he has failed to notice?—there are five swings over there, brand-new and narrow.

Ah, here they are being taken to swing.

Five of them.

Five men.

Their hands are twisted behind their backs with straps—and so are their feet—they walk in tiny little steps. Ryleyev.

His face! His face!

So calm!

He nods to Wilhelm. Wilhelm shakes his head and stares at him.

That face!

They are being taken to swing. To the music. On the children's swing.

Wilhelm is suddenly being dragged. He feels sick. His tailcoat is torn from his back and thrown into the fire.

The smoke is suffocating, it stifles him.

A cracking noise overhead—it seems his sword has been broken.

That face!

Before him stands a scarecrow in a huge hat with a huge dirty plume, in large Hessian boots—and half-naked. The bare calves stick out from under the prisoner's striped robe.

Wilhelm realizes that this is how they have dressed up Yakubovich and laughs a shrill shrieking laugh.

That face!

Wilhelm roars with laughter.

From a tall white horse, General Benckendorff's clear eyes look at Wilhelm with an expression of disgust.

Wilhelm laughs—on and on, shriller and shriller.

That face!

A howl was coming from cell No. 16, a mad, suffocating howling and barking.

IV

Like one who hugs his friend in silence
Before the other is exiled.

A small posting station between Novorzhev and Luga-Borovichi. Anyone who came here and waited while the postmaster, looking at him intently and trying to guess his title and rank, provided him with horses, would willy-nilly find his gaze wandering over the walls, examining old paintings and portraits, familiar ones—the fat Empress Anna Ivanovna, the snub-nosed Emperor Paul—or unfamiliar ones of generals with angry eyes. And the "Prodigal Son" would be hanging there too.

In autumn, with an oblique fine drizzle falling—the wait was particularly tedious.

The traveler who was stuck at Borovichi station on October 14, 1827 woke up at about ten o'clock in the morning. Glancing absent-mindedly at the flowery canopy round his bed, the pots with balsams, the postmaster sitting at the table, he remembered where he was, realized that it was quite late—and stayed in bed. He was gray-haired and stout, his eyes were small and alert.

He heard the jangling of spurs of an arriving hussar, who threw his travel documents on the table. The postmaster got up and stammered:

'You'll have to wait for a couple of hours.'

The hussar flew into rage, shouted at the postmaster, but the latter spread his hands apathetically, swore that no horses were available, and the hussar soon got tired of arguing.

He threw off his overcoat and looked around.

The fat man looked at him affably and good-naturedly.

The hussar bowed to him in silence.

Then he grew tired of sitting and saying nothing, so he called the postmaster and asked for tea to be served. The fat man did the same. Over tea they started to chat.

The fat man introduced himself as a landlord from the town of Porkhov; he was traveling to Petersburg on business. A quarter of an hour later a game of faro started. Lying in bed and shifting his entire fat torso whenever someone won, the fat man played, lost, and groaned.

The hussar got carried away. He raked in a small pile of gold coins, added to it about the same amount—and staked it on a card. The fat man beat the card first time.

At this moment, an agile little man entered. He was out of sorts, cursed the postmaster, yelled at him so that the postmaster promised him horses within an hour, then sat down in an armchair, started to bite his nails, and ordered lunch. He bowed briefly to the players, glanced out of the window, whistled a little, then grew interested in the game, and began to follow it.

He was served lunch and a bottle of rum.

The fat man was again on a losing streak.

Sipping his rum, and eating his lunch, the man cast glances at the players.

Having finished his lunch, he called the postmaster to settle the bill.

The postmaster looked at the money and said timidly:

'Your grace, you're five rubles short—for the rum.'

The traveler had no small notes.

Then, taking five rubles from the postmaster's hand, he approached the gamblers and said, smilingly:

'Allow me.'

And put the money on a card.

The fat man beat the card.

The traveler quickly stuck his hand into his pocket, pulled out an imperial,[58] and staked it on a card. It was beaten.

Then the traveler frowned, pulled up a chair, and began to play.

Two hours later the horses were ready.

He told the driver to wait.

Another hour later he got up, paid the fat man 420 rubles and wrote a note for a further 200: "By this I undertake to pay at any time 200 rubles. Aleksandr Pushkin." He left the station, fuming at the rain and at himself, wrapped himself in a cloak, and drove to the next station in silence.

The next station was Zalazy.

'It really *is* Zalazy,'[59] he muttered, went inside the station, and began to wait impatiently for horses. While waiting he chatted to the landlady. The landlady was still young, wore a wide cotton dress, and was fat from her sedentary life.

'Aren't you bored staying in the same place?' he asked her, smiling.

'Why bored? With all this hustle and bustle—one hardly notices how the days go.'

"Is that so? She hardly moves," thought Pushkin. 'How long have you been here?'

'About ten years.'

"Ten years at this station," he thought—"what deadly boredom! Merciful God, it's been ten years too since we left the Lycée (celebrations in Petersburg in four days; Yakovlev must already be making preparations)."

Ten years. And so many changes!

Delvig has gone flabby, he's a cuckold, and he drinks; Korf is a big wig (and a sycophant), Wilhelm and Pushchin are as good as dead. And his own life hasn't come out well. "How sad—God's my witness, how sad!"

There was a little book on the table. He looked inside and was baffled: it was Schiller's *Ghost-Seer*. He began to leaf through the book and got lost in it.

"No,' he thought, 'Wilhelm was wrong to call Schiller immature."

He heard a jingling of horse-bells—and at once four troikas stopped at the entrance.

A courier was riding in the front one.

The courier quickly jumped down, entered the room, and threw the travelers' papers on the table.

'Must be Poles,' said Pushkin quietly to the hostess.

'I suppose so,' said the hostess, 'they are being transported today.'

The courier looked at them sideways but said nothing.

Pushkin went out to look at the prisoners.

A prisoner in a baize overcoat stood resting against a peeling column of the station—tall, gray-haired, hunched, with dim eyes.

He cast a weary glance at Pushkin and for some reason looked at his own hand, his fingernails.

The other three troikas stood nearby; the gendarmes and prisoners were still climbing out of them.

A small, stout convict with magnificent mustaches, a Pole, took his meager belongings out of the cart.

Pushkin studied the prisoner with interest.

The prisoner untied his knapsack, took out a loaf of bread, neatly broke off a hunk, sprinkled it with salt, sat down on a rock, and started his breakfast.

His unhurried, purposeful movements seemed to Pushkin entertaining.

A young prisoner, similarly tall and hunched, also in a baize overcoat and in a ridiculously tall bearskin hat came up to the tall old man standing at the column.

Pushkin looked at him with an unpleasant feeling. The prisoner was black-haired, thin, with a long black beard.

"Who is he like?" thought Pushkin.

"Oh yes, Vogel. What the hell is going on?"

Vogel was the chief spy of the late Miloradovich, who was still snooping in Petersburg. All Petersburg knew him.

"The spy," thought Pushkin. "Being taken along for the interrogations and denunciations."

He winced with disgust and turned again to the Pole with his magnificent mustaches.

Meanwhile, the tall young man glanced eagerly at Pushkin. Sensing it, Pushkin turned round angrily.

They were staring at each other.

'Aleksandr,' said the spy in a muffled voice.

Pushkin was dumbfounded—and the spy rushed to embrace him, kissed him, and burst into tears:

'Don't you recognize me? My dear, dear friend!'

Pushkin shuddered and started to babble:

'Wilhelm, brother, is it you, my dear fellow, where are you being taken?'

And he started to speak very fast:

'How is your health? Your family are well, I've seen them recently, everyone remembers you, we are doing what we can—and might yet succeed. What books should I send you? You're allowed books, right?'

Two stout gendarmes seized Wilhelm by the shoulders and dragged him away.

The third one touched Pushkin's chest in an attempt to push him away. The convicts stood huddled together, holding their breath.

'Keep your hands off me,' Pushkin said quietly, looking furiously at the gendarme.

'It's forbidden to talk to the convicts, sir,' said the gendarme, but withdrew his hand.

The courier ran out onto the station porch.

He grabbed Pushkin's arm and shouted:

'Why are you breaking the rules? You will answer for this.'

And, still holding his arm, he nodded to the gendarmes to take Wilhelm away.

Pushkin did not listen to the courier, did not realize that the courier was holding his arm. He was looking at Wilhelm.

Wilhelm was being dragged to the cart. He was in a bad way. His face was pale, his eyes rolled, his head hung down on his chest. They sat him down. The gendarme scooped up a canful of water and handed it to him. He took a sip, looked at Pushkin, and said inaudibly:

'Aleksandr.'

Pushkin yanked his arm from the courier and ran toward him. He wanted to say goodbye but the courier called out:

'No talking!'

The gendarme silently pushed Pushkin aside.

Pushkin ran up to the courier and asked:

'Listen, sir, this is my friend, let me at least say goodbye. I have two hundred rubles here, let me give them to him.'

The courier looked away and shouted:

'Criminals are not allowed to have money.'

He approached Wilhelm and asked sternly:

'You have no right to talk to other people. Who were you speaking to?'

Wilhelm looked at him, smiled, and said:

'This is Pushkin. Don't you know? The poet.'

'I know no such thing,' the courier said, knitting his brow. 'Don't answer back!'

He shouted to the driver:

'Get going! Wait half a mile from here.'

The cart set off. Wilhelm turned his head and looked at Pushkin silently from behind the gendarme's shoulder. Two other gendarmes held him firmly by the hands. The cart vanished, rattling and scattering mud.

Pushkin ran over to the courier. His eyes were bloodshot. He shouted:

'You haven't let me say goodbye to a friend, or give him money! What is your name, my good man? I'll report you in Petersburg!'

The courier was a little taken aback and stayed silent.

'Name! Name!' yelled Pushkin, and his face grew purple.

'My name is Podgorny,' the courier answered abruptly.

'Very well,' said Pushkin, panting.

'Since the convict is doing time in a fortress, he mustn't have money,' the courier said grimly, looking sullenly at Pushkin.

Pushkin roared:

'I don't care about your fortress! To hell with you and your fortress! I've been in exile and they let me out. How dare you drag me by the arm? Answer me!'

The courier stepped back, looked at Pushkin, made no reply, and went into the station room to make out the travel documents. Pushkin followed him. His lips were trembling. In passing, he quickly asked the old man standing by the column:

'Where are they taking you?'

The old man shrugged:

'We don't know.'

The prisoners were silent.

The Pole with the magnificent mustaches followed the courier and Pushkin with his eyes, then resumed his breakfast.

On October 16, 1827 Wilhelm arrived at the fortress of Dinaburg.

V

For good behavior prisoner No. 25 of the Dinaburg fortress received ink, quills, paper, and books.

Books and journals came to Wilhelm in a strange order: *The European Herald* of 1805, *Russian Grammar* by Kurganov, *The Man of Good Will*[60] containing his own old poems. And, just as in the old days, he became a journalist. As in the years when he had worked with Grech and Bulgarin and edited miscellanies himself, so now he would sit down in the morning to write articles, reflections, and reviews. He wrote about the *European Herald* of 1805, and about Kurganov's *Grammar*, and his current journalistic activity differed from the past only in that there was no journal that would print him and he did not have to read proofs. The fact that he did not have to proofread was even agreeable for Wilhelm: he could never stand it.

The heaps of manuscripts grew bigger—comedies, poems, dramas, articles, and at the end of the month the commandant, Colonel Krishtofovich, would come and take away the latest crop.

'Plenty today!' he would say, shaking his head in amazement.

He would thread the notebooks on a string, seal the last clean page with wax and write in square old-fashioned handwriting: "This notebook contains . . . numbered pages . . . Dinaburg Fortress . . . date . . . year. Commandant, Colonel Engineer Yegor Krishtofovich.'

Krishtofovich was an old war-time colonel with cropped hair and a crimson fleshy nose.

His daughter, an overripe girl of about thirty, getting bored and growing fatter in the commandant's house behind pots of balsam, once noticed a tall prisoner being led across the prison yard. (Wilhelm was sick and they were taking him to the hospital.) The commandant's house faced the parade ground. The daughter asked her papa about the tall prisoner and said that a person with such eyes could not be a harmful criminal.

The colonel growled:

'What do you know! He is a dangerous state murderer.'

'Maybe dangerous but not harmful,' the daughter said dreamily.

The colonel remembered his daughter's words. And somehow, unaware of it himself, he grew accustomed to the thought: dangerous but harmless.

He began to allow the prisoner books. (The first one was the very same Kurganov's *Grammar*, the book that the colonel deemed the most entertaining and suitable for the circumstances.)

Once he came to the cell and said tersely:

'Walk.'

And from that day on, Wilhelm walked every day around the parade ground. The parade ground was cobbled, bare, with a striped sentry box and a view of barred windows. But that first time, having made a circuit of the parade ground, Wilhelm collapsed from sheer weakness and joy.

Letters came rarely—from his mother, from his sister, no other letters were allowed. Soon Wilhelm found the opportunity occasionally to send his own letters. One sentry took to peeping through the window too often. This irritated Wilhelm. But the soldier's eyes were lively, brown, and jovial. And one day Wilhelm asked him:

'What's the weather like?'

The usual answer would be: 'I don't know' or 'it's forbidden to talk.' But this sentry said, after a pause, in a low voice:

'Warm.'

And Wilhelm began to talk with him occasionally, sparingly of course, and then asked him to post a note to his two friends. The sentry thought about it and agreed.

Wilhelm wrote to Pushkin and Griboyedov:

Dinaburg, July 10, 1828

Dear friends, brothers, poets, Aleksandrs,

I'm writing to you to put you in touch with one another. I am well and, thanks to the gift of mother-nature—a carefree spirit, not unhappy. I live, I write. I will never forget my meeting with you, Pushkin.

Forgive me. I embrace you both.

W. Küchelbecker

And two months later a humble clerk visited Pushkin, looked around, whispered to him, handed him a letter from Küchlya. Pushkin shook the clerk's hand for a long time, saw him to the door, and then sat in his study over the yellow sheet, re-reading it, biting his nails, frowning, and sighing.

VI

Wilhelm acquired a curious neighbor. The cell next door had long been empty. And then one day Wilhelm heard the sound of a key in the door and some sort of fuss. Someone was being locked up. Then a male voice sang out in the next cell very loudly.

Wilhelm could not make out the words but immediately recognized the romance by the melody; the prisoner was singing "The Black Shawl."

As if I was mad at a black shawl I stare
And feel my cold soul torn apart by despair.

Wilhelm involuntarily smiled at such an extraordinary start to this inmate's prison life. Then he heard the angry muttering of the warder, and the singing ceased.

Wilhelm was intrigued by this prisoner.

Next morning, he knocked quietly on the wall, intending to initiate a conversation by tapping. The result was unexpected. The response from the next cell was a violent pounding—the prisoner was battering the wall with his hands and feet. Wilhelm was dumbfounded and made no further attempt to explain the tapping rules. He would have to find some other way.

Wilhelm asked "his" warder (the kindly one) to pass a note. The sentry agreed. Wilhelm asked in his note who the prisoner was, what he was doing time for, and whether his sentence was a long one. He received an answer soon, toward evening: it was detailed, scratched on the back of Wilhelm's note with a piece of charcoal or a burnt stick. (Which meant that his neighbor was not allowed any ink, or paper, or quills.)

The prisoner wrote:

> Deer neighbor I am Prince Sergey Abalensky staf captain of a hussars regiment, the devil knows what I am here for but it seems for card-playing and rulette and mainly for beeting up the commander and riting an afficial letter to the division commander baron Budberg that he is a tsarist lackey, did time in Sveaborg for a hole year, how long they will keep me in this pit—Godd knows.

The neighbor was apparently quite a character. They soon met on the parade ground. Sergey Obolensky was a young hussar, almost a boy, with a pink girlish face, black eyes, and a small mustache; he did not look at all like a thug. But he winked at Wilhelm so wickedly and rakishly that Wilhelm immediately became very fond of him and thought affectionately: "He'll come to no good, poor chap."

The warder passed notes between them. The prince's "letters," written in an astonishing language, delighted Wilhelm and somehow reminded him of his childhood and the Lycée. In addition, the prince was related to Yevgeny Obolensky, with whom Wilhelm had been in Peter's Square. Wilhelm tried repeatedly to explain to him the tapping alphabet, which he had learned from Misha Bestuzhev in the Peter and Paul Fortress, but it was too much for the prince. He would begin diligently but from the third letter he would drum violently on the wall—and only a shout from the warder could shut him up.

The prince had been in his pit for a year and a half for his official letter to the division commander, Baron Budberg, including six months in the Dinaburg Fortress.

They released him from the Dinaburg Fortress in April 1829. He was then sent to Georgia, to the Nizhny Novgorod Dragoons. Their farewell was tender.

The prince wrote to Wilhelm:

> My deer frend, I will never forget you for nothing in the world I shall always despise flunkies and tyrants for keeping in the pit such a soul as you deer frend. Whatever needs to be passed to your frends and family shall do all I can. Ah deer hart, if only I could spend a day with you outside, I would soon liven you up. Upset not to know if I'll see you again, my deer frend.
>
> Yours faithfully,
> Staf captain Abalensky

And since the prince was heading for Georgia, Wilhelm passed to him via the warder a letter for Griboyedov.

In the morning he heard the key in the cell next door, cheerful steps stomped past his cell, and the prince's voice said behind the door:

'Farewell, my friend.'

The prince left in a magnificent mood. He was being sent to Georgia and he had heard that Georgian women had no equals. Pushkin's Circassian girl alone was worth something! No, sir, if the prince was captured by the Circassians, damn it! rest assured he wouldn't leave a Circassian girl in a stream! The only nuisance was the policeman who was accompanying the prince—a fattie, with a red peasant woman's face, by the name of Aksyuk, who pushed him about deliberately to assert his authority and at stops kept looking at him as if the prince was a wild goat that might immediately shoot off into the forest. The prince tried to talk to him like a human being but Aksyuk simply would not answer. Not a word. The prince sulked. Everything about Aksyuk irritated him—the fact that he had a peasant woman's face, and that he had a woman's umbrella, and that he snored at nights and when he woke, would grab the prince's hand in fear to check that he was still there. A couple of times he asked the prince for a loan but the prince did not have a penny, and that might have been the reason why Aksyuk pushed him about. However, in the city of Orel the prince forgot about Aksyuk. Four of his friends—hussars—had somehow found out that the prince was being transported to Georgia and had arranged a real party for him, damn it! A lot of champagne was drunk and countless tears of joy were shed.

After the party the prince dozed along the way. They passed the village of Kulikovka where they stopped at the tavern kept by Lyakhov, the village money-bag. Leaving Kulikovka, the prince noticed, not without gloating, that Aksyuk's umbrella had fallen out of the cart. Needless to say, he never mentioned this to Aksyuk. They had driven for about ten *versts*, when Aksyuk started to fuss. The umbrella was missing.

He stopped the cart, pushed the prince about, told him to get out, searched and rummaged everywhere—no umbrella.

Then, swaying slightly on his feet, the prince said, looking at Aksyuk who was dumbfounded by the loss of his umbrella:

'Bye-bye umbrella, gone for a walk. Fell out when we were in Kulikovka.'

Aksyuk stared at him and croaked:

'Did you see it?'

'I surely did,' said the prince, 'naturally I did.'

Aksyuk glared at him angrily:

'Why didn't you say anything?

'It's not mine,' said the prince indifferently.

'Get into the cart!' hollered Aksyuk.

They got into the cart.

'Drive back!'

'What do you mean: back?' asked the prince. 'Ten *versts* back because of your wretched umbrella?'

'Shut up!' hissed Asksyuk. 'Convict scum!'

The prince sat down in the cart in silence. His face was flushed. They drove to Kulikovka.

They stopped by the inn. Aksyuk, rattled by the loss of his umbrella, ran into the hut to question the owner. He had left his saber in the cart. The prince remained there waiting.

He sat for a minute, spotted the sergeant's saber, and reached out for it. Then he pulled it out of the sheath and ran with the bare saber into the hut.

Aksyuk saw him and trembled.

'Back to your seat!' he wheezed.

Deftly and swiftly the prince stuck his saber into the policeman's side. The police uniform split under the blade and there was a flash of shirt. Aksyuk gasped, grabbed his side, and scampered inside. There he dashed to the closet and hid himself in it.

The prince ran after him with loose, joyful strides and attacked the closet.

'Come out! I won't touch you inside the hut,' he shouted.

Aksyuk decided to negotiate:

'Stop joking, Your Honor.'

'Who says I am joking?' asked the prince. 'And what kind of "Honor" am I? I'm merely convict scum. Come out, I won't touch you in here, but if you don't come out—I'll hack you to death.'

He opened the door to the closet a chink.

Aksyuk scampered out into the street and shrieked in a peasant woman's voice:

'Help! He is trying to kill me!!'

And he ducked behind a roadside bush.

The prince began an attack on the bush.

At that point the tavern-keeper and his son came running from the inn. They grabbed the prince firmly from behind. The old tavern-keeper knocked the saber out of his hands.

'Bring some straps.'

They tied the prince's hands.

The prince sat there, grinning:

'A tavern-keeper and a sergeant. That's authority for you.'

The prince was taken to Orel.

During the search, they found someone's letter among his things. To the question who the letter was from and who it was to, the prince replied casually that he could not remember.

He was thrown into jail and shackled. He was interrogated as to who he had received the letter from. The prince kept pretending to remember; the gendarmes waited. Then, smiling, he would say: "I forget" and shrug his shoulders.

The Third Department of his Imperial Majesty's office conducted an investigation and came to the conclusion that the letter found during the search was written by state criminal Wilhelm Küchelbecker, held at the fortress of Dinaburg, to State Councillor Griboyedov.

The prince was kept shackled in jail.

In 1830, the chief of the Third Department, Adjutant General Benckendorff, made a report to the tsar. The tsar issued an order to keep a watchful eye on Obolensky and on state criminal Küchelbecker. The chief of the Third Department, Adjutant General Benckendorff, communicated the imperial order to the commander of the Caucasus Corps, Count Paskevich-Erivansky, under whose authority the arrested Prince Obolensky had been placed, and the commandant of Dinaburg, Colonel Krishtofovich, under whose authority state criminal Küchelbecker was detained.

Prince Obolensky was closely watched—woken up at nights with knocking, not allowed walks, and kept in chains.

State criminal Küchelbecker in Dinaburg was deprived for a while of ink, paper, quills and was not allowed out for walks either.

The prince continued to languish in jail.

Six months later Benckendorff presented to the tsar a special memorandum on the outcome of the investigation.

The imperial resolution read: "Bring to the attention of the commandant of the Dinaburg Fortress that the prisoner should not have been allowed to write."

Since the inmate was already strictly supervised, the resolution was superfluous.

The Audit Department of the General Staff sent the case of the criminal Prince Sergey Obolensky to Count Paskevich-Erivansky for a decision, and he wrote on it in his own hand:

> I would propose stripping Obolensky of his nobility and princely title and exiling him to Siberia for six years of hard labor, on completion of which he should reside there indefinitely.

Sitting there in shackles, the prince would sing "The Black Shawl," cry and say to the rude commandant who addressed him too familiarly: 'I don't take offense. That's what the tsar's flunkeys are paid for—to insult people.'

Two more months later the final report of the Audit Department to His Majesty the Tsar of All the Russias was submitted:

> Finding Prince Sergey Sergeyevich Obolensky guilty of causing a wound with a naked saber in sergeant Aksyuk's side, of obstinacy in concealing a letter received from state criminal W. Küchelbecker to be passed to State Councillor Griboyedov, as well as of expressing complaints against the government, we hereby banish Obolensky to Siberia for lifetime settlement, having divested him of his nobility and princely title, as well as of his military rank, as detrimental to the service and unfit for society.

And the tsar again with his own hand approved the resolution: "So be it, Nicholas."

At the end of 1830, Sergey Sergeyevich Obolensky, now a commoner, was hurriedly rushed by two couriers to lifetime settlement in Siberia.

And the letter of state criminal Küchelbecker to State Councillor Griboyedov went like this:

> I have long hesitated whether I should write to you, but another such opportunity may never present itself—to tell you that I am not dead yet, that I am still fond of you and that you have been my best friend. I want to believe in humanity, I have no doubt that you haven't changed and that you will be delighted to hear from me. I do not expect an answer—to what end? I ask you, my friend, if you can, to be useful to the man who will bring you this letter: he was a faithful and kind friend to your W. over the course of almost six months, he consoled me when I needed consolation. He will tell you where I am and in what circumstances. Farewell! We shall meet in the world in which you were the first to make me believe again.
>
> W. K.

It was written on April 20, 1829. And State Councillor Griboyedov had been torn to pieces on January 30, 1829 by the Tehran mob, incited by the *sheikhs* and *qadis*[61] who had declared a sacred war on the state councillor. The letter was written to a dead man.

VII

DUNYA'S LETTER,
which never made it into Wilhelm's hands

March 15, 1828

My dear friend,
You are always with me in my thoughts. Whatever happens to me, wherever I am, I always think about you. Believe me, separation is not too hard for me, as I am convinced that the moment I think of you, you think of me too. And it is enough for me to know that you are alive somewhere, even if on an uninhabited island, for me to feel cheerful. What a blessing, Wilhelm, that you have survived. I await the end of your incarceration, which will surely come. We are both still young enough. I kiss your eyes, my friend.

March 17

I am finishing the letter which I have not yet posted to you. I have just returned from Countess Laval's, where Pushkin read his *Boris Godunov*. Imagine who I met at the reading—your Aleksandr! Griboyedov was there. And you know what he told me? He is interceding for you to be transferred to the Caucasus. Oh, he will succeed! He is highly regarded, he has brought home a peace treaty and was greeted with cannon salvos. It seems that he is going to be appointed minister to Persia. My dear, he will manage to get you transferred to the Caucasus. But do not give it too much thought or pin too many hopes on it, so many of them have already been dashed, but still the day will come, and they will come true. Let me tell you: Aleksandr has not changed, the same lines on his forehead and the same old readiness to laugh off the general affection for him. One can be offended by this, but you know yourself, dear Wilhelm Karlovich, that one can't help loving him. He is still rather lugubrious, but do not imagine anything unsettling—just the usual hypochondria. With what kindness he remembered you! He is a loyal friend.

You would have been comforted if you had seen him with Pushkin. Pushkin is enchanted by Aleksandr, he says that he is the most intelligent person in all Russia, but it seemed to me that he clams up and does not speak freely in Griboyedov's presence. Maybe that's only how it seemed to me. Pushkin told me when he saw me: 'Good to have you here. *You* means not only you but also Wilhelm.' He remembers you and is still very fond of you. Michel Glinka, your one-time student, had many memories of you. He has now become a fine musician, he sang so well at the countess's that you couldn't hold back your tears, though his voice was not at all good.

So, the Caucasus! I breathe more easily since I talked to Aleksandr. *Adieu* and maybe I'll soon say *au revoir*!

Eudoxie

VIII

DUNYA'S LETTER,
which did get into Wilhelm's hands

August 20, 1829

My precious friend,
I have received the letter you managed to send me, and I keep it together with the other four. It frightened me. You have learned about Griboyedov's death and you are close to despair. I read it with death in my soul. But know, my dear friend, know once and for all, that there is no need to be so sad. You will realize, of course, that Aleksandr's death is hard for me too. I cried like a little girl and all the time I imagined him before me, imagined his eyes and his voice. It is hard to believe that he is no longer with us.

And yet he is dead. You will die too, my dear friend, and so will I, we will be forgotten, and even our letters will decay just like our hearts. But there is nothing sad about this. No one is capable of taking away our happiness; we have lived—and we shall say it together—we have loved. I do not know if the poem that Pushkin dedicated to your comrades and you has reached you. I am sending it to you. You ask for details about Aleksandr's death. Will that make things easier for you? I'll tell you word for word what General Artsruni stated after he had come back from Persia. The general claimed that the English were to blame for Griboyedov's death: Aleksandr had begun to exert too much Russian influence on Persia. He did not take off his shoes in the place that the Persians regarded as sacred. Isn't that like

Aleksandr? He defended Georgian and Armenian women from forced marriages to Persians. The *seids* and *sheikhs* declared a holy war on him. His death was predetermined. Seeing the thousands of people outside, he drew his sword and rushed from the balcony into the crowd, alone. You know the rest. His servant Aleksandr, whom you surely remember, died together with him.

These are the bare facts—otherwise I would not have enough strength to write about it. Weep, my friend, and then be comforted.

Let's not remember his last days, let him remain for us forever young and living.

Lots of kisses.

E.

The End

I

From the Peter and Paul Fortress to Shlisselburg, from Shlisselburg to Dinaburg, from Dinaburg to the citadel of Reval, from Reval to the Sveaborg Fortress. The prisoner grows gray and hunched, his vision weakens, his health begins to fail him.

And yet he is young; time has stopped for him. He reads old magazines, he writes articles in which he takes issue with long-forgotten writers and praises a novice poet who has long since ceased to write. Time has stopped for him. He can die from illness, go blind, but he will die young. His friends are the same in his memory: young and strong. The same Delvig is in his mind's eye—lazy and sly, the same Pushkin with his ready laughter, and the same Dunya, as cheerful, light, and pure as the sea air.

He does not know that Delvig has grown old and flabby, that he locks himself in his study for weeks on end, sits there unkempt and unshaven, and smiles meaninglessly; that at the moment when the prisoner is recollecting the carefree poet, the very same poet gets up groaning from the chair, goes to the cupboard, takes out wine, and pours himself a glass with shaking hands, repeating his old saying: 'Funny, isn't it?'

And only when the brief news reaches him that Delvig has died does the prisoner weep and begin to understand that time is passing behind the walls of the fortress and that youth is no more. But in his thoughts, he buries the young Delvig, not the flabby pale poet who did actually die.

And the prisoner still craves freedom, but he is not at all afraid of the fact that outside the fortress time never stops and that everything will change as soon as he crosses the threshold.

That day finally comes and the prisoner is freed—to live in Siberia.

The last wanderings of Küchlya begin: Barguzin, Aksha, Kurgan, Tobolsk.

II

He arrives at Barguzin. He still sees the walls, the peep-hole, the exercise yard on which he used to walk, some fragments of human faces and voices. He peers into the log houses of Barguzin. A red-faced woman goes to the river, crunching on the snow and swaying under the weight of the yoke with its two pails of water—to wallop the laundry. A pot-bellied shopkeeper stands on the porch, scrutinizing him, screening his eyes from the sun with his hand. Some official in what seems like a postmaster's uniform rides by in a sleigh, and a *muzhik* bows low to him. It's an amazing town, small, scattered, squat, with houses that look not like homes, but like gray toys. Wilhelm is delighted. The most important thing is that there are no walls around him. His legs are weak from prison and from the road. It will pass. Having wrapped himself up in a fur coat, he waits impatiently for the moment when the coachman with the frosted beard will drive him up to his brother's house. Misha lives as a settler. Exiles are not allowed to reside in Barguzin, they live out of town.

The coachman has stopped at a small wooden house. A column of smoke is rising up from the chimney stack—a sign that it will be frosty. A tall, thin man in a sheepskin coat is shoveling away the snow from the front of the hut. His face is haggard and stern. His beard is graying. He gives Wilhelm an unfriendly look from behind his metal-rimmed glasses, then suddenly drops his shovel and says in confusion:

'Wilhelm?'

The tall man is his brother Misha.

'Oh, your beard is gray,' says Misha, and there are tears in his cold eyes. Misha leads his brother into the hut.

'Sit down, will you? We'll have some tea. Thank goodness you've come. My wife will be here in a moment.'

Misha does not ask his brother any questions, just looks at him for a long time. A woman in a dark dress and with a kerchief on her head enters the hut. Her face is simple, Russian, plain, with kind eyes.

'Wife,' says Misha, 'my brother has come to see us.'

Misha's wife bows awkwardly to Wilhelm and Wilhelm embraces her, also awkwardly.

'And where are the daughters?' asks Misha.

'At the neighbors', Mikhail Karlovich,' the wife says in a singing voice, grabs the samovar from the shelf, and takes it into the hallway.

'A good woman,' says Misha simply and adds: 'It's silly to marry in our situation. I have nice daughters though.'

Wilhelm has the curious feeling that his brother is a stranger to him: strict, business-like, taciturn. Their meeting isn't what Wilhelm has dreamed of.

'You'll stay with me,' says Misha, gazing tenderly at his brother. 'We'll live together. Later you can take a look around, we'll build a wooden house for you, I've already found a place.'

A settler enters.

'Your Honor, Mikhail Karlych,' he says and fumbles with his cap, 'I have a favor to ask, with respect.'

'What's the matter?' asks Misha without inviting the settler to sit down.

'I'm not feeling very well.'

'Go to the hospital,' says Misha dryly. 'I'll come over there and we'll talk.'

The settler is reluctant to go.

'And I'd like to borrow some money from your lordship too.'

'I don't have any,' says Misha calmly. 'Not a penny.'

Wilhelm takes out his purse and hands the settler a banknote.

He grabs it in surprise, thanks him, muttering something, and runs away.

Misha scolds his brother:

'Don't encourage them or they'll plague you every day.'

III

In the spring, Wilhelm begins to build a hut out of logs. And something strange starts to happen to him. He thought he would see his brother and Pushchin, that Dunya would come to join him. This seemed the most important thing in his future life. But in this life, the most essential thing turns out to be something else: a corner shop that stops his credit, the dance evenings at the postmaster's, petty gambling, and stinking fish. He no longer thinks of Dunya. He is horrified, he convinces himself that there is some kind of failing here, and cannot put his finger on it. At the fortress the image of Dunya was pure and clear, in Siberia it dissolves. Why? Wilhelm does not understand it, he is lost.

Barguzin life goes on, cheap and cheerful. Local big shots attend the postmaster Artyonov's evenings: the shopkeeper Malykh, the merchant Lishkin, the doctor. With wives. When your hair is gray, isn't it fun to cavort, dancing the polka to the broken sound of a harpsichord of the last century—Heaven knows how it has got to Barguzin? Isn't it fun to whirl with the postmaster's daughter, fat little Droniushka? She has a Kalmyk profile, she squeaks, she is cheerful and red-faced, she makes Wilhelm laugh.

DUNYA'S LETTER

My dear friend,

Let us talk calmly and, I fear, a little sadly about everything that is important to us now. Your latest letters have somehow stunned me, poor dear Willie. Forgive me from the bottom of your heart—but I cannot see you in them. Your letters from the fortress were quite different. I imagine, and there's no need for us to deceive ourselves, that you have become unaccustomed to me, to thinking about me. What can we do? Youth has gone, your present life and petty concerns are probably no easier for you, dear friend, than life at the fortress. I am not reproaching you. I have made up my mind to tell you frankly, my poor dear friend,—I have decided not to come and join you. My heart is growing old. I kiss your old letters, I love the memory of you and your portrait, where you are young and smiling. Both of us have turned forty. I kiss you for the last time, dear friend, a long, long kiss. I will not write to you again.

Wilhelm becomes strangely distracted, forgetful, easily carried away.

Lots of fun at the postmaster Artyonov's ball in January 1837: the gentlemen, sweaty and red-faced, dance tipsily, drumming with their heels; the postmaster in a new uniform, with dyed mustaches. Droniushka has found a fiancé, she is marrying Wilhelm Karlovich Küchelbecker.

Wilhelm is merry and drunk. He is being congratulated and two clerks try to hoist him on their shoulders. In the corner Misha gleams with his metal-rimmed spectacles. Wilhelm approaches his brother and looks at him silently for a minute.

'Well, Misha, brother?'

'Never mind, life goes on—for better or worse.'

A month after the wedding, Wilhelm learns that some Guards officer has killed Pushkin in a duel.

He has no friends: Ryleyev is in his grave, and so are Griboyedov, Delvig, and Pushkin.

Time, which marched joyfully about Peter's Square and stood still at the fortress, now scampers by with tiny little steps.

IV

Wilhelm began to feel restless.

The same yearning that had driven Griboyedov to Persia, and carried Wilhelm all over Europe and the Caucasus, now whirled him about in Siberia.

He requested a transfer to Aksha, a tiny fortress on the Chinese border. The Chinese and Russian huntsmen lived poorly there, in little shacks called *fangzi*. The climate in the Nerchinsk region was severe.

Wilhelm now had a family, loud, noisy, and alien to him. His wife wore shabby clothes, the children were growing up.

They did not stay long in Aksha.

Once Drosida Ivanovna, looking angrily at Wilhelm's pale face, said:

'We haven't a penny. I'd rather kill myself, God help me. Living with the Chinese—and rags and fleas! Request a transfer. This is no life.'

And Wilhelm asked for a transfer to Kurgan in the Tobolsk province. They did not let him reside in Kurgan itself, but he was allowed to settle in Smolenskaya Sloboda, out of town. Passing through Yalutorovsk, he called on Pushchin. Jeannot had grown hanging mustaches and shaggy overhung eyebrows. When they met, they cried and laughed, but a day later they realized that they had become unused to each other. He stayed at Pushchin's for three days. After his departure, Pushchin wrote to Yegor

Antonovich Engelhardt, a decrepit old man who one by one had outlived all his pupils:

> March 21. Wilhelm stayed at my place for three days en route to settling in Kurgan with his Drosida Ivanovna, two screaming children, and a chest of his literary works. I embraced him with the old "Lycée" feeling. The meeting reminded me vividly of the old days: he is the same eccentric except his hair is now gray. He read me to death with his verses, and out of hospitality I had to listen and remain silent instead of criticizing, sparing the author's endlessly growing vanity. I would not say that his family life could convince anyone of the pleasures of marriage. It seems to be a novel task for providence: to arrange the happiness of two human beings who have come together with none of the qualities needed for good fortune. I have to confess that this thought often occurred to me as I was looking at the two of them, listening to his verses and the cries of the *muzhik*-like Droniushka, as her hubby calls her, and the constant squealing of the children. His choice of spouse proves the poor taste and ineptitude of our eccentric friend: even in Barguzin one could find someone easier on the eye than she is. She is remarkably bad-tempered and there is no kind of sympathy between them. It is strange that he tries to excuse the behavior of his fat peasant on the grounds of ill-health and even nervous fits; he is too scared to contradict her and constantly asks you to mediate; and all the while the wretched woman rages away at will and all he can say is: "You see how irritable she is." All this is in the order of things: it's a shame, but what can you do to help? I am grateful to Wilhelm for his loyal friendship, he is certainly attached to me, but nothing comes of it. He looks at the simplest things in the strangest way, asks for advice, and does absolutely the opposite. If I told you all he did on the day of the "event" and on the day of the sentencing, you would split your sides with laughter, in spite of the fact that at the time he was a player in a quite tragic and momentous scene. Some stories might have reached you in a roundabout way. He intends to write to you from his new place of residence. I read him a few of your letters. They delighted him: the poor thing is not spoiled for friendship and attention. He had a hard time at the fortresses and in Siberia. No idea how he will find things now in Kurgan.

V

Years in Kurgan.

And so? The end had come.

His right eye was half covered with a cataract, he saw vaguely, and at a distance could distinguish only colors; the left eyelid grew heavier and drooped. When he wanted to look closely at something, Wilhelm had to raise his eyelid with his fingers. No one wrote from Petersburg—his mother had died, he was forgotten.

It was clear—his life was over. Now he tended his kitchen garden just for appearance's sake; it had cost him so much hard work—and indeed, he found it harder to bend over, his back hurt, and his shoulders stooped. Then he gave up the garden too. Drosida Ivanovna bustled, shouted at the children, gossiped with the neighbors. He gave up on that too. It was as clear as day: the marriage was pointless and so was this alien woman who walked about in house coats, yawned in the evenings, and each time made the sign of the cross over her mouth; pointless, too, was the land and the kitchen garden he could not cope with. What remained was his poems, his play, which any European theater would be honored to stage, his translations of Shakespeare and of Goethe, whom he had been the first to introduce into Russian literature a quarter of a century before. So should he read them to the clerk's son, a shy young man who revered Wilhelm but did not seem to understand much? Or else indulge in petty gambling with Shchepin-Rostovsky, the very same man who had once led the Moscow Regiment to Peter's Square and was now a flabby, squalid drunk?

No, enough's enough.

And once, raising his left eyelid, Wilhelm was re-reading or rather peering into and reciting by heart the manuscripts from his trunk, reading for the hundredth time his drama, which gave him a place alongside the writers of Europe—Byron and Goethe. And suddenly a new feeling shot through him: the drama seemed clumsy, the verses listless in the extreme, the comparisons strained. He jumped up in horror. The last support was crumbling. Was he really a Trediakovsky of his time, was this the reason why the literary big boys laughed their heads off at him?

Wilhelm's real anguish began that day. In the mornings he would crouch at the trunk, rummage through his notebooks and sheets, and arrange them, peer into them, read them. He would read until instead of the words there were specks floating before his eyes. Then for a long time he would sit without thinking. Drosida Ivanovna pestered him:

'Do you want to kill yourself like this, old man?'

She cared about him, but her voice was strident and Wilhelm waved her away.

'Don't you wave your hand at me,' drawled Drosida Ivanovna, either offended or threatening.

Then Wilhelm would leave silently—to Shchepin's, or, perhaps, just for a walk along the nearby road.

Drosida Ivanovna let him be.

And then suddenly he gave up on his manuscripts. He closed the trunk and did not look into it anymore.

One night Wilhelm stayed late at Shchepin's. They remembered their youth, Shchepin talked about Odoyevsky and the brothers Aleksandr and Misha Bestuzhev, Wilhelm recalled Pushkin. They rambled on for a long time, drinking wine in memory of their comrades and hugging each other. On the way back home, Wilhelm caught a chill from the cool wind. He immediately started to feel his legs aching and his heart pounding.

'Granddad,' a boy called to him, passing by on a cart.

Wilhelm looked at him and did not respond.

'Climb in, granddad,' said the boy, 'I'll take you home. I'm the Panfilovs' boy.'

Panfilov was a peasant neighbor. Wilhelm climbed in. He closed his eyes and began to shake with fever. "Granddad," he thought, and smiled. The boy brought him home. And once at home, Wilhelm felt that the end was coming. Tall, hunched, with a sharp gray beard, he paced his room like a beast his lair. Something else had to be decided, something which had to be worked out—maybe to make arrangements for the children? He wasn't sure. It was necessary to settle some business. He thought and gesticulated. Then he stopped and leaned against the iron stove. His legs could not hold him. Oh yes, the letters. He needed to write letters, at once. He sat down to write to Ustinka; struggling, having a job to hold up his head, spilling ink, and scraping with his quill; he wrote to send her his blessing. He did not feel like writing anything else. He signed his name.

Then he felt that he did not want to write letters at all and was surprised to realize that there was no one to write to.

The next day he wanted to get out of bed and could not. Drosida Ivanovna looked at him anxiously and ran for Shchepin.

Shchepin came, red-faced and flabby, shouted at Wilhelm that he was not doing anything about his transfer to Tobolsk, said the governor would come to Kurgan one of these days, and sat down to write a petition. Wilhelm signed it indifferently.

And indeed, two days later the governor arrived. He filed a report to the governor-general regarding the settler Küchelbecker. The governor-general wrote that on his part he did not see any objections to transferring the sick man to Tobolsk, and sent a note to Count Orlov. Count Orlov did not find it possible to allow the settler to stay in Tobolsk without a preliminary medical examination and therefore requested that the Governor-General should notify him of his conclusion after the patient's medical examination.

Wilhelm treated the progress of the petition with utter indifference. He lay in bed and spoke to his friends. He would often call his children, talk to them, and stroke their heads. He was growing noticeably weaker.

On March 13, 1846, he received permission to depart for Tobolsk, and next day he came into Kurgan to see Pushchin. When he saw Wilhelm, Pushchin's face puckered, he knitted his eyebrows, his eye blinked, and he spoke grimly, his lips trembling:

'What's the matter with you, old fellow?'

Wilhelm raised his left eyelid with his fingers, peered for a minute, caught something in Pushchin's face, and smiled:

'You've grown old, Jeannot. Come to my place this evening. We need to talk.'

In the evening, Wilhelm sent Drosida Ivanovna out of the room and the children away and asked Pushchin to lock the door. He dictated his will: what to publish, in what form, completely or in fragments. Pushchin sorted through the manuscripts, wrapped up each of them in a clean sheet of paper as if in a shroud, wrote on each one clearly its number, and put them back into the trunk. Wilhelm dictated calmly, in an even voice. Then he said to Pushchin:

'Come closer.'

One old man leaned over the other old man.

'Do not leave my children,' said Wilhelm sternly.

'What are you talking about, brother,' said Pushchin frowning. 'You will recover in Tobolsk.'

Wilhelm asked calmly:

'Shall I give your love . . . ?'

'To whom?' Pushchin was flabbergasted.

Wilhelm did not answer.

"Must have been weakened by the dictation," thought Pushchin, "how shall we get him to Tobolslk in this state?'

But after two minutes Wilhelm said firmly:

'. . . to Ryleyev, Delvig, Sasha.'

VI

Wilhelm weathered the road quite cheerfully. He even seemed to get better. When they came across beggars, he would stubbornly stop the wagon, untie his money pouch and, to Drosida Ivanovna's horror, give them a few coppers. Right at Tobolsk they met a crowd of them. A drunken, ragged man danced around in front of them all. He kicked his legs in the air and yelled in a hoarse voice:

'Fiddle-faddle, doodle-dum, tam tara rum tara rum!'

Spotting the wagon, he ran up to it, pulled his crumpled cap off his head, and croaked:

'Spare a copper for a commoner, Prince Sergey Obolensky who has suffered for the truth at the hands of flunkeys and tyrants!'

Wilhelm gave him a copper. Then, five *versts* later, he fell into a reverie, remembered the pink face, the hussar's mustaches, and grew anxious:

'Turn back,' he said to the coachman.

Drosida Ivanovna glared at him in amazement.

'Have you gone completely crazy, old man? Keep going,' she shouted hastily to the coachman, 'what's the matter?'

And for the first time in his entire illness Wilhelm burst into tears.

He felt slightly better in Tobolsk. His breathing became easier, even his eyesight seemed to be recovering. Soon he received a joyful letter from Ustinka: she had applied for permission to visit Wilhelm. She hoped to travel in the autumn.

But Wilhelm did not recover. In summer he started to feel worse.

VII

One day he went out for a walk and returned home tired, lifeless. He lay down on the bench and closed his eyes. Weakness and a secret contentment took hold of him. There was nothing more to be done, apparently, everything had already been done. He could only lie down. It was good to be stretched out. Only his heart was in the way, it kept dropping down somewhere. Drosida Ivanovna snored in the side room.

Then he had a dream.

Griboyedov sat with a green *arkhaluk* thrown over his refined undergarments, staring at Wilhelm with a piercing glance from underneath his eyebrows. Griboyedov said something seemingly trivial. Then tears rolled from under his glasses, and in embarrassment he turned his head sideways, began to take off his glasses and wipe his tears with a handkerchief.

"What's the matter, brother," Wilhelm said to him protectively and felt happy. "Why are you crying, Aleksandr, dear friend?"

Then he felt sore and woke up, his body was empty, his heart was gripped by a cold hand, which was releasing it slowly, one finger at a time. The pain was coming from there. He groaned, but rather hesitantly. Drosida Ivanovna was fast asleep and did not hear him.

. . . The fair, curly-haired cabman dumped him out into the snow right by the bridge. He had to check whether the pistol was clogged with snow, but for some reason his hand would not move, his mouth was filled with snow, and it was hard to breathe . . . "No talking aloud," said the colonel with the hanging mustaches, "and no crying." Wilhelm asked meekly: "Really? No crying either? Well, I won't then."

And he fell into oblivion.

He lay like that all through the night and next morning until noon. The doctor, whom Drosida Ivanovna had rushed to fetch in the morning, had been busy with him for a long time and Pushchin had long been sitting by his bed, biting his mustaches.

Wilhelm opened his eyes. He looked vaguely at Pushchin and the doctor and asked:

'What's the date today?'

'The eleventh,' Drosida Ivanovna said quickly. 'Feeling a bit better, dearie?'

Her face was tear-stained, and she was wearing a new dress. Wilhelm moved his lips and closed his eyes again. The doctor poured some camphor oil into his mouth, and for a second Wilhelm had an unpleasant sensation in his mouth; he immediately sank into oblivion. Then he woke up one time from the sensation of cold: a cold compress had been placed on his forehead. Finally, he came to and looked around. The window looked copper-red in the sunset light. He looked at his hand. A thin blue light was burning over it. He dropped the light and realized: a candle.

His children stood at the foot of the bed looking at him curiously, wide-eyed. Wilhelm could not see them. Drosida Ivanovna blew her nose hurriedly, wiped her eyes, and leaned over him.

'Droniushka,' Wilhelm struggled to say and realized that he had to speak quickly or he would run out of time, 'go to Petersburg,' he moved his lips, pointed to the corner and the trunk containing his manuscripts, and finished almost inaudibly: 'these will be published . . . they will help you there . . . the children need to be looked after.'

Drosida Ivanovna shook her head hastily. Wilhelm beckoned the children with his finger and placed his huge hand on their heads. He spoke no more.

He was listening to a sound, a nightingale or possibly a stream. The sound flowed like water. He was lying under the branch of a tree by the stream. A curly head was directly above him. It laughed, baring its teeth, and, in jest, tickled his eyes with the reddish curls. The curls were thin, cold.

'We must hurry,' said Pushkin quickly.

'I am trying,' replied Wilhelm apologetically, 'you see. It's time. I'm ready. No time to waste.'

Through the conversation he heard something like women's crying.

'Who is it? Ah yes,' he remembered, 'Dunya.'

Pushkin kissed him on the lips. He seemed to detect a delicate smell of camphor.

'Brother,' he said to Pushkin joyfully, 'brother, I'm doing all I can.'

The neighbors, Pushchin, Drosida Ivanovna, and the children stood all around him.

Wilhelm straightened up, his face turned an ugly yellow, his head fell back.

He lay outstretched, with upturned gray beard, sharp uplifted nose, and eyes rolled back.

Some Poems by Wilhelm Küchelbecker

In his introduction to the first complete edition of Küchelbecker's writings, Yuri Tynianov wrote: "Küchelbecker's works are epic and dramatic, and only to a lesser degree lyrical." Even so, he notes how at the end of his life Küchlya's sufferings and the deaths of his poet friends "brought him to the lyric genre, under the name of 'iambics.'" Given the constraints of space, it is this lyrical vein that is represented in the following brief selection of poems covering a period of thirty years from his schoolboy years to the time of his death. These translations aim to convey the feel and the rhythm of the quite varied originals.

ВИНО

Что мне до стихов любовных,
Что до вздохов и до слез?
Я смеюсь над дураками,
И с веселыми друзьями
        Пью в тени берез.

Нам вино дано на радость;
Богом щедрым создано,
Гонит мрачные мечтанья,
Гонит скуку и страданья
        Светлое вино.

Много, много винограду
Ел в раю отец Адам,
Грусти он и слез не ведал;
А как яблока отведал,
        Отпер дверь бедам.

Друг воды на мир прекрасный
Смотрит в черные очки:
Мало трезвых Демокритов,
А спьяна митрополитов
        Счастливей дьячки!

О вино, краса вселенной!
Всем сокровищам венец!
Кто заботы и печали
Топит в пенистом фиале,
        Тот прямой мудрец.

1815?

WINE

What care I for songs of lovers,
What care I for sighs and tears?
I just laugh at people's folly,
If with friends I can be jolly
Drinking beneath the trees.

Wine is given us for pleasure;
By a generous deity
Gloomy fantasies are banished,
Boredom, suffering, soon vanish—
Wine has set us free.

In Paradise our grand-sire Adam
Fed on grapes—great quantities.
He knew neither tears nor sadness,
Till an apple's fatal badness
Unleashed misery.

Water drinkers see all beauty
Through a somber telescope:
Democritus was never sober,
And with drink a deacon's bolder,
Happier than the pope.

Wine, you summit of creation,
Welcome sight to every eye!
Anyone who drowns his sorrows
In a precious foaming goblet,
That man's truly wise.

1815?

[Like the following poem, this one was written when Küchelbecker was a pupil at the Lycée at Tsarskoe Selo.]

К РАДОСТИ

Не порхай, летунья Радость!
Сядь и погости у нас,
Удержи, Богиня—сладость,
Удержи крылатый час.

Отдохни: ведь в Петрограде
Пышность заняла свой трон,
Праздность бродит в Летнем саде,
В залах скука и бостон.

Не порхай, летунья Радость!
Сядь и погости у нас,
Удержи, Богиня—сладость,
Удержи крылатый час.

Здесь не по указу моды,
Не для новостей сошлись,
Мы в объятиях природы,
Мы для дружбы собрались.

Не порхай, летунья Радость!
Сядь и погости у нас,
Удержи, Богиня—сладость,
Удержи крылатый час.

Ныне ты хозяйка наша.
Ах! не брось нас навсегда:
Будь сладка нам жизни чаша,
К гробу нас веди мечта!

Не порхай, летунья Радость!
Сядь и погости у нас,
Удержи, Богиня—сладость,
Удержи крылатый час.

1815?

TO GLADNESS

Do not flutter, light-winged Gladness!
Sit here with us in this bower,
Goddess, perpetuate your sweetness,
Perpetuate the flying hour.

Rest here; now throughout the city
Opulence has raised its throne,
Idleness haunts the Summer Garden,
Boston and boredom, the salons.

Do not flutter, light-winged Gladness!
Sit here with us in this bower,
Goddess, perpetuate your sweetness,
Perpetuate the flying hour.

Here we are not brought together
By fashion or by novelty,
We live in the embrace of nature,
Friendship is what makes us meet.

Do not flutter, light-winged Gladness!
Sit here with us in this bower,
Goddess, perpetuate your sweetness,
Perpetuate the flying hour.

Now you are our true protectress.
Do not leave us on our own,
Fill the cup of life with sweetness:
Dreams, go with us to the tomb!

Do not flutter, light-winged Gladness!
Sit here with us in this bower,
Goddess, perpetuate your sweetness,
Perpetuate the flying hour.

1815?

К ПУШКИНУ И ДЕЛЬВИГУ ИЗ ЦАРСКОГО СЕЛА

Нагнулись надо мной родимых вязов своды,
Прохлада тихая развесистых берез!
Здесь нам знакомый луг; вот роща, вот утес,
На верх которого, сыны младой свободы,
Питомцы, баловни и Феба и Природы,
Бывало, мы рвались сквозь пустоту древес,
И слабым ровный путь с презреньем оставляли!
 О время сладкое, где я не знал печали!
Ужель навеки мир души моей исчез
И бросили меня воздушные мечтанья?
Я радость нахожу в одном воспоминанье,
 Глаза полны невольных слез! –
Увы, они прошли, мои весенни годы!
Но—не хочу тужить: я снова, снова здесь!
Стою над озером, и зе́ркальные воды
Мне кажут холм, лесок, и мост, и берег весь,
И чистую лазурь безоблачных небес!
Здесь часто я сидел в полуночном мерцаньи,
И надо мной луна катилася в молчаньи,
Здесь мирные места, где возвыше́нных Муз,
Небесный пламень их и радости святые,
Порыв к великому, любовь к добру—впервые
Узнали мы, и где наш тройственный союз,
Союз младых певцов и чистый, и священный,
 Волшебным навыком, судьбою заключенный,
 Был дружбой утвержден!
И будет он для нас до гроба незабвенен!
 Ни радость, ни страданье,
Ни нега, ни корысть, ни почестей исканье—
Ничто души моей от вас не удалит!
И в песнях сладостных, и в славе состязанье
Друзей-соперников тесней соединит!
Зачем же нет вас здесь, избранники Харит?—
Тебя, о Дельвиг мой, поэт, мудрец ленивый,
Беспечный и в своей беспечности счастливый?

TO PUSHKIN AND DELVIG, FROM TSARSKOE SELO

I sense above my head the well-known elms
And the cool quiet of the branching birches.
Here is our meadow, here the wood, the cliff
    On which, young sons of liberty,
And devotees of Phoebus and of nature,
We used to scramble through the barren woodland,
Scorning the rest, who took the beaten track.
O happy times, without a hint of sadness!
Has it all gone, the world so good to me,
    And have I lost my airy dreams?
Only in memory can I find gladness;
My eyes fill with involuntary tears—
Alas! my springtime years will not come back.
But let me not grieve, I am here again
Standing above the lake, whose gleaming waters
Reflect the hill, the wood, the bridge, the bank
And the pure azure of the cloudless heavens.
Here often I would sit late in the gloaming
And watch the moon glide silently above me.
In these quiet places we first recognized
The high-born Muses and their heavenly flame,
Their holy joys; here first we set our hearts
On greatness and on virtue, three companions
Three youthful bards whose pure and sacred bond
Sealed by enchanting art and destiny
    Was fortified by friendship.
And it will be remembered while we live!
    Nor joy, nor suffering,
Pleasure or profit or the love of fame,
    Nothing will separate our souls!
Rivalry in sweet song or public honors
Will only bind us with a tighter bond.
Why are you far away, you whom the Muses
Most love—you, Delvig, poet idly wise,
Carefree and happy in your carefree life,

Тебя, мой огненный, чувствительный певец
      Любви и доброго Руслана,
Тебя, на чьем челе предвижу я венец
Арьоста и Парни, Петрарки и Баяна?—
О други! почему не с вами я брожу?
Зачем не говорю, не спорю здесь я с вами,
Не с вами с башни сей на пышный сад гляжу?—
      Или, сплетясь руками,
Зачем не вместе мы внимаем шуму вод,
Биющих искрами и пеною о камень?
Не вместе смотрим здесь на солнечный восход,
На потухающий на крае неба пламень?
Мне здесь и с вами все явилось бы мечтой,
      Несвязным, смутным сновиденьем,
Все, все, что встретил я, простясь с уединеньем,
      Все, что мне ясность и покой,
И тишину души младенческой отъяло,
И сердце мне так больно растерзало!
При вас, товарищи, моя утихнет кровь,
И я в родной стране забуду на мгновенье
Заботы и тоску, и скуку, и волненье,
Забуду, может быть, и самую любовь!

1818

ЖИЗНЬ

Юноша с свежей душой выступает на поприще жизни,
Полный пылающих дум, дерзостный в гордых мечтах;
С миром бороться готов и сразить и судьбу, и печали!
Но, безмолвные, ждут скука и время его;

Сушат сердце, хладят его ум и вяжут паренье.
Гаснет любовь! и одна дружба от самой зари
До полуно́чи сопутница избранных неба любимцев,
Чистых, высоких умов, пламенно любящих душ.

1820

And you, ardent and soft-hearted singer
Of love and noble Ruslan;
You on whose brow I dreamed the crown
Of Petrarch, Ariosto, Parny, Bayan?
O friends! why am I not walking by your side
Speaking with you or arguing with you here?
Why are we not together looking down
From this high tower on the sumptuous garden
Or arm in arm following the roar of water
Splashing and foaming on the rocks?
Why can we not gaze together on the sunrise
Or on the fading fires of the night sky?
If you were here with me, it all would seem
An obscure vision without form or meaning,
All, all that I have seen since I went out
Into the world, all that destroyed my peace,
The cloudless quiet of a youthful soul,
And racked my heart so painfully.
If you were here, comrades, my heart would rest,
And in my native land just for a moment
I should forget cares, grief, boredom, and passion,
I should forget, perhaps, even love itself.

1818

LIFE

A young man with soul still fresh steps out on the road of life,
He is full of flaming thoughts and bold in his lofty visions,
Prepared to fight with the world and to vanquish fate and sorrow;
But, never saying a word, time and tedium lie in wait.

They dry up the heart, freeze the mind, and bind the wings.
Love fades away! and from first dawn until midnight
Friendship alone accompanies the heaven-chosen,
Pure and exalted minds, ardently loving souls.

1820

БУРНОЕ МОРЕ ПРИ ЯСНОМ НЕБЕ

Дикий Нептун роптал, кипел и в волнах рассыпался,
А с золотой высоты, поздней зарей освещен,
Радостный Зевс улыбался ему, улыбался вселенной:
Так, безмятежный, глядит вечный закон на мятеж
Шумных страстей; так смотрит мудрец на ничтожное буйство:
Сила с начала веков в грозном величьи тиха.

15 (27) сентября 1820, Мемель

К А.Т. ПУШКИНОЙ

Цветок увядший оживает
От чистой, утренней росы;
Для жизни душу воскрешает
Взор тихой, девственной красы.
Когда твои подернет щеки
Румянец быстрый и живой.
Мне слышны милые упреки,
Слова стыдливости немой—
И я, отринув ложь и холод,
Я снова счастлив, снова молод,
Гляжу: невинности святой
Прекрасный ангел предо мной!

1823 или 1824

ТЕНЬ РЫЛЕЕВА

В ужасных тех стенах, где Иоанн,
В младенчестве лишенный багряницы,
Во мраке заточенья был заклан
        Булатом ослепленного убийцы,—
Во тьме на узничьем одре, лежал
Певец, поклонник пламенной свободы;

STORMY SEA AND CLEAR SKY

Furious Neptune was grumbling, boiling in turbulent waves,
While down from a golden height, lit by the lingering twilight
Joyfully Zeus was smiling on him and the universe;
Just so, eternal law looks calmly down on the tempest
Of noisy passion, and the wise man on trivial rage:
At all times strength has been calm in its awesome power.

September 15 (27), 1820, Memel
[Memel, now Klaipeda, is in present-day Lithuania, on the Baltic Sea.]

TO A.T. PUSHKINA

The faded flower finds new existence
In morning dew, so fresh and clean;
The soul is reborn in the sweetness
Of a quiet, maidenly mien.
When a blush, vivid, momentary,
Spreads on your cheeks so all can see,
I seem to hear your sweet reproaches,
Words of a silent modesty,
And shaking off coldness and falsehood,
I am happy and young; a glance
Shows me the features of an angel,
All lovely, holy innocence.

1823 or 1824
[Avdotya Pushkina is the Dunya of the novel.]

SHADE OF RYLEYEV

Within those fearful ramparts where Ioann,
In childhood shut out from the light of day,
A prisoner of the night, was robbed of life
By an unseeing murderer's sword—
In that dark place a bard, a devotee
Of fiery freedom, lay in captivity,

Отторжен, отлучен от всей природы,
Он в вольных думах счастия искал.
Но не придут обратно дни былые:
    Прошла пора надежд и снов,
И вы, мечты, вы, призраки златые,—
Не позлатить железных вам оков!
Тогда (то не был сон) во мрак темницы
Небесное видение сошло—
Раздался звук торжественной цевницы—
Испуганный певец подъял чело:
    На облаках несомый,
Явился образ, узнику знакомый.

    «Несу товарищу привет
    Из той страны, где нет тиранов,
    Где вечен мир, где вечен свет,
    Где нет ни бури, ни туманов.
    Блажен и славен мой удел:
    Свободу русскому народу
    Могучим гласом я воспел,
    Воспел и умер за свободу!
    Счастливец, я запечатлел
    Любовь к земле родимой кровью!
    И ты, я знаю, пламенел
    К отчизне чистою любовью.
    Грядущее твоим очам
    Разоблачу я в утешенье—
    Поверь, не жертвовал ты снам:
    Надеждам будет исполненье!»

Он рек—и бестелесною рукой
Раздвинул стены, растворил затворы—
Воздвиг певец восторженные взоры—
    И видит: на Руси святой
    Свобода, счастье и покой.

1827
Шлиссельбургская крепость

Torn off, divided from the whole of nature,
And seeking happiness only on wings of thought.
But those past times will never come again,
    The day of hopes and dreams is gone,
And you, old golden visions of delight,
Are powerless to gild his iron chains!
Then in his dungeon –this was not a dream –
There came the solemn sound of echoing pipes;
The bard lifted his face in fear and saw
    The image of a man he knew
Standing before his eyes, borne up by clouds.

    'Greetings to my comrade
    From a land free of tyrants—
    Peace and light everlasting,
    Free from all storms and mists.
    Happy my fate and fame:
    With a mighty voice I sang
    Of freedom to the Russians,
    For Russia lived and died!
    Happy that I could seal
    With my own blood my love
    Of my homeland. You, I know,
    Burned for Russia with a flame
    That was pure. Let me show you
    The future, bring you comfort:
    You were not dreaming, truly,
    And your hopes will be fulfilled.'

He spoke and with a disembodied hand
Dissolved the locks and opened up the walls,
And the bard lifted up his ardent gaze
    And saw through holy Russia spread
    Freedom and peace and happiness.

1827

[The poet Kondraty Ryleyev was executed in 1826 for his part in the Decembrist rising. *Ioann*: the young prince Ivan Antonovich, having reigned for a year, was killed in 1764 in the Shlisselburg fortress, where Küchelbecker was a prisoner when this poem was written.]

* * *

Суров и горек черствый хлеб изгнанья;
Наводит скорбь чужой страны река,
Душа рыдает от ее журчанья,
И брег уныл, и влага не сладка.
В изгнаннике безмолвном и печальном—
Туземцу непостижная тоска;
Он там оставил сердце, в крае дальном,
Там для него все живо, все цветет;
А здесь . . . не все ли в крове погребальном,
Не все ли вянет здесь, не все ли мрет?
Суров и горек черствый хлеб изгнанья;
Изгнанник иго тяжкое несет.

1829

ЭЛЕГИЯ

«Склонился нá руку тяжелой головою
В темнице сумрачной задумчивый Поэт.—
Что так очей его погас могущий свет?
Что стало пред его померкшею душою?
    О чем мечтает? Или дух его
        Лишился мужества всего
    И пал пред неприязненной судьбою?»
    Не нужно сострáданья твоего!
    К чему твои вопросы, хладный зритель
    Тоски, которой не понять тебе?
    Твоих ли утешений, утешитель,
    Он требует? Оставь их при себе!
Нет, не ему тужить о суетной утрате
    Того, что счастием зовете вы,—
Равно доволен он и во дворце, и в хате:
Не поседели бы власы его главы.
    Хотя бы сам в поту лица, руками
Приобретал свой хлеб за тяжкою сохой,
    Он был бы тверд под бурей и грозами

* * *

Bitter and dry the stale bread of the exile;
The river, unfamiliar, troubles him,
His soul sobs as he listens to its ripples,
The shore is dreary and the distance grim.
The longing that pervades his lonely silence
Perplexes the strangers who observe his gloom;
He left his heart elsewhere, in the longed-for distance,
Where all is alive for him, all flowers in bloom;
But in this place . . . is it not like a funeral
With everything dwindling and dying here?
Bitter and dry the stale bread of the exile;
It is a grievous yoke for him to bear.

1829
[a lyrical digression from the long poem *David*]

ELEGY

"He lays a heavy head upon his hands
In his dark cell, the Poet, deep in thought . . .
What has put out the great light of his eyes?
What does he see, this darkened soul? What now
Appears to him in dreams? Perhaps his spirit
Has lost its former courage, sunk beneath
    The burden of a hostile destiny?"
He doesn't need your empty sympathy:
Why all these questions, you who coldly look
On sorrow that you cannot understand?
Does he want your consolations, consoler?
        Keep them!
He's not the one to weep the trivial loss
Of happiness as you conceive it. No,
Palace and cottage are alike to him;
In either case his hair will not turn gray.
Even if with the sweat of his brow he earned
His bread by toiling at the heavy plough,
He would stand fast against the raging storms

И равнодушно снес бы мраз и зной,
Он не терзается и по златой свободе:
Пока огонь небес в Поэте не потух,
Поэта и в цепях еще свободен дух.
Когда ж и с грустью мыслит о природе,
О божьих чудесах на небе, на земле,
О долах, о горах, о необъятном своде,
О рощах, тонущих в вечерней, белой мгле,
О солнечном, блистательном восходе,
О дивном сонме звезд златых,
Бесчисленных лампад всемирного чертога,
Несметных исповедников немых
Премудрости, величья, славы бога,—
Не без отрады всё же он:
В его груди вселенная иная;
В ней тот же благости таинственный закон,
В ней та же заповедь святая,
По коей выше тьмы и зол, и облаков
Без устали течет великий полк миров.
Но ведать хочешь ты, что сумрак знаменует,
Которым, будто тучей, облегло
Певца унылое чело?—
Увы! он о судьбе тоскует,
Какой ни Меонид, ни Камое́нс, ни Тасс,
И в песнях и в бедах его предтечи,
Не испытали; пламень в нем погас,
Тот, с коим не были ему ужасны встречи
Ни с скорбным не́дугом, ни с хладной нищетой,
Ни с ветреной изменой
Любви, давно забытой и презренной,
Ни даже с душною тюрьмой.

18 июня 1832

And face the dirt and heat indifferently.
Nor does he grieve for golden liberty:
As long as heavenly fire inspires the Poet
His soul is free, even in captivity.
And when, all sorrowful, he thinks of nature,
God's wonders in the sky or on the earth,
Valleys and mountains, the unbounded heavens,
Groves plunged in the white mist of evening,
    The brilliance of the rising sun,
And of the heavenly throng of golden stars,
Innumerable lamps of the great universe,
    Uncounted, silent witnesses
Of God's eternal wisdom, glory, grandeur—
Even then he is not without consolation:
Within him lies another universe,
Where the same hidden laws of good and evil
And the same heavenly commandments hold,
By which the endless round of worlds goes on
Above the dark, the evil, and the clouds.
But do you want to know the meaning of
The twilight gathered like a cloud about
    The singer's gloomy brow?
Alas! his misery comes from a fate
    That Homer, Camoens, and Tasso,
His ancestors in fighting and in song,
Never experienced: his flame is quenched,
The flame with which he did not fear to meet
Gloomy depression or cold poverty
    Or fickle treacheries
Of love, now long forgotten and disdained,
Or even the oppressive prison cell.

1832

ТЕНИ ПУШКИНА

Итак, товарищ вдохновенный,
И ты!—а я на прах священный
Слезы не пролил ни одной:
С привычки к горю и страданьям
Все высохли в груди больной.
Но образ твой моим мечтаньям
В ночах бессонных предстоит,
Но я тяжелой скорбью сыт,
Но, мрачный, близ жены, мне милой,
И думать о любви забыл . . .
Там мысли, над твоей могилой!
Смолк шорох благозвучных крыл
Твоих волшебных песнопений,
На небо отлетел твой гений;—
А визги желтой клеветы
Глупцов, которые марали,
Как был ты жив, твои черты,
И ныне, в час святой печали,
Бездушные, не замолчали!
Гордись! Ей-богу, стыд и срам
Их подлая любовь!—Пусть жалят!
Тот пуст и гнил, кого все хвалят;
За зависть дорого я дам.
Гордись! Никто тебе не равен,
Никто из сверстников-певцов:
Не смеркнешь ты во мгле веков;—
В веках тебе клеврет Державин.

24 мая 1837

SHADE OF PUSHKIN

You too! My comrade brimming over
With poetry! and yet I have not honored
With just one tear your sacred dust:
Grown used to bitterness and grieving,
Tears have dried up in my sad breast.
But in the weary nights, unsleeping,
Your image haunts my dreaming eyes,
But heavy sorrow fills my mind,
But, somber, by the wife I dote on,
I have forgotten thoughts of love . . .
My thoughts are there, above your tombstone!
The rustle of the wings that moved
With your enchanted songs is silent,
Your genius has flown to heaven;
And yellow calumny's shrill cries
From fools, who when you were alive,
Distorted your unequalled features,
Now, in the hour of sacred sorrow,
Keep up their soulless pandemonium!
Be proud, by God! their abject love
Is shameful. Let them bite! The person
Whom all men praise is empty, rotten;
To my mind envy is a proof
Of worth. Be proud! For no-one ever
Will equal you among our bards,
You will survive the fleeting years,
You and Derzhavin stand together.

1837
[a response to Pushkin's death in a duel]

19 ОКТЯБРЯ

Блажен, кто пал, как юноша Ахилл,
Прекрасный, мощный, смелый, величавый,
В средине поприща побед и славы,
Исполненный несокрушимых сил!
Блажен! Лицо его, всегда младое,
Сиянием бессмертия горя,
Блестит, как солнце вечно золотое,
Как первая эдемская заря.

А я один средь чуждых мне людей
Стою в ночи, беспомощный и хилый,
Над страшной всех надежд моих могилой,
Над мрачным гробом всех моих друзей.
В тот гроб бездонный, молнией сраженный,
Последний пал родимый мне поэт . . .
И вот опять Лицея день священный;
Но уж и Пушкина меж вами нет.

Не принесет он новых песней вам,
И с них не затрепещут перси ваши;
Не выпьет с вами он заздравной чаши:
Он воспарил к заоблачным друзьям.
Он ныне с нашим Дельвигом пирует.
Он ныне с Грибоедовым моим:
По них, по них душа моя тоскует;
Я жадно руки простираю к нам!

Пора и мне!—Давно судьба грозит
Мне казней нестерпимого удара:
Она того меня лишает дара,
С которым дух мой неразрывно слит.
Так! перенес я годы заточенья,
Изгнание, и срам, и сиротство;
Но под щитом святого вдохновенья,
Но здесь во мне пылало божество!

19 OCTOBER

Happy the man who fell like the young Achilles,
Powerful, bold, majestic in his prowess,
In the midst of life, victorious and famous,
Brimming with indomitable powers!
Happy the man! His face, forever youthful,
Burns with the fire of immortality
And radiates like a sun forever golden,
Like the first day dawning in Paradise.

But I, alone among an alien people,
Helpless and feeble, here in the night I stand
Over the fearful grave of my ambition
And the dark resting place of all my friends.
Into that place, burnt up as if by thunder,
Our last, beloved poet has gone down:
Pushkin is no more among your number
As the school's opening day once more comes round.

No more will he bring to you his latest poems,
No more your hearts will tremble at their sound,
He will not join you in your festive potions,
He has flown up to friends above the clouds.
Now he is feasting alongside our Delvig
And Griboyedov, in a better place,
And my soul yearns for them, for them, all eager
To hold them in a loving warm embrace.

My time has come too! Fate for years has threatened
To strike me down with some relentless blow;
It keeps from me a gift that every second
Is woven into the fabric of my soul.
Yes! I have borne the weary years of prison,
The exile and the shame, the orphanhood,
But sheltered by the shield of inspiration,
I warmed myself before the flame of God!

Теперь пора!—Не пламень, не перун
Меня убил; нет, вязну средь болота,
Горою давят нужды и забота,
И я отвык от позабытых струн.
Мне ангел песней рай в темнице душной
Когда-то созидал из снов златых;
Но без него не труп ли я бездушный
Средь трупов столь же хладных и немых?

1838

УЧАСТЬ РУССКИХ ПОЭТОВ

Горька судьба поэтов всех племен;
Тяжеле всех судьба казнит Россию;
Для славы и Рылеев был рожден;
Но юноша в свободу был влюблен . . .
Стянула пе́тля дерзостную выю.

Не он один; другие вслед ему,
Прекрасной обольщенные мечтою,—
Пожалися годиной роковою . . .
Бог дал огонь их сердцу, свет уму,
Да! чувства в них восторженны и пылки:
Что ж? их бросают в черную тюрьму,
Морят морозом безнадежной ссылки . . .

Или болезнь наводит ночь и мглу
На очи прозорливцев вдохновенных;
Или рука любезников презренных
Шлет пулю их священному челу;

Или же бунт поднимет чернь глухую,
И чернь того на части разорвет,
Чей блещущий перунами полет
Сияньем о́блил бы страну родную.

28 октября 1845

Now it is time! No thunderbolt, no lightning
Has struck me dead; no, a bog sucks me down;
I am oppressed by need and care, forgetting
To play upon the strings that I have known.
In days gone by an angel brought me golden
Celestial dreams that flowed into my song;
Without them, am I not a lifeless body
Among a cold, unspeaking, lifeless throng?

1838

THE DESTINY OF RUSSIAN POETS

Fate weighs upon the poet in every land,
But heaviest of all with us in Russia:
Ryleyev was born for fame's poetic band,
But freedom captivated the young man . . .
A noose put paid to hopes of revolution.

Not him alone, but others after him,
Enamoured of that captivating vision,
Came flocking to the fateful feast of reason . . .
God filled their minds with light, their hearts with flame,
Yes, all their feelings were exalted, burning—
And then? Confinement in dark prison rooms
Or frozen in an exile with no ending.

Illness sends night and fog to dim the sight
Of seers around whom inspiration hovers,
Or else the hand of evil-minded lovers
Shatters a holy forehead with a shot.

Or mutiny excites the stupid mob,
The rabble who will tear the man to pieces
Whose brilliance could have flooded his penates
With light, and thunder roaring like a god.

October 28, 1845
[The final two stanzas refer to the deaths of Pushkin and Griboyedov.]

* * *

До смерти мне грозила смерти тьма,
И думал я: подобно Оссиану,
Блуждать во мгле у края гроба стану;
Ему подобно, с дикого холма
Я устремлю свои слепые очи
В глухую бездну нерассветной ночи,
И не увижу ни густых лесов,
Ни волн полей, ни бархата лугов,
Ни чистого, лазоревого свода,
Ни солнцева чудесного восхода;
Зато очами духа узрю я
Вас, вещие таинственные тени,
Вас, рано улетевшие друзья,
И слух склоню я к гулу дивных пений,
И голос каждого я различу,
И каждого узнаю по лицу. . . .

1845

УСТАЛОСТЬ

Мне нужно забвенье, нужна тишина:
Я в волны нырну непробудного сна,
Вы, порванной арфы мятежные звуки,
Умолкните, думы, и чувства, и муки.

Да! чаша житейская желчи полна;
Но выпил же эту я чашу до дна,—
И вот опьянелой, больной головою
Клонюсь и клонюсь к гробовому покою.

Узнал я изгнанье, узнал я тюрьму,
Узнал слепоты нерассветную тьму
И совести грозной узнал укоризны,
И жаль мне невольницы милой отчизны.

Мне нужно забвенье, нужна тишина
. . . .

1845

* * *

Before death I have felt the dark of death.
I thought: like Ossian I shall lose my way
In mist by the grave's edge and blindly stare
From wild moors down through the dim precipice
Of dawnless night and see no trees, no fields
Of freedom, no soft grass, no azure skies,
And no sun rising like a miracle.
Yet with the soul's eye I shall see you, shades
Of prophets, friends too soon flown out of sight,
And I shall hear the blessed poets' song
And know each voice and recognize each face. . . .

1845
[the opening lines of a short poem written in Siberia, where Küchelbecker was going blind after twenty years of imprisonment and exile]

WEARINESS

I need oblivion and peace; I need
To plunge into the waves of deepest sleep,
You, restless sounds of a lyre's broken strings,
Be silent, thoughts and feelings, sufferings.

Yes, for the cup of life is full of gall,
But I have taken this cup and drunk it all—
And now my sick intoxicated head
Is sinking to the grave's quietness.

I have known exile, prison I have known,
I have known blindness, darkness with no dawn,
I have known conscience and its bitter pangs,
I weep for my dear, captive motherland.

I need oblivion and peace
. . . .

1845

* * *

Счастливицы вольные птицы:
Не знают они ни темницы,
Ни ссылки, ни злой слепоты.
Зачем же родился не птицею ты?

Да! ласточкой, легкой касаткой!
Глядел бы на мир не украдкой,
Весь видел бы вдруг с высоты.
Зачем же родился не птицею ты?

Счастливицы вольные птицы:
Купаются в море денницы,
Им прах незнаком суеты.
Зачем же родился не птицею ты?

Нет божией птичке работы,
Ни страха, ни слез, ни заботы,
Не слышит она клеветы!
Зачем же родился не птицею ты?

С утра и до вечера бога
Ты славил бы в выси чертога
Чудесной святой красоты.
Зачем же родился не птицею ты?

Ты пел бы с утра до зарницы
Созданье премудрой десницы,
И звезды, и луг, и цветы,
Зачем же родился не птицею ты?

Ты грязь ненавидишь земную,
Ты просишься в твердь голубую,

* * *

How happy the birds in their freedom,
For they have never known prison
Or exile or the fate of the blind.
    O why were you not born a bird?

Yes, like the light swallow, the martin,
You'd gaze on the world in the open,
Looking down on all life spread out wide.
    O why were you not born a bird?

How happy the birds in their freedom,
As they bathe in the new day's bright ocean,
Innocent of the cares of the world.
    O why were you not born a bird?

God's birds, they all live without working
Or weeping or terror or worry;
Spiteful gossip they never have heard.
    O why were you not born a bird?

From daybreak to twilight you'd carol
Your God from the peak of a temple
Of heavenly beauty, a bard.
    O why were you not born a bird?

From first light to late in the evening
You'd sing the wise ways of creation
And the stars and the flowers on the mead.
    O why were you not born a bird?

You hate the vile world in its baseness,
You aspire to the firmament's blueness,

Ты рвешься из уз темноты,
Верь: некогда птицею будешь и ты!

Прильнут к раменам тебе крылья,
Взлетишь к небесам без усилья,
И твой искупитель и бог
        Возьмет тебя в райский нетленный чертог!

29 апреля 1846

You tear off the night's gloomy bonds.
    Believe: you'll one day be a bird!

For wings will appear on your shoulders,
You will fly to the heavens without labor,
And your loving redeemer, your God,
    Welcome you in his heavenly deathless abode!

April 29, 1846

Endnotes

1 Tsarskoe Selo, literally "Tsars' Village," a country residence of the Russian tsars fifteen miles to the south from the center of St. Petersburg. In the seventeenth century, the estate belonged to a Swedish noble; its name is traced to the Finnish word *saari*, which means "island," hence Saarskoe Selo.
2 Distorted Russian: 'Is the soup any good?'
3 Anagram of the surname "Myasoyedov."
4 Fellow (Germ.).
5 A heroine of Nikolay Karamzin's novella *Poor Liza* (1792), the most celebrated piece of Russian prose fiction in the pre-Pushkin period. In the story a young girl of lower social origins, seduced by her lover, a young nobleman, commits suicide by drowning herself in the pond near the Simonov Monastery outside Moscow.
6 Tiberius and Gaius Grachhi (second century BC) were Roman tribunes assassinated by their enemies. The brothers conducted a number of reforms in order to redistribute the major aristocratic landholdings among the urban poor and veterans.
7 Thrasybulus (c. 440–388 BC) was an elected Athenian general and democratic leader who commanded at several critical Athenian naval victories. Leader of the successful democratic resistance to a military coup.
8 Derzhavin's ode "On the Death of Meshchersky" (1779) is dedicated to Stepan Vasilyevich Perfilyev (1734–1793), Governor of St. Petersburg, a friend of Derzhavin and A. I. Meshchersky.
9 The lycéens are licentious. (Fr.)
10 Trans. Roger Clarke, in *Alexander Pushkin: Lyrics*, vol. 1 (Richmond: Alma Classics, 2018), 349.
11 Trans. Roger Clarke, *Alexander Pushkin: Lyrics*, vol. 2 (Richmond: Alma Classics, 2019), 37.
12 Drinks (Germ.)
13 Trans. Roger Clarke and John Coutts, in *Alexander Pushkin: Lyrics*, vol. 1, 343.

14 A form of unpaid obligatory land work that the Russian serfs performed for the landed nobility. A 1797 decree by Paul I stipulated a *barshchina* of three days a week as normal and sufficient for the landowner's needs.
15 Alceste, the main character of Molière's masterpiece *Le Misanthrope* (1666), a denouncer of social vices.
16 Kotzebue's murder by Karl Sand, a militant member of the student fraternities (*Burschenschaften*), gave Metternich the pretext to dissolve the fraternities, crack down on the liberal press, and seriously restrict academic freedom in the German Confederation.
17 The *Cortes Generales,* the Parliament of the Kingdom of Spain.
18 Antonio Quiroga (1784–1841), general and politician who took part in the national war against Napoleon and in 1815 attempted to establish a constitutional government in Spain; released from imprisonment in 1820 by General Rafael del Riego (1784–1823), who started an anti-absolutist uprising that quickly spread throughout Spain. Quiroga and Riego were the heroes of the Russian liberals of 1810–1820s and of the Decembrists.
19 Gentleman who is angry over trifles (Fr.).
20 The dates are given in the New Style (according to the Gregorian calendar) and the Old Style (the Julian calendar). The Julian calendar was in use in Russia until February 14, 1918.
21 The Battle of the Nations, the bloodiest in the history of the Napoleonic wars, was fought in Leipzig on October 16–19, 1813 by the coalition armies of Prussia, Russia, Austria, and Sweden. They decisively defeated the French army of Napoleon I.
22 The Carbonari was an informal network of secret revolutionary societies active in Italy from about 1800 to 1831, which aimed at defeating tyranny and establishing constitutional government. The secret society was divided into small covert cells with strict hierarchy, initiation ceremonies, and complex symbols, similar to Masonic revolutionary groups in Russia.
23 Modern-day Villefranche-sur-Mer in Southern France.
24 King Vittorio Emanuele I of Piedmont abdicated in favor of his brother Charles Felix of Sardinia who invited an Austrian military intervention. On April 8, the Habsburg army defeated the rebels and the uprising of 1820–1821 collapsed. In September 1821, Pope Pius VII condemned the Carbonari as a Freemason secret society, and excommunicated its members.
25 Laibach (modern-day Ljubljana in Slovenia) was the administrative center of the Kingdom of Illyria in the Habsburg Empire. At the Congress of Laibach in 1821 Russia, Austria, and Prussia issued a declaration affirming the right and duty of the powers responsible for the peace of Europe to intervene to suppress any revolutionary movement by which the peace might be endangered.
26 A Georgian Kingdom of Imereti on the Rioni River in the Caucasus.
27 The Grand Vizier in Turkish, the title of the effective head of government.

28 A baker, in Russian literally a "bread-baker."
29 Original title of Griboyedov's comedy *Gore ot uma (Woe from Wit).*
30 A pun on the name Ivan (the given name of the two Russian generals in charge of the campaign, Ivan Diebitsch and Ivan Paskevich). Its diminutive Vanka also means "a cabbie."
31 Peter the Great's plan, which became a tenet of Russian foreign policy for the next two centuries, was to recall to Russia the schismatic Greeks, who were spread over Hungary and Poland, and to make Russia their center and support.
32 Russian, Polish, or Moldavian captives held by various Central Asian or Caucasian peoples.
33 A small flat-roofed house, typical of the Caucasus, made of stone or clay. *Saklyas* are located on the mountain slopes in the form of terraces closely adjacent to each other. The roof of the lower building is often the floor or the courtyard of the one above it.
34 Emancipated and therefore independent peasants in Chechnya, Dagestan, and Adygea, who sometimes rose to the nobility.
35 *Atala, ou Les Amours de deux sauvages dans le désert* is an early novella by Chateaubriand, first published in 1801. The work, inspired by his travels in North America, had an immense impact on early Romanticism.
36 One *verst* equals approximately one kilometer (0.66 miles).
37 The *armiak* was a long, warm, spacious long-sleeved coat made of coarse woollen fabric, with a hood, without buttons, and girdled with a belt. It was worn in winter, often by cabmen or peasants.
38 I do not want this news to cause them new worries (Fr.).
39 A state policy implemented by Tsar Ivan the Terrible in Russia between 1565 and 1572, which included the institution of secret police, mass repressions, public executions, and confiscation of land from Russian aristocrats. The six thousand henchmen of the tsar, that is, the political police, were called *oprichniki.*
40 Aleksandr Pushkin, *Collected Narrative and Lyrical Poetry*, ed. Walter Arndt (New York: Harry N. Abrams, 2009), 289.
41 Probably K. P. Bezak, Grech's cousin, the future husband of Sophochka Grech. Subsequently, the head of a department at the Ministry of Foreign Affairs. [Note by Yu. Tynianov.]
42 So Sofochka calls Wilhelm throughout. [Note by Yu. Tynianov.]
43 At the time Grech had been working on his *Comprehensive Russian Grammar,* which was published in 1827 with a dedication to Nicholas I. It had a preface by F. V. Bulgarin, who considered it necessary to replace the author's foreword with his own.
44 Aulus Vitellius Germanicus Augustus (15–69 AD) was Roman Emperor for eight months in 69 AD, known as the Year of the Four Emperors. Vitellius was executed in Rome by Vespasian's soldiers.

45 Titus Flavius Vespasianus (39–91) succeeded Vitellius and ruled until 79 AD. He founded the Flavian dynasty that ruled the Empire for twenty-seven years.
46 Servants employed in riding service, usually dressed in Hungarian, Hussar, or Cossack clothes.
47 Saint Nicholas (270–343 AD), an early Christian bishop of the ancient Greek city of Myra. Because of the many miracles attributed to his intercession, he is also known as Nicholas the Wonderworker.
48 The dead have no will (Fr.).
49 Kovno (modern-day Kaunas) and Siaulie (modern-day Siauliai) are both in Lithuania.
50 Modern-day Jelgava in Latvia, formerly the administrative center of the Duchy of Courland Governorate (1795–1918).
51 When you see Constantine, tell him clearly that if we have acted this way, it's because otherwise blood would have been spilled (Fr.).
52 It has not yet been spilled, but it will be (Fr.).
53 In Russian, *razvodnoy most,* a bascule or lift bridge, and *Razvodnaya ploshchad'*—Liftbridge Square.
54 Do you want to take Michael down? (Fr.)
55 The Santa Hermandad ("Holy brotherhood") was a type of military peacekeeping association of armed men, which became characteristic of municipal life in medieval Spain, especially in Castile.
56 *Sarafan*, a long pinafore dress worn over an embroidered blouse by girls and women; part of Russian traditional folk costume.
57 A silver ruble.
58 At the time a Russian gold coin worth ten rubles.
59 In Russian evokes the word *neprolazny*, "impassable."
60 Russian literary journal *Blagonamerenny*, which was published by Aleksandr Izmaylov between 1818 and 1826.
61 A *qadi* is the magistrate or judge of the Shari'a court.

About the Translators

Anna Kurkina Rush taught Russian at George Watson's College (Edinburgh) and the University of St Andrews of which she holds a doctorate. Together with Christopher Rush she translated Tynyanov's novel *Pushkin* (2007) and *The Death of Vazir-Mukhtar* (Columbia UP, 2021). She is currently working on a monograph about representation of Pushkin in Tynyanov's historical novels.

Peter France is the author and editor of many books on Russian, French and comparative literature, including *Poets of Modern Russia* (1982) and the *Oxford Guide to Literature in English Translation* (2000). He has translated numerous volumes of Russian poetry, from Baratynsky and Batyushkov to Mandelstam and Aygi.

Christopher Rush is the author of 25 critically acclaimed books in various genres: poetry, prose fiction, biography, besides his work as editor, memoirist, screenplay writer and writer of academic and literary essays.

CPSIA information can be obtained
at www.ICGtesting.com
Printed in the USA
JSHW051651060622
26757JS00001B/34